THE MILITARY WIFE

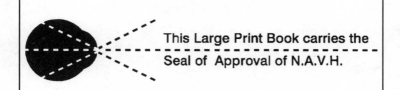

This Large Print Book carries the
Seal of Approval of N.A.V.H.

A HEART OF A HERO NOVEL

THE MILITARY WIFE

LAURA TRENTHAM

THORNDIKE PRESS
A part of Gale, a Cengage Company

Farmington Hills, Mich • San Francisco • New York • Waterville, Maine
Meriden, Conn • Mason, Ohio • Chicago

Copyright © 2019 by Brandon Webb.
Thorndike Press, a part of Gale, a Cengage Company.

ALL RIGHTS RESERVED
This is a work of fiction. All of the characters, organizations, and events portrayed in this novel are either products of the author's imagination or are used fictitiously.
Thorndike Press® Large Print Women's Fiction.
The text of this Large Print edition is unabridged.
Other aspects of the book may vary from the original edition.
Set in 16 pt. Plantin.

LIBRARY OF CONGRESS CIP DATA ON FILE. CATALOGUING IN PUBLICATION FOR THIS BOOK IS AVAILABLE FROM THE LIBRARY OF CONGRESS
ISBN-13: 978-1-4328-6611-2 (hardcover alk. paper)

Published in 2019 by arrangement with Macmillan Publishing Group, LLC/St. Martin's Press

Printed in the United States of America
1 2 3 4 5 6 7 23 22 21 20 19

To all the military wives (and husbands)

CHAPTER 1

Present Day

Winters in Kitty Hawk, North Carolina, were temperamental. The sunshine and a temperate southerly breeze that started a day could turn into biting, salt-tinged snow flurries by afternoon. But one thing Harper Lee Wilcox could count on was that winter along the Outer Banks was quiet.

The bustle and hum and weekly rotation of tourists that marked the summer months settled into a winter melancholy that Harper enjoyed. Well, perhaps not enjoyed in the traditional sense . . . more like she enjoyed surrendering to the melancholy. In fact, her mother may have accused her of wallowing in it once or twice or a hundred times.

In the winter, she didn't have to smile and pretend her life was great. Not that it was bad. Lots of people had it worse. Much worse. In fact, parts of her life were fabulous. Almost five, her son was happy and healthy and smart. Her mother's strength and support were unwavering and had bolstered her through the worst time of her life. Her friends were amazing.

That was the real issue. In the craziness of the summer season, she forgot to be sad. Her husband, Noah, had been gone five years; the same amount of time they'd been married. Soon the years separating them would outnumber the years they'd been together. The thought was sobering and only intensified the need to keep a sacred place in her heart waiting and empty. Her secret memorial.

She parked the sensible sedan Noah had bought her soon after they married under her childhood home. Even though they were inland, the stilts were a common architectural feature up and down the Outer Banks.

Juggling her laptop and purse, Harper pushed open the front door and stacked her things to the side. "I'm home!"

A little body careened down the steps and crashed into her legs. She returned the ferocious hug. Her pregnancy was the only thing that had kept her going those first weeks after she'd opened her front door to the Navy chaplain.

"How was preschool? Did you like the

pasta salad I packed for your lunch?"

"It made me toot and everyone laughed, even the girls. Can you pack it for me again tomorrow?"

"Ben! You shouldn't *want* to toot." Laughter ruined the admonishing tone she was going for.

As Harper's mom said time and again, the kid was a hoot and a half. He might have Harper's brown wavy hair, but he had Noah's spirit and mannerisms and humor. Ben approached everything with an optimism Harper had lost or perhaps had never been gifted with from the start. He was a blessing Harper sometimes wondered if she deserved.

"Where's Yaya?" She ruffled his unruly hair.

Of course, her mom had picked an unconventional name. "Grandmother" was too old-fashioned and pedestrian. Since she'd retired from the library, she had cast off any semblance of normalcy and embraced an inner spirit that was a throwback to 1960s bra burners and Woodstock.

"Upstairs painting." Ben slipped his hand into Harper's and tugged her toward the kitchen. Bright red and orange and blue paint smeared the back of his hand and arm like a rainbow. At least, her mom had put him in old clothes. "Yaya gave me my own canvas and let me paint whatever I wanted."

"And what did you paint?" Harper prayed it wasn't a nude study, which was the homework assignment from her mom's community college class.

"I drew Daddy in heaven. I used *all* the colors." The matter-of-factness of his tone clawed at her heart.

No child should have to grow up only knowing their father through pictures and stories. Her own father had been absent because of divorce and disinterest. He'd sent his court-ordered child support payments regularly until she turned eighteen but rarely visited or shown any curiosity about her. It had hurt until teenaged resentment scarred over the wound.

Noah would have made a great dad. The best. That he never got the chance piled more regrets and what-ifs onto her winter-inspired melancholy.

"I'm sure he would have loved your painting." Luckily, Ben didn't notice her choked-up reply.

He went to the cabinet, pulled out white bread and crunchy peanut butter, and proceeded to make two sandwiches. It was their afternoon routine. Someday he would outgrow it. Outgrow her and become a man

10

like his daddy.

She poured him a glass of milk, and they ate their sandwiches, talking about how the rest of his day went — outside of his epic toots. His world was small and safe and she wanted to keep it that way for as long as possible.

Her mom breezed into the kitchen, her still-thick but graying brown hair twisted into a messy bun, a thin paintbrush holding it in place. Slim and attractive, she wore paint-splattered jeans and a long-sleeve T-shirt that read: *I make AARP look good.* Harper pinched her lips together to stifle a grin.

"How's your assignment coming along?" Harper asked.

"I'm having a hard time with proportions. It's been a while, but I'm pretty sure my man's you-know-what shouldn't hang down to his kneecaps."

Harper shot a glance toward Ben, who had moved to the floor of the den to play with LEGOs. As crazy as her mom drove her, she was and would always be Harper's rock. The irony wasn't lost on her. As hard as she'd worked to get out of Kitty Hawk and out of her mother's reach when she was young, she'd never regretted coming home.

"It's been a while for me, too, but that's

not how I remember them, either."

"A pity for us both." Her mother pulled a jar of olives out of the fridge and proceeded to make martinis — shaken, not stirred. She raised her eyebrows, and Harper answered the unspoken question with a nod. Her mom poured and plopped an extra olive in Harper's. "How was work?"

Harper handled bookkeeping and taxes for a number of local businesses, but a good number closed up shop in the winter. "Routine. Quiet."

"Exactly like your life."

Harper sputtered on her first sip. "What's that supposed to mean?"

"I hate seeing you mope around all winter." Her mom poked at the olive in her drink with a toothpick and looked toward Ben, dropping her voice. "He's been gone five years, sweetheart, and you haven't gone on so much as a date."

"That's not true. I went to lunch with Whit a few weeks ago."

"He was trying to sell you life insurance. Doesn't count."

Harper huffed and covered her discomfort by taking another sip. "What about you? You never date."

"True, but your father ruined me on relationships. I have trust issues. You and

Noah, on the other hand, seemed to get along fine. Or am I wrong?"

"You're not." Another sip of the martini grew the tingly warmth in her stomach. Their marriage hadn't been completely without conflict, but what relationship was? As she looked back on their fights, they seemed juvenile and unimportant. It was easier to remember the good times. And there were so many to choose from.

She touched the empty finger on her left hand. The ring occupied her jewelry box and had for three years. But, occasionally, her finger would ache with phantom pains as if it were missing a vital organ.

"You're young. Find another good man. Or forget the man, just find *something* you're passionate about."

"I'm happy right where I am." Harper hammered up her defenses as if preparing for a hurricane.

"Don't mistake comfort for happiness. You're comfortable here. Too comfortable. But you're not happy."

"God, Mom, why are you Dr. Phil–ing me all of sudden? Are you wanting me and Ben to move out or something?" Her voice sailed high and Ben looked over at them, his eyes wide, clutching his LEGO robot so tightly its head fell off.

"You and Ben are welcome to stay and take care of me in my old age." Her mom shifted toward the den. "You hear that, honey? I want you to stay forever."

Ben gave them an eye-crinkling smile that reminded her so much of Noah her insides squirmed, and she killed the rest of her drink. She was so careful not to show how lonely she sometimes felt in front of Ben.

"Harper." Her mom's chiding tone reminded her so much of her own childhood, she glanced up instinctively. Her mom took her hand, and her hazel eyes matched the ones that stared back at Harper in the mirror. "You're marking time in Kitty Hawk. Find something that excites you again. Don't let Ben — or Noah — be your excuse."

Harper looked to her son. His chubby fingers fit the small LEGO pieces together turning the robot into a house. She had built her life brick by brick adding pieces and colors, expanding, taking pride, until one horrible day she'd stopped. Maybe her mom was right. Was it time to build something new?

"I'm not sure what I want to do," she said in a small voice, the uncertainty but also the resignation startling. As a teenager, she'd been confident and ready to chase her dreams. Fate had intervened in a big way.

"I'm not saying you have to figure it out overnight, but I'm thrilled you're even considering the future." Her mom squeezed Harper's hand before retreating. "How's your friend Allison doing? I know you've been worried about her."

"I got an email from her today." Harper popped a martini-flavored olive in her mouth, glad to focus on the messiness of someone else's psyche. "She didn't say much about Darren, but . . . I'm worried."

Nothing Allison wrote in the email raised alarms, but it was exactly what she had omitted that had Harper's stomach dipping. Not a word about how Darren, her husband, was adjusting after his last disastrous deployment. He was alive, the cuts and bruises long healed, but the damage was more insidious.

From the bread crumbs Allison had dropped in their conversations, Harper feared Darren was exhibiting the hallmarks of PTSD. Allison's tendency to put a sunny spin on things only increased Harper's unease. PTSD wasn't something a wife could coddle away with bandage changes or favorite meals.

"Why don't you take the weekend and drive down to Fort Bragg? I'm happy to watch Ben."

As soon as her mom suggested a visit, Harper realized the notion had been lingering in the back of her mind for days. "It would be a good time to go. Everyone is caught up and business is so slow in the winter. One condition" — she wagged her finger at her mom — "Ben is not allowed to tag along to your nudist painting class. That is a talk I'm not ready to have."

"You make it sound like we all prance around naked. There's only one naked model, and come to think of it, he's single and young and I can vouch for the fact you won't be disappointed. It might not make it to his kneecaps, but . . ." Her mother cast a gaze meaningfully between her legs. "A fling would do you good."

"Mom, seriously." Harper's laugh ruined her attempt at prudish outrage.

Her mom harrumphed, but an answering smile played at her mouth. "Fine. No nudists while you're gone."

"It'll be a quick trip. I'm sure I'll find Allison her usual perky self." The glance she and her mother exchanged did nothing to settle her nerves.

Two days later, Harper was on the road to Fort Bragg, North Carolina, simmering

16

anxiety keeping her alert behind the wheel. Allison was the consummate officer's wife. She was friendly and social without coming off as fake or pushy.

After Harper and Noah had settled in a town-house community popular with military families outside the Naval base in Virginia Beach, Allison was the first one to knock on her door with a beribboned wicker basket full of housewarming presents.

It had taken months for Harper to adjust to life as a military wife and Allison had played a big part in her ability to find happiness in the role. They'd formed a true friendship, and as they faced the lonely months with their husbands deployed Allison became the sister she'd never had.

Having her to lean on throughout the weeks after Noah had been killed had made a huge difference. Now Allison needed help, even if she was reluctant to ask for it, and Harper refused to let her down.

As she got closer to Fort Bragg, the number of trucks and motorcycles whizzing by her well over the speed limit skyrocketed, and testosterone rose off the roads like the heat mirages.

She'd forgotten what the bases were like. Full of brash, confident men who lived on the edge of danger. Men who were exciting and overwhelming and sexy all at the same time. Of course, they could also be bossy and tight-lipped and a general pain in the ass.

After negotiating the checkpoints, she drove down streets populated with cookie-cutter base housing. A formation of soldiers jogged through an intersection in their boots and BDUs — battle dress uniforms.

Despite the cold winter air, she fanned her flushed cheeks. The darkest, most selfish part of her missed having a man in her life. In her bed. Acknowledging the fact made her feel weak and guilty.

She peeled her gaze off the clump of pure masculinity and counted down the house numbers. Although Fort Bragg was only a half-day drive from Kitty Hawk, Harper had only been down a few times to visit. After Noah's death, Allison's and Harper's lives had diverged.

For sanity's sake, Harper had focused on leaving all things military behind, while Allison was in the thick of that world, her husband climbing the ranks, his promotion to Commander in JSOC — Joint Special Operations Command — his latest achievement.

It had garnered a move into a bigger house and upped the unspoken requirements on Allison to entertain. Not that she seemed fazed by the pressure. Her ability to make wives — and husbands — of the officers and enlisted soldiers alike feel comfortable was her gift.

The house sat on a quiet corner. Allison's three kids played out front wearing nothing but jeans and long-sleeve shirts, unbothered by the chill, their cheeks flushed, their laughter and squeals settling some of Harper's unease.

"Hi, kids." She stretched herself out of the car and smiled. "I'm your mom's friend Harper. It's been a while since I've been down for a visit."

Libby, who was ten if Harper's math was right, smiled back. "I remember. You brought us saltwater taffy."

"I did, and I might just have another box stowed in my bag for a treat after dinner." She winked, and the kids cheered. "Your mom inside?"

Libby nodded, her smile dimming. "Daddy's sleeping, so she sent us out to play."

"I'll be quiet then."

A cobblestone walkway led to the front porch. Two rocking chairs with dusty, pollen-covered cushions sat to the side. The kids resumed their game of tag, and Harper watched them a moment before cracking

Allison's front door open and slipping halfway inside.

"Allison? You here?" She kept her voice soft.

No answer. She stepped fully inside and listened. The house was dark, the low ceilings and partitioned-off rooms giving it an old-fashioned feel compared to the openness of her mom's house.

She followed the *tink* of silverware down the hall. A room on her left opened into a formal living room with a wet bar along one wall but no TV. Dust motes danced in the single shaft of sunlight winnowing between brocade curtains, giving the room a disused feel.

Family pictures led her down the hallway. The kids as babies, toddlers, and their first days of school. Darren in his dress uniform at his promotion ceremony. Allison had invited Harper, but she hadn't come. Knowing Darren was receiving something Noah had strived for but would never have had been too painful. Selfish. She'd been so selfish in her grief.

She shuffled to a stop at the kitchen entrance. Allison's back was to her as she sorted silverware from the dishwasher to a drawer. No curtains obscured the afternoon light from the small window above the sink.

Even with her back turned, Allison showed hints of stress. Always slim, she was downright skinny, her shoulder blades too prominent under a red T-shirt that was half-untucked. Her hair was pulled back into a lopsided ponytail, a look she usually only wore at the gym.

"Hey," Harper said.

Knives clattered into the drawer, lying like pick-up sticks. Allison whirled around, her hand on her chest, her breathing rapid. Surprise stripped away any pretense she might have worn for appearance's sake.

She looked haggard. Spent. Weighted. Harper had worn the same expression for months after Noah's death. Things were even worse than Harper feared. She crossed the kitchen and hauled Allison in for a hug. Allison's body loosened until she collapsed into Harper, a desperate sob escaping.

Harper let her cry, rubbing circles on her back and whispering soothing nonsense words. After too short a time, Allison stiffened, and Harper released her when she really wanted to encourage her to get it all out. But that wasn't Allison's style. She grabbed a paper towel and wiped her eyes and blew her nose.

"Sorry. I thought I had time to grab a shower and clean myself up before you got here." Allison redid her ponytail and tucked in her shirt, her gaze focused somewhere over Harper's shoulder.

"Allison."

Allison hummed but evaded Harper's eyes. "Allison, look at me." Finally, her gaze skittered to meet Harper's. "You don't have to play the perfect officer's wife. Not with me."

Allison's chin wobbled, but she nodded firmly.

"You have some wine stashed?" Harper didn't wait for an answer but opened the fridge to find a bottle of white in the door. Grabbing a glass, she poured and pressed it into Allison's hands. "Hop in a steamy shower and take your time."

"But —"

"I'll handle dinner and the kids. Darren too, if he wakes up. Go." She used her no-arguments-allowed mommy voice, and Allison complied without another peep of protest.

Once her footsteps faded up the steps, Harper inventoried the pantry. Leave it to Allison to have the fixings available for any type of casserole imaginable. Harper went with a beefy, cheesy noodle concoction that was a favorite of Ben's and the definition of comfort food.

Allison still wasn't down when Harper called the kids in for dinner. She herded them into the kitchen and sat down at the table but didn't fix herself a plate.

"Is Daddy up?" Ryan asked around a mouthful of pasta. He was the spitting image of Darren with his thick, dark eyebrows, wide mouth, and prominent nose. On his eight-year-old face, the combination looked ungainly, but Harper had no doubt he would grow into a handsome man.

"I haven't heard him stir." Harper took a sip of iced tea while she debated the friendship ethics of pumping Allison's kids for information. "Does your dad take lots of naps?"

Libby nodded. "He doesn't sleep so good at night. Mommy says he has bad dreams."

Sophie, the youngest at five, piped up. "Sometimes he's really loud and wakes me up."

Libby shushed her little sister as if she was aware of the strangeness and the need to keep secrets.

"Everything is going to be okay." Harper held Libby's gaze as the hated platitude slipped out of her mouth.

God, the number of times she'd heard the same words after Noah had been killed had made her want to scream or punch the kindhearted soul in the face. At the time, nothing felt like it was ever going to be okay again. Now she understood. You said it when you didn't know what else to say. The crazy thing was all those people were right. Eventually, everything *was* okay. Not the same, but okay.

Harper left the kids to finish up their dinner and stood at the bottom of the stairs, listening. Nothing. She climbed, trying not to make a sound, but the steps creaked under her weight.

The kids' rooms were empty, so she padded to the end of the narrow hallway. The door was cracked, so she toed it open enough to peer inside. Allison had curled herself into a ball on top of the covers next to her husband. Both were asleep.

Harper returned to the kitchen, forced herself to eat a small bowl even though worry had stolen her appetite, then played crazy eights with the kids until bedtime. Libby and Ryan got themselves ready for bed, but after a quick bath Sophie begged for a story, her big blue eyes impossible to deny.

Harper tickled her. "Can we read about a princess? Ben never lets me read those."

"Princesses are my favorite," Sophie said between giggles.

Harper snuggled next to Sophie and read until the little girl drifted to sleep. Reaching over to turn the lamp off, Harper dropped her nose into Sophie's shampoo-perfumed hair. A few months older than Ben, Sophie seemed younger. Was it simply their different personalities or had growing up without the umbrella protection of a father forced Ben to mature faster? Harper prayed Sophie traversed this difficult time without losing her innocence.

Lying next to Sophie in the dark, Harper let her imagination travel down alternate futures. One where Noah hadn't died. One where they had a daughter with his blond hair and blue eyes. One where Ben had a father and little sister and she had a husband.

She startled awake, blinking up at the glow-in-the-dark stars on the ceiling. Had she dreamed the noise? Her heart pounded a steady rhythm in her ears, masking external sounds. What time was it? Her phone was downstairs, but the moon was high, the streets quiet.

As the adrenaline faded, her body loosened, and she closed her eyes, wanting to somehow reinsert herself into her dream. The snick of the front door closing bolted her upright. After a quick check showed

Libby and Ryan both in bed, Harper shuffled to Allison and Darren's room and peeked in. Allison had burrowed under the covers at some point, but Darren's bulk was missing.

Thankfully still dressed, she made her way down the steps, shoved her feet into her running shoes, and muttered a curse. He was a grown man, but wandering the streets in the middle of the night in February was not normal. Harper had a feeling nothing had been normal since he'd made it home.

She jogged into the middle of the street. No sign of him in either direction. She spent precious seconds waffling over which way to go, finally taking off at a fast walk into the heart of the base. At the next crossroads, she turned in a slow circle on the hunt for any movement.

Yellow and red slides of a playground were lit by weak streetlights. A dark figure hunched in a swing and rocked back and forth. Harper's heart dropped from her throat back where it belonged.

Darren did nothing but watch as she approached and took the swing next to him. The squeak of the chains broke the silence of the night. She shivered and stared down at his bare feet.

"I'm not crazy." His voice was graveled

with disuse.

"I know."

He planted his feet and stopped his swing. "They all think something's wrong with me."

"Who's 'they'?" Harper sensed his defensiveness and deflected.

"I'm not crazy," he repeated.

"No one thinks you're crazy, Darren. But . . . you *were* injured."

"Banged up. Not like some of my boys who came home without legs or in body bags."

Harper was out of her depth, drowning in platitudes. How was she qualified to help exorcise his demons when she still fought her own? "There's different kinds of injuries. You might be physically healed, but concussions can affect you for months."

"Fuck that." He pushed up and stalked off. She scrambled to follow. "I should be able to deal with a head knock."

He didn't turn back toward the house, and she kept pace at his side. "Aren't your feet cold?"

He glanced down, his step stuttering slightly as if he hadn't realized he was barefoot. His stalk evened out and slowed to an amble. "No."

"Liar." She forced tease into her voice and

was rewarded with a twitch of his lips.

"Did Allison beg you to come down and save her from the living hell I'm putting her and the kids through?" Resignation sucked any emotion from his voice.

The one thing she'd hated above all else in the weeks after Noah had died was the pity in people's eyes and voices. "No. She begged me to come down and put my foot up your ass."

This time he smiled and came to a stop. "Did she really say that?"

"I read between the lines." Harper shrugged and looked around, trying for nonchalance. "Look, I'm tired and completely turned around, so unless you want to explain my frostbitten body to Allison and the MPs, I need an escort back to your house."

He huffed something resembling a laugh, which she counted as a small victory, and turned them around. She kept the conversation light and about how great his kids were. Tension seeped out of her shoulders when the house came into view. She wasn't scared of Darren, but he was a big guy and physically forcing him back inside wasn't an option.

"I'll bet Allison keeps stock in hot chocolate. Want a mug?" she asked.

"Why not. No way I'll be able to go back to sleep." His expression was flat, just like his voice.

Under the kitchen lights, the toll the injury had taken on Darren became more apparent. His eyes were bloodshot and shadowed. He, too, had lost weight, and his hair was longer than she'd ever seen it.

Sure enough, a dozen packets of Swiss Miss were in a polka-dot bin in the pantry. Darren sprawled in a chair and fiddled with the fringed edges of the place mat. She set down steaming mugs and joined him. While she'd never been shot at, she was intimately acquainted with death.

"I had nightmares every night for months after Noah died. Still do sometimes," she said. When he didn't speak or look up, she continued. "Every night I dreamed another horrible way he was killed. Dreamed he died quick and painless, dreamed he suffered, dreamed he died all alone. There were times Ben was the only thing keeping me sane."

She refused to push him any further, and the silence stretched taut.

"McIntyre got shot three feet away from me. Then a bomb went off, and I was on my back. He dragged himself toward me, one of his legs a bloody stump." His words came out choppy, bordering on unemotional even though his eyes said differently. "Over and over and over in my head. I can't get away from it. From him. Maybe it's a blessing Noah was killed."

Anger flared quick and hot in that hollowed-out place in her heart, spreading like wildfire. She popped up and slapped her hands on either side of his mug. The untouched contents sloshed and left a brown stain on the cheery yellow place mat. For the first time, his attention was fixed on her and not turned inward.

"Don't you ever fucking say that again, you hear me? I would do anything, give up anything, to have him back. I don't care what kind of shape he was in. And Allison feels the same way about you. She wants to help you. Let her, dammit."

His brown eyes were wide and his mouth gaping. Her anger died as quickly as it had flared and left her feeling as shocked as he looked.

The stairs creaked and broke the intensity of their gazes. Harper cleared her throat and retrieved a paper towel to dab at the spilled hot chocolate.

Allison shuffled into the kitchen, squinting against the light. "Is everything okay?"

Harper forced a smile. "Fine. Darren and I were chatting over some hot chocolate.

Want some?" She didn't wait but grabbed another mug. With her back to Allison and Darren, Harper dropped the pretense and the smile and took a deep breath. She owed Darren an apology.

She rejoined the couple, and as they spent the next twenty minutes making small talk the tension diminished. Darren leaned closer to Allison, and she reached out to touch his arm or hand, hope erasing a portion of the worry clouding her face.

They said quiet good nights at the foot of the stairs. Halfway up, Darren glanced over his shoulder and their eyes met. Harper couldn't read his expression, but he kept a hand on Allison's waist the rest of the climb.

Harper stretched out on the couch but popped back to sitting when footsteps sounded on the stairs again.

Allison appeared with a blanket over her arm and a pillow clutched to her chest. "I can't believe I forgot to give you these."

Harper took them and set them at her hip. "No worries. I actually fell asleep with Sophie after reading her 'Rapunzel.' "

"She's crazy about fairy tales and loves to play make-believe." The indulgent smile faded. "Sometimes, I feel like I'm playing make-believe. Pretending, you know?"

"You don't have to pretend with me."

"I'll see you in the morning." She nodded and paused in the doorway of the den. "Thanks for coming down and getting him home this time."

This time. Darren's midnight ramble wasn't a onetime thing. Harper's nerves took a swan dive.

Harper lay down, her thoughts jumbled between past and present. Darren and Allison's struggles peeled back the callus on her memories. The abyss that had almost claimed her after Noah's death yawned closer than it had in years, and after she fell into a fitful sleep, Noah haunted her dreams.

CHAPTER 2

Past

After a couple of hours, muscle memory kicked in and Harper didn't have to remind herself to smile at the unending flow of customers. Apparently, scorching summer days in Kitty Hawk had only one balm — ice cream.

The shop's AC struggled to keep up with the constant bursts of steamy air as people entered and exited. She was on the scooping rotation for the rest of her shift. The cold air from the ice-cream freezer was offset by the surprisingly strenuous task of scooping. Every few minutes she had to turn and dab at her face with the towel she kept tucked in her Wilbur's World Famous Ice Cream apron.

She doubted Wilbur Wright or the rest of the world would agree, but it was a good summer job. This was her third — and she hoped last — summer working at Wilbur's.

She'd saved and scrimped and studied hard. Between the scholarships and the money she'd earned, the University of North Carolina was her ticket out of Kitty Hawk.

With her pasted-on smile, she watched the next customer take two measured steps forward. Interest flickered. In board shorts and a sleeveless T-shirt from a band she'd never heard of, the man was good-looking, but if his posture and general air hadn't given him away, his hair did.

High and tight. The standard military-issue haircut. He was probably on leave from Virginia Beach. As hot as the guy was, she avoided military guys. They prowled the Outer Banks looking for a hookup to pass their few days of R and R, never to be seen again. Not her style.

"What can I get you, sir?" She tacked on the "sir" automatically, even though he didn't look much older than she did.

"Mint chocolate chip. Two scoops, if you don't mind." His accent was slow and sultrier than the weather. She couldn't place it, but he was from somewhere farther south than Kitty Hawk. Some place where women lounged in rocking chairs on front porches, gossiped about their neighbors, and drank sweet tea.

"I don't mind a bit, but even if I did, it's

my job." She tempered the slight bite in her tone with a smile she didn't have to force. "Waffle or sugar cone?"

"Sugar." The way he said the word made it sound like an endearment.

The flush started in her chest and made the temperature rise a few more degrees in the packed store. She ducked closer to the tubs of cold ice cream and flapped her shirt a couple of times before fulfilling his order.

In between pulls on the metal scoop, she glanced up at him through the glass. All she could see were his shoulders and chest. Both wide, but a little gangly. They were nice, though. Solid.

Their hands brushed on the exchange, hers sticky, his big, with long fingers and a broad palm. Uncharacteristic nerves zinged through her body, and she wasn't sure what to do with herself. She rubbed both her hands on her apron and glanced down the line, but things were at a standstill.

She recognized the look in his eyes. It happened often enough that she'd learned evasive tactics. The easiest evasion was the simplest. The overly interested customer paid and left and forgot about her as soon as he crossed glances with the next bikini-clad beach bunny.

She leaned back and checked on the

holdup. Sheila, a frazzled expression on her face, slapped the side of their flaky credit card reader a couple of times. Highly satisfying, but generally ineffective. Harper could step over and help. That would break the weird vibes pinging between her and the man staring at her with a charming half smile and cocked eyebrows. Her feet refused to move. Not even a shuffle.

"Are you here for the summer working?" he asked before licking across the top scoop.

"I grew up in Kitty Hawk. A native species. We're a rare breed."

"I'll bet you are." The admiration in his gaze and the softness of his tone tied her stomach into a Boy Scout–worthy knot.

The line curved out the door now. She really should help Sheila. Harper was the best with numbers and anything technical, including the equipment, yet for once she didn't care if the line ever started moving again.

"What's your favorite flavor?" He gestured and took another lick that had her swallowing, almost able to taste the cold minty sweetness.

"First summer I worked here, I ate so much ice cream, I put on fifteen pounds and got sick of the stuff. That said, my favorite *used* to be . . . mint chocolate chip."

Sheila's, "Thank the Lord," echoed through the store to a smattering of applause as Sheila tore off the receipt for the customer to sign.

He reminded her of the blond hot guy from the *Top Gun* movie. Iceman. The line moved, and Iceman sidestepped toward the register, his blue eyes still fixed on her. She glanced at the next woman in line only long enough to get her order before her attention returned to Iceman.

She grabbed a waffle cone and scooped butter pecan, all the while glancing in his direction. He paid with cash, sent a last smile in her direction, and disappeared through the line of people out the door.

She let her smile fade as the knots of nervous anticipation dissolved into a hollow wistfulness. Living in a beach town, she was used to seeing people come and go and didn't get attached to summer dwellers. Yet she had a feeling his crinkled blue eyes and sugared voice would live on in her imagination.

A frazzled mother with two kids pulling at either hand and whining for candy toppings dragged Harper back to her reality. She rallied a smile, even if it felt a little smaller now.

Harper stuffed her stained, sticky apron into her backpack and swung it over her shoulder. Shift change was at five, and she pushed out the back door of the shop by ten after. The air in the alleyway that ran behind the row of shops was stagnant and smelled of garbage and dead sea life. Everything seemed to move slower, as if the heat had an effect on time itself.

She keyed in the combination on her bike lock, pulled the bike off the rack, and straddled it. The seat was hot against her bottom and thighs as she coasted to the alley opening. A man stepped around the corner. She braked hard and the back end of the bike skidded on the loose stone.

It was her man. No, not *hers* but Iceman. She dropped her feet on either side of the pedals and waited for his move. The same knots of anticipation retied themselves at warp speed. And something else . . . relief. Relief she hadn't seen the last of him.

He held up his hands as if surrendering. "The girls inside said you'd already left but that I might be able to catch you around here. Hope I didn't scare you."

"I'm not scared." With a jolt, she recognized she spoke from a place of truth and not a knee-jerk defensiveness. Like she had in the store earlier, she tempered her words with a smile, this one big enough to use cheek muscles she hadn't exercised in a while.

"Just so you know, I'm not a weirdo." A self-deprecating laugh rumbled from his chest. "I guess that's what an actual weirdo would say, right?"

She swung her leg over the seat and walked her bike closer to him. "I trust you." Her words registered a millisecond after they left her mouth. "I mean, I trust you're not a weirdo."

"My name's Noah. Noah Wilcox." He stuck out one of his big hands.

She bit the inside of her lip and slipped her hand in his. As much as she didn't want to admit it, his palpable strength was attractive. "I'm Harper Frazier."

"Nice to meet you, Harper." He gave her fingers a squeeze before letting go and tucking his hands into the pockets of his shorts. Stepping aside, he chucked his chin in the direction of the main thoroughfare, and without words they fell into step side by side, the bike between them like a chaperone.

"So . . . what did you do the rest of the

afternoon?" she asked after too many seconds of silence.

"I hung out on the beach with my buddies."

Of course he did. She internally cringed. *Way to go, Ms. Obvious.* Making small talk with the opposite sex wasn't exactly her forte. She'd never even had a serious boyfriend.

She snuck a glance, but he didn't seem to be laughing at her. His cheeks were tinged with the beginnings of a burn, his hair glinting even blonder in the sun. "You know what's strange? Even though I grew up here, I hardly go to the beach. If I'm in the mood, I'll sometimes walk over to the bay side and watch the sunset."

"Most people love the beach." He raised his eyebrows, and she shrugged.

"For one thing, I hate sand. It gets *everywhere.*" She sent him a meaningful glance and was rewarded with another of his rumbly laughs. "Mostly, though, the ocean makes me feel . . ." She struggled to come up with the right words. "Small. Kind of sad, I guess. And seriously insignificant."

Most boys her age were put off by her philosophical musings. That's the price she paid for being raised by a librarian who didn't allow a TV in their house.

"Deep thoughts. I myself prefer the vast wildness of the ocean. I grew up on a soybean farm in Georgia. Thought my roots ran so deep that I'd never get out."

She struggled with the same pull and guilt to stay or go. "You somehow managed to rip yourself away, since you joined up."

He brushed a hand over his hair with another self-deprecating laugh. "The shorn look give me away?"

"Among other things. What branch?"

"Navy SEALs. Or at least, that's the plan. I leave next week for training in California."

Her heart pinched, reminding her not to get attached. "I've heard they only take the best and the most badass."

"It's rigorous. Didn't think I had a shot, but I nailed all the evaluations."

Silence fell between them. She should say a polite good-bye and ride off. The crazy bolt of happiness that had flared on seeing him standing in the shaft of sunlight at the mouth of the alley was because she either had read too many books or was looking for a way to assuage her own nervousness. Come autumn and she'd be flying from her own nest.

Yet, like in the ice-cream shop, she didn't leave. Something primal and ancient rattled her bones like an earthquake, and she kept strolling along, herding him down a quieter, shaded side street and away from the chaos of the beach. "Are you scared about training?"

He blew out a slow breath. "Don't tell my buddies, but I'm terrified. A huge percentage of recruits wash out."

"What happens if you don't make it?"

"I become a regular Navyman. Which would be fine, but . . ." His lips pressed tight.

"You'd feel like you failed?"

"No 'feel' about it. It would be a fact. I'd be a failure."

She didn't know how to respond or alleviate fears of the future she battled on a daily basis as well. What if she flunked out of UNC? What if she had to move home and battle the flaky credit card machine at the ice-cream shop for the rest of her life?

"Do you miss your family?" she asked.

"As insane as they make me and as much as I wanted to leave . . . Yes. So much I've thought about quitting and heading home. Dad wants me to take over the farm." He made a scoffing sound and ran a hand over his head as if it was an old habit to ruffle his now-phantom hair. "I don't know why I'm telling you all this considering we just met, but I can't talk about it to them." He thumbed over his shoulder toward the beach. "Okay guys, and we might even be friends, but we're also competing for SEAL spots. Sometimes, the testosterone is too much even for me."

"I don't mind if you tell me stuff." Again, she answered not from politeness' sake but with the truth. His searing blue eyes demanded that of her.

"What about you?" he asked.

"What about me?"

"How old are you?"

"Eighteen. I'm heading to UNC in the fall."

"Wow, that's cool. What are you going to major in?"

"Business, I think. Maybe minor in marketing." She gripped the handlebars of her bike a little tighter. "I'm scared about going off, too. Scared about flunking out. I can't imagine coming back here and living with my mom."

"You two don't get along?"

"No, we get along fine. Better than fine, actually, but she's very protective. And a little controlling."

"Where does she work?'

"Mom is Kitty Hawk's librarian." She rolled her eyes as she added, "My full name is Harper Lee Frazier."

Noah's laugh burst from his chest, startling a squirrel up the nearest tree. She found herself laughing with him even though living with the name for eighteen years had thinned her skin against teasing. She had dropped the "Lee" on all her UNC forms.

"That's awesome. I love it." He cast still-smiling eyes in her direction. "It suits you, by the way."

"I'm afraid to ask how considering she wrote an American classic and then turned into a recluse with like fifty cats."

"Harper Lee had fifty cats? Geez."

She giggled at his exaggerated grimace. "I totally made that up. But doesn't she strike you as the cat lady poster child?"

"Maybe, but she claimed a slice of glory. She'll never be forgotten."

Harper tilted her head to study him. Was Noah Wilcox after a different type of glory? She didn't ask, only pointed and said simply, "My house."

"Hard to get used to seeing all these places on stilts. You ride out storms here or move inland?"

"Unless an evacuation order is issued, we stay." She didn't add that her mom took on storms the way she took on life. Balls-to-the-wall defiant, but with more than her fair share of humor. Her mom was a Character with a capital *C*. The kind Harper Lee would have written about.

"You didn't mention your dad. Does he live here, too?"

"Messy divorce when I was two. He sends child support, but that's about it." Her daddy issues weren't on the table for discussion. "I have a feeling you left a big family behind. Younger sisters?"

"Four of them. How'd you know?"

She wouldn't tell him it was in the polite, protective way he treated her from positioning himself on the street side of the sidewalk to the way he glanced at her under his lashes as if she was special.

"Lucky guess," she said lightly.

She trailed to a stop across the street from her house under the shade of an oak. The air was oppressive, too far inland to benefit from the water-cooled breezes.

He faced her, feet braced shoulder-width apart, hands clasped behind his back. "Can I see you again, Harper Lee?"

"For what?"

"Dinner? A sunset walk on the beach or the bay if you'd rather. Doesn't matter to me." His earnestness struck her as sincere.

"That's nice, but I guess I meant *why*? You're leaving."

"For now, but there's a good chance after training I'll be stationed at Virginia Beach."

"But *I'm* leaving for UNC in August."

He didn't break eye contact with her. "Okay, so logistics aside, I like you. This afternoon after I left the ice-cream shop, I couldn't stop thinking about you. You're . . . different."

She been told that enough by the boys at her high school to know it was true. Yet Noah said it like it was a compliment and not an insult. "Nothing can come of us hanging out."

"Maybe not, but I'd still like to see you again." In a more cajoling tone, he said, "Come on, dinner's on me. Nicest place along the Outer Banks if you want."

His choice of words jolted her. "Maybe not." Not "definitely not." She weighed her options. Never seeing Noah again wasn't one of them. Even if it was only one more time.

"How about tonight?" Her impulsiveness surprised her. She was more of a pro and con list maker, but urgency stripped away her usual caution.

"Tonight?" Shock drew out the word and emphasized his accent.

Had she been too forward? Her experience — or lack thereof — didn't provide clues. Unable to tolerate a rejection face-to-face, she bounced her bike over the curb, checking for traffic even though her street was deserted compared to the crowds only a few blocks away.

"You're probably going out and partying with your buddies. I totally get it."

"Not anymore I'm not." He jogged backward until they were eye to eye. "I'm taking out the prettiest girl in Kitty Hawk."

She wasn't, but the way he was looking at her made her feel like she might be within shouting distance. Then, his expression fell and so did her answering smile.

"What is it?" Fear that she'd done something wrong made her voice pitch high.

"I only brought shorts."

Relief sent a laugh skittering out of her. "As long as you pair them with a shirt with sleeves, that's dressing up around here in the summer."

She reached the steps leading to her front door, leaned the bike against the rail, and faced him with nothing in between them for the first time. He was a good six inches taller than she was and grew more handsome the longer she stared into his smile-crinkled blue eyes.

"What time should I pick you up? Does seven give you enough time?"

It was almost six already and she needed to shower and straighten her unruly hair, but a shot of anticipation had her saying, "Seven would be perfect."

He backed away as she took the first few steps to her front door sideways so she could keep him in sight. He reached the shady sidewalk, raised a hand, then turned and jogged away. He moved like an athlete. Maybe he'd played football if he was a Georgia country boy.

She didn't have to wonder. She could ask him tonight. A blistering happiness swept through her, and she stayed planted until he disappeared. Sweat trickled down her neck in the hot sun. Once he'd disappeared, the spell he'd cast over her waned, and ordinary worries interjected.

She'd just met him. His career choice was another strike against him. Not that the military wasn't a noble calling, but only heartache would result in getting attached to someone who was up and leaving in a week.

The logical arguments against a date buzzed like no-see-ums, but she waved them away. Nothing could dull Harper's smile, even though no one could see.

CHAPTER 3

Present Day

Milk-tinged morning breath and a light poke at her right cheek woke Harper. She opened her eyes and startled back into her pillow. Sophie was nose-to-nose, a blur of messy curls and one big blue eye.

"I was worried you were under an evil witch's spell like Sleeping Beauty," she whispered.

"If I was then you broke it," Harper whispered back, forcing the laugh that bubbled up back down. The little girl was so serious, Harper didn't want her to think she was making fun of her.

"Do you want pancakes?"

"Is your mom up?"

"She's in the kitchen."

"Go tell her I'll be there in a minute."

Sophie's full weight fell on Harper in a hug before she skipped off. Harper sat up and rubbed her face, sticky where Sophie had touched her. She grabbed her toiletry bag and turned herself decently human in the kids' bathroom. By the time she emerged, the kids were back upstairs playing in their rooms, and Harper found Allison alone in the kitchen.

"Morning," Harper said tentatively. "Where's Darren?"

"Out for a run. If he's not wandering the streets at night or napping, he's running." Allison laughed, but it was tinged with irony. "Our crazy was on full display last night, huh?" She held out a cup of black coffee.

Harper took a sip to buy some time. At the very least, last night had torn back a veil of normalcy. "Crazy doesn't faze me; you know that."

Allison huffed and leaned against the counter, her gaze on her coffee. "It might not faze you, but you know how it is around here. . . . I'm the one who's supposed to deal with everyone else's crazy."

"Allison." The frustration Harper felt was akin to when Ben refused to ask for help before making a huge mess pouring his own milk. "You were my rock after Noah died and when Ben was born, and you've been the rock for countless wives on base during deployments and births and deaths. Let me

— let *us* — help you now."

Allison swallowed, her chin wobbling. "Everything's falling apart. It's starting to affect the kids. Libby's grades have slipped, and Ryan's been getting in trouble at school. Sophie seems to be the only one who takes Darren's moods in stride."

"Is Darren talking to someone? Are you?"

"I'm talking to you, aren't I?" Allison's attempt at a laugh fell a yardstick short.

The pressure to find the right thing to say stalled Harper's tongue. No one could understand the stress and isolation of being a military wife unless she'd lived it. Finally, she said, "I'm glad you're talking to me, and I want you to tell me everything, but I have to leave soon. What about the military wives' support group you started?"

"They're a great group of women." Allison jerked, spilling coffee. "Oh my God, I forgot we have a meeting this afternoon. I was going to get everything ready last night, but I conked out."

Her panic bled into Harper. "Are they coming here? What do we need to do?"

"It's at the community center, thank God, but what'll I do for food? I usually bring a homemade cake and petit fours and several dips." Allison yanked the pantry door open so hard it bounced into the wall and hit her back.

Harper grabbed one of Allison's hands and tugged her around. "We are going to hit up the commissary and buy whatever they have that we can open and plop some chips next to."

"But —"

"No buts. We will buy paper napkins and plastic tablecloths and then you're going to ask for their help."

"It's more of a social group. Or a place to complain about moving — again. Finding schools and doctors and all that. You know the drill."

"You need support, and those women can help. No reason it can't be more than social."

Harper held Allison's gaze and gave her hand a squeeze. In a thin voice, Allison said, "What if they think I'm weak or something?"

"I don't think you're weak. In fact, you're the strongest woman I've ever had the pleasure of calling a friend. I'll be right there with you."

"Promise?"

"Yep. Chowing down on some store-bought french onion dip and Ruffles."

Allison's laughter was sharp and edged

with dread, but Harper would take it.

The women didn't seem to mind the picnic-like fare she and Allison had thrown together. The chatter and laughter of ten women filled the room in the base community center. Born of routine, after an hour of gossip and small talk the women shifted metal folding chairs into a circle, everyone quieting and looking toward Allison, their leader.

Allison cleared her throat. "I managed to introduce Harper around, didn't I?" Murmurs of welcome and smiles were directed toward Harper. "Does anyone have anything they want to discuss?"

Harper gave Allison's ankle a nudge, but another woman with bottle-blond hair launched into a diatribe about her son's pediatrician that went on for a solid ten minutes broken only by nods and sympathetic muttering.

The woman finally ran out of gas and the silence was filled by the squeak of women shifting in their seats. Harper caught Allison's eye and nodded.

"I don't know if anyone's noticed, but" — Allison's voice cracked — "Darren's not doing great since he made it home."

The women erupted in "oh nos" and "ah,

honeys." The circle of chairs scooted inward so the women could reach Allison to give a pat on her knee or squeeze her hand. Tears sprang to Harper's eyes, the moment bringing back memories of the outpouring of support she'd gotten after Noah's death. Among military wives, no matter what branch, when disaster struck one a "there but by the grace of God go I" feeling incited true compassion.

After Allison's battle with Darren's demons poured out, a petite woman named Samantha sat forward on her seat. "I don't think my husband has slept a full night since he got home two months ago. He won't talk to me about it."

Walls crumbled right and left as one by one the women let go of the façade. Another woman, a plump, pretty redhead, said, "Things can be tough when they're home, but I struggle when they're deployed."

"We all miss our husbands," said another woman curtly. "No one is saying we don't."

"It's not that. . . ." The redhead dropped her gaze to her lap, her hands reflecting her agitation in their constant movement. "I haven't been able to find a job since we moved here. I get bored and depressed and sometimes wonder what I signed up for by marrying a military man. Our lives — *my* life — seems to revolve around his career, wondering when he'll deploy or what our next big move might be. Sometimes I resent it. Is that terrible?"

The woman's confession slingshot Harper back nine years to when she was a newlywed struggling to fill the hours in their small town house off base while she looked for a job she wasn't vastly overqualified for. It had never truly felt like a home. Her framed diplomas from UNC mocked her until she'd taken them off the wall and tucked them into a closet.

"Not terrible," Harper said. "I felt the same way after I got married. I graduated with honors, but it was hard to find a decent job. If it hadn't been for Allison, I would've lost it." She had loved Noah, but how long would that have sustained her? He'd died and she'd never had to face up to the answer.

Some women stated their kids kept them plenty busy, but a handful of others agreed with Harper, lamenting the lack of opportunities for military wives to contribute outside of the household. The uncertainties military wives faced were unique, which meant their paths led them off the beaten track. Excitement went hand in hand with frustration.

The meeting wrapped up with hugs and promises to talk soon. While everyone pitched in to clean up, Samantha pulled Allison aside for a quiet conversation that left Allison wiping her eyes.

Once Allison and Harper were alone in the car, Allison pulled out a scrap of paper with a number written on it. "Samantha gave me the number of a group for soldiers that meets on base to talk about their experiences. Sort of like AA except for PTSD."

"That's great."

"I don't know if Darren will go."

"You'll have to work on him until he does, that's all," Harper said lightly to counteract the darkness in Allison's voice.

"You make it sound so easy. Nothing's been easy since he made it home." Tears muffled Allison's words.

If Allison weren't driving, Harper would snatch her up into a hug. "I know it hasn't, but if anyone can make it through this, even if you have to drag Darren kicking and screaming with you to the other side, it's you. It'll get easier."

"Doesn't feel that way."

"I can't count the number of times some well-meaning person patted my hand and told me it would get easier. I didn't believe them, but it turns out, they were right. So now I'm telling you the same thing, knowing it's true."

Allison pulled in to their driveway, put the car in park, but left the engine running, the faint drum line from a pop song in the background. She took a deep breath, her face resolute. "I'll talk to him tonight, and if he doesn't agree to go, I'll talk to him tomorrow night and the next and the next."

"Excellent plan." They stared toward the house, and Harper gave a little laugh. "Should we make sure the house isn't destroyed?"

Instead of turning the car off, Allison shifted toward Harper. "Were you serious back there?"

"About what?"

"About being bored and feeling useless when you and Noah were together?"

Harper didn't detect judgment, only curiosity. "Don't misunderstand me, I wasn't unhappy, but I craved something outside of all military, all the time. Things got better after I started volunteering. Then I got pregnant and had something else to focus on."

"Did you ever tell Noah how you were feeling?"

Guilt pinged. "I tried, but I'm not sure he

ever understood. Not really. It was easier to act like everything was perfect. And in lots of ways — the ways that count — they were."

"I bet lots of wives on base feel like you did. Too bad there's not an outlet for them beyond volunteering and their kids." Allison turned the car off and got out. The echo of music faded into silence.

At Allison's meeting alone, three women expressed the same dissatisfaction. That was a slice of wives in one group and at one base. How many around the Southeast — the country — dealt with the same issues as they crisscrossed the world following their husbands?

Allison hesitated at the front door and shot a quizzical look over her shoulder. Harper got out of the car and stepped into the chaos of the house, the three kids playing tag while Darren was sprawled on the couch and flipping through the channels.

His eyes were red rimmed from lack of sleep, and he gave Allison a kiss on his shuffle to the stairs, disappearing for what Harper assumed was a nap, which would probably lead to a repeat of last night's wanderings.

Allison only watched him go, but the look on her face was more resolute and less downtrodden than it had been the day before. "I'll talk to him later. Want to help me get dinner going for the kids?"

After a noisy, fun dinner, Allison sent the kids upstairs to get ready for bed and to finish any homework before heading back to school on Monday.

"I wish you didn't have to leave so soon." Allison scooped out chocolate ice cream for their dessert and set the small bowls on the cleared table.

Harper took a spoonful and was cast back more than a decade to her summer job in the ice-cream shop. Bittersweet memories.

"I'm afraid to leave Ben under my mom's sole influence. She'll turn him into a socialist, nude-painting, granola-eating tree hugger in a week." Her exaggeration achieved the intended result when Allison laughed with only a hint of her earlier strain.

"Your mom is incredible."

"She totally is." Harper jabbed at her ice cream. "I can't stop thinking about what you said in the car. About base wives looking for something to do. What if I came up with something?"

"Like what? Knitting?"

"Not a hobby. I'm talking about a business to employ military wives. Something they could keep doing no matter where they were stationed." The seed Allison had planted earlier bloomed into full-on excitement.

Allison stared at Harper as if she'd switched to a different language and Allison couldn't understand her. "What kind of business?"

Harper shot from the hip, ideas coming fast and furious. "Something homegrown. Maybe military focused but appealing to everyone."

"What do you know about running a business?" Her question came out more astonished than disparaging.

"I graduated from UNC with dual degrees in business and marketing, and I've been dying to put them to good use. Plus, I've been doing bookkeeping and taxes up and down the Outer Banks since Noah died. I understand a good business plan." Harper left her ice cream to melt and paced the floor. Her body felt tingly and alive, as if someone had taken paddles to her chest and jumpstarted her life.

"I don't want to be a Debbie Downer, but what about money to get started? Doesn't it take tens of thousands of dollars?"

"At least that much, but I invested the money I got from Noah's bravery award. Even if I keep some back for Ben's college, we should have enough to get started. Once we come up with a solid, marketable product. Do you think the women in the group want to help?"

"I'm sure they do. We can set up a group chat or something. Hang on a minute, though. What bravery award? I don't remember that."

"He received it posthumously."

"And it came with money?"

"Yeah, lots of it. I was shocked."

"Define 'lots'?"

Allison's tone finally registered and Harper sank back into her seat. "A hundred thousand?"

"Not government death benefits?"

"No. This was different. The man handed me a cashier's check and told me it was for a bravery award. I think he gave me a certificate, too." Had she kept it? Had it even been real? Harper had printed Ben a certificate off the internet when he'd finished potty training, for goodness' sake.

Allison uttered a word Harper didn't think was even in her vocabulary before continuing. "Who was this man?"

Unease blunted Harper's excitement. Had she done something wrong or, even worse, illegal? "That time was a blur, but his name was Caldwell, I think."

Allison looked down and fiddled with her spoon. "Of course. Bennett Caldwell. Makes sense."

"What are you talking about?"

"Did Noah never mention him?"

"Was he a SEAL?"

Allison nodded. "Served with Noah and Darren."

"Noah used everyone's nicknames at home. Even called Darren 'Family Man.' "

A small smile helped erase the worried crinkles in Allison's brow. "Noah's nickname was my favorite."

"He hated being called Peaches."

"Bennett Caldwell, aka Grizzly, and Noah were close. According to Darren, Bennett was there when . . ." — Allison's gaze skated to the floor, her voice turning vague — "you know."

Harper knew. Or had at least imagined what Noah's last moments had been like. She had played the scenarios over in her head so many times she wondered if she'd go mad. But what drove her insane was knowing that whatever she imagined hadn't come close to the terribleness of his death.

And Grizzly had been there. While the name Bennett Caldwell was unfamiliar, she was well acquainted with Grizzly. Or at least stories about him. Noah had talked about

Griz like he was a big brother and a father and the biggest badass ever all rolled into one.

"Why would he give me so much money?" Harper asked. "Are you certain there's no bravery award? Maybe within the unit?"

"The military enjoys its pomp and circumstance. A bravery award given to a fallen hero would have merited a huge ceremony and the front page of the paper."

With the sharp lens of hindsight fixed on the moment, Harper blamed her naïveté on grief. The man with the check had given her more than money; he'd given her something to cling to. *Bravery. Honor.* Something to be proud of in those dark days and months. Was it all a lie?

"I don't feel right taking his money."

"He obviously chose to give it to you and hasn't come asking for it back." Allison shrugged. "Seems to me he wanted you to have it for some reason."

"But why?" Harper whispered, not expecting an answer from Allison.

The obvious answer was to alleviate guilt. What did he have to feel guilty about? Another thought tripped onto the last. *Bennett. Ben.* Had she unknowingly named her son after him?

Noah had suggested the name Ben their

last night together, cuddled under the covers. She'd been barely six weeks pregnant, but they'd spent the night imagining what their child would be like. Boy or girl, blond or brown haired, outgoing or shy. Afterward, the name had provided another connection to Noah.

"What happened to Caldwell? Where is he?"

"Last I heard he got out right after Noah was —" Allison cleared her throat.

"I never got the full story, you know. On Noah's death."

"Not even now?"

"I've asked every year on the anniversary. Why do I keep torturing myself? It's always the same answer." She put on a pompous voice. " 'Details are classified, but rest assured, Mrs. Wilcox, your husband died a hero. Let me send you the same vague report we've sent the last four times.' "

"Darren gave me the same runaround when I asked him. He takes classified intel seriously, but I can try again. Not sure if he's up to reliving it, though." Allison sent a weighty glance toward the stairs.

"No, don't do that." The last thing Darren needed was Harper selfishly adding to his troubles. "My imagination is digging up conspiracies that aren't there. Knowing won't bring him back, so I guess I should let it go?" Her voice lilted the statement into questioning territory.

"Maybe." Allison popped up. "But maybe not. You deserve closure, and if details are what you need, then Bennett Caldwell has them. Also, this award thing is superweird. Let me grab my laptop and we'll do a little cyber-stalking."

Harper scooted her seat around and bounced her knee as the computer booted up. "What if he turned into one of those hermit preppers who live in an old missile silo?"

Allison typed in his name and hit enter. "Or . . . holy moly, what if he runs a survival school in Virginia?"

The first hit was for a Caldwell Survival School, Virginia Beach, Virginia, owner/operator Bennett Caldwell. Harper muttered a curse that made a regular appearance in her vocabulary but made Allison giggle-gasp.

Allison clicked on the link and a well-designed, welcoming website popped up. A wideshot of a man in camo, hat, and sunglasses standing on the ridge of a mountain was in the bottom corner along with a brief tag line — "Decorated former Navy SEAL Bennett Caldwell."

"It's been five years. You sure you want to open this door? It might be more painful than satisfying." Allison's voice hitched with hesitancy.

"Could be, but I can't in good conscience use money if it isn't really mine. I need to know why he pretended Noah was awarded that money for bravery." Harper sat back and crossed her arms over her chest. Betrayal nipped even though she wasn't sure why. "I read the bare minimum of facts the military provided, but I want to know . . . *everything* that happened to Noah."

Allison breathed her name. A warning Harper would ignore.

"Looks like my next stop is to see Bennett Caldwell."

CHAPTER 4

Past

Bennett Caldwell stashed his clothes in the closest locker and examined the men he'd be spending the next six months with. Some of them, anyway. Statistically, the washout rate was cited as anywhere between 75 and 90 percent, depending on how bad the man you asked wanted to scare the shit out of you.

While Bennett wasn't overly confident, he wasn't a wet-behind-the-ears recruit straight out of boot camp like some of the kids. He was twenty-four and had served his time in the regular Navy on an aircraft carrier in the Middle East.

Two of his roommates, Hollis and Carter, were ordinary in every way, except for a special swagger only bestowed by BDUs. They had arrived first and claimed the top two bunks, not that Bennett cared. This was a temporary stop on his way to receiving his trident.

Bennett hadn't offered his name or much more than a grunt in greeting and didn't miss the eye rolls as Hollis and Carter left for the chow hall. Not that he gave a damn what they thought.

"Where you from?" Bennett's third roommate was a blond-haired, blue-eyed All-American type with ruddy cheeks and a broad, lanky body. His smile was friendly and open.

Bennett narrowed his eyes and didn't return the overture. He wasn't here to make friends. He didn't need them. His plan was to keep his head down and do the work. "Mississippi."

"That's awesome. I'm from Georgia." His tone implied because they were both from south of the Mason-Dixon that afforded them a special bond. It didn't.

Bennett's years being passed around foster care in Mississippi didn't incite the warm fuzzies. If he never stepped foot in Mississippi again, it would be too soon. He didn't offer up additional information, but the kid didn't get the hint.

"I'm Noah Wilcox." He stepped closer and held out a hand.

Bennett hesitated longer than was polite

but took it in a shake. There was no reason to be a total dick. "Bennett Caldwell, AW."

"You've been serving already?"

"Six years. Last assignment was on the *Carl Vinson.*"

"Cool." Noah's tone was awed with more than a hint of worry. "I signed up straight out of high school. This seemed like a good idea at the time. Now, I'm not so sure."

The kid was wide-eyed and untarnished. Bennett was pretty sure he'd never looked like that. Not much he could offer except the truth. "BUD/S is going to be hard as hell."

Passing Basic Underwater Demolition was the first step in becoming a SEAL. Actual SEAL training followed, with men washing out at every phase. Optimism wasn't in Bennett's nature or vocabulary, but his grim hold on reality had gotten him through tough times before, and he would make it through BUD/S or die.

"I guess the worst that can happen is I get shuffled into regular Navy." His laugh was an anxious one.

Bennett grunted, his respect for the kid taking a dive. If Noah was already thinking in terms of contingencies then he might as well quit right now and give his spot up to someone who wanted it more.

After he got his things neatly stored, Bennett lay down on top of the blankets and closed his eyes. Sleep would be a thing of the past soon enough, and he wasn't going to spend energy on a kid who was already a ghost.

Wake-up the next morning came before dawn. The alarm dragged Bennett out of a deep sleep where old dreams didn't trouble him. It was dark in the room, but Noah was up and rustling through his locker for clothes.

Within ten minutes, the BUD/S class gathered on the black-painted concrete and asphalt yard outside the quarterdeck doors, affectionately referred to as the grinder. Bennett quick-stepped to the far side where there were fewer men. He didn't realize Noah was on his heels until he stopped and the kid bumped into him, mumbling an apology. Besides high color on his cheekbones, he was pale and looked ready to shit his pants.

Bennett wasn't that far gone, but his heart galloped along, nerves fraying his usual calm. This was the start and, for many, it would soon be the finish.

He'd done his best to ignore the bell hanging from the rafter next to the open space of their soon-to-be torture area. But the bell drew his gaze as if magnetized. It was smaller than he'd anticipated, innocuous looking even, but ringing it would signal the death knell of his dreams.

He snapped his attention forward and his body straight when a monster of man in BDUs stalked to the front of the class. Another man, shorter, slighter, but no less cut, stood to the side in parade rest.

"You maggots want to be SEALs?" the monster in the front yelled with a Southern twang. Just Bennett's luck to be tortured by a man from the South.

The group hesitated and when they answered it was at different times and on top of one another.

"I said, do you little fuckers want to be SEALs?" His voice increased in volume and intensity if that was possible.

"Sir, yes, *sir*!" This time they managed to answer in unison.

"Then let's see what you got."

The man standing off to the side went from zero to a hundred miles per hour. Two other men flanked them from the back, yelling and clapping and getting them moving. High knees. Push-ups. Sit-ups. Burpees. Basic stuff over and over that should have been easy. And it was for Bennett. He'd learned at ten years old to tune out scream-ing men and this was no different.

After two hours and in the middle of another set of push-ups, a glance to his right showed other men struggling, their arms trembling like taffy. Noah was hanging in there, his mouth pulled into a grimace but his push-ups still crisp.

A whistle sounded. "On your feet." The monster was back at the front. "I'm Instruc-tor Lennox. Your mama and daddy and Heavenly Father for the next five weeks. You got that?"

Everyone replied in the affirmative.

"See that bell?"

He pointed and Bennett turned to look like everyone else but promptly returned his attention to Instructor Lennox. Smarter if he ignored the damn thing.

"Some of you will quit me. Maybe even today. Three-quarters of you assholes won't make it out of Phase One. You scared yet?"

No one answered and then Instructor Lennox took two ground-swallowing steps. The unfortunate man who'd gained his at-tention was still staring at the bell, but with the dragon's breath of Lennox on his face, he snapped to attention.

"You scared yet, Matthews?"

"Sir, yes, *sir.*" At a spate of laughter from

the men, Matthews amended his answer, but his voice wavered. "I mean, sir, no, *sir.*"

Instructor Lennox didn't move and Matthews visibly wilted as if Lennox could melt spines with his eyes. "You assholes just earned an extra mile, thanks to this maggot." Finally, he swept his gaze over the group. "What the fuck are you waiting for? An embossed invitation? Go!"

Bennett was the first one to move, leading the pack of men out onto the beach. He settled into a pace that would meet requirements but wouldn't burn him out. Hopped up on adrenaline and fear, men streaked past and set an impossible pace, hoping to impress. Bennet's job wasn't to impress but to survive.

Noah stayed at his side. It was half-annoying and half-endearing, like a stray puppy. Soon, though, their feet beat the same rhythm in the sand and became a comfort.

He lost track of time, but their boots ate up the miles. Finally, they met runners on the return loop. Most of them were red faced and gulping air through their mouths. He and Noah had fallen to the back third of the men, and a moment of doubt streaked through him. Had his already-tired muscles fooled him into a too-slow pace?

He kicked it up a gear. Noah grunted next to him. "We're good, man."

Bennett slowed to match Noah. "You sure?"

"Made it to the state championship in track." He puffed the words out.

Bennett settled in and kept his head down, his gaze fixed on the six feet of sand in front of him. Soon enough they blew past men who'd burned out too early, and when they crossed the line in the sand and got their times they had moved into the top third.

Bennett slowed to a walk, his legs quivering. He'd done his best to maintain fitness on the *Vinson,* but endurance might prove an issue. Treadmills weren't anywhere near as grueling as sand.

The rest of the day was an endless round of PT. Five weeks of the same shit filled the foreseeable future. As the edge of the sun touched the water, they regathered on the grinder. Somehow he and Noah had ended up on the second row. Too close to the Monster, as Bennett had already dubbed Instructor Lennox.

Bennett's body was numb. All he wanted was to shovel as much food as possible into his mouth and collapse in bed to regroup, but Instructor Lennox had more yelling to do. How the man hadn't busted a vocal cord

74

by now was a medical miracle. Bennett tuned him out.

"— quit? You gonna quit, you fucking pussy? Go on, then. Do it."

The *q* word yanked Bennett back into the moment. Instructor Lennox was back in Matthews's face. The instructor was an expert at identifying the weakest men and his job was to cull them out before they could become a danger to them all. Bennett could respect the mission if not the method. He'd tasted the bite of humiliation, and unwanted empathy for Matthews surfaced from his exhaustion.

Matthews stood directly in front of Noah and diagonal to Bennett. Wet sand coated his left side and clumped in the back of his hair. He shifted, favoring his left foot. He couldn't have been much over eighteen and was not ready for the mental mind games of BUD/S, that much was obvious. His foot moved, enough to signal what was coming. Bennett barely stopped himself from grabbing the boy's shoulder and forcing him to stay.

When Matthews turned, the anguish on his face made Bennett close his eyes. Tears had tracked through the sand and grime on his cheeks. The bell rang. The noise reverberated through Bennett's head long after his ears stopped processing the noise.

"And what about you?" The instructor's voice was so loud, Bennett's eyes popped open, expecting to find the man in his face.

But he'd only taken a step forward in Noah's grill. Noah had proved himself physically on the run. It was his mental strength that was in question.

"I'm not quittin', sir," Noah barked out.

"Where're you from, sailor?"

"Georgia, sir." The unmistakable pride in Noah's voice made Bennett wince. He was well acquainted with men like Instructor Lennox. They didn't appreciate pride. They made it their mission to stamp it out.

"You look about sixteen, son. Who let you off the peach farm? Is that what you've got on your balls? Peach fuzz?"

"No, sir."

Bennett cursed internally.

"Drop and give me twenty."

Noah dropped and gave him twenty. Which under normal circumstances would have been a cakewalk, but after the men had spent an entire day spent flogging their bodies Bennett could see the strain across Noah's back and the tremble in his arms. He got up like an old man but threw his shoulders back once he was upright.

"You ready to quit yet, Peaches?"

"Sir, no, sir!" His voice was strong. The instructor stared Noah down, but he didn't give an inch, and Bennett had the urge to give him a high five.

"Break!" The instructor backed away from Noah, pivoted, and stalked past the forlorn helmet of Matthews.

Bennett kept his head down and shuffled along with the other men toward the chow hall. The smell of spaghetti made his mouth water and his stomach rumble. Noah was sitting by himself at a table in the front. Bennett carried his tray past him and took a seat in the far corner of the room as far away from everyone as possible.

The buzz of conversation filled the room, but every once in a while a man's voice would rise above the fray, "Hey, Peaches," or, "What's up, Peaches," followed by laughter and accompanied by shit-eating grins. Bennett was too far away to hear Noah's response, if he even had one.

The poor bastard.

Bennett only slowed down when he was halfway through the enormous mound of spaghetti on the tray. He was still alone at the table. Which was fine. Friends weren't on the menu.

Noah twisted in his seat and said something to the man next to him that caused raucous laughter to erupt. Noah stood and stalked away. Apparently, he was the joke and not the comedian.

As Noah approached, Bennett shifted his attention back to getting food into his belly, hoping his Fuck Off vibes were strong enough to repel Noah. They weren't.

Noah slammed his tray down and took the seat across from Bennett.

"Assholes." Noah shoveled a forkful of spaghetti into his mouth, his color high and his eyes bright with anger.

Bennett ignored him.

A laugh huffed out of Noah. "I'm not even from a fucking peach orchard."

"Oh really?" Bennett had pegged Noah as a country boy.

"No. My family owns a soybean farm."

A laugh snuck past Bennett's determination to stay distant. "Same thing to a lunkhead like Lennox."

Noah glanced to either side and leaned over his tray. "Careful."

"I plan to be. You, on the other hand, are screwed."

"How so?"

"You've earned a big target on your back."

Noah muttered a curse.

"Do the work and don't let that lump of humanity intimidate you. His job is to try to make us quit. Prove him wrong; don't." A slow grin came to Bennett's face. "Anyway, it could be worse."

"How so?"

"He could have called you peach balls. Or douche canoe. Or panty waister. How would you like to be out at a bar and get introduced to a hot chick as Panty Waister? Be thankful."

Noah snorted and returned a grin. They finished eating and headed back to their room, not talking much, but the camaraderie that had been planted on their run broke ground and resulted in a comfortable silence.

The next weeks passed much like the first day until it was hard to keep track. It felt like they'd been in the middle of indoctrination forever. Bennett could feel his body changing, growing harder and leaner, but it was easier to see the changes in others. Noah grew skinnier, his cheekbones like blades in his tanned face and his muscles more pronounced.

A couple of guys quit from injuries before indoc was complete. Turned out indoc was a cakewalk compared to First Phase of BUD/S. Intensity jacked up to insanity levels. Heatstroke claimed a few men, still others went out with broken ribs, and one left with a broken arm.

Twenty quit before Hell Week, which marked the halfway point of First Phase. The night before Hell Week, a palpable anxiety rose to frenetic levels.

Bennett tried to sleep, knowing it was the last rest he would get for days, yet he couldn't shut his brain off. It pinged through his memories. Age nine at a scarred kitchen table being told he'd end up in jail or dead. Age eleven, his first experience at being pulled from a foster home after getting beat up by the man of the house. Age sixteen, the caseworker with the kind eyes who'd placed with him with her uncle, an old Vietnam veteran.

Life pivoted on single moments.

Rustling came from the Noah's bed. "You got anyone back home, Caldwell?"

Talking about the old man would lead to questions he didn't want to answer. "A girl, you mean? Nope. You?"

"I don't know."

"How do you not know?"

"I met someone right before we shipped out here. She's leaving for college in a few weeks. Timing's a bitch."

The silence deepened.

"Damn, I can't stop thinking about her, though." Noah continued softly. "She's real pretty. Innocent, though, you know? Not like the women hanging out at the bars around the bases."

The women around the base were perfect in Bennett's eyes. Sex and no questions. No ties. The heartfelt shit Noah was spouting would only make him weak.

"Put her out of your head and concentrate on getting through tomorrow."

"Right. I will." Noah didn't sound at all convincing. "But this girl, man. Listen to this email she sent me."

A mini-light clicked on from Noah's side, and Bennett pulled a pillow over his head.

Noah,

I'm really happy (and a little surprised) to hear from you. I figured you'd ridden (flown) off into the Great Beyond. I have four more weeks in Nags Head before I leave for UNC. My mom says my head and heart have already moved on, and I suppose she's right. Hope the training isn't as rough as you're expecting, but you'll rock it no matter what. Every time I scoop the mint chocolate chip ice cream, I think of you. Wish Wilbur was still around to fly you a gallon. An older gentleman came in the shop last week. He reminded me of you except forty

years from now. He ordered mint chocolate chip and had blue eyes, too. Just as
I was getting all teary and nostalgic, the
creep hit on me! (Just like you, too. Ha!)
Don't worry, I didn't let him walk me
home. Instead, I gave him directions to
the retirement home. Write when you
can. . . .

Harper

Bennett grunted out a laugh. He'd been
expecting some sappy love note full of
expectations. The girl — Harper — sounded
down-to-earth, with more than her share of
humor. He hoped Noah made her proud.

Bennett needed to focus. While he liked
the kid, it would be hard enough getting
himself through Hell Week intact. And to
do it, he needed sleep. At some point, he
must have drifted off, because an alarm and
screaming instructors woke him.

Every warning and story he'd heard about
Hell Week couldn't compare to reality. Until
they'd lived through it, no one could understand the strain it put on body and mind.
The constant physical stress shredded
bodies and the sleep deprivation messed
with heads. The mournful clang of the bell
rang out time and again at all hours of the
day and night and soon the line of aban-

doned helmets on the grinder outnumbered the men still fighting to survive.

Nights were spent in tents being woken every few minutes. Days were spent running holding heavy inflatable rafts overhead, his shoulders and arms screaming for relief. Hours were spent lying in the surf, locked arm in arm with Noah battling the unrelenting ocean.

Bennett lost track of time, but the sun was beating down on them when they were lined up in front of a bog strung with ropes. The kind of muddy mess he'd lived next to in Mississippi. The problem was he could barely hold himself upright, much less harness the agility needed to cross on ropes.

The first two guys to take it on splatted into the mud. One crawled toward the end; the other turned over and lay like a mudbug in the sun. Bennett and Noah exchanged a glance and slid onto the ropes. Raw blisters along Bennett's palms sent sharp pains up his arms. It was a mental struggle not to let go.

Noah lost his balance. One foot slipped off and his weight tipped him to the side. He lost his grip and momentum took him to the ground. He fell on his side with a loud grunt.

Bennett continued his shuffle forward.

One foot and then the other. "Get the fuck up."

"My shoulder is toast." Noah turned to his back, his arm cradled on his chest, his face scrunched. Mud painted every wrinkle of agony.

Bennett couldn't stop. If he did, he might not make it. He slid a few more feet and glanced back. Noah hadn't moved.

He couldn't just leave him, could he? A sense of duty trumped his self-preservation. Cursing himself, he dropped into the mud, landing in a graceless roll that twisted his ankle. Mud and sand and sweat caked every part of him. He crawled to Noah, grabbed his collar, and hauled him to sitting.

"I can't," Noah said between clenched teeth.

"You can and will." Bennett ignored the pain in Noah's eyes, a piercing blue against the almost black, stinking mud. Any sympathy on Bennett's part would made things worse. "Did you come this far to give up? You want to disappoint your family and your girl?"

"Fuck no."

Using each other as support, they stumbled through the mud and out of the pit, Noah holding his left arm tucked up on his chest and Bennett limping. The pressure in his boot where his ankle was swelling was already uncomfortable.

But they'd made it to the other side and out of the pit. Like salmon fighting a current, they fought their way across the sand to the training center. Less than a third of the class that had entered indoc gathered on the grinder, exhausted and trailing watery grime.

Instructor Lennox paced at the front and Bennett had a feeling the man was waiting for someone else to bail and ring the bell before announcing their next impossible task.

"Cl-l-lass Three Thirty-Seven secured from Hell-l-l Week." The instructor's cadence was a combination of drawn out and punctuated. "Dismissed."

It was like hearing "And they lived happily ever after" or "the wicked witch is dead." Unimaginable. Unreal. Unbelievable.

He wasn't the only one in shock. The instructor might as well have hollered, "Freeze." Then, everyone reacted at once, whoops and high fives and hugs. Brown T-shirts that signified graduation of a sort were passed out. Bennett and Noah stared at each other. A grin spread over Noah's face, cracking the already-drying mud. Another man slapped Noah on the back, and he doubled over with a groan.

"Come on, let's get you to Medical," Bennett said.

They limped along and Bennett left Noah with the medic after assurances his shoulder wouldn't get him kicked out of BUD/S. Bennett's ankle was throbbing, but the swelling went down after icing.

Bennett collapsed in his bed, closed his eyes, and enjoyed the feeling of being sand-free with endless peaceful hours ahead of him. Except for Hollis's snoring. Both Hollis and Carter had made it through Hell Week, too. Bennett's body was exhausted, but his mind whirred.

How close had he come to sacrificing his dream of becoming a SEAL to help Noah? Scenarios scrolled rapid fire through his head, each one involving Bennett quitting or getting cut.

"Hey, Bennett, you still awake?" Noah's voice was soft.

"Yeah, man."

"Thanks for today. Not sure if I would have made it without you. Glad I'm not headed home right now."

Bennett's thoughts calmed. He hadn't quit. And neither had Noah. Bennett was glad he hadn't lost his friend. "I'm glad, too," he whispered before turning over and falling into a dreamless sleep.

CHAPTER 5

Present Day

Harper sat behind the wheel of her car in the parking lot of Caldwell Survival School. It was Tuesday and not even lunchtime. Two other vehicles were there. A black truck with mud tires and a Jeep. The building was a rustic log cabin with a wraparound porch. Good branding for his line of business. As was the location, outside of Virginia Beach proper with expansive views into the distance.

She'd found the certificate Bennett Caldwell had given her with the money and had been surprised not to find something misspelled. It wasn't even a good fake. How had she just accepted him at his word? Her thoughts churned in circles, gnawing at the possible reasons this man, with the same name as her son, for God's sake, had shown up on her doorstep with a huge check.

Righteous anger had fueled her since

uncovering the deception, but now that she was here, a tingle went down her back. Her mom would have said someone had traipsed over her grave. Harper was too logical for such nonsense, but the feeling of being on the cusp of change filled her with trepidation. There was still time to turn around and go home.

But the questions she hadn't been able to formulate in her shock after Noah's death might finally be answered. Questions she'd never get answered through official channels. And the money. She was honor bound to return it. Knowing she would no longer be able to put her fuzzy business plan into motion soured her mood further.

After a half-dozen pep talks, she gave herself one last bolstering look in the rearview mirror and unlatched her door. A chilly wind flung it wide, and she took a deep breath. The gray skies portended rain and the air was salt tinged even this far inland. A storm fit her mood.

Yet she was entering enemy territory and needed to proceed with more caution than she was feeling at the moment. When her emotions ran hot she could be counted on to say something she would regret.

The wind helped dampen her anger. She hesitated at the *Closed* sign in the window.

An unexpected roadblock. The shade was up, the lights were on, and the door was unlocked. Gathering her gumption, she took a deep breath and stepped over the threshold as if it were booby-trapped.

A chime sounded and made her start, but no one was there to greet her. The interior of the building was stocked with survival and outdoor gear for sale. The nearest rack held all-weather coats in different colors, and backpacks hung from hooks along the wall.

The smell of cedar wafted through the store, reminding Harper of the old trunk her mom kept at the foot of her bed filled with winter quilts. Harper had fallen asleep wrapped in the scent since she was a child. The memories of comfort were ill placed alongside her nerves.

A huge animal sat up next to the door, and she gave a breathy, "Dear Lord," before she recognized it wasn't a small bear but an enormous dog. Its fur was an unrelenting black and so thick, she couldn't guess how much the dog actually weighed. It could be anywhere from 80 to 180 pounds.

The dog gave one deep, chesty *woof* but didn't make any threatening growls or movements. Footsteps sounded above her head, each one growing the tension across her shoulders. The dog trotted toward a set of stairs she hadn't noticed in the corner, its plumed tail wagging like a wind-up toy.

The *clomp* grew louder. First boots, then jeans-clad legs appeared on the stairs, followed by the bottom of a plaid shirt. The man reached the bottom and swept his gaze over the room, finally landing it on her.

He rubbed the dog's head, never taking his eyes off Harper, and moved closer. A familiar upright confidence common in military men, especially SEALs, marked his movements, but his hair and beard were distinctly non–military issue.

A mixture of browns, his hair was thick, with a natural wave, and brushed his collar. Wiry gray broke up the darkness of his beard. His features were stamped with a distinct masculinity and grimness that Noah had never acquired even through his deployments.

There was something else she noticed in his expression — a lack of recognition. Anger and relief battled, but relief won. It was like drawing the Get Out of Jail Free card. A reprieve.

Even though the enormous dog stayed at his side, Harper recognized which one of them was the true threat. She'd go a round with the dog over the man any day.

Instead of jumping straight to the accusations she'd practiced on the drive from Fort Bragg to Virginia Beach, she tempered her anger with charm. A direct assault would never gain her victory. "That's a big dog you've got there. Thought it was a bear at first."

The hand he was using to stroke the dog's head stilled. Her smile froze. If she could kick her own butt, she would. Why had she mentioned bears, considering his nickname was Grizzly?

He scratched the dog behind the ears, and it rose even higher on its paws, its eyes drooping in pleasure. "Mostly Newfoundland, I figure. No reason to worry, though, he's a gentle giant. Good with the customers. Plus, he earns his keep. Helps on trips to calm skittish people, provide warmth, scare off predators. That sort of thing."

"Interesting." A lull stretched and provided an opportunity, but instead she bought more time, or perhaps more accurately, she chickened out. "What's his name?"

"Jack London."

A puff of laughter escaped. "I love it. Seems appropriate for his line of work."

"Not many people read London nowadays unless it was required."

"My mother was a librarian, so I read everything. In fact —" She clamped her mouth shut. She'd been getting ready to reveal her namesake, which would have given her away for sure. Knowing the shift was abrupt, she said, "Speaking of trips, I'm interested in your programs."

"We're actually closed today." His expression was a pleasant enough mask, but hardly friendly.

"Oh, well, the door was unlocked." She thumbed over her shoulder and tried on her sweetest smile, which her mom had likened to tart lemonade. "Since I'm here, do you mind? Not sure when I'll make it back into town."

He glanced down her body. Not in a sexual way, but an assessment as to her level of fitness for his school's programs. She had a feeling the jeans she had tucked into brown riding-style boots and her pink-and-blue sweater didn't project "hard-core survivalist." To his credit, he didn't say anything except, "Have you had a chance to look over the options on the website? Some are more intense than others."

She had read through them all with a fair amount of horror. Paying to freeze her butt off in the middle of nowhere wasn't her idea of fun. Central heat and air-conditioning

93

had been invented for a purpose, thank you very much. Not to mention how much she enjoyed bug- and wildlife-free sleeping arrangements. Her one and only camping experience with Noah had ended with her sleeping in the backseat of the truck after a centipede had gotten into her sleeping bag.

"Could you review them for me right quick?"

He gestured toward a sales counter tucked into the corner of the room. Instead of going around to the other side, he reached over, pulled a brochure from behind the counter, and spread it between them.

His hands were broad, with a few silvery scars along the backs. The sleeves of his red-and-blue plaid flannel were rolled up revealing thick, sinewy forearms dotted with dark hair. Her shoulder brushed his biceps.

She totally got his nickname. Grizzly. He was very bear-like, huge and intimidating, especially with the beard. Her stomach did calisthenics and not just from nerves. Or at least a different type of nerves. It had been a long time since she'd been anywhere near this level of sheer manliness.

His forefinger moved down the page as he detailed each option. She only half-listened. Fire starting. Navigation. Shelter building. Bowhunting. The inflections in his voice were similar to Noah's — a Southerner then — but with key differences. Bennett's accent was rougher around the edges and not quite as polished, but hypnotic. When he finished, he folded the brochure and held it out to her. She didn't take it.

He cocked his head, his brows hovering low over his deep-set eyes. Dark-brown irises framed by an amber circle classified as unusual yet striking. As if she flew light-years in the past, she remembered them staring into hers the day he'd given her the check. Clean-shaven, he'd been skinnier then, almost gaunt, and in his eyes she'd recognized a familiar reflection of grief. That's what she remembered.

"I'm thinking you aren't really interested in a survival weekend." Suspicion slowed the cadence of his words even more.

"Not really, no." She took a step back to break the dynamic pull he exhibited. Did he affect everyone that way or was it only her? "You're Bennett Caldwell."

"I am." He put the pamphlet down and faced her with his hands clasped behind his back, his feet braced apart. It was a stance Noah had favored as well.

"I'm surprised you don't recognize me."

"Why should I?"

"We met a few years ago and I want —"

He held up a hand. "Look, lady, I don't know what you're after, but we did not hook up. I damn sure would have remembered that."

She barked out an incredulous laugh, on the cusp of asking whether he would have remembered in a good way or bad way. "You think that we . . . ? Well, I never. I'm not here as one of your conquests, for goodness' sake." Her sweater had turned into a hotbox.

"How exactly are we acquainted?"

"My name is Harper Wilcox."

His eyes flared and his body swayed backward as if she'd given him a physical shove. His throat worked, but no words emerged.

"I recently discovered something very interesting." She continued when it became clear he was unable or unwilling to speak.

"What's that, ma'am?" His voice was rougher and tougher and she might have been intimidated if she hadn't been around and lived with a SEAL.

" 'Ma'am'?" More than a little put out, she stepped forward and was gratified when he stepped back. A second ago, she'd been a possible hookup. "Did you actually go there? Pretty sure I'm younger than you are, *sir.*"

He raised his eyebrows. "What can I do for you, Mrs. Wilcox?"

"Call me Harper, please." She advanced again and this time he didn't give any ground, even leaning forward to loom over her. "Considering I unwittingly named my son after you, *Bennett,* it's only fitting."

"You what?" He abandoned his casually aggressive stance and grabbed hold of the counter.

Time to press her advantage while he was unsteady. "Noah suggested the name Ben our last night together. I could tell it was attached to someone important. Just didn't realize it was you. Now, why did you make up a fake bravery award in order to give me a truckload of money?"

His gaze darted over her face as if assessing her threat level. She hoped she registered as DEFCON 1.

"Would you have taken the money otherwise?" he asked.

"Of course not!"

"Well, then, there's your answer." His face shuttered, his tone indicating the matter was closed for discussion. He turned away from her.

She grabbed his arm. Through the thick flannel, the muscle was taut. "Hang on. That answer isn't good enough. You realize

I have to return the money."

"Don't want it. Don't need it." He looked to where she had hold of his arm. His profile would be at home carved in marble or etched on a coin. That's how strong and hard his face was.

She should let go of him. Instead, she held on even tighter. "It's not about wanting and needing. It's about right and wrong."

"Exactly. Right and wrong. And I made a promise to Noah —" His face blanked and turned cold.

A shiver traveled up her arm. "What promise?"

"It was nothing." He looked off into the distance — or maybe into the past.

Whatever he had promised Noah was far from nothing. In fact, it might be the key to everything. How could she extract information he was unwilling to divulge? SEALs were trained to keep their secrets.

Her frustration boiled over, and she dropped his arm to poke him in the chest. "I'm going to write you a check right now."

"I'll tear it up."

"I'll send a certified money order."

"I'll send it back."

"I'll withdraw the cash from the bank, put it in a duffel, and throw it on your porch in the middle of the night."

A twitch of his lips broke the stone cast of his profile, and he raised his gaze to hers. "You're still as sassy and stubborn as I remember."

She shuffled backward, her mind whirling.

Dammit. What had happened? His tongue was out of control. He was unbalanced. Everything about her had him reeling. She belonged to a different part of his life. One he'd done his best to box up and leave behind. The money had been a last-ditch sacrifice to the gods to appease his guilt.

"What are you talking about? To my knowledge this is only the second time we've met. Unless I'm mistaken?" Uncertainty edged her voice.

Time to climb out of the six-foot hole he'd dug for himself in two seconds flat. "You're not mistaken."

At his reticence, she waved her hands in a "gimme more" gesture. "How do you know I'm stubborn?"

"You're not denying it?" He moved to the nearest rack and straightened hangers for something to do.

She gave an impatient-sounding huff. Or maybe the sound landed closer to pissed off. "Whether or not I'm stubborn has nothing to do with the issue at hand. Did Noah talk about me or something?"

"A bit." More than a bit. All the damn time, if he was truthful. But, beyond that, Noah had gotten into the habit of reading Harper's emails and occasional letter out loud. They'd been chockfull of humor and wit and normalcy. She had helped Bennett understand what they were fighting for even though he didn't have anyone to protect. No one to live for.

"What does 'a bit' mean exactly?" She raised one eyebrow, the corner of her mouth ticked up to match.

Their only other meeting had been a few weeks after Noah was killed. Bennett had been injured in the same raid. Bad enough to get sent stateside and be given a Purple Heart. She'd been heavily pregnant and sallow faced and red eyed, her hair scraped back into a limp ponytail. A familiar black cloak of grief had weighed across her shoulders. The same outfit had stared back at him from the mirror every morning.

A different woman stood in front of him now. This one crackled with energy, with no hint of the guilt and grief that still plagued him. Somehow she'd come out the other side of Noah's death with her hope intact, or at least refurbished.

"Did Noah talk about me?" she asked

again. "About us?"

He refused to look her in the eye and admit her letters to Noah had provided him a lifeline. "Nights were long and lonely. It helped to talk. And Noah wanted to talk about you. He loved you."

"Yeah, I know." Her voice had softened.

He made the mistake of looking at her. Her eyes were a striking hazel framed by her thick golden-brown hair. What would she look like in the sunlight with a smile on her face? She was pretty in a way that made his chest ache.

Pity hid poorly in her eyes. Shouldn't it be the other way around? He shook off the feelings of melancholy. "You seem to be doing well. You have a son."

"I am, and I do. He's five. Happy and good natured and sweet."

"Like his dad then." As soon as the words were out, Bennett wanted them back. "Or maybe like you, I don't know —"

"No, he's a mini-Noah in attitude if not looks."

Noah had been over-the-moon excited that he was going to be a daddy. One bullet was all it took to steal that dream. The promise he'd made to Noah standing in the middle of a soybean field in Georgia still bound him to Harper no matter that he'd tried to break it with his gift of money.

"His name is Ben?"

"You didn't know Noah wanted to name him after you?"

"Not really. No." He remembered joking about the possibility with Noah, but the reality was sobering. And humbling.

The ensuing silence made him shift away from her stare. A shudder made its way down his back. Sarge had told him tall tales about a Mississippi swamp witch who stole poor wanderers' souls. Harper looked prepared to extract his painfully.

"I'm glad things are well with you," he said. "We've established I'm not taking the money back, so if there's nothing else you need, I have work to do." He walked away. His destination? Anywhere but next to her.

His rudeness was inexcusable, but he needed this woman gone and out of his life. The longer he was around her, the worse his insides became tangled. In BUD/S, an unknottable knot was called a whammy. Harper was his whammy.

"Actually, we have not established that fact." She had followed him into the storage area in back of the shop where he kept equipment for overnight bookings. The lighting was dim. "But I'll let it go for now, because I have other questions."

He found a shadow and parked himself in it. Old habits. Even after all these years, his hands felt empty without a gun. Instead, he clasped Jack London's fur, the softness and warmth a salve. "What kind of questions?"

"You were with Noah when he died."

He hoped she couldn't see his face. "Who told you that?"

"Allison Teague. Darren's wife. Is it true?"

Truth, lie. Black, white. Dream, nightmare. It didn't matter. He wasn't telling her or anyone else. "You need to leave, Harper."

The warning in his voice seemed to have no effect on her. She stepped closer. "Not until you tell me about the night he died."

"Ask for the report." He left the shadows feeling like a wild animal being chased out of its hidey-hole and pushed the back door open. The cold air washed over him and helped control the blaze of memories she'd sparked.

"I have and they sent me some vague bullshit meant for civilian consumption. I want to know if he was in pain. If he said anything. I want to know what his last moments were like."

The wind tumbled her hair around her face and shoulders, her shiver noticeable. In spite of the hardships Harper had endured, she retained an enviable purity and innocence. People like Harper were familiar with TV death. Movie death. Not the stark reality of your best friend bleeding out in your arms. The pain of watching life leak out of Noah's eyes, painfully, slowly, with a recognition of all the years he would miss with the love of his life and the child he'd never meet.

Some burdens were his to bear alone for the rest of his days.

"I know you miss Noah. I do, too. But I have nothing else to say." He presented his back, his entire body tensed, his heartbeat blocking any noise. After what felt like an eternity, gravel crunched under tires and he looked over his shoulder. She was gone.

He should be glad she'd given up and left. Instead of relief, disappointment coursed through him.

CHAPTER 6

Past

"I'm not sure about this." Noah smoothed the brown button-down shirt of his uniform.

Bennett slunk down in the backseat and hung on to the head rest to keep from getting flung across the seat into Noah on every turn. Hollis was driving, the only one of them with a car on base, and he darted down side streets like the local he was.

Hollis glanced up at the rearview mirror. "Not sure about what? Getting laid?"

"I'm only nineteen for one thing. The club probably won't even let me in."

Hollis chuckled, shook his head, and stopped short at the next red light. "Dude. That uniform you're wearing is your ID and your panty dropper. That's half the reason I joined up. Seen it all my life around here. The chicks go nuts over your bravery and shit. It's not even a challenge, but I'll take it." Hollis exchanged a slapping handshake with Carter, who was sprawled in the shotgun seat.

Bennett kept his response to an eye roll. Hollis and Carter didn't like him, but the way they avoided him at chow time and the whispers that stopped when he walked into their shared room didn't bother Bennett at all.

But Noah had pleaded with him to come along, his nerves obvious, and Bennett couldn't leave him hanging with Hollis and Carter as wingmen. That would have been plain cruel. Besides, seeing something beyond the concrete walls and the grinder while enjoying cold beer sounded appealing.

Carter draped an arm along the back of Hollis's seat and twisted around, putting his large hooked nose in profile. The setting sun highlighted the constellation of acne on his visible cheek. "By the way, if we find some willing women, you boys will need alternative transportation home."

Bennett couldn't help but admire the man's confidence, no matter how misplaced. "If you find a woman with beer goggles that thick then congratulations and have fun."

Carter's eye narrowed on Bennett. The attempt at intimidation fell short. Way short. Hollis's laughter was like an engine misfiring. "Ah, the boys in the back don't get it. But they will." Hollis and Carter exchanged another slapping shake that seemed congratulatory before they'd even walked into the bar.

Bennett stared out the side window feeling a couple of decades older than Hollis and Carter. Not that he could fault them. Bennett had been them, or a lot like them, anyway, his first couple of years in the service. It was heady stuff until you realized the women only saw the uniform and didn't care what was underneath.

Hollis pulled in to the parking lot of a squat white cement club with a neon sign and arrow proclaiming *Gin Boogie Bar.*

Clumps of people gathered around the parking lot, smoking and cutting up. From the corner of his eye, he caught the interested glances of a few women already. The bass beat of music thrummed his chest.

Noah fell behind and Bennett slowed his pace. Hollis and Carter disappeared into the blackened maw of the club.

Noah stopped and grabbed Bennett's arm. He was looking around like someone might pull a gun at any minute. "This place is sketchy."

To Bennett it didn't look any different from the dozens of other bars and clubs he'd walked into over the years. He clapped Noah on the back. "Come on. Let's grab a couple of beers and get the lay of the land. We can always get a cab back to base."

Noah's reluctance was palpable, but he stayed on Bennett's heels. The black, three-hundred-pound bouncer on the stool out front waved them in.

"He didn't even ask for our IDs." Noah had to raise his voice to be heard over the music and everyone else.

Bennett hit Noah's chest with the back of his hand. "It's the uniform, man. Hollis is a horny idiot, but he's right about that. Let find a spot at the bar."

Bennett scythed through the crowd, his uniform and size clearing a path, and he and Noah took up a corner of the bar. The female bartender walked over as soon as Bennett signaled with two fingers, wiping her hands on a formerly white towel thrown over her shoulder before propping her arms on the bar and leaning over.

"What can I get you boys?"

"An ice-cold longneck, if you have it."

She nodded, raising her eyebrows in Noah's direction. He held up two fingers. She was back in thirty seconds with the beers, condensation dripping down the sides. Bennett drank half of his in one go, the cold slipping down his throat and through his body like nectar. It had been before BUD/S training since he'd had a drink, and damn, it was good.

Noah killed his, too, and the bartender returned with two more without asking. This one Bennett savored. He turned and took in the scene.

A dance floor took up the far corner, mostly populated by women and surrounded by men checking them out. Tables and chairs were strewn in the space between the dance floor and the bar with clumps of friends or couples sitting close. Waitresses circulated with trays lined with shots.

A half hour passed with Noah and Bennett sharing two more beers. Two women approached, both cookie-cutter pretty but too drunk to carry on a conversation. When one of the women fell into Noah and he brushed her off like she had cooties, they moved on. Noah visibly relaxed.

"You not interested in anyone or just them?" Bennett gestured toward the retreating women and sent a side-eye glance toward Noah. "Might be good to blow off some steam."

Bennett crossed glances with the bartender again. The heat between them sparked, the invitation as clear as if she'd spoken aloud. A non-Navy-issued bed, preferably with a willing woman in it, was almost too much to deny. Yet he didn't want to leave Noah on his own. Or worse, at the whims of Hollis and Carter.

"Nah." Noah scuffed his shoe on the floor, his gaze lowered. "It wouldn't feel right."

" 'Cuz of that girl back in North Carolina?"

Noah nodded and Bennett took another drag off his beer before answering. Considering his longest relationship was however long he'd spent on leave, Bennett was flabbergasted a relationship strong enough to survive months of separation had sprung up after a week.

"Forget firecrackers, she must be a damn Roman candle in the sack." Bennett chuckled.

An unmissable blush ruddied Noah's cheeks and cut Bennett's amusement at the knees.

"No fucking way." Bennett turned to Noah. "You haven't even had sex with her yet? And you're hanging on like she's the Holy Grail or something?"

Noah turned to face the bar. "Jesus, could you keep your voice down. I know it makes me sound like a first-class pussy, but I can't help it. She's special, man."

"How can you even know that?" In Bennett's experience, women *seemed* special. Until he got into their pants, and then they invariably tried to manipulate him or mold him into what they wanted. Because what they sure as hell didn't want was a taciturn loner without any family and with even less charm.

"We've been emailing and writing."

"And you two have some exclusive deal or something?"

"We haven't exactly talked about it."

Bennett rubbed his forehead. "Let me get this straight. She could be screwing the brains out of every football player on campus while you turn down a willing woman?"

Instead of getting mad or defensive like Bennett expected, Noah laughed and with a smile still lingering said, "She is not out banging football players. Not her style. If she was going to bang any group, it would probably be the debate club or science bowl guys."

Bennett snorted, but something that felt like jealousy excavated a place in his chest. He crossed glances with the bartender, her smile holding promises of a mindless night.

The appeal faded, and he scraped at the label on his beer, his eyes downcast. "What makes her so different from any other woman?"

"She's smart. And funny. And a little quirky. She grew up with no TV and only read books."

TV had been his constant babysitter. Mindless garbage, yes, but it had connected him to an outside world that wasn't as bleak as his own.

"Is she hot?"

"She's the kind of pretty that doesn't need all the makeup and tight clothes." Noah gestured toward a gaggle of women on the hunt. "Check out this last letter I got from her."

Noah dug out a piece of paper from his pocket and smoothed it out on the bar. The lined notebook paper took him back to high school. Bennett picked it up and tilted it toward the bar light. Her handwriting was bold and loopy and distinctly feminine.

Noah,

Hell Week sounded . . . hellish. Do you have any free time or is it all work, torture, work? My life is mostly study, test, study. But I did make friends with a couple girls in my dorm, and we went to a college bar to hear a band. They were loud. That's about the nicest thing I can say. I had fun, though, and a couple of drinks. Purple Hazes. They were delish (and dangerous). Although, not to worry, my roommate has turned our room into the Virgin Vault. Instead of posters of hot musicians, she has the Madonna and Child on one side and Jesus on the other. I haven't told my mom I'm living with a bible-thumper. She's not exactly into traditional religions (understatement!). Back to studying for me. More push-ups and running and genuflections toward the Monster for you?

Harper

Bennett grunted. She sounded . . . nice. Too nice and sweet with no fire. Maybe that suited Noah, but he wanted a woman who challenged him and wouldn't put up with his crap. He doubted such a woman existed. He refolded the letter and handed it back to Noah.

"All right then, Peaches, no women tonight. Only booze and a little fun." Bennett clinked the neck of his beer against Noah's. His face flooded with relief.

Women came and went and so did the beers. Bennett was feeling pleasantly fuzzy in the head when flailing arms in a tan shirt on the dance floor grabbed Bennett's attention. Laughter spurted out of him, and he pointed. "Jesus, I never would have pegged Carter as a dancer."

Noah squinted and then collapsed against Bennett, laughing his ass off. Bennett hung on the edge of the bar, doubling over as Carter gyrated like he needed medical attention. Bennett wasn't sure he'd ever laughed this long and this hard. Tears blurred his vision.

Between his laughter and the alcohol slowing his brain processes, he didn't sense the situational change until the first punch was thrown.

He straightened and grabbed Noah's arm, pulling him toward the dance floor. "Oh hell no. Fight. Let's go."

While he didn't particularly like Hollis or Carter, he couldn't leave them outnumbered. Maybe they'd all make it through BUD/S and end up brothers-in-arms; maybe they wouldn't. But, until one of them quit, they were bonded by a trial of fire.

The dance floor had turned into a melee, women ducking out of the scrum and men joining it. Bennett waded in throwing elbows to heads to clear a path. Carter was being held by one man while another took a sucker punch.

Bennett let out a deafening holler and

grabbed the man who was doing the punching by the back of his shirt, spinning him around and landing a jab on his nose. He went down but had plenty of friends.

Bennett and Noah ended up back to back fending off one man after another. Everyone was drunk and the hits and kicks were clumsy and off target. The adrenaline rushing Bennett like a tsunami eased his restlessness. Not as good as sex but satisfying in its own way.

He laughed and head butted the same guy he'd initially punched. A man grabbed him from behind in a wrestling hold that effectively disabled him. Whoever had him was bigger, stronger, and sober.

He was frog-marched toward the entrance, yelling obscenities and threats along the way. Six feet out the door, the man released his hold and shoved Bennett away. He stumbled before getting his feet under him and turned. Noah, his eyes bright and wild, walked out on his own steam. Hollis wandered in circles, rubbing his neck, and Carter sat on the ground, his head between his knees.

The bouncer planted himself like a tree in front of them. "My brother is serving, which is the only reason I'm not calling the po-po to haul your sorry asses in. Now get gone before I change my mind."

Sometimes retreat was the best and only option. Bennett grabbed Carter's collar and hauled him to his feet. "Wise advice. Thanks, man."

Bennett crossed glances with Noah and gestured his head toward Hollis. Noah threw an arm around Hollis's shoulders and steered him toward the sidewalk. Bennett followed. Carter was close to passing out, but Bennett wanted to get out of retaliation range from the guys at the bar.

They were in a popular area close to the water, and it wasn't so late to be deserted. Bennett scanned over their group. All of them looked worse for wear. Blood dotted Carter's shirt. A tickle had Bennett wiping his own nose, his fingers coming away stained red.

An unoccupied bench sat in a small grassy area, and Bennett steered them toward it to regroup. Hollis and Carter were deposited side by side.

"My car. We have to go back for it." Hollis tried to get up, but he plopped back down, his balance nonexistent.

"None of us are in any shape to drive. I'll call a cab." Bennett stepped away.

Carter leaned over and heaved, puke splattering his shoes.

The call made, Bennett went to stand next to Noah, who was looking out over the water. The artificial lights behind them turned the bay black and fathomless. As his adrenaline ebbed, a rhythmic throb in his face and shoulder gained in intensity. Feeling unsteady, Bennett leaned against the light pole.

"Why the SEALs?" Bennett asked. "Why not college?"

"According to my dad, college is a waste of money. You don't need a college degree to farm. My choice was the military or farming. I'm the only son and my dad expects me to take over."

"You don't want that?"

"Not right now. I'm only nineteen. I want to see the world. Do something important before I get caught up in the day-to-day grind of worrying about the weather and crop prices. You think that makes me a selfish asshole?"

"Nope. Makes you normal, I'd say. But why the SEALs?"

"The men in my family have always served. Had an uncle in the First Gulf War. A grandad in Vietnam. All the way back to the American Revolution. Seemed natural to join, and I wanted a challenge. Recruiter told me SEALs was the hardest." A small self-deprecating laugh emerged like a whisper. "I didn't know what I was getting into."

"Regrets?"

"I was regretting it hard when I landed in that damn mud pit and strained my shoulder. But now?" He shrugged. "No regrets. What about you? Why the SEALs?"

Dammit. If he'd been sober, he wouldn't have allowed curiosity to get the better of him, knowing it could boomerang back around. "I was adopted by an Army veteran. A drill sergeant."

It was more than he'd admitted to anyone since he'd joined up. But he wouldn't go further back than the moment Sarge signed the papers making the adoption legal.

"Geez. Did he make you square your sheets and spit shine your shoes?"

The image was so far from reality, Bennett laughed. "Not hardly. He'd turned into one of those hard-core preppers that live off the grid. The smartest SOB I've ever met. Taught me how to hunt and survive."

"He sounds cool. Why didn't you go into the Army then?"

"Wanted to get the hell out of Mississippi. Thought the Navy was the best way to see the world. Sarge was just happy I didn't end up in jail."

"I'll bet he's over the moon you made it

into the SEAL program."

Bennett could nod and leave it there, but more leaked out of his beer-weakened defenses. "He died. A couple of years after I joined up. Massive heart attack. It was a while before his niece got worried and found him, and she buried him quick. I was in the middle of the ocean and couldn't get back for the funeral."

Sarge's niece had changed Bennett's destiny when she'd put him with her uncle. Then, she changed it again when she'd written to him about her uncle's death and the money he'd left Bennett. Money he didn't deserve. It was then he'd decided to go for the SEALs. He had nothing to lose but his life and no one to disappoint but himself.

"I'm sorry, man." Noah's hand on Bennett's shoulder imparted a sympathy Bennett hadn't asked for or needed, yet he was grateful nonetheless.

"It was a long time ago." The years felt more like weeks in that moment, and he stared into the darkness over the water.

"Have you been back? To Mississippi, I mean."

A honk came from behind them, saving Bennett from giving Noah a big "hell no."

A cab waited at the curb. Bennett grabbed Hollis by the upper arm and maneuvered him into the car. Noah did the same with Carter. Bennet took the front seat and prayed no one puked again.

The cabbie was already on the road, knowing where they were headed based on their uniforms.

"Yo, Caldwell," Hollis said.

"What?" Bennett turned.

Hollis grinned, blood smeared on his teeth from a split lip. "I can't believe you waded into that fight. Thought for sure you'd desert us. You came in roaring like a grizzly bear. Scared the shit out of me until I realized you were on our side."

"Yeah, well. You might be an asshole, but you're our asshole. Noah and I couldn't leave you hanging."

Hollis's head lolled on the headrest. "Thanks, Peaches."

Bennett met Noah's eyes, and they both smiled. Their friendship had set deep roots. Bennett's mission was still about getting himself through BUD/S, but he would do what he could to make sure Noah got through, too.

CHAPTER 7

Present Day

Harper had done a very bad thing. Misleading, dishonest, manipulative. Her accounting job required scrupulous honesty, and she did her best daily to set a good example for Ben. That hadn't stopped her from calling Caldwell Survival School and booking a weekend one-on-one survival lesson with Bennett under her mom's name.

Various scenarios had unspooled through her mind before landing on this one. If she called him, then he could hang up and once he had her number he'd ignore her. If she showed up at the survival school unannounced, privacy was an issue. Plus, he could sic Jack London on her. Although the dog looked more likely to lick her to death than bite. Booking Bennett for a weekend seemed the best option.

Now that the hour was upon her, though, doubts crumbled the logic of her decision.

She checked the GPS in her car. He had sent instructions to meet him at a ranger station on the edge of the Great Dismal Swamp. She'd hoped it had gained the name like a big man earned the nickname Tiny, but the farther she traveled on the two-lane road, the denser the trees grew, lending a sinister feel.

Or maybe that was her guilt over the deception. No doubt Bennett was not going to be happy to see her. His last words to her couldn't be interpreted as anything but a warning. Yet here she was.

The small brown cabin blended into the backdrop of forest, and she almost missed it. Braking hard, she took the turn too fast, fishtailing in the gravel. She recognized the black truck as the one in front of his log cabin survival school. Judgment was minutes away.

She'd spent a small fortune on her evil plans. Not only paying Bennett for his services but also outfitting herself. "Outdoorsy" wasn't a word that described her wardrobe. Lying out on the beach had never held any allure, and while the inlets were pretty, she'd never had the urge to explore farther than the dock. She preferred to hole up in her room for hours with stacks of books. The hazard of being a librarian's kid.

She parked next to his truck and gathered her courage. With the car off, it didn't take long for the cold to seep through cracks, driven by the whistling wind. Spending the night outside might not be bad if there was a fire to huddle next to. Or would it be like the one miserable camping trip she went on in Girl Scouts? Cookies be damned, she'd dropped out after the trip.

Her new water-resistant hiking boots squeaked as she got out of the car, pulled a backpack over the console, and swung it over one shoulder. His email — to her mom's email address, which had been fun to explain — had laid out exactly what she'd needed to bring. A tent hadn't been included.

The wind cut through her layers of clothes in the short walk to the door. She debated the merits of turning around. A woof at the window ruined her retreat. The door opened and a stranger in a brown park ranger uniform greeted her warmly.

"You must be Gail Frazier. I'm Seth. Bennett will be right out. Come on in."

A smile was difficult in the face of her mom's name. Denials and excuses would be upon her soon enough, so she took Seth's hand in a shake.

"Hey, Jack." The dog's tail whipped back

and forth as he bumped her hand for a pat. The dog was way friendlier than his owner, that's for sure.

"Ah, you've met the beast." Seth gestured toward a small kitchen. "Can I get you some hot tea or coffee before you head out into the wilderness?"

"Coffee would be great. Black is fine."

He poured from a stained pot into a chipped mug with *The Great Dismal Swamp* written across the side in fancy script. She thanked him on the handoff. "Have you been the ranger here long?"

"Two years." He had a thick beard a few shades darker than his hair, which made it difficult to pin an age to him, but unlike Bennett, no gray hairs peeked out. The twinkling good humor in his eyes landed him in his midtwenties at a guess. "I couldn't ask for a better gig. It's less about public relations and more about science collection. Marshes and swamps like the Dismal have amazingly diverse ecosystems. Big predators and —"

"How big?" Her hand tightened on the mug.

"Black bears are common. And then there's the —"

"Common?" She riffled through what she knew about bears, which was dominated by

Ben's Winnie-the-Pooh bedtime stories and Goldilocks's encounter. "But it's winter. They're in hibernation, right?"

The excitement of a zealot vibrated Seth's voice. "Black bears don't hibernate; they enter torpor. They're lethargic and sleep more than usual but will come out and snack."

"Snack on people?"

Seth's laugh reverberated through the room. "I doubt it."

A door in the back opened, and Bennett backed into the room, maneuvering his pack. It was considerably bigger than hers. A black toboggan covered his head, but the ends of his hair flipped up at the bottom. A dark-green Henley stretched across his broad shoulder and was half-tucked into black pants with more pockets than any reasonable person could fill. But, damn, they fit him well. The heartbeat before he turned, she forced her gaze off his butt to meet his eyes.

She wasn't worried about a black bear eating her like a fruit roll-up anymore. She was worried about the very real Grizzly making the room feel small.

"Ms. Frazier, I hope the drive was —" The smile on his face morphed into a grimace. "What are you doing here? You're not Gail

Frazier."

"Gail is my mom. I'm here in her place."

Bennett stared her down. The anger roiling through the silence generated its own energy. All directed at her. Seth glanced between them, then shuffled to the nearest window and pressed his nose to the glass like a kid trying to spot Bigfoot.

She made a sweeping gesture between them. "I realize how this looks —"

"You lied."

"No."

His eyebrows rose.

"Okay, well, I sort of misled you —"

"Lied." He barked the word like an epitaph.

"You wouldn't have seen me otherwise, would you?" She set her mug on the counter with a small clatter. Damn her shaking hands. He was trained to exploit weaknesses.

"No. Because I have nothing else to say to you."

"Fine." Obviously, a direct assault was impossible, but she could flank him. "That's not why I'm here anyway. I'm here because I need to learn survival skills."

"Why?"

"Because . . ." She bobbed her head and harrumphed. "You know, the apocalypse is

126

coming. The end is nigh and all that."

"When did you turn into a bible-thumper?"

"I've always thumped the Bible. It's how I was raised." If her mom could hear the nonsense coming out of her mouth, she would have taken Harper over her knee for a different kind of thumping.

"No, it wasn't." His absolute confidence stoked a flame of anger in her chest.

"You don't know —" The realization that he might indeed know hit her like a punch to the throat. "*How* do you know that?"

He'd already admitted Noah had talked about her. How much had he shared with this bear of a man who had been undeniably kind but refused to give her what she wanted the most — the truth?

"It doesn't matter how. This" — he waved his finger between them — "is not happening."

"Wait. I've already paid. And . . . and . . . if you don't take me then I'll be forced to file a complaint with the Better Business Bureau." It was an empty threat, but he didn't need to know that. Throwing more fuel on her pretend outrage, she added, "Is this because I'm a woman? Are you discriminating against me?"

"For the love of . . ." His eye roll was epic.

He shuffled his feet farther apart and crossed his arms over his chest. "It's going to drop below freezing tonight with a chance of snow. The night will be bleak unless *you* can get a fire started."

"But you're the guide."

"Instructor, not guide. The first thing you need to learn about survival is that there are consequences when you can't get the basics done. You have to put the work in. It's what you paid for. And you'll need the skills to survive the apocalypse, right?"

A teeny-tiny spark of humor in his face threatened to set off an explosion of maniacal laughter in her. She'd won the skirmish.

"When do we get started?" She tried not to look smug.

"Right now." He glanced toward the door. "That your pack?"

"Stuffed full of everything on your list." Plus the makings for s'mores, which in retrospect might have been a tad optimistic. Or delusional.

He examined her head to foot, shook his head, but didn't say anything. "Let's hit it. Thanks, Seth. Will you be around on Sunday?"

Seth had turned and was half-sitting on the windowsill, watching them. "If the weather clears I'm scheduled to inventory the geese population. You two take care out there. If the front moves farther south than predicted, it's likely to be a rough couple of days."

"You can still cancel and get a full refund." Bennett shot her a side-eye.

"I can handle a couple of days in the great outdoors. I'm not a total wimp." Physically, she was in good shape. She ran and worked out regularly. It was the cold and unknown she feared. And the possibility of finally finding out how Noah had died. Did she really want to know if he'd been in pain or if he'd said her name at the end? Uncertainty washed over her, but if she bailed now, it was over. Bennett wouldn't be fooled again.

He pulled on a plaid flannel shirt that seemed to be his uniform and a lightweight jacket and then swung his pack over his shoulders without any indication of strain. Trying to imitate his level of casualness, she flung her own on. The weight tipped her balance and she stumbled backward until he caught her pack and shoved her upright.

"You sure about this?" he murmured so close his beard hair tickled her ear.

Like sticking her finger in an electrical socket, a jolt passed through her. It was vaguely familiar even though she hadn't felt anything like it for years. Since Noah. It was attraction. Lust. Basic and primal and damned inconvenient.

"I'm sure," she said even though she was nothing of the sort.

Bennett led the way out the door, but instead of heading toward his truck, he made for the tree line behind Seth's ranger station. She followed, glancing over her shoulder at her car. It was her last chance to make a run for it. Forcing her eyes back to Bennett's pack, she put one foot in front of the other, and when she looked again the forest blocked any view of civilization.

They trudged in silence. The gray sky peeked every so often through the trees but offered no hint as to how much time passed. She wasn't in the habit of wearing a watch and her phone was stashed in her pack.

The ground was spongy. Pine needles littered the trail, and the going was easy, the pace brisk enough to generate enough body heat to stay comfortable.

A slight clearing opened in the trees with a circle of stones containing the charred remnants of a fire. She stopped, slipped her pack off, and stretched. That hadn't been bad at all. He'd tried and failed to scare her away.

"Do you need a bathroom break already?"

She whipped around. He was on the opposite side of the clearing where no path cut through the thick brush. Jack London was sitting on his haunches at Bennett's feet.

"Are we not setting up camp here?" She pointed at the fire ring.

A slow smile that was as chilly as the wind snaking down the collar of her shirt spread over his face. "This is for day hikers and Boy Scouts. We're still on the refuge's land."

"Where are we headed?"

"Deeper. Off trail. Onto my land."

"Out of the park?"

"Yep. Liability issues. I use Seth's place as a jumping-off point, but your training will take place on *my* land."

His tone skittered like crawly bugs down her spine. She would be at his mercy. Holding his gaze, she swung her backpack on and joined him.

He paused with his hand on a low branch and faced her. "What direction are we headed?"

"Uh . . ." She looked to the sky, but the cloud-obscured sun offered no hints. Noah used to joke she could get lost in their tiny town house. "West?"

His eyes narrowed.

"East?"

He made a huffy sound.

"North?"

"Ding-ding-ding. You got a compass?"

"On my phone." She reached for the zipper pocket on the side.

"In a survival situation you might not have a phone. It might have broken. Or it might have lost its charge. What then?"

"I guess I need a real compass."

He stared at her long enough to ignite nerves in her stomach. "Last chance. You should turn around."

"No." She cursed the questioning lilt in the denial.

"You can't handle this. Admit it." His voice contained equal amounts exasperation and anger.

"The hell I can't." She had no idea if she could actually handle it, but not even with her last breath would she admit that to him. She could handle anything for a weekend. As long as she didn't freeze to death, and she had enough faith in Bennett not allowing that unfortunate event to occur. At the very least, it would be terrible for his business.

"I know why you're doing this, and it's not going to work." His voice was soft but barbed with menace.

All right, their cards were on the table. Good. She didn't like deception. "Answer my questions right here, right now, and we can turn around."

"Not gonna happen."

"Then, lead on, Macduff."

"You're going to be miserable."

"I'll survive."

She held his narrowed gaze until he shook his head and led them through the heavy undergrowth. The determination in his eyes made her fear it would take more than an overnight trip to wear him down to the truth.

A brambly bush grabbed at her jeans, and she stopped to unstick herself. Whatever his pants were made of repelled the thorns like Teflon. Somewhere along the makeshift path, she quit admiring the fabric of his pants and ended up admiring what was in them. He'd been out of the service for years, but he was solid, with thick, ropey muscles. Admiration on a purely physical level made for an excellent distraction.

However, the longer she trudged behind him, the further her admiration nose-dived. In fact, she started to entertain fantasies about kicking his butt. Except putting one foot in front of the other became a study in determination. Her new hiking boots were rubbing blisters on both heels and a few toes. Damn if she would admit it or ask him to stop, though.

Another hour or more of hiking through scrub and soft ground led them to a canal of stagnant-looking water that smelled of decomposing earth. Bennett stopped and gestured. "We have to get across this ditch. Have any ideas?"

The ditch was too wide to jump and continued as far as she could see in either direction with no sign of a man-made bridge. That would have been too easy for Bennett the Torturer.

"Tree catapult?" The pain in her feet revved up her snarkiness. "I've seen Wile E. Coyote make one."

His lips twitched. "Inventive, but doesn't he usually make a coyote-sized crater?"

About fifty yards downstream, she could see a downed tree. "Shimmy over on a tree?"

He gave a small nod. "Go for it."

When she reached the fallen tree, it was obvious it had been used as a crossing many times, but it was too narrow for comfort and the water was murky, with a pungent, unpleasant odor. She could only imagine how cold it was. Dare she tackle the trunk like a balance beam? She glanced over her shoulder.

"Or if you want to head back rather than risk hypothermia after falling in the water, we can. No telling how deep the muck goes." He tutted. "Might take weeks to get the stench out."

He was attempting to get in her head. And succeeding. A nervous shudder had her knees going gelatinous.

"Ass," she hissed under her breath.

"What was that?"

The way to extract information from him was with honey, not vinegar. She fought her tongue and, as usual, lost. "I said, you're an ass." She enunciated every word.

" 'Bout time you caught on."

The combination of his smirking Southern accent and the light of triumph in his eyes cinched the decision. Stepping onto the end of the tree, she did her best to ignore the heat of his gaze on her back and concentrated on her feet. A few steps from solid land, she looked up and lost her balance. Her heart accelerated like a car leaving the starting line. Flailing her arms, she scampered the last few feet and landed on her hands and knees on the bank.

She stood and wiped her hands on her jeans, the knees muddy and wet but not the rest of her. Bennett walked across with his thumbs tucked into the straps of his pack like he was taking a Sunday stroll. He hopped off the end and landed next to her.

Jack was the last to cross, bounding over with no problems.

"I did it." Her heart was beating with the shot of adrenaline.

She wasn't sure what she expected. A pat on the head? A high five? The spilling of secrets in the face of her meager accomplishment?

"Barely. Jack made it over with more grace."

Sadly, she couldn't dispute the facts. "Yeah, well. Yay for me."

His lips pinched together, but she almost swore his eyes danced with laughter. He cleared his throat. "From here, we need to head northwest. Use my compass."

The face of the metal compass he handed her was elaborately drawn with fancy script and embellishments. She rubbed her thumb over the back and could feel an engraving, but with his attention boring into her, she didn't flip it over.

She lined up the needle with north and pointed northwest. "This way?"

"Your lead. Make sure we stay on track. It's easy to drift off or even circle back on yourself in the woods."

She did as he instructed. They continued in single file, the dog in the back. The going was slower because instead of following in

Bennett's wake, she was forced to push through the brush. A brief clearing allowed her to catch her breath. And flip the compass over. She rubbed over the inscription as if that would somehow help her decipher it.

Honor . . . something, something . . . *Laurence.*

His father? An uncle or brother? Or maybe he'd picked it up in an antiques store.

She became hyperaware of him a few feet behind her. More than his footsteps or the rustle of his clothing, it was as if his aura expanded to include her. It was the sort of hippie crap her mother tried to sell, but she'd never bought into.

"There is more among heaven and earth than we've dreamed," she whispered.

"What was that?" His voice sounded so close, she stopped. He bumped into her, grabbing her upper arms to keep her from bouncing forward. She twisted her head around to see him.

Even with the hump of her pack between them, his face was only a few inches from hers, her eyes level with his beard. How soft or scratchy was the hair? She swallowed, her voice thin. "I said, 'There is more among heaven and earth than we've dreamed.' "

"Shakespeare?"

"Yes. Are you a fan?"

"I prefer Mark Twain's earthiness. 'Go to Heaven for the climate, Hell for the company.' "

The pithiness of his choice had her smiling. "I pegged you as an adventure reader, if you read at all."

"Wasn't *Huckleberrry Finn* basically an adventure?"

"True. And Jack London wrote amazing adventures, of course."

Hearing his name, the dog barked and wagged his tail. They both laughed. Their relationship — if it even qualified as one — veered sharply from adversarial into uncharted territory. Not friendship by any stretch, but they danced on the edge of ease.

While they were still locked in a strange almost embrace, a snowflake drifted and landed in his beard, melting on contact. With more effort than it should have cost, she peeled her gaze from his and looked skyward. Through the gaps in the treetops, snow filtered to the ground.

A hush fell over the woods. Not a single bird chirped or squirrel chattered. It was a lonely feeling even though she wasn't alone.

"Who's Laurence?" she whispered. Not sure what had prompted her to even ask, she remained still. The moment took on the feel of a priest's confessional.

His hands flexed on her arms, but he didn't release her or push her forward. "The man who adopted me," he whispered in return.

"I'm sorry." Except she wasn't sure what she was apologizing for. Perhaps the pain she could sense under his stoic answer. Perhaps the events that had necessitated an adoption at all.

"Don't be. It was the best thing that ever happened to me."

"How old were you?"

"Sixteen."

She sucked in a breath, the cold making her lungs tingle. So old. What had happened to him before he'd turned sixteen? Where were his parents? Had they died? And how? Questions stumbled over one another to get out, but before she could formulate the words, he released her, the confessional door flung open.

"We need to get a move on. We have another hour at least before we can make camp."

She checked the compass to confirm their direction and trudged along, her head down, her mind troubled. For a while, those troubles distracted her from the pain in her feet. But soon enough each step was like walking barefoot on hot coals. She gritted her teeth. No one died from a blister.

After an eternity, he said, "Holler if you see a promising spot to make camp."

A tent would require ground space. She spotted a clearing through the trees. Snow dusted the pine needles and scrubby grass in the clearing like sifted powdered sugar. Except way colder.

She dropped her pack to the ground and rolled her shoulders. Shedding the weight lent her a second wind. They'd have the tent up and a fire going in a half hour tops. "Where do you want to set up the tent?"

"What tent?"

"The one in your pack?"

The look he gave her landed squarely in the middle of pity and amusement. "You really are a city girl. We build our shelter."

She was too hungry and cold to rise to his bait. "How?"

"I'll show you. Did you bring a hatchet?"

"I did." She pulled it out and scraped the price tag off the wooden handle while turning to face him. His was twice as big as hers. She clinked the blades together. "Seriously? If I was a man, this would give me a complex."

Again, a smile threatened to crack his stony expression. "It's too late to build anything off the ground, but the fire ants are dormant and the bugs are minimal. We can use pine needles as ground insulation. And boughs as cover. Look for low limbs, less than an inch in diameter."

He did an about-face and stopped at an evergreen to chop. She headed in the opposite direction and found a young tree with thin branches and set to work. A raw place formed on the pad of her palm. She tugged on gloves, but the fleece made it difficult to keep a strong hold and she tucked them back in her pocket. Sweat broke over her forehead in spite of the freezing temperatures.

She dragged over the half-dozen limbs she'd managed to fell. He joined her with bigger, fuller branches. "I'm surprised you aren't making me do all the work," she said caustically. Her blistered hand and feet soured her mood by the minute.

"I'm here to teach you, not torture you."

Her huff was a poof of white in the cold air. "Then teach me, wise one."

"Flattery will get you nowhere."

"I didn't mean . . . It was sarcasm."

His sparkling eyes were too warm and attractive for her comfort. She preferred him harsh and unfriendly.

"Just show me." She gestured.

"The fastest shelter is a lean-to or teepee type shelter. It's also good in cold weather because it keeps heat in. Now, which direction should it face?"

"Away from the wind?"

"Exactly. So, we'll face this way. I have cordage to make the braces."

She caught on quickly, and they worked in silence. The sky was still spitting out snow and had turned a dimmer switch on the sun. Dusk crept closer. Her fingers were clumsy, and ice encased her feet. Except where her blisters burned. And all she could think about was food. Something hot, like soup.

For that they'd need a fire? "What about a fire?"

"You gather twigs we can use as kindling. I'll gather fuel. You brought a fire stick?"

She nodded and trudged back into the woods, doing her best to scoot her feet without exacerbating her blisters. With her exertion level falling, a chill crept over her body. She shivered. Coming back with the kindling, she was thankful to see the pile of wood and a half-finished fire ring.

She retrieved her fire stick and sat cross legged on the ground next to where he was squatting. Dampness registered too late. She popped to her knees. The butt of her jeans was wet. If she weren't so tired and hungry and cold, she would have laughed.

"What'd you bring back?"

She made her offering without words. He picked through the twigs and dead fronds and made a mound in the circle of rocks. "We'll leave the rest to feed the flame once we get it started. It's a delicate balance of fuel and air. Give it a shot."

She clutched the fire stick, having read the instructions but not actually taken it out for a practice run. She set the stick on the edge of the mound and pushed down. A tiny spark emerged.

"More and faster," he said.

She pushed and pushed, the sparks coming but nothing lighting like a firework dud. Breathing hard, she sat back on her haunches, fighting tears and not wanting to admit defeat, even though that's exactly how she felt. Defeated. "Can you try?"

She held out the fire stick. He took it and her hand both, tilting her palm toward the fading light. "Are these new?"

"Believe it or not, my accounting job generally doesn't require hatchet work."

"Jesus, why didn't you tell me? I would have helped you."

Many reasons surfaced. She didn't want to give him the satisfaction. She didn't want to appear weak. She'd talked herself into this mess and would push through to the end. What she said was a deeper truth that went beyond chopping wood or starting a fire. "I don't like asking for help."

His hand was bigger and calloused, yet his thumb glanced over her palm with an almost unbearable gentleness. "Is that why you don't want to accept the money?"

Her gaze clashed with his, but with darkness falling it was impossible to get a read on his emotions. She pulled her hand out of his grasp, the slide of her fingers through his unexpectedly comforting. She pressed her fist into the cold, wet ground as punishment for betraying her. His kindness was disorienting.

"Could you get a fire going? Please?" The last word cost her, but it was a price she was willing to pay for warmth and light.

After ten minutes, he too was unsuccessful and sat back, stretching his shoulders. "It's too wet. Always a problem out here, but doubly so with the rain we've had the last week."

"What now? We huddle under the lean-to all night?" A night under the insubstantial array of branches seemed impossible. She would survive — maybe. Was her misery worth whatever information Bennett would be willing to give?

She moved back under the boughs and sat next to Jack to steal his warmth with her arms wrapped around her legs, her head on her knees. The insulating pine needles kept her butt mostly dry but poked through the denim.

"Come on, then." The low rumble of his voice brought her head up.

He stood over her, a hulking shadow blocking the remainder of the light. His hand was extended. She looked at it, finally making the decision to grab hold. He hauled her up.

"Grab your pack and watch your step."

Jack London bounded ahead, and Bennett didn't call him back as he'd done throughout the day. She matched his stride and put her feet in his steps, her head down.

It wasn't until he stopped that she looked up. A small cabin stood on a rise. She slapped his arm. "You freaking have a cabin out here?"

"For emergencies."

"But you let me chop trees and nearly kill myself starting a fire. What if we'd slept outside and I'd turned into a Popsicle?"

"Stop being dramatic. You're paying to learn survival techniques."

"You know that's not —"

He turned so fast on her she took a step

back. A crackling energy, like the moment after a lightning strike, held her immobile in his focus. Jack London barked at the door and broke the spell.

"Come on then." Bennett had to duck his head to clear the frame.

She made herself step after him even though danger pulsed with every beat of her heart. The interior of the cabin was cool and dark, but her relief to be surrounded by four walls and a roof was acute and trumped the sense of danger.

Bennett headed straight to a fireplace in the middle of the far wall. The cabin's chinked walls, low ceiling, and woodsy smell made her think of school-days field trips taken to old plantations. The cabin was old.

Light flared and drew her closer like a moth. Within minutes, heat from the blaze seeped around the room. She shrugged off her pack and jacket and set them on a small wooden table big enough for two. He tossed his pack in the corner and stripped down to his Henley but kept his hat on.

She took an inventory of the room. It didn't take long. Besides the table, an oversized twin bed took up one corner and a rudimentary kitchen another. She looked for a door leading to a bathroom but saw none. Neither did she see a faucet over the sink.

Still, a cabin with no water or bathroom was a sight better than no cabin at all, and she was thankful Bennett hadn't forced her to sleep in their lean-to.

"You hungry?" His voice rumbled from where he was squatting in front of the now-roaring fire.

Her stomach audibly awakened on cue. "Starving."

He got out a pot and pulled down three cans. She moved close enough to see two were chili and one was dog food. She hoped she rated the chili.

"There's a kerosene lamp next to the bed and matches in the drawer." He opened the two cans of chili and dumped the contents into the pot and lit a two-burner camp stove. The can of dog food went into a silver doggy dish. Jack London pranced in anticipation at his side and attacked the dish as soon as it hit the floor.

She managed to light the lamp on the second try and set it on the table, moving her pack next to his. While he stirred, she drew a chair closer to the fire and unlaced her boots. Blood glued her sock to her heel, and a curse escaped when she ripped the sock off. The second was even worse, and she fought the sting of tears.

He knelt in front of her and took her left foot in both his hands. "Let me guess: you wore new hiking boots."

"I bought nearly everything new for this trip. I don't have a selection of fire starters or hatchets hanging around, either."

Still holding her foot, he rocked back on his heels. "You spent a lot of money to get me alone."

"Yeah, I guess I did."

Was he aware he was running his thumb up and down her arch in a near caress? Abruptly he dropped her foot and rose to rummage through a cabinet. He returned with a first-aid kit, cleaned her blisters, and applied an antibacterial gel. "I'll put something over it tomorrow for the hike out. Chili should be hot."

He doled out two bowls and set them on the table along with bottled waters. She took a bite and moaned. Over canned chili, for goodness' sake. But after the hike and the stress and worry over spending a night outside, sitting in a cozy cabin eating chili was beyond her expectations.

The crackle of the fire made conversation unnecessary. The moment was surprisingly comfortable. She gestured around them. "Did you build this cabin?"

"No. If I had, I would have raised the ceiling a good five feet. I got snowed in for five days a few years ago and nearly lost my mind."

"Are you claustrophobic?"

"Not really, but this place reminds me of the caves in Afghanistan and gave me bad dreams. No escape." He put his head down and concentrated on scraping the last of the chili out of his bowl.

Questions about Bennett, not Noah, burned to escape. Noah had been killed. Darren fought to keep PTSD from destroying his life. It was becoming clear Bennett hadn't escaped unscathed. Maybe he was better at dealing with his issues or hiding them, but she could sense them nonetheless.

"If not you, then who built the cabin?" She steered away from the more personal questions.

"Don't know exactly, but the Dismal Swamp was a path to freedom for runaway slaves. A man could lose himself here for months. Back then, it was bigger, of course. Bleaker. Could be this cabin was built by former slaves or as a hideout or maybe a stop on the Underground Railroad."

She swept her gaze around the room, her perception altered with his brief explanation. "It's in good shape for being built so long ago."

"I overhauled it when I bought the land. Thought about moving it somewhere more convenient, but . . . I don't know. Didn't seem right somehow." He shrugged, sat back in his chair, and fiddled with his spoon.

She closed her eyes and stretched her other senses, her imagination taking flight. History was steeped into the logs. What joy and tragedy had the cabin seen?

"It's so isolated out here. Imagine a wanderer, lost and alone, smelling chimney smoke. It must have seemed a mirage. Salvation."

As the silence lengthened, she popped her eyes open. He stared at her, his expression an enigma, but the firelight made his eyes dance.

"Salvation," he murmured.

Whimsy inherited from her mother bubbled up, nurtured through the multitude of books she'd read. It was a trait she'd squashed her entire life and thought dead and buried since Noah had been killed. She'd needed to be practical for Ben's sake. But in the middle of nowhere, cozy in a cabin with Bennett Caldwell, a sense of magic stripped away reality.

"This cabin gave people hope and life. Can't you feel it?"

CHAPTER 8

Past

Noah,

I can't believe you can come! You're probably going to regret it, though. I've heard the commencement speaker this year is bo-ring. Although I should warn you . . . I've shaved my head and gotten a nose ring and neck tattoo. Corporate America will appreciate that, right? Actually, my mom bought me a pantsuit for interviews and it must have worked, because I have two amazing job offers! We can discuss later. Can't wait to see you . . .

Harper

Harper adjusted her graduation cap, tilting it jauntily to the side. Whoever had invented the flat-topped hats obviously didn't have long hair in mind. The tassel swung in front of her eyes, the color designating her honors status.

Her mom pushed into Harper's dorm room holding two coffees and a paper bag. "I wasn't sure if you wanted a bagel or donut, so I got one of each." She met Harper's eyes in the mirror.

"On a scale of one to ten, how dorky do I look?" Harper smiled and flapped the sleeves of her black graduation gown like a bat.

Her mom's smile was watery and her voice choked. "I'm so proud of you, Harper Lee."

Answering tears sprang to Harper's eyes. She hugged her mom, hiding her face in her mom's shoulder. "I love you, but please don't call me that in front of my friends."

Her mom's body shook with laughter. "Oops. I forgot."

Harper pulled back and took one of the coffees, sipping the strong brew. She would need it to get through the marathon ceremony. Once it was over, she would be free and let loose on the world. Trouble was she was standing at a crossroads with no clear vision of what lay ahead.

"Have you heard from Noah?"

"Not since last night. I hope he made his connecting flight." She checked the time.

"Ten more minutes and we'll have to leave or I'll be late lining up and you won't get a seat."

They ate, Harper taking the donut and her mom eating the bagel. Finally, Harper brushed her hands together. "We'll have to go without him."

On the walk from her dorm to the arena where she'd be recognized as part of the graduating class of the University of North Carolina, she worried over Noah. She'd never been the kind of girl who dreamed of a Prince Charming. In fact, family history taught her that men were not to be depended on.

Her father hadn't even sent a card after she'd written to tell him she was graduating with dual degrees. Silence was standard operating procedure when it came to him.

But Noah was shattering her expectations. She'd been shocked to hear from him after their week together. It had been fun and lighthearted and she'd liked him — a lot — but the practical side of her hadn't expected anything but the kiss he'd given her the last evening before he'd headed back to Virginia Beach.

Except it hadn't ended there. He'd emailed and called, and during a break in BUD/S training he'd flown across country to see her. At first, she'd been scared and panicked to get serious with a man in the military and, even worse, a man who put himself in constant danger.

But keeping herself from falling for him had been like stopping flowers from blooming. One day the ground was barren and the next buttercups were unfurling in the chilly February sun.

She and her mom joined the current of people headed into the arena. They exchanged a hug and parted ways for the ceremony. Harper might not be able to pick her mother out of the crowd, but she would be there, supporting Harper and cheering her on. Like always.

The ceremony passed with less pomp and circumstance than the theme song would imply, with only one injection of heart-stopping adrenaline when her name was read, along with those of the other honors students in the business department.

It was over both faster and slower than she anticipated. Not just the ceremony, but her four years of college. She was officially an adult. Unfortunately, a lightning bolt of wisdom didn't accompany her degrees, and a decision loomed.

She pushed through the crowd to the side of the floor and scanned the stadium seats for her mom. White flashed in her periphery, and she turned. Noah walked toward her in his dress uniform, his hat tucked under his arm, his swagger undeniable. The crowd parted for him like he was a celebrity, the ladies, young and old, taking surreptitious second glances.

Harper didn't blame them a bit. Since she'd met Noah at eighteen, he'd matured into a Man with a capital *M.* The body-jammed too-warm arena had her needing a fan like some antebellum debutante greeting her returning solider.

When he got within earshot, like a toddler in possession of only a handful of words, she said, "Hi."

His response was to sweep her into a hug that was at once fierce and tender. Her cap fell to the floor. It had been three months since she'd seen him, but the awkwardness slipped like sand through her fingers and she wrapped her arms around him.

"I didn't think you'd make it," she said into his neck.

"Almost didn't. I got here halfway in. Heard your name. Dual degrees with honors. I'm proud of you."

She tightened her hold. His pride in her meant a lot. He'd accomplished great things since they'd been together, and now it was her turn. Together they'd be unstoppable.

As soon as the thought popped into her head, her path was chosen. Maybe subconsciously she'd decided ages ago.

"Yes," she whispered in his ear.

He pulled away and stroked a hand over her hair. "Yes what?"

"Yes, I'll marry you."

In slow motion, his smile morphed into gaping shock. "Are you serious?"

Even though nerves fluttered like a swarm of bees in her stomach, she nodded. "Completely and totally."

He picked her up and spun her around. Giggling, she hit his shoulder to put her down. People around them smiled and gave them wide berth. He caught the eye of a salt-and-peppered father and pointed to Harper. "She agreed to marry me."

"Congratulations, son," he said with a smile, and moved along with the flow.

"Stop, Noah! You're embarrassing me." The heat her body was putting out made her feel like a foil-wrapped potato being roasted over coals. She flapped the front of her gown.

Noah never hid his emotions. His joy radiated to her and she tried to match him but couldn't. Not that she wasn't over-the-moon happy with him and her decision to accept his proposal. She was, but the gene to be able to express her emotions — both good and bad — had passed her by.

Her mom found them, and Noah relayed the news. She had no problem with public emotional outbursts and promptly started crying while trying to hug both of them.

Over her mom's shoulder, Harper stared at the floor. His hat had fallen next to hers. Black and white. What was the symbolism? Good versus evil? Opposites attract? Or was it only the vagaries of gravity?

The three of them went to dinner. Still in his dress whites, Noah had gotten them preferential seating and a free bottle of wine from the manager whose son was serving overseas. Afterward, they gathered on the sidewalk outside the restaurant. Her mom shuffled through her oversized purse for her keys.

"Be careful and call me when you get home, okay?" Harper gave her mom a hug and kiss on the cheek. She didn't want to let her mother go. It was like she was letting her childhood drive away and stepping into the shoes of an adult. She wasn't ready.

The spike of fear faded like the taillights of her mother's car. She put her arm around Noah's waist and leaned into him, taking a deep breath. "Want to head back to my place?"

"I thought you'd never ask." Noah skimmed his hand over her bottom, leaving no questions as to his intentions. Which suited her fine.

She snuck him in the side door of her dorm and tried to muffle his laughter as she pulled him into her room. As soon as she turned the bolt on the door, he attacked the buttons of her dress. She did the same to his jacket and shirt. They fell together on the bed and made love with an urgency that reflected their time apart.

Afterward, tucked into his side, her heart still dancing an Irish jig along her ribs, she let her hands wander his chest, admiring the cut of muscle under skin. Things didn't have to change immediately because they'd gotten engaged. She had a job offer from an accounting firm in Raleigh and another in Atlanta. They were due answers by the end of the week.

"When do you want to get married?" He traced unknown symbols on her back.

Her breath stalled.

He continued. "A deployment could be passed down any day. I think we should make it soon; otherwise we might have to wait a while."

"How long?"

"Months. Maybe even a year."

"I've got job offers."

"You might be able to find something on base. Or you could do people's taxes for extra money. Whatever."

She propped herself up on her elbow and pulled the sheet over her nakedness. "I don't want to do people's taxes."

"Then, don't. You don't have to work at all. In fact, I'd prefer you didn't, so I can have you all to myself when I'm off." His smile was sweet and charming, yet her stomach didn't swoop because of excessive warm fuzzies.

"That's not what I meant. I want a real job. I worked my ass off and want to work."

"Okay, fine. You can look around Virginia Beach for something." A hint of anger or frustration colored his words and tensed his body.

"Would it really be so bad to wait a few months or even a year? What difference does it make if I take the job in Raleigh if you're not even here?"

His chest rose and fell, and when he spoke his voice was soft. "Because if . . . something happens to me, you'll be taken care of if we're married."

His gaze didn't waver from hers and in

his eyes were grim possibilities of the future. The implication scored her heart. Noah could die.

She sank back into him and laid her head on his chest, his heartbeat steady and strong. She loved him more than she'd ever thought possible and wanted to be with him more than she wanted any dream job. She would find something in Virginia Beach. Flexing her independence wasn't as important as what he did day to day, laying his life on the line to protect her and his country.

"We can get married tomorrow if you want to elope," she whispered.

He kissed the top of her head. "That's my girl."

A week later, Harper twisted the gold band on her left hand and walked the perimeter of the town house they were leasing. Choices on base were limited and taken by single men, so they were off base, but close. The collection of town houses was filled with military families but projected a characterless, faintly institutional feel. Noah put his arms around her from behind and kissed her temple.

"A coat of paint. Some furniture. We can make it work, right? And how about we hang your diplomas right here?" He tapped the wall behind him. Her framed diplomas had been her graduation present from her mom.

She leaned back into Noah's chest and turned her head enough to give him a glancing kiss on the mouth. "That sounds perfect."

Optimism flourished. She would spend some time turning the place into a home and then look for a job. Virginia Beach had a thriving economy. Surely finding something would be easy with her qualifications.

Three months later, she was no closer to finding a suitable job. She had to wonder if her status as a military wife was a black mark against her. Where the husband was stationed, the wife followed, leaving any company in the lurch.

After another fruitless interview, she'd kicked off her heels, poured a glass of wine, and plopped on the couch. The house was quiet. Suffocating.

An adjustment period was normal, right? She'd gone from living in a dorm teeming with people to a town where she knew no one except Noah, who worked from dawn to dusk. She checked her watch. Too early to call her mom. She did the next best thing and picked up a book.

An hour later, after she'd finished the glass of wine and closed her eyes for a second, the jangle of the front door startled her to full adrenaline-fueled wakefulness.

Noah rounded the corner into their den. Harper blinked, trying to orient herself in time. "You're home early."

He usually greeted her with a smile and kiss. Not today. "The team got its orders."

Another shot of adrenaline weakened her knees and made the wine burn a path up her throat. She sank to the edge of the couch. "When? Where?"

"Can't tell you where. We're leaving in two weeks."

In the routine of their days, it had been easy to ignore the deployment they both knew was coming. "How long will you be gone?"

"Six months. Maybe a year, if they extend it." He sat next to her and his weight tipped her into him. She didn't fight the natural laws and tucked herself close.

Months that he would be in danger every single day while she was safe. "Maybe I should go back to Nags Head with Mom."

His sigh tickled the hair at her temple. "You need to acclimate yourself to life in Virginia Beach. Make connections. No luck at today's interview?"

"That empty glass over there wasn't cele-bratory."

"I'm sorry, babe."

The silence wasn't suffocating with Noah at her side. If they could just stay like this forever.

"Did you contact Allison Teague yet?" he asked.

"Not yet." She gnawed the inside of her mouth. "We don't have anything in com-mon."

"You both have husbands who are about to deploy."

"She has a *baby.*" She didn't mean to add the pinch of panic to the word "baby."

"Don't you want to have kids?"

"I guess. Sure. Eventually." The thought of having a baby while she was still so unsettled terrified her. It was like she'd stepped into quicksand and instead of sav-ing her Noah was waving and saying, "Bon voyage." "I didn't go to college to pop out babies right away, Noah. You know I want a career."

"Yeah, I know, but . . ." His shoulder moved under her cheek in a shrug.

She could sense he wanted her to press him for whatever strife was hiding behind his innocuous agreement. Melding their lives was already a complex process and if the fundamental beliefs were weakened she wasn't sure what to do.

She did want kids. Really, she did. Just not at twenty-two with a husband who was getting ready to leave her all alone.

CHAPTER 9

Present Day

Hope and life thrummed through the cabin, but Bennett decided it had nothing to do with the logs around them and everything to do with the woman they harbored.

"All that salvation stuff is ancient history." He rose and gathered the tin bowls and cutlery, bagging them for a cleaning. It busied his hands and allowed him to find his footing.

"Is it? I'm not so sure." She stirred, and he watched her out of the corner of his eye. She flicked the short curtain aside and shivered. "Weather has gotten worse."

"Yep." The wind whistled through cracks in the chinking around the windows, making the curtains sway.

"Will we be stuck here another night?" She pulled a chair and her pack closer to the fire and rummaged around inside.

"Don't rightly know yet. The front wasn't

supposed to drop this far south. The cabin is stocked with enough food and firewood for a week. You don't have to worry about freezing or starving to death." He pulled his chair next to hers, held out his hands, and rubbed them together.

"I'm not worried about freezing to death. Or starving. I was wondering if I should save these or not." She dropped a package of graham crackers, marshmallows, and two chocolate bars on the table.

It took a few beats to put the items together logically. "You brought s'mores?"

"I thought they were mandatory on camping trips." She ripped open the crackers and poked around the fireplace. "Have you got anything to roast marshmallows on?"

Roasting marshmallows on a survival trip. Ridiculous. Impractical. Fun? A warmth tied itself into a knot in his chest. "Let me see what I can find." He ducked outside and foraged for an appropriate stick.

Back in his chair, he shivered and pulled out his pocketknife to whittle the end to a point. He handed it over and slumped back in his chair, his legs outstretched and crossed at the ankles.

She hummed a little off-key as she opened the marshmallow bag and speared two. Crouching at his feet, she turned the marshmallows above the flame, her patience keeping them from burning. Using his feet for leverage, she pushed up and assembled the s'more.

"This is a masterpiece. My best one ever." She displayed it on the palm of one hand while performing a Vanna White flourish. She held it out toward him.

"Yeah, it looks amazing." He couldn't seem to stop his lips from turning upward.

"Go on. I made it for you." She waved her hand under his nose.

He uncrossed his arms but didn't reach for it. "For me?"

"You deserve it for putting up with me and not making me sleep outside and for getting the stick." Her smile was coaxing and sweet.

He took the s'more and took a big bite out of the corner. The warm marshmallow and melted chocolate hit his tongue like a gourmet dessert. Still smiling at him, she licked melted chocolate off the side of her hand. The dart of her tongue did weird jumpy things to his heart.

"Is it heavenly?" she asked.

" 'S good," he mumbled around an even bigger bite. In fact, he couldn't remember anything tasting so good.

She readied two more marshmallows on

the stick and resumed her position at his feet, this time putting a hand on his knee for balance. The warmth of her touch was incinerating compared to the flames of the fire.

"In high school, we used to build bonfires on the beach and drink beers and make s'mores." While she assembled her own s'more, she asked, "When's the last time you had one?"

The last and only time he'd had one was in Mississippi. "It was a long time ago."

"How long?"

"I was sixteen. Just out of foster care."

She betrayed no hint of pity or surprise. "How did you end up in foster care?"

He laid his head back and stared through a smoky haze toward the ceiling. If she'd pressed him harder, he might have blown her off. But she didn't. She only sat and watched and waited. Had Noah taught her how silence could be used to extract information?

She nibbled the corners of the graham crackers, acting as if she had all night. Which technically she did. What would it hurt to tell her? After all, it was ancient history and didn't bother him anymore.

"My mom was a druggie. Opiates mostly. OD'd when I was nine. No one wanted me, so I was shuffled into the foster system."

He didn't mention the fact that he was the one who'd found her on the bathroom floor before school one morning. He hadn't touched her, only backed out of the dingy little bathroom, called 911, and waited for the police on the front steps.

"How could no one want to adopt you?" Outrage for his younger self colored her tone.

"People want to adopt babies, not troubled kids. Nine is ancient in foster care."

"What's the difference between living with a foster family and getting adopted?"

"Foster families can return you if you're defective." The first days in a new family were always the worst. His attempt to act perfect always failed. "I got returned a lot."

Her soft sound of sympathy landed like a punch to his chest.

"I deserved it. I lied. Stole. Was generally an asshole."

"You were hurting." She'd cut through to the truth in seconds.

He'd struggled with nightmares about his mother until other even more painful ones took their place. "When I was sixteen, I got one last shot. The state fostered me with a retired Army sergeant. He'd never married and occasionally took on problem kids."

"Laurence from the compass. The man who adopted you."

"I called him Sarge. The compass was a gift the day the adoption became legal." He swallowed down a lump, surprised to realize his history still had the teeth to wound. "So I could always find home, he said."

"That's amazing."

"Yeah, I guess it was." When he reviewed his past, he tended to focus on the difficult times, but his pairing with Sarge had been a stroke of fortune for which he could never repay the universe. "That weekend he took me out into the woods for a camping trip. I had s'mores for the first time. It was . . . special."

"I'll bet. You finally had a family." She finished her last bite, propped her chin in her hand, and regarded him with an intensity that veered toward uncomfortable. "Is he still in Mississippi?"

Bennett's good luck never lasted. Maybe that's why he was cynical. "Died during one of my first tours in the Navy. I was on a six-month rotation in the South China Sea and couldn't get home in time."

"I'm so sorry. Life seems to snatch the best people too soon." Her hand brushed the back of his, and before he thought better of it he caught it close.

The firelight sparked off the lighter brown in her hair, turning it golden. Her eyes were bright with life, and her T-shirt and jeans molded her body. She was more beautiful now than in the few pictures Noah had shared. He ran his thumb over the back of her hand, aware of the strength beneath the softness.

Harper was at once practical and a dreamer, vulnerable and ballsy, and vastly more complex than he'd imagined her. No longer a two-dimensional caricature drawn from her emails and letters to Noah, she was flesh and blood and exuded an innocent sexuality that was more dangerous than anything he'd ever faced. To his sanity at least.

Noah's ghost stepped out of the shadows where he always lurked. Guilt ran rough-shod over reopened wounds. Noah's widow was off-limits. Especially to him. A tangible shift in mood occurred. He pulled his hand away, balled it on his lap, and stared into the fire, his vision turning fuzzy.

"What do you think would have happened if you hadn't met him?" she asked.

His heart stopped. If he hadn't met Noah, would Noah still be alive?

"I assume you joined up because of Laurence — Sarge, I mean?" she added with a smiling glance.

He blinked, searching for equilibrium. She hadn't been referring to her dead husband. The man who'd extracted promises before dying in Bennett's arms. "Sarge wanted me to go into the Army, but I had dreamed about being a SEAL. With all the shuffling around, my grades weren't great. Plus, my state file was thick. And not with commendations. I had to enlist in regular Navy and prove myself first."

"First a SEAL and now you own your own business. I wonder how many foster kids are as successful as you are."

He shrugged away a weird embarrassment. Compliments and praise were two things he'd never gotten much of growing up or in the navy.

Like a wild animal seeking an escape, he grabbed the pot and a flashlight and headed for the door. "I'll go clean up."

"Since there's no running water, how do you handle personal functions, if you know what I mean?" She waggled her eyebrows.

His survival weekends attracted serious-minded men and women who were at least familiar enough with outdoor living to know the basics.

"There's an outhouse in the back if you're desperate and not afraid of dark places and spiders. Otherwise, the trowel is hanging by the door. Try not to get frostbite on your butt."

Jack shot outside as soon as the door opened enough for him to shimmy through. She left the trowel but headed toward a thin copse on the left side of the cabin. How could she switch so easily from eviscerating Bennett with her probing questions to teasing? Fighting a smile, he scrubbed at the pot with a handful of snow.

She stood at the edge of the clearing, making no move toward the outhouse or the cover of the trees. He highlighted her in a beam of light. She turned away from the glare, rubbing her arms. Neither one of them had bothered with a coat.

He dropped the circle of light to her feet. "What's wrong?"

"Seth said bears don't hibernate; they go into torpor. That means one could be wandering around, right?"

"Unlikely."

"Could you just . . . you know . . . come watch over me while I . . . do my business?" The request came out like every word had gone through a shredder.

"You're worried a bear might eat you?" At her shrug, he dropped the chili pot, joined her, and pointed. "Head into the trees. Take

174

the light. I'll be right behind you."

Even with the help of his flashlight, she struggled over the brush and rocks, falling once and catching herself on her hands and knees. Her boots were untied, with no socks. Every step must have been rubbing her blisters raw.

She stopped in the cover of trees. He kept a good six feet between them, turned his back, and propped his shoulder on the trunk of a pine. A cross between a cry and a frustrated curse came from her.

"You okay?" he asked without turning.

"My fingers are numb. I can't get my pants unbuttoned."

Even knowing it was a terrible idea, he took his hands out of his pockets and rubbed them together. "I can help."

They closed the distance to each other. It was too dark to see her waistband, much less the button. "I need some light."

She pointed the light toward her jeans and closed her eyes. "This makes the top ten list of my most embarrassing moments."

"Peeing in your pants would be way worse." He worked the button of her jeans open and then the zipper. Her panties were hot pink and low cut. He shouldn't have noticed, much less stared like he was doing with his hands still on the waistband of her pants, but damn, her panties were in the spotlight. He let go and she stumbled backward.

Resuming his position against the tree, he took a deep breath. Woodsmoke was thick in the air, the smell pleasant. Snowflakes fell, and Jack jumped and played like a puppy.

An *oof* and unladylike curse had Bennett half-turning toward her.

"No, don't look. I just lost my balance and landed my bare ass in the snow. You boys have it so much easier when it comes to relieving yourself in the woods." The light bounced around, and she materialized at his elbow.

She'd gotten her pants up but not re-buttoned. An offer to help her almost shot out. Instead, he said, "I'll walk you back to the door and finish cleaning."

She shuffled next to him, her shivers noticeable. "Thanks for the escort," she whispered before ducking back inside. The blast of warmth was like a siren's call. But he was nothing if not disciplined and returned to finish what he'd started.

After using the snow and leaves to scrub the pot clean, he stepped back inside to defrost, Jack on his heels. Harper wasn't by the fire as he expected, and his gaze bounced around the room, landing on a lump under the quilt on the bed. Not even the top of her head was visible. Was she asleep?

As quietly as possible, he put the pan away and fingered her jeans, now hanging over the back of the chair toward the fire, wet splotches darkening the fabric.

He sat and pulled his boots off. Jack circled the hearth a few times before curling up on the warm bricks. Bennett glanced over at the bed again as he squirmed in the upright wooden chair. He'd slept in worse conditions, but not for a long time now. Crossing his arms, he closed his eyes and let his chin sink toward his chest.

He startled to full wakefulness in a snap, his ears reverberating, not sure where he was or what had happened. His mind was still trapped in an old dream where he was eleven.

He blinked, his surroundings coming into sharp focus. The fire had burned to red coals. Kneeling next to Jack, he threw wood on the fire and stirred the coals. A flame licked up the back of the wood, casting light over the cabin.

"Bennett?" Harper was sitting up, watching him, her voice sleep roughened. "It's f-freezing in here."

"I'm getting the fire going again."

"Why don't you lay down over here? Isn't sharing body heat an important survival lesson?"

His gaze went from the bed to the chair and back again. His neck was stiff and he didn't relish spending another minute on the hard seat. Shivering, he shuffled toward the bed, his stomach jostling. It had nothing to do with there being an attractive, funny woman in pink panties under the covers.

The bed was an odd size. Roomy for one, but not quite comfortable for two. His plan was to lie down on top of the covers until she lifted them for him. The welcome was too much for him to deny. He slipped underneath, her warmth like a mini-generator.

"You're an ice cube," she said.

"Sorry."

She gave a husky laugh. "Noah used to tell me the best way to share body heat was to get naked."

Lightning passed through his body, an image frozen in his mind's eye. The two of them in bed for entirely different reasons than to share body heat.

She inhaled sharply, her body tensing. "I didn't mean —"

"I know." If only circumstances were different then . . . Their paths would have never crossed. The only things binding them were shared memories of her dead husband, his best friend. He forced his muscles to loosen. "As a matter of fact, it's both a great pickup line and true. One time, Noah and I —" He cut himself off, but it was too late. He'd invited Noah's ghost to sit and stay a spell.

"You what?"

The fire had fully caught and cast a glow around the room. She popped up on her elbow. Her hair was out of the ponytail she'd worn all day and his hand itched to touch the tendrils that waved over her shoulder.

"We got separated from the team and had to spend a night in a cave in the Afghani hills. I've never been so damn cold in my life."

"Did you two get naked?" The hint of tease in her voice surprised him.

Thinking or talking about Noah even all these years later brought a rush of guilt and pain. But a different realization joined the crippling emotions. Between training and deployments, Bennett had spent months at a time with Noah. Maybe even more time than Harper had with him in their too-brief marriage. The answers she sought were too costly for Bennett, but he could give her other memories.

"Not naked, but I'm not ashamed to admit we spooned." Even as cold and miserable and sleepless as the night had been, Noah had managed to crack a couple of jokes. Bennett was smiling before he realized it and forced a frown.

"He was always so upbeat and optimistic, wasn't he?" No pain hid in the fondness in her voice.

"It's what got him through, I think."

"Got him through what?"

"Training. Deployments. Dealing with the shit we had to deal with on a daily basis over there." The years in foster care had killed any optimism Bennett had been born with. "He had an easier time than some readjusting to life back home."

"Why did I never meet you when the team was stateside? You never came to cookouts or Super Bowl parties or baby showers. Why not?"

"I don't know." Except he did know.

A big part of why he stayed away was because of her and his inappropriate attachment. But another reason had been his own inadequacies. Being around his buddies' families had been a stark reminder of how lonely his life was. No family left. No serious girlfriend. No friends, outside the SEALs. He'd often thought how easy his death would have been to handle. No one for the chaplain to visit. No one back home to mourn him.

"When did you decide to start your business?"

Grateful for the subject change, he said, "It had been brewing for a while. It's something we used to talk about over there. Once a SEAL, always a SEAL, but everyone moves on eventually, either in the military or out of it."

"Like Darren."

"Yep." He tucked his hand under his head and stared at the flickering shadows on the ceiling. "Sarge had taught me survival techniques and SEAL training honed them. Weekend warriors were eager to learn, and no one else offered what I could in the Virginia Beach area. Now, though, I have people fly in from New York, Atlanta, Boston. It's grown even faster than my business plan predicted."

"Wow." She didn't say more, but the energy that thrummed indicated she was wide awake. Finally, she said, "Do you want to hear something crazy? I'm thinking of starting a business."

"Not crazy. Challenging, though. What kind of business?"

"We're leaning toward a coffeehouse. Who doesn't like coffee, right?"

"Who is 'we'?"

"Allison and me. And a handful of other ladies from a support group for military wives. We've been chatting via text and Skype and . . . I don't know, I think we're onto something. We have a lot in common."

He tried not to be curious but failed. "New businesses are risky even with something amazing to offer. Why would you want the stress?"

"Because" — she made a little sound of disgust — "my life is fine. Easy."

" 'Easy' sounds good."

"Too easy. Unfulfilling. Boring."

"Not good enough reasons to sink money into a business with no mission."

"A mission and purpose I have in spades. It's the product that's been hard to nail down."

He turned and propped his head up on his hand, matching her stance and putting their faces close. "Give me more info."

She chewed her bottom lip, her gaze unwavering on his. "It started with Allison and Darren."

"Heard Family Man got another promotion." His life had diverged from his SEAL counterparts', partly from circumstance but mostly by his own doing.

"Yeah. He's part of JSOC now." Troubles weighed the words and clouded her eyes.

"What's wrong?"

"He's having a hard time. PTSD, I think. Depression, maybe. Allison is at her wit's end. I went down for a visit because Allison's emails seemed . . . off. Darren sleeps too much during the day, and the night I was there he wandered around the base in the wee hours. Not sure what would have happened if I hadn't been there."

Bennett had only met Allison twice, but she'd struck him as the quintessential officer's wife. Welcoming and friendly, but with a steel backbone. "Has he tried counseling?"

"Did you?" Her eyebrows rose. When he didn't answer, she continued. "You know how these things work."

Unfortunately, he did. Darren was probably attempting the common "stuff your problems in the closet and nail it shut" method of dealing with his issues. Worked better for some men than others. Or maybe his closet had gotten too full and the door would no longer close.

"Drinking too much?" Bennett asked.

"I'm not sure, but he doesn't look good. He's a shadow of the man I remember."

Fuck. Maybe he should reach out. Not that he had any great wisdom to impart, but at least Bennett understood what he'd been through better than some base shrink. And Darren wouldn't feel comfortable sharing with a group of strangers.

"I'll call him when we get back."

"That would be great." She touched his arm. The muscle jumped instinctively and scared her hand away. *Good.*

"I still don't understand how this undefined business venture has anything to do with Darren."

"I went to a support meeting of base wives. It was enlightening. Several of the wives lamented the lack of job opportunities. They want to contribute. I felt the same way when I was in their shoes, but now I'm in the position to do something." An infectious enthusiasm lit her voice.

"And you want to start a business that employs them."

"Yes. Exactly." She snapped and pointed.

She understood better than most what military wives faced — the good, bad, and tragic. It was a noble reason, but nobility and success weren't natural partners when it came to actually making money.

"You graduated with honors, didn't you?"

"How did you — ?" She gave a little shake of her head. "Double major: marketing and business. After Noah and I married, I couldn't find a job that I wasn't grossly overqualified for. They could smell a military wife from a mile away."

"Why the black mark for being a military wife?"

"When husbands move, so do wives. Why spend the time and money to train someone when she might leave at any moment? I don't blame them. I really don't." She sighed and flopped to her back. "But it was frustrating. I wasn't cut from the same cloth as Allison. She's the perfect military wife."

"I don't know. According to Noah, you were perfect."

Her gaze darted to his and then away. "No. I wasn't perfect by any stretch."

Chapter 10

Past

"Redecorate or something. I see a bunch of the wives taking a kickboxing class during morning PT. Allison coordinates all sorts of charity shit you could help with." Noah ran a hand through his hair. "Why can't you just be happy?"

His hair was longer than normal. Their most recent deployment had been in Afghanistan. To fit in with the locals, many men grew their hair and beards out. Noah's blond hair fingered him as a foreigner no matter how long it was.

His usually epic patience with her must have been at a breaking point. He'd cursed. Of course, she'd heard him curse before, but never at her. Anger and unease took up equal space in her chest.

"I'm not wired to take kickboxing and fritter away my day on charity work. I've worked since I was sixteen. I put myself

186

through college. I busted my butt for two degrees that I'm not even using." She gestured toward the wall where she and Noah had proudly hung her diplomas after they'd moved in. Her pride had turned to bitterness over the last two years.

"You've had opportunities." His voice was almost accusing.

"Selling people mattresses or working the register at a department store? Really ambitious stuff."

Noah plopped down on the couch and put his head down, his hands linked behind his neck. "What do you want me to do about it? The SEALs are my life. It's what I've always wanted. Do you want me to give it up so we can move to a bigger city? Is that what you want?"

Great. Now she felt like a slug that crawled out of the muck after a big rain. "Of course not." She sat next to him and put a hand on his knee, squeezing slightly. "I get frustrated and there's no one else to talk to around here. No one that I have anything in common with."

He slouched backward on the couch, his arm across the back. She took the invitation and snuggled into his side. Fighting with Noah left her feeling queasy. He was so good and noble and she . . . wasn't.

"You haven't even tried to make friends, Harper Lee." His voice had lost its sharpness.

"Ugh. I was never good at making friends. And it's only gotten harder."

"Will you do one thing for me?" He tipped her face toward his.

They'd been married almost two years, but because they spent so much time apart, in many ways they were still getting used to living together and sharing their lives. She was struck by not only how handsome he was but also the kindness in his eyes. How could she deny him anything?

"I'll try."

"Invite Allison over for coffee. Spend some time with her. If you still don't like her then —"

"I never said I didn't like her. She's nice. It's that we don't have anything in common."

"Just one morning, one hour."

"Okay, fine." Her agreement came out sounding more petulant than she intended. He picked up her phone on the side table and held it out to her. She snatched it out of his hand. "You want me to call now?"

"Yep. Otherwise, you'll put it off."

She tried not to resent his high-handedness. He was used to a chain of command. That was something they never told you about living with a man in the military, and maybe the SEALs in particular. They were bossy as hell. Of course, in the right conditions, that made them sexy as hell, too.

She had Allison's number stored and hit it, praying to get sent to voicemail. Her prayers weren't answered.

"Why, hello!" Allison's voice was chirpy.

Harper popped up. "Hi, Allison. It's Harper. Harper Wilcox."

"I know. You came up on my caller ID. Are you enjoying have Noah home as much as I'm enjoying Darren?"

Harper shot a look toward Noah, who was sprawled on the couch, his slight smile veering toward smug. "I am. Of course I am. I calling because" — she cleared her throat — "because I was wondering if you wanted to come over for coffee one morning this week." She felt like she was asking a boy out to a Sadie Hawkins dance.

An extra beat of silence rang loudly through the phone. "I would love that. Absolutely love it. What day works best for you?"

They settled on a day and time and Harper assured her that the kids were welcome and even managed to insert a joke about putting away her collection of Ming Dynasty vases. She hung up, her relief shadowed by a slight sense of dread.

"There. Was that so hard?" Noah asked.

Harper gave him the finger. On a burst of laughter, he jumped up and pulled her close, his hands wandering down her back to cup her butt. They sank to the floor and didn't come up for air until dinner.

The day of her coffee with Allison approached at warp speed. She cleaned the house and dusted the books on the shelf twice. Waffling on appropriate clothes, she settled on a simple skirt, T-shirt, and flip-flops. The coffee was brewed, snacks were arranged on a platter, and the house was spotless. There was nothing else to do but pace by the front window.

She spotted the stroller first and jumped to the side of the window to watch Allison's approach around the edge of the curtain. A toddler squirmed in the stroller while a baby slumped in a contraption strapped to Allison's front.

The doorbell rang and Harper skipped to the door, opening it and gesturing Allison and the kids through. "Come on in. Can I help you?"

"Could you lift the front of the stroller?" Allison's breathlessness gave the impression of being frazzled even though she was put together like a catalogue model, with smooth blond hair and in a pretty sundress.

Harper helped get the stroller up the two porch steps and into the den. With an efficiency that would do the Navy proud, Allison unstrapped the girl in pigtails from the stroller and set her down. Next Allison pulled a blanket out of a back compartment of the stroller, laid it out, and proceed to unstrap the tiny human from her chest.

On his back like a stuck bug, the baby kicked his arms and legs, his face turning red until a scream emerged.

"Sorry." Allison tossed Harper an apologetic smile.

Meanwhile, the girl, who was around two years old, took off toward the kitchen like an Olympic sprinter.

"Oh my God." Allison scrambled toward her on all fours.

"I'll get her. And some snacks, too." Harper retreated to the kitchen to find the little girl — what was her name? Libby? The little girl was rearranging the magnets on the fridge. A few papers and pictures had fallen to her feet. She was counting one-two-three over and over at the top of her lungs.

Harper's usually quiet, mundane morning had been shattered. But, strangely, she didn't mind. She fought a giggle. "Hey,

Libby. Are you hungry? Would you like a snack?"

Thank goodness she'd bought juice boxes and Goldfish along with sweet rolls and cheese and crackers. She shook the Goldfish box and the girl focused on the box like a hungry predator.

She held them out. "Can you carry them back to your mom?"

"Yesh. Dank you." Libby took the box with a smile that would break hearts someday if it hadn't already.

Harper followed with the plate of snacks. Libby plopped down crisscross applesauce next to Allison and tried to rip into the Goldfish box. Allison smoothly divested her of it before she could make a mess.

"Is it okay if she eats in here?" Allison looked up. For the first time, Harper could see the exhaustion behind Allison's perfect smile.

"Of course. I can't keep Noah from dragging the entire fridge to the couch when Georgia football or basketball is on."

"God, Darren is a Green Bay Packers fanatic. We went to a game for one of our first dates, and he tried to get me to wear a huge cheese hat. I refused. I fully expected him to dump me at halftime."

Their shared laugh dismantled any tension that Harper had carried around since the invitation. "How do you take your coffee?"

"In an IV straight to the jugular," Allison deadpanned with a dryness Harper hadn't ever noticed. Maybe she hadn't been looking hard enough. A grin broke over Allison's face like sunshine. "Barring that, just a splash of milk. Or cream if you have it."

Chuckling, Harper poured two mugs and returned. Allison was trying to get a squirmy Libby to sit on the blanket with her juice box and crackers. The baby was nuzzling at Allison's breast making little discontented sounds.

"Do you mind if I nurse?"

"Of course not." Harper set one of the mugs on the side table and gestured for Allison to sit on the couch. "Make yourself comfortable. Or as comfortable as you can with a tiny human attached to your body."

Allison's eyes flared before laughter poured out of her. She adeptly maneuvered the baby onto her breast, covering herself with a burp cloth.

"You're a natural." Harper pushed away any feelings of inadequacy.

"A natural? Ha!" Allison held the baby with one hand and took a sip of coffee with the other. "It took practice. Being pregnant is weird at first. Then, just about when you're getting used to feeling this actual human inside of you, you give birth and are expected to produce food for it. Which is totally surreal. But, then, somehow it becomes the most routine thing in the world."

"Noah wants to have kids." Harper couldn't believe the admission slipped out. The only other person she'd talked to about it was her mother.

"Now or later?"

"Now. Or yesterday if I could manage it." Harper stared into her coffee. "I've been putting him off. I was raised by a single mom who worked. I worked my way through school. I really thought I'd have a career going before I had kids. I mean, what's the hurry, right?"

"I understand where you're coming from, but these men . . ." Allison switched the baby to her other breast. "They approach life differently. They see a goal and go after it with everything they have, even if it means they might die. It's part of why we were drawn to them, right? They pursued us with the same single-minded purpose."

That certainly described Noah. What should have ended as a brief summer fling had turned into more than she'd ever imagined. Marriage, with a baby on the horizon.

"You think we should go ahead and start trying?" Harper asked.

"Now don't go putting words in my mouth. You wait as long as you need to. I'm just attempting, in my fumbling, obtuse way, to explain the pressure. Whether Noah talks to you about it or not, every time they get orders he worries about dying. Dying without leaving some part of him behind. It's primal, I think."

"Did Darren tell you that?"

"Goodness no. But I've lived it and seen it enough to form my theories. I should write a book. Or maybe a pamphlet for military wives. Forget death and taxes, it's all about 'Death and Babies.' " She gestured like presenting a marquee and grinned.

"That is supermorbid." Yet somehow Harper found herself smiling back at her.

"We've got to laugh about it. Most people don't get it. The threat of death is abstract, but for women like us, the threat has moved into the spare bedroom."

"Some nights when he's gone, I can't sleep because I wonder if he's okay or I imagine terrible things. Then, other times, I forget to worry and feel guilty as hell."

"I know exactly how you feel."

Harper believed her. No one else, not even

her mother, could truly understand.

"Did you work before you had kids? Before you and Darren got married?" Harper tucked her feet under her and nibbled on a cracker.

"Darren and I were high school sweethearts. He went through ROTC in college and applied for the SEALs right after graduation. I got a degree in education, but we got married before he got sent to boot camp, and I went home to live with my parents until he made the cut and got assigned. I've never worked. Well, except at home."

"Do you regret that?"

"Yes. No. I don't know. I wouldn't change my life for anything, you know? It's hard to have regrets." She gave a slight eye roll. "Except for the lack of sleep. I really miss sleep."

Allison put the baby over her shoulder and alternated between rubbing and patting his back. The wet protracted burp that emerged made Harper laugh, but Allison jumped up.

"Sorry. I hope we didn't turn your couch into a toxic waste site." Allison craned her neck to look over her shoulder. "The baby spit up."

"Couch looks fine. Your dress on the other hand . . ." Harper winced.

"Here. Could you hold him a second while I change?" Allison didn't wait for an answer and held the squirming baby out. Harper took him, and Allison squatted down to rummage through the bottom of the stroller. "No one tells you that you need spare clothes for not only the kids but yourself."

"Bathroom's right off the foyer."

"I'll just be a sec." She stopped in the doorway, her expression equal parts serious and amused. "Don't worry. You'll be okay."

" 'Cuz he doesn't bite?" Harper attempted a joke.

"Oh no, he bites all right. Four little nubby teeth can do more damage than you think." Allison's laughter trailed and echoed in the foyer, fading when the bathroom door shut.

It took Harper some juggling before she found the most comfortable hold was to prop the baby on her hip. His head seemed entirely too big for his spindly neck. Harper had never babysat or been baby wild. The closest she'd been to babies was funny internet videos.

Birds darted around a hanging bird feeder, and she moved toward the window and pointed. "Do you see the pretty red bird?"

The baby grabbed her finger and gurgled.

Harper held her breath, but it seemed to be a happy noise and not foretelling another imminent eruption of spit-up. She rubbed her chin against the baby's head. His hair was soft, the smell inherently snuggly, but Harper couldn't say why.

The baby guided Harper's finger toward his mouth, but Harper jerked her hand away. The baby's face went blank for two blinks, then screwed up into a bawl.

Harper bounced him. "I'm sorry. I'm sorry. Here's my finger."

She shoved her finger at the baby's mouth. The cry stopped like turning off a spigot. It was more of a gnaw than a bite and Harper made a funny face. The baby's big belly laughs made Harper laugh, too.

"You're a natural, too." Allison stood a few feet away in shorts and a T-shirt. How long had she been there?

Harper gave her the baby back. "No, I'm not. More coffee?"

Before Allison had the chance to answer, Harper grabbed both mugs and retreated to the kitchen. She rubbed her hands over her face and stared at her wavery reflection in the window. Holding a baby for two minutes wasn't the same as being responsible for one every minute of every day and entirely on her own when Noah was deployed.

What if he didn't come back and she was left to raise a child by herself? The thought shot her knees with Novocain, a sick feeling making her head swim. She grasped the counter and let her head hang low to get a handle on the panic.

"Harper? Are you okay?" Allison had come up next to her without her noticing.

"Not really, no." The words emerged around a block of tears.

Allison leaned back against the counter. "I've scared you with all this baby talk, haven't I?"

"It's not you. I'm scared that Noah will leave me to take care of a baby all by myself. You have two kids. Doesn't that possibility freak you out?" Harper raised her head enough to cross gazes with Allison.

"Of course it does. But it's more likely that you and Noah will retire to a peach orchard and grow old together rocking on your front porch. You'll never be happy if you can't find a way to deal with the SEAL lifestyle."

"Maybe I'll never be happy then."

Harper wasn't sure what she was looking for from Allison. Maybe some motherly comforting, even though she wasn't much older than Harper.

Allison's face tensed, faint lines bracketing her face. "Shut down the pity party. You need to get out of this house. If not a job, then volunteer somewhere. Join a book club or the wives group I coordinate. If you love Noah, you have to learn to deal with the uncertainty, and staying busy and engaged helps."

After an initial flare of resentment, she absorbed the tough love and her panic receded, still lapping at the shore but no longer swamping her.

"I still don't want to have a baby right away."

Allison made a harrumphing noise. "Then don't. But don't rule out a family down the road because you're scared."

Harper nodded and tried on a smile. It wasn't her biggest or brightest, but it was better than nothing. She was the hostess of this shindig after all.

"Here, let me get you more coffee." She bustled over to the pot.

"Actually, I've got to get home and put the baby down for a nap. Thanks for the coffee and chat, though." Allison breezed back into the den, where Libby was flipping through a pile of board books and the baby was strapped into the stroller.

Allison packed everything away like the stroller had some magic compartment and maneuvered it to the door.

Harper mouthed a curse before slapping on a smile and following Allison. Instead of providing a normal "get to know you" coffee, she'd aired her neurosis for the other woman to pick over like a rummage sale.

"I hope —"

"Why don't you —" Allison spoke over her and gave a little laugh.

"Thanks for coming," Harper said.

"Thanks for inviting me. How about you come over to my place next? What about Thursday morning? Come around now. I'll put a show on for Libby and the baby will be down for a nap. We can actually sit down and relax."

Maybe she hadn't screwed up. Relief relaxed her smile. "That'd be great."

After Harper helped her get the stroller down the steps, she stood there, feeling awkward, until Allison leaned in to give her a quick hug.

"See you soon," Allison whispered in her ear.

A bond of friendship, as fragile as it still was, had formed between her and Allison over the short morning and she didn't feel as alone. Or lonely.

Instead of retreating to the empty house, she sat in one of the rockers on the porch.

The set had been a wedding gift from her mother. With her foot she made the other chair rock in tandem with hers, and imagined Noah, old but never gray, beside her.

CHAPTER 11

Present Day

Harper tried to get a read on Bennett. Between the flickering firelight and his beard, she couldn't interpret his expression.

"Noah and I fought about me getting a job. And having kids. I was happy with Noah, but not so happy with my life in Virginia Beach. Things got better after Allison and I became friends. I volunteered with Meals on Wheels and with an adult literacy program. That gave me a purpose, I suppose."

"You didn't want kids?"

"No, I did, just not on the same timeline as Noah. I ended up giving in, though."

"You don't seem the type to give in or give up. No offense." His lips quirked into what qualified as a smile for him.

How much to admit? "Every time your team deployed and came home safe, it was like cheating Fate. Like it was only a matter of time before something bad happened."

"I felt like that at the beginning of every mission, too." His soft admission was threaded with understanding.

"I tried to keep that pessimistic side of me hidden from Noah."

"Why?"

"He wouldn't have understood. He comes from a long line of happy, optimistic people. Eventually, I couldn't stand myself. I was being selfish. A baby would make him happier than anything, and I wanted to make him happy more than anything."

"Do you regret it?"

For the first time, she spoke the truth aloud. "Not anymore. Not after how everything turned out. I can't imagine my life without Ben."

He flinched at the sound of her son's name.

"Does it bother you?" she asked.

"What?" The wariness in his voice betrayed him.

"That my son is named after you."

He shook his head and rolled to his back, throwing his arm over his eyes. His jawline was prominent and hard, his mouth pulled into a tight line. "Not bother. It humbles me. He was a good man. I did my best to protect him." His voice had thickened. "It wasn't enough."

"I don't blame you for what happened, you know."

"Maybe you should." He presented her his back and pulled the covers up around his ear.

She stared at the back of his head so intently she expected to see his hair catch on fire. He didn't move. He wasn't asleep, though. His body was too tense and his breathing unsteady. "What was your nightmare about?"

The silence that followed her question was oppressive. Finally, he asked, "What nightmare?"

"The one that woke me up earlier. You called out."

"What did I say?"

"I couldn't make it out."

"It was nothing."

"Liar."

The huffy sound he made turned the tension down from incendiary to uncomfortable. "An old dream. This cabin . . . the ceiling is so low. It's dark and smell makes me think of a freshly dug grave. Unless the weather is particularly nasty, I avoid staying the night."

She ignored the niggling guilt over her wimpy survival skills. "Did something happen on one of your missions in Afghanistan?"

"No." The word was barely a whisper.

She moved close enough to feel the heat radiating off his broad back. "Growing up in foster care then?"

"Yeah."

She waited. If she pushed, he would retreat.

After a few minutes listening to the fire crackle in the silence, a soft rumble of words emerged. "I was eleven and on my third foster home. Early enough that I still had hope I would land with a good family that would want to keep me."

"They weren't good?"

"The parents were okay, but they had two kids. Both boys. Teenagers. I was big for eleven, but not as big and strong as they were. It started small. A few shoves. Blaming me for messes they made. Fighting back only made it worse. One day, I threatened to call Social Services on their asses. I wouldn't have, of course, but they got scared and locked me in an old cedar chest."

"For how long?"

"Long enough to pass out."

"Oh my God, Bennett, you could have died."

He'd been eleven. Still a child. Between

his mother dying from an overdose and his stark existence in the foster-care system, Harper couldn't help but think of Ben. It was her job to protect him and she'd do it with her life. Bennett hadn't had a champion.

Without thinking beyond the moment, she scooched closer and put her arm around him from behind. It was like hugging a gargoyle, and she half-expected him to shove her arm away as if comfort were a communicable disease.

He didn't. As the seconds ticked off, his body lost its edge. His hand glanced across hers and she caught it, linking their fingers and squeezing.

Her hug was an offering to the eleven-year-old Bennett. Yet the longer it went on, the less innocent the touch grew. She hadn't been this physically or emotionally close to a man since Noah.

She was older — wiser was up for debate — and Bennett was more complicated than Noah had been. With Noah, she'd kept her own complexities and warring emotions under wraps, but she had a feeling that Bennett would not only sympathize but also empathize.

"I'm sorry," she whispered. Who was she apologizing to? Herself? Bennett? Or Noah?

"No. I'm sorry for saying anything. It's not important anymore."

If it weren't still important, he wouldn't have had a nightmare twenty-five-odd years later. Instead of calling him on his BS, she snuggled closer, their fingers still entwined, and held him tighter.

Harper popped her eyes open. Daylight suffused the cabin. The fire had burned down, but her body was warm under the covers against Bennett. She'd been dimly aware of changing positions throughout the night like a dance, ending with him on his back with her head pillowed on his shoulder. Her hand was sandwiched under his on his chest, his heart tapping a steady rhythm.

It was achingly intimate. Part of her wanted to rip herself away from him, but another part wanted to drift back to sleep and ignore the messy world outside the cabin door.

A sigh interrupted the sleepy cadence of his breathing. She could tell the exact moment he exited dreams for reality. His body turned into a taut rubber band, thrumming with dynamic energy. She forced herself to stay relaxed against him.

He curled his hand around hers for a heartbeat before letting go and shifting out of the bed. As if she'd just woken, she hummed and stretched, watching him through slitted eyes. He stoked the fire. Jack sat by the door, not making a sound.

Bennett let him out and let in a blast of cold air. She shivered and pulled the covers over her nose, trying to capture the warmth he'd left behind. He stood by a window, the light limning his profile, and ran a hand through his hair.

The image that popped into her head was an abandoned toy soldier, still upright but grimly alone and cast aside. Her breath got stuck somewhere between her lungs and heart.

He moved to the door, the illusion broken. Jack trotted back inside, shaking himself. After giving Jack another can of dog food, Bennett approached the bed with a foil packet. She looked up at him with the covers still over most of her face.

"Can I interest you in a Pop-Tart?"

"What flavor?"

"Brown sugar. Frosted, of course."

She snaked her hand out of the cover and took the packet. "I don't want to get crumbs in your bed."

"I won't kick you out." His slow smile could only be described as insinuating. Her insides went crazy, her heart dancing across her ribs, something slow and sexy like a tango. Before she could do more than stutter nonsense, he retreated to poke at the logs in the fireplace.

She ate one of the Pop-Tarts, but her throat was so dry she had a hard time swallowing. "I don't suppose you have a hand-cranked coffeemaker stashed somewhere?"

He huffed a laugh. "I don't even have instant, unfortunately. You miss it?"

"Desperately. Could you pass me my jeans?"

He glanced over his shoulder. "Let me get them warmed up first."

When he tossed them to her, they were dryer-fresh toasty. She shimmied them on under the covers and girded herself to emerge from her cocoon. Barefoot she ran on her toes to join him at the fire, squatting to hold her hands out.

"Was it this cold yesterday?"

"No. The clouds cleared and the temperature has fallen even with the sunshine."

"Is it too cold to hike out?"

"Not going to get much warmer today. It won't be so bad once we're moving. I need to take a look at your blisters before we head out, though."

Unable to unstick her gaze from him, she nodded, aware of him in ways that made parts of her tingle. Or was that the beginnings of frostbite? Bennett didn't seem to be battling the same weirdness she grappled with. For all she knew, he cuddled up with women all the time.

Yet . . . she didn't think so. He wore his loner vibes like a familiar sweatshirt. The kind you refused to throw away despite the frays.

"Did you ever get married?" She couldn't believe the question popped out of her mouth with no vetting from her brain. But, now that it was out, she was desperate to know.

His brows lowered and the side-eye he shot her was cutting. "No."

"Do you have a girlfriend?"

"You think I would've . . . ?" He let out a long sigh and grabbed the first-aid kit from the counter. "No."

It was the first true acknowledgment that whatever had sprung to life last night wasn't in her imagination.

"I don't, either." At his slightly quizzical expression, her mouth kept running. "Have a boyfriend, I mean. I haven't dated anyone since Noah died, actually. Much to my mom's horror."

"She thinks you should date?" He cracked the top of a water bottle and took a sip.

"Date. Have fun. Participate in the exchange of bodily fluids."

He choked and doubled over in a coughing fit that was interspersed with laughter. It was such a rare event, she couldn't help but chuckle along with him. After he got control of himself, he said, "She did not say it like that."

"You don't know my mom. Retirement has unleashed unruly tendencies. She's currently taking a nude painting class. And by 'nude' I don't mean she paints in the nude — although I wouldn't put it past her — but that she's painting naked young men. And loving it."

Their laughter intertwined, his a little rusty but pleasantly rumbly. Even after his laughter faded, his smile remained. His eyes crinkled and his teeth gleamed white in his dark beard, his two bottom teeth overlapping a little. The room seemed to heat a few degrees. Jack settled at her hip, and she leaned over to bury her face in his ruff to hide her blush.

"You don't seem as unconventional as she sounds."

"I'm not. I tried my best to be as normal as possible to offset her eccentricities. Jack London's not the only one in here named after a literary giant, you know." She tapped her thumb against her chest.

"Harper . . . ?" He blinked at her with his smile still in place. "What's your full name?"

"Harper Lee."

"Of course. I didn't know that," he said softly.

"I'm glad you don't know *everything* about me." She glanced at him through her lashes.

Any humor leaked out of his expression. "I'm beginning to think I don't know you at all."

She shifted to face him, her hand fisted in Jack's fur. "In a good way or bad way?"

He studied her, and she forced herself to remain still, her nerves building, but not wanting him to know how deeply he affected her.

"Not bad. Let's get your blisters taken care of." He pulled a chair up and made a "give me" gesture with his hands. He caught her foot around the ankle and pulled her closer, her butt sliding forward. He twisted her foot and ignored her muttered, "Hey, it's attached."

He was gentle in his handling, almost too gentle, because the brush of his fingers along her arch sent her foot flailing.

He tightened his hold around her ankle. "Ticklish, huh?"

"Little bit," she said through foot twitches. She ended up with bandages on both heels and several toes. "Am I all better?"

"As good as it's going to get. The hike out won't be comfortable for you, unfortunately."

"I'll survive." She pulled her pack closer to find socks before her toes froze.

"Of that I have no doubt."

She glanced up at him, but he had turned away to pack away the trash they'd generated. The dryness of his voice had contained something else. Something that sounded suspiciously like admiration.

"You're not mad that I booked this trip under false pretenses and insisted we come out here in spite of the weather?"

"I *was* mad and ready to teach you a lesson."

"If it's any consolation, I learned that I'm not cut out to live off the land."

"Not many people are. And that's okay."

"Do you enjoy it?" She pulled her boots on, trying to mask a wince as her tortured heels made contact with the leather. "Living off the land, I mean."

His movements slowed and turned almost absentminded. His hands were efficient yet graceful in their work and held her mesmerized. "It suits me, I suppose."

"How do you mean?"

"I'm a loner."

"I'm not so sure about that."

He pivoted to face her, his body language stark. "What do you mean?"

The truth emerged in spite of the warnings blaring in her brain. "You're not so much a loner as you are lonely."

"I'm not lonely." His response came too fast to be anything but defensive bullshit. She utilized it often enough to recognized the stench.

"Okay, you're not lonely." She gave him a tight smile and turned around to finish zipping up her pack.

The tenuous bonds they'd knitted overnight cleaved in two. He doused the fire with ashes from a bucket, and smoke billowed through the room. She heaved her backpack on and retreated outside, Jack on her heels.

A deep breath of cold air cleared her lungs and mind. With the sun filtering through the trees, the woods took on a magical cast. She'd read enough fairy tales to know the stories were often darkness wrapped in beauty.

The squawk of the door had her tensing.

"Ready to hit the trail?" His voice rumbled a shiver up her spine.

The point of her reckless subterfuge had been to uncover details of Noah's last minutes on earth. In that respect, she had failed. But she'd discovered so much more. About Bennett. And herself. For better or worse, she was leaving changed in a fundamental way. The future teemed with possibilities, and instead of burying her head under the covers, she was ready to meet them and maybe even get to know them better.

"Let's do it." She headed back the way they'd come. "Do you want me to navigate?"

He held out the compass. "If you want. After all, you paid to learn."

Her hand passed over his to retrieve the compass. "I'm guessing if we headed northeast to get here, then southwest to get back to Seth's ranger station?"

He nodded. She got her bearings and set off. They were silent until they hit the trench they'd crossed on a log the day before.

"We can follow the canal down about a quarter mile to a bridge and path if you'd rather."

"What?"

"I said —"

"There's a bridge and path?" Her jeans were thorn pricked from cutting through the brush.

He had the good sense to look sheepish. "Sorry about that. Like I said, I was mad yesterday and trying to get you to turn around."

"I'm stubborn."

"Yeah." A slow smile spread across his face, and her anger dissipated too quickly for her comfort.

Once they reached the path, they could walk shoulder to shoulder. "You'll call Darren when we get back?" she asked.

"Today? I don't know. . . ."

"If you don't do it today, you'll put it off and not do it. He needs you, Bennett." She added softly, "Promise me."

"I . . . I promise." The words sounded painful for him to say.

Several minutes passed with only the dry crunch of brush under their feet filling the silence. "You said last night you and the other ladies were considering a coffee business," he said in a pensive way that prepared her for more questions.

"Yep. That's one idea we came up with. Most people love coffee, right? But there's a coffee place on every corner these days. How would we compete?"

"Exactly. What else do people like?"

"Uh, pie?"

"Well, that too. Especially pecan." He

pronounced it "pee-can," which made her smile for reasons she didn't want to delve into. "But, more specific to you, they like to support a good cause."

"I'm not following."

"You have a noble cause. Exploit it."

"How?"

"You'd need a good spin. A catchy name. Acquire the beans, roast, and sell them yourself. You could ship around the country. Maybe even get a deal to supply them to the bases themselves."

Her steps slowed to accommodate the thoughts racing breakneck through her. His suggestion was daunting in scope. Bigger and riskier than she'd envisioned. Yet . . . it was a good idea. Even better, it was something that could be duplicated across bases around the country and world. But, for now, she could start small at Fort Bragg to gage its success.

"I love the idea, but realistically, how much money would it take to start up this sort of business?"

He rattled off a number that made her choke on a gasp of air. That would be a good chunk of the money he'd given her. Money she'd planned to put toward Ben's college fund. Or give back to Bennett out of a sense of honor.

"I'd have to use the money you gave me. It wouldn't be right."

"Bullshit. It's perfect. I'm not taking the money back, so get that out of your head, and this way you can appease any guilt from accepting it."

"I've read the statistics. Small business usually fail."

He took her arm and drew her to a halt, facing him. "What happened to the woman with balls enough to confront me and when that didn't work to plan this escapade?"

"You're confusing balls with confidence. And competence. I've never done anything like this before."

"You graduated top of your class with two degrees."

"Two degrees I never had the chance to use." Her voice rose, but she wasn't sure what she was mad about.

"Dust 'em off and put 'em to work." His eyes narrowed. "Anyway, you wouldn't be doing this alone. You have Allison and the other ladies, don't you? Plus, I can offer advice."

"Considering the seed money would be coming from you, I'd say you're doing enough."

"I'll make sure you avoid the mistakes I made starting up the survival school."

"Why are you suddenly willing to help me?" She couldn't help her suspicions. The day before he was willing to play dirty to get her to leave him alone.

His focus shifted from her to the floor. "Noah would expect me to help."

"Because of that mysterious promise you made? Don't bother. I'm doing fine on my own." She went to step around him, but he shuffled to block her. They repeated the movement in the other direction.

His smile was like the sighting of a rare bird, and it filled her with the same kind of wonder. "I'm not offering my expertise just because of Noah. Starting a new business will be a challenge, and I like challenges."

"It's a huge risk."

Behind the tease in his smile was a risk-taking badass. "Yep. Trust me, we'll have fun. What's the worst that can happen?"

"Total humiliation. Poverty. Failure."

He made a throaty noise between laughter and frustration. "This is money you were going to throw on my porch in a duffel bag. In fact, unless you use the money I gave you to start a business, I want it back."

"You what?"

"Use it or lose it, sweetheart." His tease took on a wolfish quality. He had her cornered. And, like any cornered animal, she would fight her way out.

"Fine. I'll use your money and start up the best new business Fort Bragg has ever seen."

"Yeah, you will."

Her frustration and nerves eased. The amorphous vision of what she and the other women could accomplish was becoming solid. Could they pull it off?

He stamped his feet. "Only a few miles until Seth's cabin. Let's go."

They walked and shared favorite movies and books. The small talk seemed inconsequential, but taken as a totality, it deepened her understanding of him. Jack bounded through the woods and a few minutes later the park ranger's station came into view through the trees. Disappointment zinged through her. Not how she expected to feel at the end of their time together.

She only had moments of solitude left with him.

"Bennett?" She laid a hand on his arm, and he glanced over, his steps slowing but not stopping. "I want to know . . ." The cold and her nerves stalled the question. She'd lied and manipulated and engineered the weekend to ask about Noah.

Yet she couldn't force the words out. Not right now at any rate. She hadn't considered the emotional toil the retelling would take on him; she'd thought only of herself. But the guilt and regrets he bore from that time were obvious.

"You want to know what?" As if he suspected the bend of her thoughts to the past, his brows drew in and his mouth tightened, emphasizing his intimidating good looks.

"I want to know what you find out about Darren."

"Yeah, okay, sure." He looked as if he wanted to say more, but she picked up the pace and led them to relative civilization.

The warmth of the ranger station made her want to dance, and the sight of the toilet made her want to cry.

Seth offered them coffee, and she gratefully accepted. Wrapping both hands around the mug, she closed her eyes and inhaled the distinct aroma. The smell reminded her of her mother and her childhood and comfort. It reminded her of home.

Home Front. "Home Front Coffee."

Bennett stopped whatever he was saying to Seth. "What's that?"

"Sorry. Didn't mean to interrupt, but what about Home Front Coffee? People would know based on the name it's related to the military. What do the men and women deployed long for more than anything?

Everyone longs for home in a way, don't they? It's why *The Wizard of Oz* still resonates."

Bennett tilted his head. She tensed. His judgment shouldn't matter, but it did. A smile slashed through his beard. "That's damn good."

She relaxed back against the counter and took a sip of coffee. Without taking his eyes off her, he said, "We'll get out of your hair, Seth. Thanks again for letting me use your place as a jumping-off point."

"Anytime, man." Seth's gaze ping-ponged between her and Bennett, a question in his smile.

She grabbed her stuff, located her car keys, and followed Bennett outside. How could it have only been yesterday when she'd arrived? It felt like weeks had passed.

She threw her backpack in the trunk of her car and lingered. He came around the side of his truck and held out a business card with a number handwritten across the top.

"That's my cell. Shoot me a text so I'll have your number. Soon as I talk to Darren, I'll let you know," he said.

She slipped the card into her back pocket. Jack snuffled into her hand, and she squatted down to give him a hug and nuzzle the top of his head. "Ugh. Someone needs a bath. I hope I'm not smelling myself." She laughed up at Bennett. He didn't return her smile. In fact, his expression was more solemn than usual.

She stood and ran her hands down the legs of her jeans. "This was . . . interesting."

"That's one way to put it." His dry sarcasm took any sting out of the comment.

"Thanks for not letting me freeze to death."

"It would have been bad for business."

The moment veered toward awkward. She was ready to see Ben, take a hot shower, and eat a home-cooked meal, yet getting her feet to move to her driver's seat was like dragging anchors. Should she offer a hand for a shake or lean in for a hug? In the end, she did neither, taking a step backward. "Okay, well. Bye."

He didn't stop her. She pulled out of the drive and onto the park road, her attention on her rearview mirror. He stood at the tailgate of his truck, watching her drive away. She stared until he disappeared behind the trees, a sense of melancholy blanketing her. Why?

Yes, he was connected to an important part of her past. But there was more. He was interesting and complicated and . . . attractive. Flames of embarrassment and guilt prickled her chest and neck.

All her mother's talk about flings and things hanging down to knees must have cracked open a door in her subconscious. That's all this was. A Freudian complex.

Driving the familiar roads back to Nags Head, she wondered what Bennett was doing. Was Jack his only company? Did he sit in silence or did he need music or the TV on to drown out the thoughts that plagued him?

She pulled in to the driveway, but before she went inside to the chaos of Ben and her mom, she pulled out her phone and his card.

Made it home. Hope I wasn't too much a bother. Thanks again.

She tapped her fingers against the steering wheel and waited.

JL and I are home, too. Not a bother. At all. Talk soon.

She clutched the phone to her chest, the nerves and excitement not brand new, but like a bear coming out of torpor, she felt clumsy and out of practice.

CHAPTER 12

Past

Harper smoothed her hair and tugged at her sweater. The bustle of travelers coming off the escalator in the airport broke around her like she was the rock in their stream. It had been six months since she'd seen Noah. He was a phase away from completing SEAL training in California, and she was on winter break, her first semester at UNC in the books.

The last time she'd seen Noah had been at the end of five magical days and nights before he'd left for BUD/S. They'd said their good-byes standing on the end of the pier, the summer air superheating her out-of-control emotions. That's how he'd wanted it even though she'd offered to see him off at the airport.

She'd girded herself to never hear from him again and brushed away tears on her walk back home, but only an hour of moping had passed before an email from him popped into her in-box. The thrill was like nothing she'd ever experienced. Not love, but something beyond infatuation.

Now six months later, her hair was longer and she no longer sported her summer tan. She was in jeans and a sweater instead of shorts and tank tops. Between her part-time job in the campus library and studying, she basically lived in the reference section. It had paid off. She'd made the dean's list with all As and had saved enough to put off needing a loan.

Basically, she worried she wasn't the same girl Noah remembered from the summer. But that's not all. What if she had idealized Noah? What if he wasn't as cute and funny and nice as she remembered? Because of their insane schedules, they'd only communicated through emails and letters since the summer.

The flow of people trickled to a handful. Had he seen her and hidden? Was he waiting for her to give up and leave so he wouldn't have to face her? Her stomach felt worse than it had before her statistics final.

She checked the clock and stared at the top of the escalator. If he didn't show up in five more minutes, she would leave. A man appeared. Broad shouldered and blond headed and even more handsome than she remembered.

Her breath hitched and her knees wobbled her a step closer. He didn't wait for the escalator to carry him down but took the steps two at a time. A military-issue ruck-sack hung over one shoulder, but he was in civilian clothes — jeans and a long-sleeve T-shirt in dark blue.

She didn't move to meet him. More accurately, she couldn't move, because he had changed too. Although his hair was the same blond and his eyes blue, he'd turned from a lanky Georgia farm boy into a man. His face was leaner, but his body had filled in with what appeared to be all muscle.

Now not only was she fighting nerves but shyness too. Not something that had affected her while she'd been writing him endless emails and letters over the fall.

He stopped in front of her and dropped his bag but didn't touch her. "I've missed you, Harper Lee." His voice, too, had matured, reflecting a vastness of experiences.

He'd sketched out hardship and challenges to her through his words in the vaguest terms. Faced with him, she understood he had come through a crucible and emerged forever changed.

"You're different." She wanted to stuff the words back in her mouth.

"Yeah." He fingered the ends of her hair and a shock buzzed through her as if her hair contained millions of nerve endings. "Your hair is longer."

"Didn't have time to get it cut."

"I like it. Did they post your grades?"

"All As."

"Babe. That's amazing. Not that I had any doubt you'd kill it." It was his smile that burned away all her nerves and shyness. One corner of his mouth hitched a little higher than the other and his blue eyes crinkled with the force of his happiness. This was the Noah who'd populated her dreams and fantasies.

She took a step into his chest, wrapped her arms around him, and laid her cheek against his neck. A deep breath reassured her further. His scent fired memories of lying on the beach in his arms and making out until the sun edged over the horizon signaling the dawn.

His arms came around her as he nosed the hair at her temple, kissing her where her heartbeat pulsed.

"I missed you, too, Noah."

"For a second there coming down the escalator, I thought you were going to bolt like a wild turkey at Thanksgiving."

"For a second, I thought I was, too."

He pulled back and met her eyes, his smile diminished by worry. "Why?"

"Because you're not the same Noah who left this summer."

He flexed his arm. The fabric stretched and outlined his impressive biceps. "BUD/S has whipped my sorry butt in shape."

"I mean, yes. You look . . . God, you look amazing." Verbalizing her thoughts was difficult when her hormones were making a case for dragging him somewhere private to let her hands do the talking. "But it goes beyond your abs. You seem older."

Thankfully, he didn't make a joke. "I feel older. Or more mature, I guess. The training is more than physical. It's testing and building our mental strength, if that makes sense."

"Will you tell me about it?"

"Later, I will." He reached for her hand and linked their fingers. "Right now, though, I'm dying for some sweet tea and fried chicken."

"Mom is making all that and more."

"Your mom is a saint."

"She's shooting more for sinner than saint now that her retirement is in sight. I caught her setting up an online dating profile last week."

His laugh was cut short when they stepped outside. While an endless blue sky stretched itself around the bright sun, the breeze held a bite of winter. "Damn, it's cold."

Harper poked him playfully in his solid stomach. "One part of you has gone soft. Has your blood gotten thin from living out there in California?"

"When the instructors aren't torturing us, it's as close to paradise as I've ever seen."

She led him to her used Honda. It had been a present from her mom. The only caveat of accepting it had been a promise to make the drive back to Nags Head when she could. While she had grudgingly agreed, once at college Harper hadn't found coming home a hardship. Homesickness had hit her hard once the realities of college had set in.

She popped the trunk for Noah to store his rucksack and then they were off for the drive from Norfolk to Nags Head. The conversation ebbed and flowed with the comforting rhythm of the ocean.

Harper stole glances at him throughout the drive, not quite believing he was there in the flesh and blood. Her stream-of-consciousness emails had sometimes seemed like diary entries. His replies were never as detailed or revealing.

God, she'd told him about walking into the bathroom and interrupting her roommate and her boyfriend mid-coitus. And the time she'd woken up late for class and run across campus still in her penguin pajama pants. A sudden burst of embarrassment had her patting her forehead and turning the air down in the car.

She cleared her throat and clutched the steering wheel so tight her palms squeaked against the plastic. "By the way, I'm not as crazy as my emails might have implied."

"Crazy? You kept me sane."

"I did?"

"Knowing I might have one of your stories waiting on me kept me from giving up more than once."

"They weren't actually made up. All that stuff happened."

He slipped his hand onto her leg, and her foot jerked, sending the Honda ten miles over the speed limit to match her heart rate. "I know, but it was the way you told it that was so entertaining. Everyone thought so."

Her foot eased off the accelerator. She wasn't thrilled at the prospect of other men reading what she'd thought was for Noah's eyes only. "What do you mean 'everyone'?"

"Just the guys in my room. One in particular doesn't have anyone."

"No girlfriend, you mean?"

"No girlfriend, no family. No one." Uncertainty replaced his newfound confidence. "You're not mad, are you?"

"I don't appreciate being made fun of. Did you read them *everything*?" While she wasn't explicit in her emails, she had expressed her feelings in a way she didn't feel comfortable doing face-to-face yet.

"Of course not. Just the funny stuff. And no one was making fun. In fact, one of the guys, Hollis, wanted me to give you his number in case you got tired of me." His laugh contained an apologetic twist. "I'll stop. I'm sorry. I just wanted them to know how awesome you are."

How could she stay upset when he said stuff like that? "That's okay. I didn't realize how hard up you guys were out there."

"Hard up? Women crawl all over us as soon as we step off base. It's the uniform."

Harper pumped the brakes hard enough to lock their seat belts. "Are they all over you?"

Noah seemed to recognize his major misstep. Red burnished his face as if the cold wind had come inside. "I don't want any of those women. Why would I when I have someone like you? More than anything, I want to make you proud, Harper. Do you believe me?"

Her head talked her heart from off the ledge. He wouldn't have brought it up if he'd been messing around with base bunnies. Trust was easy to come by with him next to her, his hand still on her leg, his blue eyes aimed in her direction, and his smile veering toward adorable. "Of course I do. Now, what do you want to do while you're home besides eat fried chicken?"

They made general plans, but it didn't really matter what they did as long as they were together. They only had four days. Noah had to be back for his final phase of BUD/S right after New Year's.

She parked along the street in front of her house. Her mom had been accommodating but hardly enthusiastic to find out Noah would be staying with them for a few days over break. A warm reception was not guaranteed. All Harper could do was cross her fingers and hope how important Noah was to her had sunk in.

Noah had met her mom over the summer, but Harper and Noah had only wanted to be around each other. Her mom's protective lectures and opinions had been ignored.

"I'm nervous." Noah ran his hands down

the front of his jeans.

"She doesn't bite. Usually." Harper tossed a grin over her shoulder as she jogged up the steps. The front door swung open before she even made it to the top.

"Hello, darling. Noah. It's wonderful to see you again." While her mom's voice wouldn't classify as excited, it was welcoming.

Harper breathed a sigh of relief. Her mom held out her hand for Noah to shake.

"Nice to see you again, Ms. Frazier. I really appreciate you putting me up. In fact, before I forget . . ." He swung his rucksack off his shoulder and dug his hand inside, pulling out a rectangular object in a brown bag. "This is for you."

"You shouldn't have." Her mom took the present and pulled out a book with a gasp. She opened the cover of a hardback version of *To Kill a Mockingbird.* "It's a first edition. And in excellent condition. I love it. Thank you. And call me Gail."

Her mom shepherded him into the house and sent Harper a virtual fist bump with a look over her shoulder. Harper couldn't stem her grin, not shocked Noah had won her mom over, but surprised at how quickly it had happened. Although Noah had won her over in a single afternoon.

The smells of fried chicken drew them into the kitchen. The table was set and the food was ready for an early dinner. After Noah's fourth piece of chicken, Harper laughed and her mom joked about making another run to the grocery store.

Noah wiped his sheepish grin with his napkin. "I relish good food whenever I can get it."

"They're obviously not starving you," Harper said.

"No, but it's like being back in school. Cafeteria-style. Quantity over quality."

The longer they lingered over the meal, the more impatient Harper grew to get Noah alone. As soon as the dishes were cleared, Harper backed out of the kitchen and grabbed Noah's hand on the way.

"I'll help you clean up in a bit, Mom. I want to take Noah down to the dock to watch the sunset."

"I'll take care of it. You two run along."

Harper hoped Noah had missed her mom's not-so-subtle wink.

Once she and Noah were out of sight of the house, she notched herself into his side. He wrapped his arm around her shoulders and matched her pace. They headed not to the beach but to the waterway to the west. The quiet serenity appealed to her more than the touristy beach side.

"Where did you find the book?" she asked.

"A used bookshop in San Diego. I always look for *To Kill a Mockingbird* because I like to see your name."

Her insides turned warm and melty. "That's really sweet. And, in my mom's eyes, you are officially the favorite of all my boyfriends. Although it's not like the competition was steep. Not being a public nose picker put you in the lead."

He laughed as was her intent, but then his voice turned serious. "Good, because I plan to hang around for a good long time."

They reached the old wooden dock and sat at the end. She took his hand in both of hers. New calluses and tendons had to be mapped into her memory. "I was afraid you'd decide it was all a mistake."

"Mistake? What are you talking about?"

"Me. You. Mistake. We only had a week together. Am I how you remember me?"

He wrapped the hand she didn't have a death clutch on around her nape and brought their foreheads together. "You're better. Prettier. Funnier. Sweeter. Don't you know?"

She didn't, but she wanted to believe him. Words beyond her, she shook her head.

"The boys on base say I'm whipped, and

all I can do is grin and agree. I don't care that we're young and on opposite sides of the country. All I know is that I'm falling for you."

She'd needed him to say it first, but once he had, she surrendered to her own feelings. "Me too."

She tilted her face to brush her lips against his. It might be cold out, but his arms were warm around her as the kiss deepened and took on a meaning far beyond simple pleasure. It felt like a promise. A promise she intended to keep forever.

CHAPTER 13

Present Day

Harper stared out the front window, squinting to try to extend her gaze.

"This man has sure got you stirred up."

Harper startled. Her mom stood not two feet behind her, holding two martini glasses. Harper hadn't even heard her walk up. She accepted the one with double olives and took a too-big gulp. Warmth spread fast and furious.

"I'm not stirred up because of Bennett Caldwell." Harper faced the window before her mother caught sight of the half-lie. "This business will be a big undertaking. The work, the risk — it will change our lives, Mom, and I'm not sure for the better."

Her mom planted her butt on the window sash and stirred the olive around the bottom of her glass. "This is the first time I've seen you this nervous and excited about anything since Noah died. Whatever sacrifices we need to make, we will."

"What about Ben?"

"Better for him to see you working hard and passionate about your job than mopey and sad."

"I'm not mopey."

"Not anymore. Not since you had an idea for a business." Her mom's voice dropped to suggestive levels. "And not since Bennett Caldwell strolled into the picture."

Deciding to ignore her mom's teasing, Harper leaned against the sash, hip to hip with her. "I hate to burden you with more babysitting time. It might cut into your painting." She nudged her mother with her shoulder.

"My foray into nude portraiture can wait." Taking a more serious tone, she said, "I love spending time with Ben. You know that. And I love seeing my daughter reaching for a dream."

"I might fail. Spectacularly."

He mother shrugged and popped an olive in her mouth. "People fail all the time. Doesn't mean it wasn't worth trying."

To cover her watery eyes, Harper killed the rest of her martini. If she couldn't locate the real thing, she'd take courage of the liquid variety.

A knock on the front door made her jump up and slide her empty glass on the coffee table. Before she made it to the hallway, Ben's voice echoed in the two-story foyer. "Wow! That's the biggest dog I've ever seen. Will he eat me?"

Bennett's rusty-sounding laugh echoed, and she stopped in the doorway of the den to surreptitiously watch her son and his namesake. "He won't eat you. His name is Jack London, and he's a perfect gentleman."

"He named his dog Jack London? I like him already," her mom whispered in Harper's ear.

Stepping forward before her mom could embarrass her, Harper put her hand on Ben's shoulder and squeezed gently. "Ben, this is Mr. Caldwell. He and your daddy served together."

"You knew my daddy?" Ben's face tipped up with an awestruck grin.

Bennett was leaning toward Jack, his hand clasped in the dog's fur, as if he sought support. "I sure did. He was my best friend." Emotions too complicated for Ben to pick up on roughed Bennett's voice. But Harper understood. No doubt, Bennett could see the best pieces of Noah in her son.

Bennett's gaze rose slowly to meet hers. "You sure you don't mind if Jack comes in?"

"I told you earlier, I don't mind a bit. I have a feeling Ben is going to love Jack and we'll be fending off requests for a dog this Christmas."

"Will he follow me?" Ben asked.

"Sure. Just ask him." With visible effort, Bennett let go of his dog.

Ben backed into the hall and patted his legs. "Come on, boy. Do you want to see my house?"

Bennett ruffled the dog's ear and said softly, "Go on, Jack. It's all right."

The dog trotted after Ben, who laughed and skipped into the den. Her mom hovered in the doorway but retreated after giving Harper a pointed look.

"Hi." Their texting over the last two weeks didn't make their face-to-face meeting any less awkward. The opposite in fact. Most of their communication had been about ideas for the coffee shop and Darren's condition, but occasionally they'd veered toward more personal topics.

Like Bennett's funny story about the man who wandered into his shop with a waist-long beard and overalls looking for supplies to live off the grid. Or her telling him about Whit, the insurance salesman who called her once a week asking her for a date — to discuss her policies.

She asked him what he cooked himself for dinner, and he confessed to ordering Chinese takeout and pizzas too often. He'd texted her one night at almost eleven to see what she was doing. The answer had been reading a thriller sure to keep her up until she finished.

"I see Noah in Ben, but mostly you."

"He's got Noah's smile and good nature."

"You're not good natured?"

"No, I'm stubborn as all get-out, remember?"

A slow smile spread over his face and an answering warmth that had nothing to do with the martini spread through her body until she was tingly.

"Something smells amazing." He lifted his nose and sniffed like a hunting dog.

"My mom's famous lasagna. Come on in and meet her."

"That's something a woman's never said to me."

She stopped short. "You've never been serious enough with a woman to meet her family?"

"I guess I haven't." He gave a one-shouldered shrug.

Nonplussed, she didn't know what to say, so she bypassed the landmine. "Come on then. You can meet the real Gail Frazier, retired librarian, nude painter, and martini maker extraordinaire."

She took his hand and tugged him toward the den. Her mom was on all fours on the floor with Ben and Jack London. Turning and sitting cross-legged, she eyed Harper and Bennett with a sharpness that made her drop Bennett's hand like a hot potato. Needing some space for her own sanity as well as to squash the weird vibes her mom was putting out, Harper went to give Jack a rub on the head.

Her mom rose like a woman who did yoga three times a week and offered a hand to Bennett. "I'm Gail. And let me apologize for the deception a couple of weeks ago. I tried to talk Harper out of any trickery, but by now, you know what she's like."

"Mom, I'm standing right here." Harper's interjection didn't faze either one of them.

"She's something else, that's for sure," Bennett said.

Her mom patted the back of Bennett's hand with her free one. "Everything seems to have worked out fine."

"Nice to meet you, Ms. Frazier."

"Gail, please. Or I won't offer you a drink. What's your poison? I make a mean martini, but I have a few beers rattling around the fridge if that's more your speed."

"A beer would be great, Ms. —" At her mom's tsking, he said on a slight laugh, "Gail."

"Another martini, dear?" Her mom raised her brows toward Harper.

"Yes, please."

"Can I have a Coke, Yaya?" Ben piped up from the floor.

"No, but you can have some lemonade. Can you help me, Harper?"

Help? Ha. Her mom sashayed off before Harper could come up with an excuse.

"I'll be right back. Make yourself at home." She barely kept herself from flouncing off like a teenager getting ready to receive a lecture.

With the efficiency of a bartender, her mom poured beer and lemonade into two frosty mugs, then added the martini ingredients to the drink shaker. "You didn't tell me Mr. Caldwell is a certified hotty-pants."

"Do they give certifications out for that? Is there an international governing body?"

The sound of crashing ice as her mom shook the martinis put a pause on their conversation.

As she poured, her mom said, "I'm not an innocent or an idiot. Something is going on between the two of you."

"He's helping me formulate a solid business plan."

"And that's all?"

"Pretty much." Harper folded and un-folded the hem of her shirt.

Her mom put a hand on top to stop her fiddling, and Harper looked up. Her mom wore a sad little smile. "It's okay if you like him. And I mean, *like* like him."

"I don't — Okay, even if I am sort of, kind of attracted to him, nothing can happen between us."

"Why not?"

"He was Noah's best friend. He was there when Noah was killed."

"So, it's complicated. Are you worried that your subconscious is substituting Bennett for Noah?"

She ran her hand through her hair, fisting the back. The two men were so different the thought hadn't even been lurking in the shadows of her subconscious. "Well, I *wasn't,* but now I am. Do you think I'm substituting?"

Her mother's gesture was noncommittal. "He's a very serious sort of man, isn't he?"

"I suppose. He's been through tough times." Was her mom taking a dig at him? "But he can be funny, too. It's just a dry sort of humor."

"It wasn't a criticism, dear." Her mom

246

peered over her glasses at Harper. "You can be rather serious yourself."

Ben's laughter peeled through the layers of confusion and uncertainty. Harper was on the cusp of huge changes, both terrifying and exciting. Part of her wanted to stay locked away in her safe gray house. It was comfortable. But was that fair to Ben? And to herself?

She picked up her martini and the beer and made her way back to the den. She stutter-stepped to a stop in the doorway. Bennett had a deck of cards and was performing a trick. Ben stood between his long legs, his hands on Bennett's knees, their heads close.

Bennett fanned the cards out in his hand with a graceful dexterity that surprised her. The sight of them together hammered her heart. Underneath the pleasure of seeing the easy camaraderie between them was a morass of sadness. It should have been Noah mesmerizing Ben with card tricks.

"Is this the one?" Bennett pulled a card out of the middle and held it up for Ben to see.

"Yes!" More belly laughs from Ben followed. He ran over and grabbed the edge of her shirt to tug her over to Bennett. "He's magic, Mama. Do her, Mr. Caldwell, do her."

Naughty amusement twinkled in Bennet's eyes, and she had to muffle laughter at Ben's enthusiastic plea. The shared moment lowered her nerves from a boil to a simmer. She set the beer and martini down on the coffee table and fell to her knees next to Ben to put an arm around him. Bennett shuffled the cards like he was a professional Vegas dealer.

He fanned them out. "Pick one."

Ben inched forward, pulling her with him until she was kneeling between Bennett's long legs. She pulled a card out of his hands and hoped he didn't notice the tremble of her fingers. The queen of hearts. Was the universe trying to give her a nudge?

"Memorize it and slip it back in."

She returned it to a different spot. Ben's attention wandered to Jack and he lay down next to the dog to rub his belly.

Bennett shuffled, his hands blunt instruments of beauty, and he shifted his knees closer as if caging her in. Her body buzzed with a different kind of high than alcohol.

"Is this your card?" He held up the queen of hearts. The intensity of his expression didn't match what should have been a lighthearted card trick.

She nodded, took the card from him, and held it in both hands to keep herself from touching him. What if she inched forward and pulled him down to her? Confusion held her in place. Noah had been the first and only man she'd seriously dated, and despite having been married with a child, she felt her inexperience keenly.

Ben popped up next to her and plucked the card out of her hand. "Did he pick your card, Mama?"

The moment shattered and she rocked back on her heels, shoving the card toward Bennett. "He did. He is magic."

She moved to sit on the opposite end of the couch from Bennett with her drink. Her mom had come in at some point and lounged in the armchair, sipping her martini. How much had she seen?

Not that there was anything to see. It was her imagination that was out of control. Thank goodness, her mom didn't have access to that. Except her "cat that ate the canary" smile insinuated she could make a pretty good guess as to its direction.

Ben bounced onto the couch, choosing to sit close to Bennett. Ben chattered about his preschool and friends, all the while touching Bennett on the arm or leg. Was Ben starved for a male role model and attention? Did he miss Noah in an abstract but no less potent way than she did?

And what happened if Ben became too attached to Bennett? Danger clutched her stomach. Protecting Ben from hurt was her job, and she fought the urge to snatch Ben to her side.

"Harper tells me you two are working up a business plan for this coffee business." Her mom's calm voice was a welcome balm.

"That's right. It's a viable start-up with a built-in customer base. In a military town, people support their own. So, at the least, the shop should get lots of military traffic." Bennett stroked his beard. "If we can find a good location."

Nerves fizzed through her body. She was worried about finding an available space for a reasonable rent. But that's not why she was nervous. She and Bennett would be alone for a good part of the weekend. The two of them had been in the middle of the woods for two days, but this was different even if she couldn't pinpoint how.

"You're going to stay with Allison?"

"That's the plan." Harper exchanged a glance with Bennett. Allison had invited them to spend the night, and Harper prayed they would find Darren improved. She wasn't optimistic.

"Dinner will be ready as soon as I toast the bread. I hope you're hungry, Bennett." Her mom rose and retreated to the kitchen.

"I'm starving," Ben said, and scampered after her. Jack followed close on his heels.

Harper waited until she was sure Ben wasn't coming back. "Ben seems taken with you."

"I've never been comfortable around kids. Guess because I never really felt like one. But Ben makes it easy." He leaned forward and braced his arms on his legs, his hands dangling.

She grabbed at words to try to put her fears into coherence. "I don't have a brother, my dad's not around, and I've never brought a boyfriend over. Not that you're my boyfriend or anything." She cleared her throat to put the brakes on her tongue. "He's never been around anyone like you."

He swiveled his head toward her. "Like me?"

"You know, honorable. Strong. It's good — healthy even — for him to have someone like you to look up to. But I want to protect him from every little hurt in the world, even though I know it's impossible."

"You're worried I'll hurt him?"

"Not on purpose. I'm worried he might

251

get too attached to you, is all."

"It's one night. He won't have a chance to get attached."

His words sent a shot of cold reality through her body. "Of course not, what was I thinking? This is . . ." She waved a hand between them not even sure what to say. They weren't dating. They weren't involved. Were they even friends? "It's business, right?"

She popped up, but before she could take a step toward escape he grabbed her wrist and pulled her back down to the couch. He'd scooched closer and she landed next to him, their legs pressed together.

"Is that all it is?" His breath tickled her ear.

"I don't know. You tell me." Part of her wanted to stalk off in a huff, but an even bigger part wanted to lean into him and close her eyes. She compromised by twisting her hand out of his but staying flush against him.

"By the way, I'm an idiot sometimes. Especially when it comes to women like you."

"Like me?" She parroted his question.

"Complex."

She gave in and relaxed into his chest.

"Beautiful too." His voice dropped to a

whisper and he covered her hand with his own, their fingers sliding over and through one another like a dance.

"Dinner's ready." Ben popped back into the room.

Harper snatched her hand away and straightened, but Ben didn't seem fazed. "Come on." He grabbed Bennett's arm and pulled.

They filed into the kitchen and found her usual place usurped by Ben so he could sit next to Bennett. Her mom kept the conversation easy and superficial, and Bennett earned her favor by asking for seconds.

"I was never a good cook. The boys used to say I could burn an MRE, even though it was impossible." Another forkful disappeared.

"Will you tell me a story about my daddy?" Ben asked.

Tension ballooned over the table like a mushroom cloud. Harper's fork clanged against her plate, loud and discordant. Only Ben was unaffected. Wide-eyed and smiling, he stared at Bennett expectantly.

Bennett cast a look toward Harper, and she wasn't sure whether to give him a red or green light.

"Uh, sure. I guess," he finally said. "Let's see . . . you know your dad grew up on a farm in Georgia."

Ben nodded. "I go two weeks every summer to stay with my grandpa and grandma. I've driven a tractor."

"One of our instructors gave your daddy the nickname Peaches."

"Why?"

Bennett pursed his lips before smiling and saying, "Because he was so sweet. Problem was he hated being called Peaches and one day he got fed up with one of the guys named Hollis in our room who wouldn't lay off."

"What'd he do?" Ben was rapt.

"Growing up on a farm, you get used to lots of animals, right? Even snakes."

Ben gasped.

Bennett's voice took on the cadence of a master storyteller, his drawl more pronounced than usual. "Your daddy went out and caught a black rat snake. It was a baby. Not more than two feet long and no bigger round than my thumb. But this guy Hollis was a city boy. Well now, your daddy slipped that snake under Hollis's pillow where it coiled up, cozy as you please. That night when we bedded down for the night, everything was quiet for about five minutes."

Drama built in the pause. Ben shifted on his chair. "Then what happened?"

"Hollis jumped up and screamed like he was born to sing soprano in the church choir. Half the men came running, including the instructor in charge. Everyone knew your daddy had done it and I thought for sure he was going to get busted, but he put on such an innocent face that the instructor overlooked the obvious."

"He didn't get into trouble?" Ben asked.

"Nope. And not only that, but Hollis never teased him again."

"Wow."

Harper sat back with a smile on her face. Noah had never told her that. How much had they kept from each other over the years they'd been together?

"Time for your bath, munchkin." She ruffled Ben's hair.

"Can I come down when I'm done? Please? I don't have school tomorrow."

"For a few minutes. I'll bet Yaya has ice cream," Harper said.

"I always have ice cream." Her mom rose to clear the table. When Harper stacked her plate on Ben's and rose, too, her mom shooed her away. "Nope. I'll clean up. It'll take a jiffy to load the dishwasher. Why don't you walk Bennett down to the dock? It's a full moon tonight. Should be pretty out." She nudged her chin toward the back door.

Once the sliding glass door was closed and her mom couldn't hear, Harper made a small sound that was supposed to be a laugh. "We don't have to go, if you don't want to."

"A walk would be good. If you want." He pulled on a Caldwell Survival School fleece zip-up, sounding as stiff and uncomfortable as she felt.

"Follow me and watch your step." She led the way down the flight of stairs to the fenced-in backyard. The night was still and silent. A wooden swing hung from the limb of a water oak and drifted as if pushed by invisible hands.

A gate at the back let out at a narrow cross street. They walked down the middle. Many of the houses would be deserted until summer.

"Noah never told me the story about the snake," she said.

"I got to laughing so hard when it happened, the instructor thought I had done it at first."

"Could Noah have gotten kicked out?"

"Nah. He would have had to run extra. Or maybe the instructors would have respected him even more." He kicked a loose piece of gravel down the road, his hands shoved into his pockets. "It's good you let Ben have time with Noah's folks."

"Ben loves going down there. Noah's sisters are all married with kids now and live close, so Ben has lots of cousins. Unlike here, where it's just me and my mom."

"He seems like a happy, well-adjusted kid. I'm sure Noah's folks are proud of the job you're doing raising him. They're good people."

Tears burned her eyes at his compliment. "You've met his parents?"

"I went to Georgia with Noah once. Helped him clear some trees for his dad."

Harper shook her head. "I remember now. I was supposed to go, but it was early in my pregnancy and I wasn't feeling well. Isn't it strange our paths never crossed until . . . after."

"Not so strange." The cryptic bent of his tone registered, but she couldn't decipher it.

The moon provided enough light to avoid potholes. Although it was a mild night, Harper shivered as they drew closer to the dock, the wind picking up a chill from the water.

"Here, take this." Bennett slipped his fleece jacket off and put it around her shoulders. It was warm from his body heat.

A manly combination of smells surrounded her. She put her arms into the too-long sleeves and buried her nose in the collar.

"But you'll get cold." Her protest was weak, and if he tried to take it back he would have to pry it out of her hands.

"I'll be fine." The dock came into view. "This is the waterway?"

"Currituck Sound, actually."

The wooden dock had weathered years of winters and storms and hurricanes. The wood was cracked and buckled and in need of a stain, but it had stood the test of time.

She led them to the end and sat on the edge. Her feet dangled over the water. He joined her. The moon was rising behind them and cast ripples of light out onto the water.

"You used to come out here a lot, didn't you?"

While the fact that Noah had shared intimate details of her inner life with Bennett was strange and backward, the more she was around him, the more she didn't mind him knowing.

"It was my refuge as a kid, but I'm still drawn down here. I find the sound calms me in a way the ocean can't."

"Do you like to fish?" he asked.

"I don't mind it as long as I can take a

book along with me. Sitting and staring at a bobber all day long is worse than watching paint dry. I'll bet fishing is your favorite thing, isn't it? You seem the type." She pulled a leg up and rested her chin on her knee.

"Yeah, I like to fish. You're not doing it right if you're staring at your bobber. And lastly, what type am I?" Amusement lightened his voice.

"The patient, quiet type. I'll bet you win quiet mouse, still mouse every time."

"It's been a while since I played, so I can't say." His rumble of laughter echoed off the water and faded into silence.

"Tomorrow's going to be a big step," she whispered. "It's been all talk up to now."

"Are you nervous?"

"Try 'terrified.' "

He put his arm around her shoulders, and her lean into him was instinctive, her head notching naturally under his chin. "You don't seem scared of anyone or anything."

"Then I'm hiding it better than I think I am. Before I walked into your store the first time, I almost talked myself into turning around before I even got out of the car."

"I'm glad you didn't." His admission was so soft she almost missed it.

"Me too," she whispered back, squeezing

her eyes shut.

She wasn't sure which one of them moved first — perhaps they moved in synchronicity — but her lips were on his cheek, and his hand cupped her nape. The coarse hair of his beard was tactile and arousing. Searching, searching, she was searching. Her lips finally collided with his.

A sigh escaped. It had been a long time since she'd kissed a man. A long time since she'd even had the urge to kiss a man. Turns out it was like riding a bike.

She trailed her hands up to rest at his flanks, shifting her hips closer and tipping into him. The muscles of his torso shifted, and she explored the ridges. Everything except for the two of them fuzzed out of existence. She was only aware of his body and his hand on her lower back, slipping under the edge of his jacket and her shirt to singe her skin. Sensations rippled through her.

Their lips continued their advance and retreat, neither assuming control. It was an exploration. Time ceased to have meaning. He speared his hand into her hair and held her, deepening the kiss. As if she would run.

She ran her hands up his back to loop around his neck. The position levered them down to the buckled, rough planks of the dock, side by side. She craved his weight pressing her down, no matter how uncomfortable, and tugged his hips.

He pulled his mouth away to whisper her name. "Harper?"

The questioning lilt broke the spell. She pushed him away and lurched to her feet, surprised to find the moon still on the rise. A seismic shift not reflected in the turn of the Earth had thrown her little world off its axis.

She touched her lips, sensitive and slightly swollen, and backed away from him. He rose more slowly, eyeing her like she was a wild animal he was trying not to spook. Actually, that wasn't far off the mark. She did feel a little like running away and hiding under her covers.

But she was an adult and could at least try to act like one. "I need to get back to tuck Ben in."

"Sure." He stuffed his hands into his pockets and didn't try to touch her as they walked the length of the dock.

Her mind raced for something innocuous to say. The one thought that hovered above all others was of Noah. Guilt assailed her, and she attempted to tease out the root cause. It's not that she believed she had betrayed him. He wouldn't want her pining for him the rest of her days.

In fact, Noah hadn't even been on the fringes of her thoughts during the kiss. Wrapped up in Bennett, it was like Noah hadn't existed. However briefly, she had forgotten him. Her knees threatened to give out on her, and she tripped on a root at the edge of the road.

Bennett caught her arm, but she shook him off and picked up the pace. "I'm fine."

She was being unforgivably rude, but all she could think of was Ben. Her one solid link to Noah was waiting for her, and she wouldn't let him down. She entered the back door with a clatter, and her mother popped around the corner with a worried expression.

"Could you get Bennett settled in the guest room while I tuck Ben in, Mom?"

Harper brushed by her mom and took the stairs to Ben's room two at a time. She stopped outside his bedroom and regulated her breathing before pushing the door open. Ben sat up in bed and played pretend with his dinosaurs.

Before she could stop herself, she sat on the edge of the twin bed and pulled him in for a hug and kiss. He squirmed away and wiped her kiss away, giggling.

"Are you ready for a book?" she asked.

"I was hoping Big Ben could come tell me another story about Daddy."

Her heart floundered. "His name is Bennett."

"Yeah, but he's big and his name is almost like mine. Can he?"

"Not tonight." She grabbed whatever book was on his nightstand and leaned back into his pillow. She read the story but didn't comprehend the words, her mind on the man down the hall. Ben had turned on his side, his knees jabbing into her legs, his eyes closed.

She turned off the light and curled around him as if she could protect him. Except she was the one who needed protection and grounding. Knowing she was hiding like a coward, she drifted on the edge of sleep, her thoughts spiraling around Bennett and their kiss.

Was she afraid of being hurt? She let the logical explanation settle over her, but it didn't exactly fit. It was more complicated. The truth hit her like a hurricane. She was afraid of being happy.

As she held their son, Noah loomed large in her memories. She had been happy with Noah. Did moving on with someone else overwrite that happiness or was it cumulative? She wasn't sure.

Bennett's words from earlier made a reappearance. He'd said Ben wouldn't get attached because they'd just met. That wasn't true, though. Sometimes a moment was all it took. That's all it had taken with Noah. Life could change in a blink.

What did Bennett think of her now? That she was crazy or just not interested? Crazy was a distinct possibility, but that he could think she was uninterested made her stomach feel funny. She hadn't rejected him at the dock. It had been a classic situation of 'it's not you; it's me." Did he realize that?

Her heart kicked into a higher gear. She eased out of bed. Ben squirmed into the warm spot she'd left but didn't wake. The squeak of Ben's door opening made her cringe and hold still. Everything in the house was quiet and dark. She must have been asleep longer than she'd thought.

She tiptoed down the hall and stood in front of the guest room door. Like a normal person, Bennett was probably asleep. Maybe it would be better — easier — to do this in the morning or during the car ride to Fort Bragg. She hesitated. If she didn't do it now, she might not do it at all. And then what?

Whatever was growing between them would be stamped out for good. As scared as she was to let it flourish, she couldn't let it die.

His fleece jacket still wrapped her in its warmth. She slipped it off, knocked on the door, and waited. Softer, she knocked again. Nothing. She leaned her forehead against the door and closed her eyes. Everything was ruined.

Bennett popped his eyes open. He'd dropped back into a doze after waking from familiar childhood dreams, but something more benign woke him this time. A second knock was definitely not dream induced. He grabbed a T-shirt and pulled it on as he padded barefoot to the door and opened it. Harper crashed straight into his chest with an *oof,* knocking him back a step. Surprise pumped adrenaline through his body.

Jack whined from the floor but didn't rise. Bennett glanced toward the window and the angle of the moonlight put the time around midnight. She was in the same T-shirt she'd been wearing earlier.

"What are you doing here?" he whispered. After their disaster-ish kiss, she hadn't been able to get away from him fast enough. And now she was practically in his arms, even if it was because she was off balance.

"Did I wake you?"

"Sort of."

"Bad dreams?" How did she see straight through him like that in the dark? "Here's your jacket."

She shoved his fleece zip-up into his chest. He tossed it into a chair. "You came to my room in the middle of the night to return my jacket?"

"Yes." She was so close, he could feel her body sigh. "No. Can I come in? We need to talk."

The four scariest words a woman could utter. Now he was the one off balance. "It can't wait until morning?"

Her hands tightened around his forearms. "No."

He disentangled himself from her and closed the door to keep from waking Ben or Gail. The distance was good. She was too soft and warm and tempting. Which was exactly what had gotten him in trouble earlier.

He perched stiffly on the side of the bed with his legs outstretched and his arms crossed over his chest. "Go ahead."

She stepped closer, the shadows giving way to moonlight. Her nerves were obvious. Was she going to tell him to take his money and get gone? Had one kiss screwed up everything?

"Earlier . . . you know, on the dock . . . well, I didn't mean . . . that is to say —" She cleared her throat and whispered, "Aw, screw it."

She straddled his legs and put her hands on his face. Before he could do more than unlock his arms and grab her waist, she kissed him.

Instead of the slow deliberation of their kiss on the dock, desperation thrummed around her, infecting him as well. He pulled her closer, fusing their bodies. She hooked an arm around his neck while her other hand played in his hair. Her sexy whimper was like flint to dry tinder.

He rolled them until she was on her back and he was between her legs. She arched against him, and a shiver coursed through him. As much as he would love to peel off all their clothes and wake up in the morning with her, too many questions burned for answers.

Except her lips felt perfect and he was having problems locating sufficient willpower to actually detach them. He moved his lips against hers. "Harper. What are we doing?"

"Kissing." She trailed her hand down his back and into the waistband of his boxer briefs.

Another inch or two and he would lose any semblance of self-control. Harper was a woman who'd lived in his imagination for years. Except she'd turned out to be sweeter, funnier, smarter, sexier . . . basically more of everything than he'd imagined. He had no defense against the real thing. Not even guilt over Noah could keep him from wanting her.

He tried one more time. "We can't have sex with your mom and son down the hall."

"Sex?" She startled enough to break the kiss but not the hold she had on him.

"Isn't that where we were headed when you put your hand in my underwear?"

She didn't snatch her hand away but moved it slowly up his back, her nails scraping pleasurably. "I didn't come in here for sex. I swear. I really did come to talk."

"Darlin', believe me, I'm not judging you. Given the green light, I'd be all in." He paused when she turned her head to the side. Had he come on too strong? "But I don't think you know what you want. Am I wrong?"

He barely heard her whisper, "You're not wrong."

With the effort of separating industrial-sized magnets, he rolled off her to his back and concentrated on the slow turn of the ceiling fan to regulate his breathing. "Why did you come sneaking to my door at midnight, then?"

She turned to her side and propped her head up on her hand. "I was afraid if I waited until morning, things would be ruined."

"What things?"

"Us things." She made a *gah* sound and rolled to her stomach, her feet hanging off the bed, her face hidden in the covers. "Put me out of my misery."

He smiled. He wasn't a smiler or laugher or hugger. Except around her he found himself doing all three more than he remembered for years. Maybe forever. "You haven't ruined 'us' things."

"I haven't?" She propped herself up on her elbows. "I didn't run off because I didn't enjoy kissing you out on the dock. Boy howdy, I enjoyed it all right. And *that* was why I ran off."

"You're afraid of getting physical?"

"Not exactly. Although, I mean, it has been a while." She hummed and sat up on the bed, her arms around her knees. "You may not want to know. It's weird."

"Why is it weird?" He moved to lean against the headboard, maintaining a safe arm's-length distance.

269

"Because . . . it's about Noah."

"You feel guilty. Like you're betraying him." He might as well have been speaking about himself.

"Yes and no. It's hard to put into words."

He closed his eyes and said what he'd been thinking even though the words cut like razors. "It's too complicated, isn't it? I can't compete with him. I won't. He'll always be between us."

Her laugh held no humor. "My problem is that I didn't feel him at all. When you kissed me, I forgot . . . everything. Even him. That's why I ran. I'm scared I'm going to lose my memories of Noah, and that's all I have left."

He took a moment to process what she'd admitted. He couldn't deny the spike of satisfaction, but neither could he deny the very real issue of Noah's ghost between them. "You'll never forget him. Neither will I."

"It's both harder and easier knowing how close you and Noah were. Knowing you were there." She swallowed hard but didn't break eye contact with him.

"We can be business colleagues. Put aside everything that happened tonight. It won't be awkward."

"Yes, it will." Her smile flashed like a

lightning bug, gone in an instant. "The thing is . . . I don't want to forget. Do you?"

Hell no. He fisted his hands in the covers to keep from pulling her into him. "No. I don't."

"Where does this leave us?"

"It leaves us taking things as slow as you need."

"I might *need* slow, but I *want* fast."

He lost the battle and reached out, tugging her into his arms. The naturalness of the way she notched herself against him as if they'd been carved out of the same piece of wood soothed the chaos and uncertainty.

Would Noah approve or would he hate the fact that Bennett wanted what Noah could never have again? Did the dead even care? The feel and scent of Harper loosened his hold on conscious thought, and he slipped toward sleep, praying his nightmares — and Noah — would stay at bay.

CHAPTER 14

Past

Bennett swung the ax and cleaved the wood in two, the impact jolting his arm. He cleared the pieces and put another cut of wood on the stump. The last time he'd put his body through such grueling physical labor was BUD/S. Noah worked at his side with a chainsaw. Bennett couldn't stem a smile. Just like old times.

After years of invitations, Bennett had finally accompanied Noah to his family's soybean farm in Georgia. Noah's dad was getting older and Noah, feeling guilt at his desertion to the SEALs, had promised to help clear land. Bennett had only agreed once he'd been assured Harper wasn't coming, too.

Bennett had spent the last three years avoiding coming face-to-face with Noah's wife. He'd made sure he was committed for SEAL business the weekend of their wedding, even though Noah had asked him to be best man, and had never accepted an invite to social functions involving the families.

His constant refusals made him seem like an antisocial SOB, which wasn't that far off the mark, to be honest. Even if he had attended one of the company barbeques, he'd have spent it holding up a corner with a beer in hand. Maybe even double-fisting it.

No, he avoided Harper Wilcox partly because he was afraid she'd never live up to the picture he'd formed of her from her letters. But mostly he was downright terrified she'd far surpass his expectations. His fascination with his best friend's wife was inappropriate at best and a betrayal at worst.

Most of the time, his feelings were easy to ignore. And when he and Noah deployed, he allowed himself to enjoy Harper's stories knowing the brief moments of normalcy could be blown to bits the next day — hell, the next hour.

And it's not like he secretly imagined Noah out of the picture. Noah had people — a wife, a mom and dad, and sisters — who depended on him in various ways. Bennett had no one except for his SEAL brothers. He would sacrifice his life for any one of them, but especially to protect Noah.

Noah powered the chainsaw off and ran the back of his hand over his sweaty forehead. "Break time."

They retreated to the shade and shared iced tea from a jug Noah's mom had packed along with snacks. She'd slipped an extra homemade Rice Krispies treat in with Bennett's name written on the wax-paper wrapping like he was in school. It made his chest ache a little.

"Thanks for coming down here with me. Sorry my mom was all up in your business last night at dinner. So annoying." Noah's eye roll was teenager-like.

"I don't mind." Bennett wasn't being polite. He really hadn't minded. With all her kids married and on their own, he got the impression Noah's mom needed someone to mother. It had been . . . nice.

"Are you sure? I can tell her to back off. I know how private you are."

Noah's mom had grilled him about his love life, then turned around and promised to knit him a scarf and toboggan cap for Christmas all the while plying him with homemade banana pudding and hugs.

"I said it's okay." The words came out harsher than he meant. "Sorry. It's just . . ."

Noah cocked his head and waited. He was accepting of Bennett's limits. It was one reason Noah was easy to be around. Another was the fact that he was a good person and even better friend.

Bennett squinted toward the tree line across the field of soybeans until they blurred into one blob of green. His laugh contained more bitterness than a pot of undercooked greens. "It's a novelty to be mothered even for a weekend."

"I wasn't thinking, man."

The silence bore down on Bennett until he had to break the tension. "I had no idea I was missing out on knitted scarves all these years."

Their combined laughter petered out but left a new connection. One Bennett couldn't help but hang on to. "If it hadn't been for the drugs, I think my mom would have turned out okay. Maybe not homemade Rice Krispies treat–level good, but at least Oreo good."

"Were they all shitty?"

"What? The cookies?"

"No. The foster homes."

"Some were better than others." The answer was a cop-out, and after everything Noah had shared with Bennett, the most valuable being friendship, he wanted to give more. "The best homes were ones where I was ignored. I got pretty good at staying under the radar."

"What were the worst kind of homes?"

"The ones with lots of other fosters or older kids. Especially other boys. Every day was a battle. Luckily, I was always big for my age." That hadn't helped him when it was three on one, of course. "Occasionally, I got put with a family who preferred hands-on discipline."

"Jesus. What did you do? Could you tell someone?"

"No one cared." Except that wasn't true. One woman had cared enough to give him one last chance. A chance that had changed his life. "Even then, I didn't have it in me to cower and take it, so I fought back. Got me blackballed from any decent foster situation. Somehow my file came across the desk of a woman who saw past my anger to something worthwhile that had survived."

"She hooked you up with your Sarge."

"Sarge was her uncle and agreed to take me on. He was . . . special." The former Army Ranger had been part drill sergeant, part therapist, and part father. "I wish he had lived long enough to know I'd made it as a SEAL."

"I'll bet he's looking down on you now proud as hell."

Bennett grunted. He didn't believe in

some afterlife bullshit. Nothing he'd seen or experienced led him to believe some benevolent deity was watching out for him. Instead of voicing his unpopular opinion, Bennett offered half of his extra treat to Noah. The silence between them wasn't at all quiet or uncomfortable this time. Birds and squirrels made noises in the trees and critters rustled in the leaves at their feet.

"Can you keep a secret?" Noah asked.

"Who would I tell?" Bennett ignored the sad commentary his answer revealed.

"Harper's pregnant."

Shock zinged through him. He pulled Noah in for a sweaty slap across the shoulders. "Dude. Congratulations. Why are you keeping it a secret? Your mom would lose her shit."

"It's early yet and Harper wants to wait until her doctor's appointment."

"I'm happy for you guys. I really am." And he was. The Harper he sometimes dreamed about wasn't real. She was like a favorite mixtape he'd assembled in his imagination. The greatest hits of her letters.

Noah looked grim considering the news should be joyous. "This put the future in perspective, you know?"

"How so?"

"Harper can take care of herself. She's

strong. But a baby . . ." Noah scrubbed a hand over his buzz cut. "What if something happens?"

Bennett didn't have to ask what he meant. He knew. Every SEAL knew. The thought was like an infestation of termites in the backs of their minds. It's not like they worked behind a safe desk in a safe cubicle in a safe building. Things could go FUBAR in seconds.

But it's what they'd signed up for. What they loved. "You thinking about getting out?"

"Not a chance." In Noah's pause, Bennett could hear the doubts. Drawing his words out, Noah continued. "Bu-u-ut . . . I have been thinking about contingencies. Listen, you can say no. Don't feel obligated or anything, but I can't think of anyone else. An-n-nd . . . well." Noah petered into silence after tripping over his tongue.

"Damn, Peaches, are you working up the courage to ask me on a date or something?" Bennett stared at Noah in amused fascination. He hadn't seen Noah this worked up since the day he'd shown Bennett the ring he'd bought for Harper.

Noah cracked a smile. "Not exactly. I want you to be a sort-of godfather. If you're willing."

Bennett straightened from his slouch against the tree. Religion hadn't made an impact on his life, but he'd seen enough movies to know a godfather was supposed to guide a child spiritually. Or head up a Mafia family, but he assumed Noah wanted the former. "I'm not qualified to teach a kid about God or anything. I would only warp its little mind."

"That's not what I'm asking you to do."

"Then what? Get the little tyke a present on his birthday? Are you going to name him after me or something?"

Noah barked a laugh. "That's not a terrible idea actually, but what if the baby is a girl?"

" 'Benjamina'? Or how about something trendy like 'Bentley'?"

"I'll talk to Harper and see what she thinks." Noah moved to stand in front of Bennett and look him in the eyes, his laughter fading into solemnness. "I want you to promise me something, Griz."

"Anything."

"If something happens to me, I want you to promise to take care of them. Harper and the baby."

Bennett's mouth felt like he'd chewed on a dozen cotton balls. He tried to swallow, but his words came out garbled. "Nothing is going to happen."

"Probably not, but I need to know they'll have someone to count on." Maybe because Noah had been thinking about the offer for a while, he maintained a calm Bennett was having a hard time locating. "I want that someone to be you."

"Why me? I'm kind of messed up, bro." There were a half-dozen better choices than him. Darren's nickname was Family Man, for goodness' sake.

"Bullshit. You're not just my brother-in-arms, Griz. You're my brother. Maybe not by blood, but in every other way that counts. I'd trust you with my life. And my life is Harper and this baby."

Bennett's heart shattered and reassembled itself in that moment. A brother. A family. He'd never had either but had wished for both every day when he was young. He'd put the foolish dream away with his childhood, but the dream had survived and now it flourished under Noah's request.

"I promise I'll take care of them." What he left unsaid was the promise he made to himself standing in that soybean field in Georgia. He would make sure nothing happened to Noah even if he had to sacrifice himself to do it.

CHAPTER 15

Present Day

For the second time, Harper woke in bed entwined with Bennett. Neither time had involved sex. Which was just plain sad. She'd thought she'd been ready for more than cuddling after the panty-melting kiss and the feel of him on top of her. But, with sunlight and reality diffusing through the room, she was thankful one of them had practiced self-control.

She slipped out from under his arm and held her breath, but he remained deeply asleep. On tiptoes, she made her way back to her room. A sound froze her in the middle of the hall. Her mom was coming out of her room in a robe, her face caught in mid-yawn when they made eye contact.

Harper shook her head and continued into her room, shutting the door and pressing her flaming cheek against the cool wood. Any other mother might have been discreet or embarrassed enough not to question her. No such luck with her mom. It would be the Inquisition over coffee.

Harper took her time showering and dressing but was still the first one downstairs. The kitchen was empty, although a fresh pot of coffee steamed and pancake batter was mixed and ready to cook. Harper sent up a quick prayer and headed toward the coffeepot.

"Well, well, well." Her mom's voice came from over Harper's shoulder.

She fumbled her thankfully empty mug and decided to play ignorant. "Good morning."

"I planned to chew your butt this morning about how rude you were last night. But looks like you apologized already. How was it?"

"How was what?" She poured a cup of coffee and hoped her mom didn't noticed her shaking hands.

"The sex," her mom said in a stage whisper.

"Oh my God, shush. Nothing happened."

"Nothing?"

"Almost nothing." Harper rolled her eyes. "A kiss. Or two. That's it. It was late, and I fell asleep in my clothes."

Her mom made a grumpy harrumphing

noise. "That's disappointing. But I take encouragement from the fact at least one part of your body made physical contact with a red-blooded, very handsome man."

A blush raced over her body, setting her on fire. "Mom. Please, don't embarrass me."

"Who me?" Her mom was the picture of refined innocence. Except for her smile. It was pure mischievousness. "I'm tickled pink to see you interested in a man."

"But —"

"No buts. Noah would want you to be happy, and Bennett would get his stamp of approval. After all, Noah thought enough of him to name your son after him." Her mom ladled pancake batter on the hot griddle.

If only it could be that simple. Or could it? Could she ignore the intersecting of their lives now they were on the same road?

Bennett's heavy footsteps on the stairs were accompanied by the patter of dog paws. Without making eye contact with her, Bennett let the dog out the back to do his business. Of course, that could be because she was studiously avoiding Bennett's eyes. What had seemed simple in darkness was drawn in stark terms in the light of day.

He took a seat at the kitchen table. Harper flipped two pancakes on a plate and slid it in front of him like a short-order cook.

He grabbed her wrist before she could retreat, his grip implacable but his thumb gentle on her pulse point.

"Morning." An unspoken question hung between them.

The same uncertainty she felt reflected in his eyes. She relaxed and turned her hand enough to give his forearm an answering touch. "Good morning."

The tension withered with the flash of his smile.

"Did you sleep well, Bennett?" Her mom set down two more plates of pancakes, the tease in her voice not in any way tempered.

Harper gave her ankle a nudge under the table.

"Best night of sleep I've had in a long time, actually." He took a big bite of pancake, his gaze never wavering from Harper's.

Underlying his claim were darker hints of things to come. A blush raised her body temperature to near boiling. She backed toward the door. "I'll go wake Ben."

She jogged up the stairs and peeked in at Ben. His cheeks were full and reddened and his mouth soft. She perched on the edge of his bed and ran her hand over his hair. If only someone could bottle the innocence of a child at sleep.

Except not all children got to enjoy an innocent childhood. Her thoughts drifted to Bennett and the little he'd told her of his life in foster care and before. She resisted the urge to grab Ben close and hug him tight. He would probably accuse her of trying to give him cooties.

Instead, she brushed her finger over his cheek until his eyes fluttered open with a yawn.

"Yaya has pancakes ready." It was their Saturday morning routine.

"Yay!" He scooted around her. "Is Big Ben still here?"

"He's downstairs."

She caught the back of Ben's shirt on the start of his streak downstairs. "Bathroom first."

Ben trudged by her to the bathroom. She waited for him and they made their way downstairs side by side until Bennett came into view. Ben launched himself at Bennett for a hug, her son chattering about books and school and whatever crossed his mind. Harper stood in the doorway of the kitchen, her eyes dry but her heart clawing to break free.

Her mom had turned away to flip pancakes but wiped at her eyes. She and her mom had done their best to fill any void left by Noah's death, but their best hadn't been enough. The realization hurt.

Harper put her hand on Ben's shoulder and guided him toward his seat. "Your breakfast is getting cold, pumpkin."

Ben took his seat but continued to talk even as he ate. "After breakfast, can we go play outside?" He was looking at Bennett and not her.

Bennett's gaze flicked toward her, and she jumped in to save him. "We won't have time, sweetie. Bennett and I have to drive down to Fort Bragg to see about leasing a space for the coffee shop."

The disappointment on Ben's face twisted a knife into her chest.

"If it's okay with your mom, when we get back tomorrow afternoon you can show me your favorite games." Bennett shot a questioning glance in her direction.

She hoped Bennett meant it and wasn't trying to put Ben off only to disappoint him later. Even with her worries, she nodded, the smile on Ben's face too much to deny. "Fine with me."

Bennett excused himself to put their overnight bags in his truck, both Jack London and Ben on his heels. He had managed to inspire devotion in both boy and beast.

"Ben is taken with him," her mom said softly, loading the dishwasher. "I hope it wasn't a mistake to introduce them so early on in your relationship."

Relationship? The word set her heart racing. "I didn't mean for anything to happen."

"It's not a bad thing, Harper. In fact, no matter how things turn out, this has all been good for you. But I don't want to see Ben disappointed. He's taken to Bennett like a duckling imprinting on its mama."

"I didn't realize how much Ben has missed out on by not having a father until I saw them together." Harper grabbed the counter, the edge biting into her palm. "I know I have nothing to feel guilty about, but I do."

"Can't change the past. You can only move forward. Preferably happily." Her mom's sigh signaled she was done allowing Harper to wallow. She dried her hands on a dish towel and leaned against the counter, her voice brisk. "Are you going to come home with a signed lease?"

"This is a big step from looking at black-and-white numbers on a page." She had spent countless hours working up a business plan. "Signing a contract scares the bejeezus out of me. And I'll have to get Allison and a couple of the other ladies on board. Even though I'm putting up the money, I want them to feel a sense of ownership."

"I know it's scary, but a coffee business sounds like a fabulous idea. Bennett must think so, too, or he wouldn't be investing his time. And money, in a roundabout way."

Harper checked the time. "We need to hit the road."

"Go on." Her mom walked with her to the front door and jabbed an elbow in her side. "And, while you're in the middle of doing business, try to have some *fun.*"

"Mom." Why did the situation make her feel like a teenager again? "We're staying with Allison and Darren and their kids. No chance for that kind of fun."

She grabbed her purse and stepped out the front door. Still in his dinosaur pajamas, Ben stood in the driveway and kicked rocks. Bennett was crouched down at his level, whatever he was saying lost in the distance.

With a fluid grace, he rose. "How about I ask your mom?"

"Okay," Ben muttered. Another rock skittered off his foot and into the grass.

"What do you think about Jack hanging out here for the weekend? He'd be bored with us, anyway."

Harper tilted her head and tried to get a read on him. "Are you sure?"

"We'll be so busy, it'll make things easier."

Ben sprang to life to hang on her arm. "Can he stay, Mommy? Please?"

"It's up to Yaya."

Her mom had a shoulder propped against the column at the top of the stairs. Ben linked his hands under his chin and repeated his plea. "Please, Yaya. Can he stay?"

"Only because he's such a gentleman." Her mom winked at Ben, who did a spastic dance of joy before throwing his arms around Jack's neck.

"I'll take really good care of him. I promise."

"I know you will." Bennett hauled the dog food and water dish out of the bed of the truck to the top of the porch steps. On his way back, he ruffled Ben's hair. "If it's sunny out tomorrow, we'll throw a ball around as soon as we get back. Sound good?"

Ben's grin was contagious, and Harper wasn't even upset that she had to remind him to give her a hug. Ben, Jack, and her mom disappeared inside the house.

Without Jack, the cab of the truck felt cavernous. Bennett's hands were tight on the steering wheel.

She tiptoed into the silence. "Are you sure —"

"Not a big deal." His voice was clipped and uninviting.

Except it was. Jack London was part therapy dog, part best friend. She'd noticed the way Bennett reached for him during uncertainty or stress. "Have you ever spent the night away from him?"

"I don't need a security blanket. I'm not a wuss." A military-tinged edge was in his voice.

She shoved his shoulder — hard — and broke his stranglehold on the steering wheel. The truck jerked toward the center line.

"What the hell, Harper?"

"Don't fire evasions in my directions, Caldwell. Not appreciated." She sat back and crossed her arms and legs. "You're as bad as Darren. Not admitting a single weakness. Are you SEALs born that way or do they brainwash you in training?"

"A little of both, I suppose. Meek, helpless bastards need not apply."

"Is that what they put on the recruitment posters?"

The rumble coming from his chest was his particular brand of laughter. Humor interwoven with a dry sarcasm. His hands moved lower on the steering wheel and his body sank into the seat.

"It's weird not to have Jack's doggy breath on my neck."

Tentatively, she touched his arm again, this time with a gentle stroke. "You have me, if it's any consolation."

With his face in profile, the tiny hitch at the corner of his mouth could be amusement or annoyance. "Your breath is a sight better than Jack's. And based on last night, if I wake up from a nightmare you're a lot more fun, too."

"Bennett." It was the first acknowledgment of her midnight invasion of his room and the embarrassment factor was nuclear.

"Are you blushing?" His voice veered from disbelief to amusement. "You literally jumped me last night, and now you're red as a radish."

" 'Jumped' is a strong word. I advanced with intent."

"Yeah, your intention was to jump me."

She slapped his arm and would have again if he hadn't grabbed her hand.

"See there, you can't keep your hands off me. I'm irresistible," he said.

Had this teasing, flirty side of him been lying dormant? Did she inspire it? "You are pretty irresistible." She popped over the console far enough to kiss his cheek.

A familiar solemnness came over him, but

instead of ignoring the moment, he lifted her hand and pressed a kiss on her palm. His lips were soft and warm; his beard, scratchy. Her nerve endings fired, overly sensitized to the difference.

He let go and she pressed her palms together as if she could transfer the feeling. A faint awkwardness descended. The new territory they'd entered together held surprises and pitfalls, and it would take time to explore and map.

The rest of the trip they discussed her business plan in depth. He pointed out some places, like advertising, where she would need to put more money. By the time they arrived at a potential property, she felt as comfortable as she ever would with moving forward.

Risk would always be lurking like a dark cloud, but if she succeeded the reward would be worth it. She glanced over at Bennett. Could the same be said for whatever was brewing between them?

They spent an hour looking over the empty retail space. In a strip mall close to the base, it was easy to get into and out of and saw lots of morning traffic. A storage area in the back could hold a roaster and bagging operations. Even better, there was a bakery across the street and possibilities fired in her brain. The coffee shop could sell bakery items and the bakery could sell Home Front coffee. A win-win.

Once they were back in the cab of the truck, she said, "It's a great location. I need to run numbers on comparable rents in the area, though."

"He's asking too much. We need to talk him down." He reached across her, opened the glove compartment, and dropped a paper in her lap. "Comparable rents in the area for similar square footage."

She scanned the numbers. The ire that rose was aimed mostly at herself. She should have run the numbers already. It was basic stuff, and she hadn't thought of it until now. She rattled the paper close to his face. "Why didn't you share this with me earlier?"

"Didn't think about it."

"I realize this is your money and you're trying to help, but I need to feel my way through this, Bennett. You have your own business to run."

"Sorry." He shot her an inscrutable look as he got them on the road. Of course, all his looks qualified as inscrutable in her mental dictionary. "You would have gone home and then run the numbers and come to the same conclusion. Use this information to negotiate."

She sank down in her seat, the passing scenery blurred. She had been a stay-at-home wife and mother and then a simple accountant. Was she up to this or was she fooling herself?

They passed the base checkpoints and Harper gave directions to Allison and Darren's house. "You weren't down here much?"

"Nope."

His monosyllabic answer fired her curiosity. What had filled Bennett's time when their team was stateside? The questions would have to wait. He parked the truck at the curb in front of Darren and Allison's house.

"Not bad for base housing." He slid out.

She hummed, but a shiver passed through her. Allison gave an energy to wherever she lived. One of the shutters at the front window was hanging askew and the bushes hadn't been trimmed since their fall growth, giving the house an unkempt, harried feel.

Allison greeted them at the door, offering Harper a hug and Bennett a welcoming smile. At first glance, she looked better. Less tired and not as stressed out. Although she'd also had time to prepare for their arrival, which along with a spread of appetizers and drinks included spackling the cracks in her life.

Their small talk echoed in the entry hall. The stairs creaked.

"Here's Darren." Allison's demeanor changed subtly. Her smile grew brittle and a new tension enveloped her. Darren reached them and immediately offered Bennett a half handshake, half hug.

"It's good to see you, Grizzly."

"You too, Family Man."

Bennett tapped his fist on Darren's back and exchanged a glance with Harper over Darren's shoulder. In it she could see the same worries that plagued her.

"Kids are out back playing. If you boys want to supervise, I'll bring you each a beer."

"That'd be great, Allison," Bennett said.

"Thanks, babe." Darren led the way through the kitchen and out the back door. His bedhead, bare feet, and sweatpants gave the impression of a man beyond caring.

Allison uncapped two beers and pointed to a platter full of mini-quiches. "You've got to try those. They are to die for."

Harper's stomach, already a mass of her own nerves, now clenched with worry over Allison and Darren. When Allison returned, Harper let her prattle on about the food and pour them both glasses of wine before she cut her off. "Enough. What is going on with Darren?"

Allison's laugh was tinged with tears. "Leave it to you to cut through my BS."

"That's what friends do, dummy. Is he going to the therapy group?" Harper took a seat at the table and Allison joined her, slumping back and drinking half her glass of wine in one go.

She wiped her mouth with the back of her hand. "He went once. Said he wasn't going back. His nightmares were worse than they had been in months that night, so I didn't insist. I thought maybe being around other guys like him had made it sharper somehow."

"Or maybe hearing the other guys made him face up to his own demons."

"Maybe." Allison drank the rest of her wine and poured more.

Wisdom didn't present itself to Harper in a lightning strike. "Have *you* seen anyone?"

"I tried, but Darren got mad. Said he didn't want me talking about him to a stranger. Or worse, some base shrink that might spread rumors." She drank more wine and turned her head to the side. "He would kill me if he knew I'd talked to my wives group about him."

"Sounds a little paranoid." The acidic wine did nothing to settle her stomach. "What does he think about me?"

"He thinks me talking to you is okay. I guess because of what you went through with Noah. I'm hoping Bennett might be able to help him."

Harper sat back and took another sip even though she didn't want more. She wasn't holding out hope that Bennett would be able to make a breakthrough with Darren. Problem was men like Bennett and Darren were trained to not exhibit weakness. They talked sports and reminisced about derring-do in the field, not how they struggled with nightmares and sleepwalking and depression.

Harper had seen the changes SEAL training had wrought in Noah over time. He'd been a good man from start to finish, but as the deployments racked up so did the walls between them. Some of the distance might have been the time spent apart or simply growing up or his desire to protect her.

She'd never probed too deeply about his deployments. He'd certainly faced similar trials to Bennett and Darren, and just as surely those experiences had changed him subtly but inexorably. Had she been naïve or had she not really wanted to know? How much about Noah had she not understood or even tried to understand? Hindsight was an evil bitch.

"You can't count on Bennett to solve Darren's problems."

"Not solve but help him figure out how to move on. There's always hope, right?" Allison's accompanying laugh sounded close to tears. Hope was her only foothold to happiness, and Harper couldn't bring herself to weaken it further.

"Of course there's hope."

Allison propped her chin on her palm and leaned onto the table, her tone lighter and teasing. "Enough about my boring problems. I want to hear everything."

"We saw the property before heading here. It was really nice. Perfect, in fact. Small retail space in front and a larger well-ventilated area in back that we could convert into a roasting —"

"Not that. I mean, that's awesome, and I do want to hear everything. But first, I'm dying for deets about you and Bennett. What's going on?" Allison wagged a finger. "And don't blow me off like you did on the phone. I can hear it in your voice when you talk about him."

"Hear what?"

"Lus-s-t." The way Allison drew the word

out sent them into pealing laughter. It was like a release valve.

"I didn't blow you off on the phone because nothing had happened last time I talked to you."

"But something has happened now?" Allison's eyes widened.

Harper put a hand over her mouth and whispered, "We kissed. It was weird and wonderful and way confusing."

"Confusing how? Because of Noah?"

"Yeah, sort of." She didn't have the emotional fortitude to delve back into the deep-seated reasons. "It's been a long time since I've liked a man and had the urge to . . . you know."

"Do you feel like you'd be betraying Noah?"

"No. Yes. Bennett's history with Noah is almost as long and strong as mine."

Allison toyed with the stem of her wineglass. "Have you gotten anything else out of him about why he gave you the money?"

"I think it stems back to a vague promise Bennett made. Guilt money is all I can imagine. It's like he holds himself responsible somehow for Noah's death. The couple of times I've broached the subject, he's iced me out."

"That's weird."

"Yep." Harper drained her glass in the silence.

"There's only one thing that really matters. . . ." Allison paused until Harper looked up. "Is he a good kisser?"

Giggly laugher ensued. Harper's cheeks warmed with the memories of the night before. Nothing they had done had been particularly scandalous, but the step she'd taken with him had been like Neil Armstrong's first step on the moon — a giant leap for her.

Allison held up the bottle with her eyebrows raised in question. Harper covered her glass. "No more for me, thanks."

"Will you please eat something? The kids won't touch those stuffed mushrooms."

The riot in her stomach had subsided. The wine and laughter had settled a sense of relative normalcy. The fraying of Allison and Darren's life didn't seem in imminent danger of rending completely in two.

She popped a mushroom into her mouth as Allison rose to pull out a covered pan from the refrigerator. "Are those your pork chops?" Harper's mouth was already watering. "You are such a fabulous cook. You should write a recipe book. I could help you put it together."

Allison slid the pan into the oven and

closed it with her heel. "Another business venture? Don't we have enough to handle?"

"Ugh. You're right. Bennett is telling me I need to go to auctions to buy the equipment I need, but I have no clue what I'm doing."

Allison leaned against the counter and crossed her arms. "Why don't you enlist Madeline or Joyce?"

The two women from Allison's group had taken a leadership role in planning and brainstorming and had been the most active during their long-distance chats and texts. Still, Harper wasn't sure about entrusting them with major purchases.

"Did you get a meeting set up? It'll be good to sit down around a table to hash out the details instead of texting," Harper said.

"Tomorrow morning. Here. I thought a coffee meeting would be apropos." Allison's smile was energetic and as close to easy as it had been since they'd arrived. The sound of men's voices carried closer. Bennett came around the corner first, his and Harper's gazes melding.

"Perfect," Harper said.

Darren chucked their empty beer bottles into a recycling bin in the pantry. "What's perfect?"

"Allison has set up a meeting with a

couple of the base wives who are interested in helping get the business off the ground." Harper examined Darren as subtly as possible. His face was flushed, from either the beer or the cool breeze, but the color gave him life and vibrancy, helping to offset his rumpled appearance.

"Bennett was telling me all about it. You're doing something good in Noah's honor. I think that's pretty amazing." Darren grabbed two more beers, uncapped them, and handed one to Bennett, clinking the necks. "To Noah."

"To Noah," Bennett repeated before taking a swig, his eyes anywhere but on her.

Guilt splattered her mood like a Pollock painting. Others would see this business as a memorial to Noah and part of her motivation was to honor his memory, but it was also a selfish endeavor.

The kids came in and Allison got them set up in the den with snacks and video games, which based on their reaction was an unusual privilege. A tutu-clad Sophie stopped to give Harper a hug and whispered in her ear, "Will you read me a story tonight?"

"Sure thing, princess."

Sophie skipped off singing a Disney song.

Darren and Bennett joined the women at the table to pick over the appetizers Allison had laid out. Although the conversation remained superficial, a tension pushed and pulled between Allison and Darren. It was dark and worrisome.

"I would love to book one of your survival weekends, man. They sound awesome," Darren said between bites.

"No need for you to book one. Winter is slow. How about next weekend? Anyone else from the team around? We could make it a mini-reunion." Bennett stared at Darren, his brow furrowed.

Allison had straightened and touched Darren's arm lightly, her gaze pinging between Bennett and her husband. "That sounds like fun. You should go."

Darren shifted his arm away from her, and a flash of hurt crossed Allison's face. She slumped back in her chair.

"It would be amazing to get together. I'll ask around." Darren peeled the label off his beer. "But I might have to work. You know how it is."

He had no intention of calling anyone or going anywhere, but no one exposed his lie. During dinner, the kids dominated the conversation, which seemed to suit everyone fine. It made things easier.

While she and Allison loaded the dishwasher, Harper said, "I hate we're kicking the girls out of their rooms."

"Are you kidding me? They're setting up a fairy tent in the den. It's all Sophie has been talking about. I wouldn't be surprised if Ryan doesn't end up sleeping with them." Allison gave the counters a final wipe down. "I wasn't sure whether to put you and Bennett in the same room or not?"

"Not." She shot back to the night before and waking next to his strength and heat and her innards turned gooey. She waited until Allison tossed the rag over the faucet. "Are you and Darren okay?"

Allison sighed and shook her head. "*Okay? What does that mean anymore?* We sleep in the same bed, but he never touches me. Never wants me to touch him."

"Is he . . ." Harper couldn't even put her fears into words. Allison and Darren's marriage had seemed so solid.

"Cheating? I don't think so. It's more that he's become sensitized to everything — noises, touch, bright lights."

Darren needed professional help, but nothing and no one seemed able to make him seek it. The rest of the evening passed in the same vein — tension and anxiety overlaid with a fake brightness. It was exhausting, and Harper was glad when the kids' bedtime offered her an escape. She crawled into the fairy tent, which was actually quilts and covers thrown over furniture to form a lean-to of sorts, to read Sophie her story.

The four adults climbed the stairs together, Bennett ducking into Libby's room and Harper taking Sophie's. Darren and Allison disappeared into the master bedroom and closed the door.

After getting ready for bed, Harper stared at the movable shadows on the ceiling. Her mind bounced between worries like a pinball machine. Her bland, boring life had become anything but.

A noise outside her door had her bolting to her feet, her heartbeat pounding in her ears. She cracked the door half-expecting another foray into the night by Darren. But the hallway was empty. Her heart slowed as her senses strained outward.

The eerie noise came again and this time she recognized the moan as Bennett's. She flew across the hall and opened his bedroom door. A night-light on the wall illuminated him tangled in a sheet with pink hearts. He tried to escape their cotton prison as his arms reached from something he could see only in his dream. Or maybe he was trying to keep something at bay.

He was bare chested, but she could see

pajama pants riding low on his hips at the edge of the sheet. She eased onto the edge of the bed and poked his bare shoulder. When her gentle touch failed to rouse him, she shook his shoulder.

"Wake up, Bennett." She kept her voice at a whisper knowing how sound traveled through the thin walls. Dropping her face closer to his, she shook him harder. "Wake up."

His surge to sitting surprised her. He grabbed her upper arms, his grip biting. She squirmed. "*Bennett.* Let me go."

His hands loosened, but he didn't release her. "Harper?" His voice was rough with sleep and emotion.

"You were having a bad dream. Was it the same one?"

"Did I wake everyone up?"

"No one. I wasn't even asleep yet." She stroked his sides, smooth skin over muscle.

She tried not to notice how good he felt, but with the danger passed she became intimately aware of their position. She had managed to get herself in bed with him once again. This time she was only wearing an oversized T-shirt and panties. Maybe her subconscious was telling her something.

He ran his hands up and down her arms, the rasp unbearably arousing and soothing at the same time. Her hands moved, too, dancing up his back and bringing her chest closer to his. He was warm and solid.

"Maybe I should stay with you," she said softly. "Otherwise, you won't go back to sleep, will you?"

His slight laugh was raspy. "I'm used to bad dreams, but I won't object."

He drew her down on the bed with him. It was a twin bed and they lay on their sides, facing each other. She buried her face in the hollow of his throat and pretended her motivations were purely altruistic. One hand was trapped between them, but the other roved selfishly over his body making notes of what made his breath hitch and what made him shiver.

His hand was on a similar mission, snaking under her shirt to measure the length of her spine with his fingertips until they reached the band of her panties. Her back arched, an invitation to move his hand lower still. He accepted, palming her buttock.

She wanted him even though it was too soon and too complicated and too crowded in the house. He wanted her, too. She could feel him against her, his hips restless and searching.

The soft opening and closing of a door froze them like two teenagers caught by a spotlight. Footsteps sounded down the hall and creaked on the stairs.

Bennett rose, pulled on a T-shirt, and slipped out. She lay in the bed for a few minutes, her ears straining for a clue as to what was happening, but only silence reverberated.

She eased out of bed and glided down the stairs. The kids were motionless in their tent. She moved to the front room and peeked out of the windows. Her breath caught. Bennett and Darren were in the yard grappling.

Before she could decide what to do, they broke apart, their chests heaving. Words passed between them. She toggled the latch and raised the window a few inches.

"— unacceptable." Bennett's voice was low but commanding. "You need help."

"Go to hell. You're not my commanding officer. Never were." Darren stalked up to the porch and Harper shrank down behind the window, pressing herself against the wall, but the doorknob didn't turn.

"No, I am — was, anyway — your friend, unless I'm mistaken." Bennett's voice was close now, and she peeked over the edge. He stood toe-to-toe with Darren on the porch, only a few feet from her hiding spot. "I should have checked on you as soon as you got home. I'm sorry for that, but I'm here now."

"I appreciate that, but there's nothing you can do."

"I can listen. You don't think I had issues after I got home?"

"Nightmares?"

"Of course."

"How often?" It was almost like Darren was in competition to see which one of them was the most screwed up.

"Often enough." Bennett stepped back and leaned against the wall. The hovering testosterone cloud dissipated. "I got a dog. Believe it or not, he helps. So do people that care."

"Allison doesn't get it."

"Have you tried talking to her?"

"No way am I going to lay my fucked-up thoughts on her."

"A shrink?"

At Darren's muttered curse, Bennet said, "Okay. Then, find someone to talk to who'll understand. Like me."

The ticking of a clock inside marked the silence. When Darren spoke, she had to strain closer to the opening to hear him. "I can't turn my brain off at night. I lay there in the dark and think about things I did and the horrible things I saw. I relive them every night. Like it's happening over and over again like *Groundhog Day.*"

"Same thing I went through."

"How'd you get past it?"

"Booze. Denial. Compartmentalization. Then, one night I was out in the middle of the Dismal Swamp by myself and just . . . stayed. For two weeks I lived off the land. I saw no one, talked to no one; no one missed me." His voice dropped. "I almost didn't come back."

"But you did. Why?"

"Along with peace, I located a selfish will to live. That's when I got motivated to start the survival school. The school gave me purpose. Maybe that's what you're missing."

"I have purpose. My job is important."

"What are you going to do if they send you back over?"

Darren plopped in one of the rocking chairs and dropped his head into his hands, his voice cracking. "I-I . . . don't know."

"For your sanity, get out and find a different purpose. Concentrate on Allison and the kids."

"The service is all I know. It's all I ever wanted. How can I leave it behind?"

"Look at yourself. It's killing you, man, as surely as a sniper's bullet."

A rhythmic squeak sounded from the slight motion of the rocking chair. "Don't you think about Noah? Doesn't he haunt you?"

Harper's fingernails pressed into the soft wood of the sash at the mention of Noah, and her heart spurred like a horse given its head. Bennett's face was cast in shades of gray, his expression camouflaged.

"Of course he does, but not in a bad way. I miss him like hell." Bennett sounded as solemn and serious as she'd ever heard him, which was saying something.

"How can you . . . and her . . ." Darren gestured toward the house.

"Trust me, I didn't plan it. You think Noah would have my balls?"

"Does she know what happened?"

Her head swam as the question birthed a million more. She dropped to her knees and closed her eyes.

"Not the details. And I'm not planning on telling her, either." Bennett's voice came from a mile away, almost indistinct. "It's colder than a witch's tit out here. How about we go inside?"

"You always did have a way with words, Griz."

The sound of the rocking chair shifting got her on her feet, even though her knees didn't feel strong enough to support her. She bolted up the stairs and into Sophie's room and leaned against the closed door. Footsteps creaked the wood floors, but otherwise the men didn't make a noise. They were trained to be stealthy and keep secrets.

She buried herself under the covers, shaking even though she didn't feel the cold. Princesses danced everywhere around the room. Their beauty and innocence and bravery would earn them a happily ever after. Real life was darker and messier. What happened when the princess wasn't brave or innocent enough for a happily ever after?

CHAPTER 16

Present Day

The morning was more awkward than she expected. She wanted to sit Bennett down — tie him up if necessary — and get him to spill his guts. He'd be immune to such tactics. Noah had told her about the training they'd received to combat common torture techniques.

Darren and Bennett headed to the shooting range, and Harper was relieved. She couldn't concentrate on her meeting for the coffee business with anger and frustration about Bennett's silence muddying the waters.

Harper paced before Madeline and Joyce arrived. They might not even have the skills to help her, but she needed these women to back her, not for money but for a confidence boost. The doorbell rang.

Allison bustled from the kitchen to answer it. Harper recognized Madeline, the pretty redhead who didn't have kids and complained about the scarcity of jobs, from the one meeting she had attended with Allison. The second woman was tall and dark haired and in her late forties. Although Harper hadn't met Joyce, they had chatted enough for their greeting not to be uncomfortable.

"It's great to actually see you guys." Harper shook both their hands.

Madeline was vivacious, her excitement bubbling up to flush her cheeks and pull her mouth into a smile. Joyce was more reserved and hung behind Madeline, yet not in a meek way. Her gaze was observant and sharp.

"Anyone want coffee?" Allison led them into the kitchen and small talk ruled until they were each sitting with a mug and a blueberry muffin.

Sitting directly across from Harper, Joyce folded her arms on the table and leaned forward. "How did yesterday go?"

"The space had potential. Lots of it." Nerves hit Harper like a freight train. She hadn't felt like this since her first date with Noah. She fumbled a blue folder with printed spreadsheets into the middle of the table. She detailed the floor plan, but when she rattled off the lease details Joyce sat back and folded her arms over her chest.

"It sounds perfect, except for the price. He's asking too much for the square footage." Joyce's voice was no-nonsense and practical.

"That's what I thought, too. Especially up against comparable properties in the area." Harper handed over the research Bennett had put together. Joyce took the paper, her eyes darting over the page her only movement.

Finally, she looked up. Her smile shoved her somberness to the side, not quite gone but nudged out by enthusiasm. "I love bargaining. My husband says I can talk the devil down on buying a soul." Uncertainty stole across her face. "But I haven't done anything like this in a long time, so you'll probably want to handle it yourself."

Joyce was obviously suffering from her own crisis in confidence. Considering Harper had been dealing with the same, she empathized and reached across the table to give Joyce's hand a quick squeeze. Allison nodded once at Harper. It was like her friend was giving her a shove out of her comfort zone.

Harper took a deep breath and laid her hands flat on the table. "I can't do all of this myself. Not only am I not in Fayetteville full-time, but I don't have the skills. I need help. I need *your* help. Joyce, I break out in hives at the thought of haggling over a lease. I would love for you to see what you can do to get him down. And if he's not reasonable, then we walk and find somewhere else."

Joyce straightened in her seat and nodded. Her expression could only be described as determined. "I'll get him down."

Harper felt like giving her a high five but restrained herself. This was a business meeting after all. She couldn't stop a smile from breaking out, though. "Once we nail down the space, we'll have to see about a design and signage. We're all agreed on Home Front Coffee, right?"

"It's perfect," Madeline said. "I'll research sign makers and get quotes."

"Great." Harper fiddled with the sheaf of papers left. She had planned to wait to bring up Phase Two of the business plan, but her confidence in Joyce and Madeline had her pulling it out. "I want to get your thoughts on expanding into roasting and packaging our own coffee."

Madeline's eyes grew big and she sat forward. "Yes. I was thinking the same, but I wasn't sure how much money we had to invest. My master's dissertation in college was about sourcing cocoa beans for dark chocolate. I came across several coffee growers. Using sustainable growers would be an excellent marketing tool."

"It's not going to be cheap." Harper slid the spreadsheet over to Joyce and Madeline.

Joyce whistled. "Expensive equipment."

"That number is for a new roaster. I'm hoping to find used equipment at auction."

"I can handle the procurement of the beans." Madeline leaned over Joyce's shoulder to see the spreadsheet. "I'll start putting out feelers this week."

"Keep me in the loop about auctions. I can meet you. It's easier to have two sets of eyes and someone to keep you from overbidding," Joyce said.

The tangible benefits that the business could offer these women were apparent. If it succeeded. "That would be great. Fabulous. One thing we haven't talked about yet is compensation. Right now, I have all the monies earmarked for investment in start-up."

"I'm going slowly insane here," Madeline said. "You'd be doing me a favor by giving me a project."

Harper tapped her pen on the table and blew out a sigh. "It doesn't seem right."

Allison topped off everyone's coffee mugs. "You could give them a cut of the café's first-year profit on top of a salary once you opened."

"That's a thought." As her mind circled the possibilities, she asked, "How would that sort of arrangement work for you two? That way, if you decide a week from now the time and effort aren't worth the trouble, you can drop it with no hard feelings. But if you stick it out, and we're successful, then you'd own a percentage of the business."

Joyce and Madeline exchanged a glance and nodded in unison.

"I feel like this idea has the room to grow into something bigger and more meaningful. What about giving away a portion of our proceeds?" Madeline asked.

"To a charity, you mean?" Even as Harper voiced the question, her mind was already in full agreement. "Wounded Warriors, maybe?"

"What a great idea." Allison sat forward. "Not to be crass, but that would make for some killer advertising. Especially around here."

"Should we vote? I'm a yes." Harper looked at each woman in turn, and everyone else murmured their assent.

"I'm excited to get started," Joyce said. "I'll admit when Allison mentioned this, and we started texting, I never thought it would become a reality. But now not only can I see our café, but cafés all around the country serving the military and civilians alike and giving back."

"To be honest, getting this one café up and running feels as daunting as climbing Mount Everest." Harper slumped back in her chair.

"We'll take it one piece at a time. And don't be afraid to delegate." Madeline was the picture of confidence. Harper wanted to borrow some.

They reviewed their immediate-action items. Madeline would look into sourcing the beans and locating a roasting company that took on contract work at a reasonable price until they could purchase their own roaster. Joyce would pursue negotiations over the location. If she couldn't talk the man down on the space Harper and Bennett looked at the day before, she would find suitable places in their price range and send Harper the specifics. And finally, Allison volunteered to handle the charity portion of the plan.

Harper waved the two women off from the front porch. Madeline possessed a bouncy optimism Harper lacked. She was a natural people person who would be perfect spearheading the supply chain. And Joyce was a hard-nosed negotiator who would do well dealing with vendors. The weight of responsibility and the suffocating feeling of being overwhelmed had lessened. She wasn't alone.

She rejoined Allison in the kitchen, sitting across from her and sipping at her lukewarm coffee. "Madeline and Joyce are fabulous."

"I know." Allison's laughter faded into pensiveness. "Joyce has been depressed since her nest emptied last fall. She stopped coming to our meetings. Today was the first time I've seen her smile in months."

"I don't want to let them down." Harper's worst fears bubbled up.

"You haven't been happy in Nags Head for a couple of years now. Your talents are wasted keeping books for other businesses. What's the worst that could happen?"

"I lose all the money that was going to go toward Ben's college." Was she being foolish? Harper rubbed her hands over her face and through her hair, her mom's accusations reeling through her mind. She'd been safe and content. But not happy. Not for a long time.

"Except you were going to give the money back to Bennett, anyway."

"True."

"If the café fails, then you keep on living

with your mom and working. But if it suc-ceeds, you'll be giving these women some-thing to get up for in the morning. Some-thing that's theirs and not their husband's or the military's. And you might make enough to pay for Ben's college along the way."

Allison was a wise mama bear to all the women who crossed her path. Harper put aside her own worries — they could wait — and concentrated on Allison. Someone needed to mama bear her. "Are you sure you want to take on a chunk of responsibil-ity with everything going on?"

"I need this, too, Harper." Allison kept her gaze on the coffee in her mug.

"Do you think Bennett has done any good for Darren?" Harper asked softly.

"He got out of bed this morning to go shooting with him. That's an improvement."

Harper tiptoed around the minefield. "Do you worry about Darren doing some-thing . . . rash?"

"I worry about Darren every second of the day." Her voice fell to a whisper.

The word "suicide" reverberated around them even though it remained unsaid. "If you're that concerned, you've got to force him in some kind of program."

"How? Put him on a psychiatric hold at

the hospital? He'd never forgive me. Anyway, most of the time I don't worry he'll actually hurt himself."

"But sometimes you do."

"At night when I can't sleep, my mind goes round and round, imagining the worst."

Harper had experienced a similar spiral of anxiety after word had reached her of Noah's death. It had robbed her of sleep, happiness, and nearly her sanity.

"Can you talk him into going out for a weekend with Bennett?"

"I'm going to try, but it's like he doesn't have the energy to keep himself together that long. After you and Bennett leave, he'll crawl into bed and not come out until morning when he has to show up at work."

"How can his commanding officer not see what's going on?"

"Maybe he does. Or maybe Darren has learned to hide it at work." Her voice choked off. "I'm terrified he'll be handed another deployment. What would happen?"

Nothing good, that was for certain. "If that happens, you'll have to talk to someone."

"It might ruin his career."

Harper didn't know how much sympathy would be afforded Darren. Things were changing, but the SEALs were known for being the baddest of the badasses. Either weakness was trained out of them or they quit.

"The alternative is not an option." Harper wished she had something more useful to give Allison besides advice and platitudes.

The front door opened and chesty, male laughter drifted into the kitchen. Allison's gasp and fleeting smile spoke of hope.

Bennett's shadow filled the doorway before he appeared, tall and broad and more attractive than he had any right to be. Harper's complicated feelings toward him defied easy labels and refused to be compartmentalized. What was clear from her eavesdropping the night before was the Noah-sized gash in her heart refused to let her move forward until it was healed. She suspected the truth would be a good start.

Darren leaned down to kiss Allison's cheek, and she groped for his hand. This time, he didn't pull away from her touch but pulled up a chair and draped his arm over the back of hers. She tilted toward him, her attention fixed on his face. He appeared almost carefree and his mood highlighted the stark difference in him from the night before.

"Did you boys hit the bull's-eye every

time?" Harper asked lightly.

Bennett poured himself a mug of coffee and took the empty chair. His knee bumped hers. "Darren schooled me. I'm rusty."

"Griz was the best shot on the team. Beating him has been my life's ambition." Darren's grin cast Harper back to all the cookouts and dinners she and Noah had shared with him and Allison. Some of Allison's hope infected Harper.

"If you were that good, you should start including firearm training in your survival packages." Harper slid her gaze to Bennett.

"Nah. Survival pits man against nature and a gun unbalances the equation." He took a sip of coffee, the pause lengthening and gathering weight. "Anyway, I got my fill of shooting things in the service."

Bennett's words were like poison-tipped arrows. Harper fought the urge to draw him closer. Secrets hid behind the admission, too. Secrets that he held close and refused to share.

Allison and Darren seemed immune to the change in mood. Or maybe Harper had become finely attuned to Bennett.

The kids wandered into the kitchen in a video game–induced hunger. Sophie climbed into Darren's lap, and he tweaked her nose, inducing giggles. As Allison put sandwiches together for the kids and Darren and Bennett caught up with military people she didn't know, Harper studied the kids.

Libby watched her father out of the corner of her eye, a half smile containing a hint of happiness wrapped in suspicion. Ryan roamed the periphery like a stray dog desperate for a pet but wary after getting kicked too many times. Sophie played with her father's hand. The difference in size and his gentleness settled a hard knot in Harper's chest. Darren was a good man going through hell, but at least he had made it home alive.

Sometimes Noah's memory only wisped on the edges of her day-to-day life, too ephemeral to perceive. But sometimes, usually unexpectedly, his memory punched so hard she lost her breath. The voices around her crescendoed in a buzz of white noise. No one seemed to notice her disquiet.

Except someone did notice.

Bennett's hand covered hers under the table, linking their fingers. She should shake him off. Instead, she borrowed on his strength and recovered her composure piece by piece. Relying on a man who might not stick around was dangerous and foolhardy, yet she found herself tightening her grip on him.

She ignored the question in his eyes and pushed up from the table, disentangling them. "We need to get on the road. Ben will be anxious."

They packed up their overnight bags and loaded into Bennett's truck. After giving hugs all around, they set off toward Nags Head. The feeling they were leaving Allison and Darren in a better state than when they'd arrived helped quiet her worries.

Others took their place. Worries about Bennett and the past and future.

Bennett glanced over at Harper on the passenger side of his truck. A discordant note struck between them. He'd been disappointed to find his bed empty the night before. Not ideal circumstances, but if Darren's middle-of-the-night rambling hadn't interrupted them, he was pretty sure his conscience wouldn't have put up a fight.

The way her nails had scratched his back and she had arched into his hands added lighter fluid to the simmering attraction between them. But she was skittish and unsure and he totally understood why. Fate had dealt a cruel hand.

The morning had cast their combined

desperation and need in a different light. She had been polite, but the distance between them had widened and a hollow loneliness burrowed in his chest. He was a kid again, reaching for his kite, but the wind snatched it away as his fingers touched the string.

"There's an auction in a couple of weekends. Do you want to hit it together?" he asked.

"I don't know." Her voice was vague.

"Let me know, because I'll need to check my bookings and free up time." No response. He tightened his grip on the steering wheel. "How did the meeting go this morning?"

"Fine." Her one-word answer was clipped and didn't invite more questions. A dozen awkward miles passed before she broke the silence. "Did you and Darren have a good talk last night?"

"I wouldn't call it 'good.' Progress maybe. He's having trouble sleeping. Reliving everything that happened. Not unusual, but he's not dealing with it well."

"Obviously." The heat in her voice was directed at him.

"What's got your feathers ruffled?" His own frustration, sexual and otherwise, rose to meet hers.

"My feathers are not ruffled."

He gave a snort and racked his brain. "Are you still mad about the spreadsheet I put together on cost comparisons?"

"No." She shook her head and looked out the passenger window. He wanted to force her to look at him, talk to him, but he didn't. "I'm not mad. Not really."

"What would you call it then?"

"Disturbed? I wonder at the kinds of things you experienced when you were deployed."

"Don't waste your time wondering. Look around and be thankful you live in a beautiful place with a son and mother that love you. Don't you get it? Men like me deal with the ugliness in the world so you don't have to."

"Noah used to say the same thing."

Miles passed in a silence he didn't know how to breach. Navigating the delicate machinations of a relationship wasn't his strong point. His internal guffaw was tinged in bitterness. He wasn't built for emotional complications and difficulties. He'd learned as a boy to pack weak shit away and never let it see the light of day.

How could he and Harper develop anything that resembled a healthy relationship with the history between them — with Noah between them? He couldn't see a way forward.

"I was at the window last night." Her soft words took him a second to process. "I need to know, Bennett."

Anger and guilt exploded like twin bombs in his chest and licked through his body. She had no right to eavesdrop. No wonder she'd retreated and acted like he'd contracted the plague.

"Not going to happen."

"I have a right to know." She turned to him, her mouth and chin set.

Had she always been like this? Her emails had never hinted at an intractable streak. Yet he liked her more for it. It was the difference between seeing a flat work of art in a book and the real thing in a museum.

"You got a report."

"I always sensed there was more and last night confirmed my suspicions. What happened and what did you promise Noah?"

"I can't." The words croaked out.

"You mean 'won't.' "

"I won't drag myself — and you — through reliving it. What will it change? Nothing. Noah will still be dead." Except he foresaw the subject of his nightmare as soon as he closed his eyes that night. He would be reliving it — with grisly embellishments — whether he wanted to or not.

She shook her head and scooted away from him. For the remainder of the drive to Nags Head, neither of them spoke. Before he had the truck notched into park at the curb, she threw open the door, unable to escape fast enough. She disappeared through the front door, leaving it ajar. For him to follow?

An ending stained the moment like a book closing. He wasn't sure if it even qualified as a breakup considering they weren't technically together. Still, a melancholy he hadn't felt in years had him swallowing past a lump. He would miss her.

He sat in the still-running truck and debated the merits of peeling rubber down the road. But Jack London was inside and no way would he leave his dog behind. He was all Bennett had left.

Ben and Jack burst through the door, the boy trying but failing to keep up with the dog. Bennett turned the truck off and slipped out. Jack jumped on Bennett and knocked him back a step, his paws on Bennett's shoulders, his tongue rasping the side of his face.

Normally, he would discipline Jack, but the welcome was so warm and unrestrained, Bennett rubbed Jack's flanks and leaned in to give him a hug. His best friend was a dog. Which probably qualified him as a pathetic loser.

"Come on, Big Ben, you said you'd play ball with me."

Oh shit. In the maelstrom in the truck, the promise had slipped his mind. Ben had his hand and was tugging him. He could have protested and come up with an excuse — albeit a lame one — but he allowed himself to be led around the side of the house to a gate in the fence.

Although tossing a ball with Ben was a small thing, it offered atonement nonetheless. Bennett had convinced himself the money he'd given Harper and Ben fulfilled his promise to Noah, but the money had been the coward's way out.

Jack followed them and found leaves and birds and squirrels to chase while Ben ran inside and returned with a worn adult-sized football. His first throw to Bennett wobbled and fell six feet short.

Bennett scooped it up on his walk to Ben. "This ball's too big for your hand."

"It was my dad's."

A rush went through his head and made him feel light-headed and weak. Maybe he *had* contracted the plague. He took a deep breath and turned the ball in his hands.

Noah's grip was visible in the wear of the leather and the fading across the laces where his fingers would have lain. Along the seam, his name was etched in permanent ink. *Noah Wilcox.* More permanent than his body.

Bennett tried to clear the emotion out of his throat, but when he spoke, his voice was rough with it. "To get the perfect spiral, you have to grip the laces, here toward the end." He wrapped Ben's small fingers in the shadowy memory of his father's hand.

Bennett took six paces back. "Move your arm forward and back at the elbow and think about the end you aren't holding spinning through the air. Go on, try."

The ball sailed in a near-perfect spiral. "I did it." Ben's voice was full of wonder.

Bennett launched a soft throw back at him. "Do it again. Remember where to put your hand?"

Ben's face was a study in concentration as he fixed his grip over the laces. Another decent throw followed. Bennet took a step back with each throw until a good fifteen feet separated them.

"My arm's tired." Ben grinned. "I'm getting pretty good, huh?"

"You sure are. Just like your daddy."

Ben tucked the ball under his arm and walked toward the stairs leading up to the back-porch sliding door. He stopped with his foot on the bottom step. "Aren't you coming? I saved some Oreos and milk for you."

A shadow drew his eye to the sliding door. It was Harper behind the glass watching them. She didn't step out to invite him in and his pride grated.

"Not this time. I have to go."

"Why?" Ben's face fell, his disappointment writ large on his face and in his body language. Noah had been easy to read like that. Harper was more guarded and Bennett wondered if it was a learned defense or natural.

"Because . . ." Jesus, what could he say? Certainly not the truth. "I have to work."

Ben walked over and Bennett dropped to a squat to put them at eye level. "Will you come back and play sometime?" Ben asked.

Bennett's mouth was inexplicably dry. "I can't promise anything."

Ben's nod was so serious and adult-like, Bennett wanted to promise him anything to return his childlike joy. But he couldn't. Resiliency was the hallmark of a five-year-old, right? He would be happy again by bedtime.

Ben leaned in and gave Bennett a hug with one arm, the ball tucked under the other.

Bennett's arms came up automatically and wrapped around the boy's slight body, ball and all.

He didn't want to drive away and never see Ben again. Noah had named his son after Bennett, and whether it was official or not, Bennett was his godfather. Now, when he was ready to accept the role, Harper didn't want him around.

Bennett patted his slight, bony shoulder and pulled away. Ben ruffled Jack's ruff and ran to the steps, a bounce already back. He would be fine without Bennett. And so would Harper. In fact, she'd be better off without him. He'd given her something easy — money. What she demanded was impossible. Their history intersected painfully through Noah and there was no getting over those fault lines.

He stuffed his hands into his pockets and walked away. At the gate, he stopped. Jack wasn't at his heels or leading the way. The dog sat at the base of the stairs and stared where Ben had disappeared.

Bennett whistled. Jack sat up taller and let out a howl, then turned and trotted toward Bennett. He rubbed the dog's head and ears and whispered, "I know, buddy. I'll miss them, too."

Chapter 17

Present Day

Spring was coming to the Outer Banks. Brave buttercups broke ground first, and like the flowers, Harper soaked up the warm sun on the back porch. Her concentration was shattered by real troubles, and she gave up pretending to read, closing her eyes. The sun danced behind her eyelids in a multicolored show.

Bennett hadn't contacted her since their return from Fort Bragg. Things had been good between them. Why had she ruined it by bringing up Noah's death and the mysterious promise? Why couldn't she leave it alone? It had no bearing on the future. Except somehow it did.

If the burden was hers alone to bear, then perhaps happiness could coexist with the questions. But Bennett carried the burden as well. They would never work unless they could lay down their burdens together.

Even without Bennett's support, her plans for the café moved forward at a rapid clip. Joyce had accompanied her to a restaurant equipment auction and Harper tried not to dwell on the fact that the auction represented someone else's failed dreams.

The sliding glass door from the kitchen swished open and the deck planks creaked. Harper squinted. Haloed by bright sunlight, her mother took a chair and tilted her face toward the sky like one of the buttercups.

"How's Bennett?" Although her mom's voice was casual, Harper sensed the worry behind the question.

Harper hadn't told her about their argument. Even thinking about it upset her. She missed him in ways she never thought possible. "I don't know."

"What happened?" Patience was in the question.

Maybe she'd sleep better if she excised the poison. "Bennett was there when Noah was killed."

"Stands to reason since they were on the same SEAL team."

Harper closed her eyes and followed the dancing light. "I mean he was with Noah when he died. When we were at Allison's, I overheard him and Darren talking. He's not telling me something. Something important.

Not to mention, he accidently let drop a promise he made to Noah. One that involved me and maybe Ben too. I pushed the issue on the way home from Fort Bragg."

"Wouldn't budge?"

Harper shook her head. "He got mad. Basically told me not to worry my pretty little head over it. I don't see how we can move on together with Noah between us. Got any sage advice?"

Her mom was silent for so long, Harper propped herself up. The expression on her mother's face was part pity and part exasperation.

"Yeah. Cut him a break. How about you back off forcing him to talk to you and wait until he's ready. I can only imagine Noah's death was extremely traumatic and dating his widow must leave him confused and conflicted."

Harper flopped to her back. Her mom had never been one to sugarcoat her opinions or throw her only daughter 100 percent support when it was undeserving. When she was a teenager, defensive anger would flare at her mom's tough talk. Time and experience had proved that more often than not, she was right. Even if Harper didn't want to admit it.

Tears clogged her throat and scratched at

her eyes. She hadn't cried this much since seeing the navy chaplain at her front door.

"Have you talked to him?" Her mom's tone had softened.

"Not since we fought."

"That's where I would start."

Her thinking needed to be readjusted. She had assumed the moral high ground — all she wanted was the truth after all — and put Bennett squarely in the wrong. Did she have it backward? Maybe they straddled right and wrong. Or perhaps right and wrong didn't exist, only the complications of living.

She stood up so fast she saw sunbursts. Urgency thrummed now the fog had cleared. "I hate to ask, but could you pick Ben up from preschool so I can work things out with Bennett? If he doesn't slam the door in my face, that is."

"Ben and I will be fine. You go on."

Harper dropped a quick kiss on her mom's cheek and took off at a run to change into jeans and a T-shirt. Determined to set things right, she was on the road in ten minutes. Unfortunately, she had an hour and a half to second-guess herself, and by the time she pulled up to the survival school she was a tangled mass of insecurity and indecision.

It was his day off, but two SUVs were

parked next to his truck. Was he with customers or friends or had he moved on with another woman? She couldn't barge in and splatter her heart all over the place. After sitting in her car like a stalker for twenty minutes with no sign anyone was leaving anytime soon, a new issue presented itself.

She needed to pee. *Dammit.* It was either leave and find a gas station, use the woods, or pull up her big-girl panties and face Bennett.

Her boots crunched gravel on her walk to the door. The sound loud in her ears. The nerves ricocheting around her body only made her need to pee worse. Like last time, the *Closed* sign was displayed, but the door was unlocked.

She opened the door slowly. The chime echoed. She braced herself, but only Jack London was there to greet her. She rubbed him behind the ears with both hands and he sat, narrowing his eyes in enjoyment. If only his master were as easily won over.

A voice carried from the back, masculine but indistinct. She weaved her way around racks and displays on the shop floor to the slightly ajar storeroom door. The closer she got, the louder the voices grew. All male and deep and interspersed with laughter. Relief he wasn't with a woman left her knees trembling.

Jack pushed the door farther open with his head and trotted inside. She peeked in. Three men stood with their backs to the door. Jack worked his way next to Bennett, who was in the middle, two inches taller than either man at his side. She would put money on the fact that all three were current or former military.

The man on Bennett's left glanced over his shoulder. His gaze crossed hers and held, his confusion turning to surprise. Alex Ramirez. Another member of Bennett and Noah's SEAL team. He had been to their house for cookouts and to watch football with Noah. Without taking his eyes off her, he turned and elbowed Bennett.

There was nowhere to hide. She forced herself forward, hoping her mouth was in something resembling a smile.

"Harper Wilcox?" There was enough of a question in Alex's voice to indicate he wasn't sure he believed his eyes.

"Alex. It's been years. How are you?" She shook his hand, keeping her eyes averted from Bennett for now. Alex was good-looking, with crinkly laugh lines around his eyes, but experience and years had added a wariness she'd never noticed.

"I'm good. How are you? I meant to stop by and offer my condolences after Noah, but by the time I got home, you had moved." He ran a hand over his jaw and broke eye contact. "Anyway, I'm real sorry. Peaches was a good SEAL and an even better man."

"Noah loved you guys and loved being a SEAL." Offering absolution, she touched his arm lightly and tilted her head to catch his eyes. His misplaced guilt faded. "What are you doing now? Are you out?"

"I'm a SEAL instructor." He chuffed a dry laugh. "We hated their guts when we went through training, and now I'm one of them. It's crazy."

"You love yelling at those kids; don't lie." The third man, the one she didn't recognize, held out a hand. "I'm Tag Barnes. I came up a couple of years after these yahoos and served on SEAL Team Three. I'm out now." Although he smiled, a strain showed in the set of his shoulders and around his eyes.

Bennett exuded a similar tension as if he was on defense against an enemy. Finally, she forced herself to look him in the eye. Noah had worn his emotions on the outside. His happiness or anger or sadness had been tangible. Bennett hid everything away like a bear in his cave.

Standing in the midst of the three men and with Bennett staring at her with a seriousness that didn't portend well, she had a sense of what Goldilocks had felt like after she had been caught.

In the awkward silence, she said, "I need to use the restroom, if you'll excuse me. I drove up from Nags Head."

"Out by the changing rooms." He pointed back out the door, and she took a step backward. She didn't sense any welcome or softening toward her in his voice.

She escaped to the small bathroom. It was clean and well stocked. After taking care of business, she stared at herself while she washed her hands. What now? He didn't want her here. Did she give up and retreat with her tail between her legs?

Her heart felt like it could use a box of Band-Aids and some Super Glue, but if she left without settling things one way or another it would need stitches.

By the time she emerged, the three men had moved to the shop floor and Bennett was talking about his services, making notes on a brochure. She pretended to browse.

"Some of the men will be amputees like me." Tag pulled up his pant leg and revealed a matte gray metal leg.

"No problem. The terrain is flat, and there

are bridges across any waterways. The hard part is setting up a shelter and getting food and water. It'll be a challenge, but doable."

"I've got five committed." Alex waved the brochure around. "I have a feeling several more will want in once I tell them about this place and you and show them this. You sure this isn't too much trouble?"

"Dude, it's the least I can do. I can line up another guide to come. We can handle up to ten. That number makes hunting more difficult, though. Too hard to keep everyone quiet. If you'd rather split this into two weekends with smaller groups, I'd be game for that."

"Let me talk to the boys, and I'll let you know." Tag tapped the brochure on his thigh.

"My meeting this afternoon should wrap up by happy hour. You want to hit the bars tonight?" Alex asked.

Her breath stalled and she couldn't stop herself from looking over.

"No thanks. Not my scene anymore." Bennett's excuse may have been only for her benefit, but she was grateful nonetheless.

"Dinner tomorrow?"

"I'll shoot you a text and let you know."

A round of hand shaking and shoulder

bumping followed. Both men offered good-byes to her as well. Bennett walked them to their SUVs, and when he returned he crossed his arms over his chest. The door drifted shut, the chime signaling the start of round one.

"Looks like business is good?"

"I'm donating a trip, maybe two, to Wounded Warriors."

"That's amazing."

"What you're doing with the coffee business and for those women . . . You inspired me. I've stayed holed up here all alone for too long." Although his face was still cast in serious tones, his voice had warmed. Between that and his words, she was encouraged enough to come within an arm's length of him.

"I'm sorry." The words came easier than she thought possible. "I shouldn't have pressed you about Noah. I can't help but want to know what happened, but my curiosity doesn't trump whatever burdens you still carry from that day."

"You'll never ask me what happened again?" The incredulity in his voice was plain.

She shuffled so close she had to tilt her head back to maintain eye contact. "Honestly, I think it would do you good to talk about it, but I won't insist. If you tell me no, I'll respect it."

"I appreciate that." He dropped his arms but didn't touch her. Still, it was like lowering the drawbridge over an alligator-infested moat, and she pressed her advantage.

"I don't want the past to destroy whatever we're building in the here and now. I've been sick with missing you." She laid a tentative hand on his arm.

He sighed away the last of his defenses, wrapped an arm around her waist, and pulled her into his body. She fisted her hands in his shirt and held him close, her nose buried in the collar of his black T-shirt.

"I've missed you, too. So damn much." His voice was muffled in her hair. "I thought I could slip back into my old life."

"You couldn't?" She fished for a bolster to her confidence.

"What I thought was peace was loneliness. It sucked."

She tightened her hold on him. "It totally did."

His beard rubbed against her temple. "Did you go to the auction?"

"Yep. I took Joyce. She's a firecracker. We did well, but I nearly had a heart attack when it came time to pay. That's more than I've spent in one go ever."

"I remember the feeling. Buying stock to fill this place up was daunting."

Everything about him felt right. His size, his strength, the way he held her with a barely disguised fierceness that stoked an answering burn in her. Noah had been her inverse. His light had counteracted her dark.

She and Bennett were alike in ways that made her nervous. He understood her fears because he battled them, too. She had admired Noah's optimism, but she craved Bennett's intensity.

"Do you want to come upstairs?" His chest rumbled. A storm was coming and she had two choices, revel in thunder and lightning and chaos or run back to her calm existence.

It was a no-brainer. She slid her hand into his hair and leaned back. His eyes were shadowed and tension drew his lips thin. The moment was pivotal.

"I'd love to."

The brackets around his mouth smoothed, although the ferocity of emotion in his eyes only deepened. His grip on her tightened and then eased. "Let's go then."

He locked the front door and led them to the back of the store to the stairs. Now that she was out of his arms, a shiver ran through her. Not fear of the future or regret of the past, but an excitement she hadn't experienced for too long.

He gestured to the stairs and she preceded him, his hand warm on her lower back. At the top, she opened the door and stepped into a warm loft-style space. A TV was mounted on one wall with an L-shaped comfy-looking couch in front. Neatly stacked magazines were on a side table. A pair of running shoes jumbled against each other in front of the couch as if he'd toed them off and collapsed. Stainless-steel appliances reflected the light coming in the windows. Through an open door to the side of the kitchen, she could see a sink and shower.

Browns and greens dominated the color scheme. Log walls and beams along the ceiling gave the impression of being in the woods except with all the comforts of the indoors. A king-size bed with rumpled covers took up the back wall. Nerves sprouted in her stomach and clogged her throat.

She whirled around and attempted a smile, even though her lips were dry and stiff. "It's very you."

"How so?"

She swallowed. "Masculine" and "sturdy" were the first words that popped into her head, but those were too telling, and he already had the home field advantage. "Woodsy and natural," she finally said.

"Like an air freshener?"

A laugh sputtered out of her. "Only the best sort. The little pine trees you hang from your rearview mirror."

His half smile was easy and charming. "How about a drink? It's five o'clock somewhere, right?"

"Sure. Why not."

He rubbed his hands together and quickstepped to the kitchen. He was nervous, too. The realization washed over her, and although it didn't eliminate her nerves, the knowledge she wasn't the only one battling worried anticipation about the next step helped her function like an adult.

"I don't have martini supplies, I'm afraid. But I have an excellent red wine." He held up a bottle.

"Perfect. My mom is the martini fanatic. I think she read a how-to book with steps on becoming the most eccentric retiree. Martinis and embarrassing T-shirts were top on the list." She joined him in the kitchen and leaned a hip against the counter as he opened the wine.

Watching his hands manipulate the corkscrew bordered on foreplay. Soon those big, capable hands would be on her doing things she'd dreamed about. He shot her a look, his eyebrows raised, and as if he could read her mind, heat raced through her. Luckily, he didn't call her on it but poured them two glasses.

She sipped the wine more out of something to do than any real desire. He led the way to the couch, sprawled in the corner, and watched her over the rim of his glass. She took her time, running her fingers along the back of the couch and making a more thorough examination.

The top magazine focused on outdoor sports; the one underneath was *National Geographic.* Picking a seat seemed a first test. She sat next to him but not close enough to touch.

"You're nervous?" Amusement edged his voice and fired her ire.

"And you're not? We're going to —" She gestured toward the bed. "It's been a while and what if I . . ." The look on his face stopped her rambling. Had she misread the situation? "Oh my god, if you don't want to have sex then — I just assumed that —"

"Slow down, darlin'." He grabbed her wrist when she tried to stand and pulled her back down. She landed between his legs, and her back settled against his front. "Yes, I want to have sex."

He plucked the wineglass from her stiff fingers and set it next to his on a side table. She wanted to relax and at least give the appearance of worldliness, but the tension in her body coiled even tighter, as she waited for him to make his move.

His arm snaked around her middle and locked her tighter against his body, and his hand covered her fist. The gentle, non-aggressive brush of his fingers unlocked the tight hold and her hand unfurled and linked with his.

"I've never known a woman to speak as bluntly as you do." His breath tickled the hairs at her nape and sent tingles streaking down her body. Her neck went lax and she rested her head on his shoulder, his beard bristly against her cheek.

"Take it or leave it, big guy."

"Oh, I'm definitely keeping you. I was never good at the games women play. That's one reason I preferred to keep things casual and simple. I took what I needed and left before anything got serious and someone got hurt."

She would stake her life on the fact that lots of someones had probably gotten hurt. Just not Bennett. How could those women not want more?

"I don't do casual. Noah was my first. And

only." It was both a fact and a warning and she hoped he understood. Her throat tightened, and her next words came out on a whisper. "Until you."

His arm flexed and he breathed her name. In his voice was a command she was happy to follow. Twisting in his arms, she found his lips in a kiss that weaved them together as surely and purely as the strongest Kevlar. All of her doubts fell away, fragile and unimpressive against long-pent-up desire.

In his bed, she discovered she'd been parched for a man's touch and surrendered to the moment. To the man. To her own need. Time was measured by the passing of light into darkness, yet she didn't feel any desire to face reality.

Tucked against him like they were spoons, she hardly needed the blanket to keep her warm. He played with her hair, the sweetness of the gesture turning her insides to mush.

"Are you happy?" he asked.

She didn't answer immediately, taking a quick stock of the massive changes in her life over the last months. Her mother had shoved her out of the nest, and she had found her wings. It wasn't just Bennett; it was the business, too. Her life was fuller and more exciting than she'd imagined it could be after Noah had died.

"I'm very happy. What about you?" She turned so she could see his face.

A flash of sadness crossed his face. "I'm happier than I deserve to be."

This time she held the questions that threatened to pierce the cocoon they'd cobbled together. The scars on his leg and hip had their own story to tell. It might take a week or a year or a decade, but she would wait for him to trust her with his secrets. What was growing between them was worth that.

She wrapped her hand around his neck and pulled him in for a fierce kiss.

"Can you spend the night?" He rolled on top of her.

She shouldn't. Would Ben miss her in the morning? Her body arched against his answering for her. Time enough for regrets and guilt later.

"Yes, I'll stay."

CHAPTER 18

Present Day

As the sky streaked with dawn light, they made love again. The rough impatience of the night before was only slightly muted by sleep. Afterward, she pulled the sheet up, her heart and breathing decelerating.

The passion between them was raw and primal and messy. Nothing like what her experience had prepared her for. She and Noah had fumbled their way through their first time, and when they'd made love shades of that innocence remained.

Bennett wasn't acquainted with innocence. He probably hadn't been for a long while. Harper was older now, too, and the pain of living left only memories of who she'd been. In old pictures she recognized herself but couldn't recall what that girl had thought and felt.

Bennett was facedown on the bed, his dark hair stark against the white pillow. She reached out and skimmed her hand down his back. He arched with her touch like an animal getting petted and turned, unconcerned with his nakedness.

Harper couldn't keep her gaze from wandering south. *Damn.* The scars on his body only made him more interesting, not less attractive. He would be the perfect nude model for her mom's painting class. Not that she was going to make the suggestion, because he was hers and hers alone. For now.

She scooched into his side and took a bite at his neck followed by a soothing kiss. Over his natural scent was something more elemental. Sex. He smelled of sex and so did she. They'd marked each other.

She didn't regret spending the night, but the implications went far beyond mind-blowing sex. There was Ben to think about. She needed to leave and put some distance between her and temptation.

"I have to go. Ben . . ." Her voice was muffled by his superheated skin. The man operated a few degrees higher than her.

"I know. I'm thankful that I had you as long as I did." He tightened his hold on her before letting go.

She wasn't ready, but then would she ever be ready to leave him? Slipping away, she grabbed her clothes and streaked to the bathroom. He might be perfectly comfortable letting everything hang out with her, but she wasn't.

She cleaned up and dressed, and by the time she poked her head out he was up, in jeans and a flannel shirt, puttering in the kitchen. Their gazes met, but hers tripped away, awkwardness spreading like a stain that only got worse with scrubbing.

"All I've got is cereal and coffee." He gestured toward a box of bran flakes.

"A quick cup of coffee, please."

He poured her a mug. Her morning-after gawkiness didn't seem to infect him. He sat down with a bowl of cereal. "What're your plans for the day?"

"Head home and research coffee roasters." She joined him at the table and perched on the edge of the seat.

"You're not going to contract the roasting?" His eyebrows rose, but she didn't feel like he was questioning her decision; he was merely curious.

"If we need to, but we have the room and the smell alone would be a selling point. Madeline has a handle on bean procurement and is excited to learn to roast. Think about walking into your favorite bakery and smelling the bread and pastries cooking. You walk out with more than you intended every single time. It's part of the experience. I've come across a couple of used roasters at reasonable prices."

"What about the equipment you bought at auction?"

"Expected delivery is two weeks from Monday."

"Shop's closed that day if you need the muscle to receive and move things around." The look he cast her was testing.

She could do it on her own, but she'd missed his advice and steadiness. He calmed her tendency to panic over price or get overwhelmed at the enormity of the under-taking. "That'd be great. I'd love your help."

She put her mug in the sink and ran her hands down her jeans. "I'd better go."

He led the way down the stairs and through the shop, unlocking the front door and flipping the sign from *Closed* to *Open*. Birds having conversations filled the crisp morning air with song. The sun had risen over the line of trees, the bright light blind-ing.

He propped a shoulder against a column. Each step she took away from him was harder than the last. This leave-taking was like ripping a Band-Aid off an extremely hairy, sensitive body part.

She pivoted around. "How is this going to work?"

"You'll drive home, do your thing while I'm doing my thing up here, and I'll see you Sunday evening." Thankfully, he didn't play dumb.

"Okay, but —"

"Harper. Darlin'." He descended but stayed on the step above her, forcing her to tilt her head way back to see him. He circled his hand around her nape and massaged. Like his touch was magic — maybe it was — she relaxed and her worries dissipated like morning fog. "We'll manage."

"How?"

"Texting. Phone. We're not that far apart. It's all good for now."

"For now?" The temporary qualification shot a chill through her.

He laughed, but no amusement tracked to his eyes. "I don't know what comes next. I've never done this before."

She was the inexperienced one when it came to matters of the body, but he was the innocent one when it came to matters of the heart.

"You've never . . ." *been in love?* The words hung between them.

"You asked me once why I never came to the team cookouts and parties. The truth was I never fit in with the happy husbands and families. I told myself I felt sorry for them. Anchored to one woman with responsibilities that kept them up at nights when we were deployed. But the truth was I was envious. I've never had a woman look at me the way you are right now. You scare the hell out of me."

"Why?" A whisper was all she could manage with her heart in her throat.

"Because until now, I've always been able to walk away."

Until now. The words raced through her heart and veins like the "Hallelujah Chorus." She tingled all over and hoped she wasn't going to embarrass herself by needing medical attention. "You're not walking this time?"

"I tried. After that first day, I tried." His lips quirked. "You tracked me down."

"Oh." Unable to come up with anything more emotionally intelligent, she wrapped her arms around his waist and leaned into him, her ear pressed against his heart.

If it was possible, his heartbeat paced even faster than hers. He was as nervous and scared and unsure as she was. She wanted to laugh.

"I'm not walking, either." She spoke softly but knew he'd heard when his arms tightened reflexively.

Except she did have to walk away, in reality if not metaphorically. She had responsibilities. Welcome ones.

He skimmed his hands up her arms to cup her face and leaned in for a kiss. This one was sweet and held promises of days and nights and moments shared.

When he pulled away, she fluttered her eyes open, swaying on the step. She'd taken hold of his wrists at some point. Now she laid a kiss on one of his palms before turning and retreating to her car on unsteady legs.

She tried not to look back — this wasn't a permanent good-bye — but she watched him grow smaller in the rearview mirror as a tear slipped out. Even a temporary parting was like losing a vital internal organ. Maybe her heart.

The week passed in fits and starts. The days flew by as she worked every aspect of the burgeoning business, keeping in close contact with Joyce and Madeline and Allison. The nights made up for the quick days, the seconds ticking away like a clock whose battery was run down.

Lying in bed with the moonlight wavering ghostly shadows on the ceiling, she listened to the night sounds from the cracked window. The continuity from childhood offered a shot of peace to her restlessness. Although things were changing at warp speed, some things stayed the same, like the push and pull of the moon on the tides.

Sleep eluded her, and she pulled her phone closer, the screen blank.

RU up? She tapped in.

Only a few seconds passed.

Miss U.

It was an admission he wouldn't have been comfortable making even a week earlier. And probably still wasn't comfortable making face-to-face.

Miss U2.

I admire Bono as much as the next man, but . . .

She giggled. *U know what I meant. How's work?*

Taking an overnight group tomorrow. Three corporate types. Should be interesting.

I'm nervous about the delivery.

Why?

Success or failure crept closer. This was the first chance she'd taken in a long time. Since she'd gone off to college and later when she'd married Noah. Both had scared her.

Delivery makes it real. Scary. The point of

no return.

Your plan is solid. You have lots of support. A decent chance of making it.

Decent?!

I meant great.

Sure you did.

Bennett was realistic and honest — if not entirely forthcoming. If he thought she stood a decent chance, then maybe she should take that as a good sign.

I need my beauty sleep. Talk when I get back?

Harper smiled. *Is Jack London with you?*

Snoring next to me. Way hairier and not as sexy as you were in my bed.

Kiss him from me. A tiny electrical current powered her response. Sleep would be a long time coming.

I'd rather be kissing you.

Bennett wasn't a lighthearted flirter. If he said he'd rather be kissing her, then he meant it. When nothing else came through, she set her phone on the nightstand and pulled the covers up over her head.

Morning came with a swiftness that left Harper's eyes gritty and underscored by dark half circles. But even with her lack of sleep she was jittery. Coffee only made it worse. Getting Ben up and ready for preschool offered a brief distraction.

Every once in a while, Ben's sunny, funny nature would be interrupted by a pensive silence. He folded the place mat into a square, a frown on his face.

"What's up, buddy?" She cast him a look under her lashes as she fixed him a bowl of cereal. He didn't answer. She slid his cereal in front of him and took the chair at his side. "Are you sad or worried about something?"

"Are you and Big Ben going to get married?"

The question sent an organ-rattling shock through her. "No. I don't know." She forced herself to stop and take a breath. "How would you feel if we did get married?"

"Where would I live?"

"With me. Always with me, pumpkin."

"What about Yaya?"

The future was bright but indistinct, and she couldn't honestly assure him of anything. "Yaya will be around one way or another. I promise." She watched him drink the milk out of his bowl. "Do you not like Bennett?"

"He can do card tricks and stuff. Plus, he has a cool dog." Ben shrugged off his worry and hopped up to grab his backpack for school.

Back home after dropping him off, there

was nothing she could do except for wait and worry over things that were in motion and couldn't be changed.

Her phone buzzed midmorning. It was an unknown Fayetteville number. She tensed preparing herself for a problem with the lease or equipment or something bigger she couldn't even anticipate.

"Hello." She clutched her phone with both hands.

"Har-r-per." Allison's voice was wavery.

It was disconcerting how a tone could rocket her back to the moment she'd opened the door to the Navy chaplain saying her name. Some moments lived like an indelible ink stain in her memory, every nuance stored away forever. A splinter biting into her palm where she'd clutched the doorframe. The spring breeze on her face carrying the scent of blooming flowers. The face of the man who had stood on her front porch, the message he had yet to impart written in the lines of his face.

In Allison's whisper of her name, a shift occurred, although Harper couldn't map the seismic changes yet.

"What's happened?"

"It's Sophie."

Harper's stomach went into riot mode. She'd been expecting to hear Darren's name. "Is she okay?"

"No."

"How bad?"

Allison's silence was answer enough.

"Where are you?"

"The children's hospital."

"I'm on my way."

Allison disconnected and Harper stared at the blank screen, her body frozen as her mind whirled in the aftermath of an EF-5 emotional tornado. *Ben.* Harper controlled an urge to go check on him even though he was safe and sound.

Her mom's footfalls on the stairs accompanied her off-tune singing of a pop song. The mundane was comforting, and Harper only watched her mom pour coffee and wrap her hands around the mug, taking a deep sniff and smiling.

After her first sip, she glanced over, her smile turning into a tense, thin line. "What's wrong? Is it Bennett?"

Harper shook her head, not sure if she could sort out the words rampaging through her head. "Allison's youngest. Little Sophie's been hurt. I'm not sure what happened or how bad it is."

"Do you need to go to her?"

Harper nodded.

"Don't worry about Ben. I'll take care of him."

"I know." Harper's voice croaked and her mom swept her into a hug that smelled of coffee and her lotion. Harper dropped her forehead to her mom's shoulder and took a deep breath. For a second, she wished she could leap back in time to when things were simple and easy and her biggest worry was whether she'd play red rover or tag at recess.

"Are you okay to drive?" Her mom pulled away, the fantasy slipping away.

Her emotions realigned from inward to outward. What must Allison and Darren be going through right now? "I'll be fine. Promise. I might be there a couple of days depending . . ."

"Whatever you need to do for Allison."

Harper took the stairs two at a time and threw some clothes into an overnight bag.

"Call or text me as soon as you know what's going on." Her mom was waiting at the door with a to-go mug of coffee.

After another brief hug, Harper got on the road, cursing the red lights and traffic. The tourists were sparse but increasing as the weather warmed. She finally reached the highway and had a hard time keeping her car near the speed limit. Was the blank screen of her phone a good or bad sign?

Bennett would be out in the wilderness with his phone tucked away. At best, he might check it later that night. Even so, he couldn't leave a set of corporate clients in the Dismal Swamp to fend for themselves.

She willed Allison to call with an update. The longer the silence lasted, the worse the scenarios her imagination produced.

With still no word from Allison, Harper entered the hospital and was directed to the children's wing waiting room. She stepped off the elevator into a cheerily decorated hall. Brightly colored butterflies took flight on the wall and gauzy 3-D dragonfly models hung from the ceiling. In opposition to the pretty displays was the smell of antiseptic and sickness.

She followed arrows to the waiting room. Allison stood straight and still looking out a large window overlooking the parking lot while Darren sat crunched over, his head in his hands. A family whispering Spanish to one another took up another set of chairs. Worry permeated the room from all corners.

"Allison," Harper said softly, her voice breaking the solemn calm of the room like a rock thrown into a placid lake.

Allison tripped over the leg of a chair making her way to hug Harper. Except it was less a hug and more a surrender. Her weight fell across Harper's shoulders. She guided Allison toward a chair near to Darren, but Allison resisted, instead steering them back toward the window.

"I feel like the walls are closing in on me." Allison's breathing was shallow and fast and sweat popped on her forehead.

Darren hadn't moved to acknowledge Harper's presence, so she focused on Allison. Harper forced her to sit, grabbed the nearest magazine, and fanned her. The picture of a smiling, happy celebrity couple on the cover was tone deaf to the surroundings. Maybe someone would find comfort in the superficiality of their life, but if the couple had been standing in front of Harper she might be tempted to punch their perfect, fake smiles.

"How's Sophie?" Harper asked gently as if the words themselves were scalpels tearing flesh.

"In surgery."

"Can you tell me what happened?"

Allison's eyes darted toward Darren, but she didn't turn toward him to offer either comfort or commiseration. "Darren and I were fighting. It got . . . heated. Libby and Ryan had already left for the bus stop, but I was going to drive Sophie. I thought she was waiting for me in the den." She held a fist to her mouth.

"She went outside?"

Allison nodded and took a shuddery breath. "I'm not sure if she was planning to walk to the bus stop or if she was trying to get away from us. A motorcycle came around the corner."

Harper's heart galloped ahead. "She was hit?"

"The man — kid really, not more than nineteen — said she darted out in front of him."

"Broken bones?"

"Leg and wrist. She hit her head and hasn't woken up." The last emerged on a sob.

"What have the doctors said?"

"Swelling on the brain. If it doesn't go down, they'll have to . . . to drill into my baby's skull." Allison seemed to wilt at that point, her head dropping to her knees.

Harper rubbed her back and didn't press for more information. Darren didn't look up or offer support. The distance between Allison and Darren yawned deeper and broader than a few feet in a waiting room.

Once Allison had a tenuous hold on her emotions, Harper asked, "What about Libby and Ryan? Do you want me to get them?"

"They don't know. Could you meet them at the house after they get off the bus and bring them here? I can't leave in case —" Allison covered her mouth and looked outside. Unmarred by a single cloud, blue sky stretched to forever. It seemed blasphemous.

A doctor in a white coat and carrying a tablet turned the corner. Everyone in the waiting room stood. Darren wavered and hugged his arms over his chest as if he were holding himself together. He looked terrible. Gaunt, with deepened furrows alongside his mouth and along his forehead.

The doctor's gaze locked on them as he approached. "Mr. and Mrs. Teague?"

"Yes?" Allison grabbed Harper's arm and pulled her forward to meet with the doctor, ignoring Darren.

"Your daughter is out of surgery. Her leg was a simple break, but her wrist required pins."

"Is she awake?" Desperation colored Allison's voice and transmitted loud and clear in the painful clutch she had on Harper's arm.

"She's still under anesthesia."

"But her head?"

"We stitched a gash along her crown. She has a concussion, but the swelling has stabilized, which is a positive sign. It's a waiting game at this point, Mrs. Teague. She's being moved to a room in the pediatric ICU. Once she's settled, a nurse will come get you."

"That's all you can tell me? 'Let's wait to see if she'll wake up'? Can't you do anything?"

"He's a doctor, not a magician, Allison." Darren's voice was scratchy.

Wearing a grimace, the doctor inclined his head and backed out of the waiting room.

The short fuse to a bomb ignited. Allison faced off with Darren. "This is your fault."

"How do you figure that? You attacked me first thing this morning and started the stupid fight."

"You aren't the same man I married. I don't know who you are." The truth exploded and left a barren crater.

"I'm dealing with my issues —"

"*Issues?* You have more than 'issues,' and you are most definitely not dealing with them." Allison's voice was both mocking and filled with despair. "I've tried to help you — I've made myself *sick* trying to help you — but you don't see or care. Libby and Ryan are scared of you. So am I sometimes. Sophie is the only one . . . and look what you've done."

Allison made a noise and ran out of the room.

Harper was left behind to bridge the gap. "It was an accident, Darren. Allison is hurting and needs to blame someone." Harper had been there and done that.

Sinking down in a chair, he didn't respond. Feeling awkward and like she was betraying Allison somehow, Harper patted his shoulder, not sure what else to offer that wasn't a lie. If Sophie didn't wake up, things wouldn't be fine.

She slipped away to find Allison. The bathroom was dimly lit, the smell of bleach stark in the small space. Harper peeked under the stalls. One of Allison's tennis shoes was untied.

"It's me." Even though Harper kept her voice low, it echoed against the cold white tile.

"Is he gone?"

"He's not going to leave Sophie, and it's not fair to ask him to."

A pause. "I don't think I can be in the same room with him."

A sense of helplessness came over Harper. Words didn't assemble themselves into advice to live by. Wisdom wasn't bequeathed to a person as a consolation prize for enduring tragedy.

"It was an accident." Harper settled for a fact.

"If we hadn't been fighting . . ."

We. She blamed herself as much as Darren. "People fight. It's not a crime."

The sound of toilet paper unspooling was followed by the sound of a nose blowing. The toilet flushed and the door swung open. Allison had a wild, panicked look in her eyes, but when Harper reached to touch her she jerked away.

"I failed him. And her. Everyone." While the declaration might qualify as melodramatic from another woman, Allison believed the harsh assessment the way she believed the sky was blue — an undeniable truth.

Grief and worry and depression could close the curtains on the good in life. Wrapped in her personal tragedy for months on end, Allison's reality had been skewed. Her failure to fix Darren had preyed on her mind and soul. She was smart, capable, and because she'd never failed, the magnitude and depth of their life spiraling out of control was like a natural disaster in paradise.

"You haven't failed anyone. And this is not your fault." This time when Harper reached for Allison's hand, the other woman didn't snatch it away. "You can't fix everything. Not everything can be fixed. Sometimes a new normal has to be found."

In the silence, hope broke ground in Harper's chest.

"I'm leaving him." Allison's words ricocheted like bullets off the tile.

"Allison, no," Harper said more to herself than as an entreaty.

"I can't do it anymore. The kids need to play and not worry about what kind of mood Darren will wake up in." A sob escaped even though her eyes were dry. "Maybe it makes me selfish or a terrible wife or a horrible person. I don't care anymore. I'm so tired. I need peace."

The exhaustion weighing Allison's shoulders and aging her a decade wasn't physical. Or at least not mostly physical. It was mental and emotional and went soul deep.

What was the right thing to do? Did right and wrong even exist in this situation? It all blurred together. "When is spring break for the kids?"

"Next week."

"How about I take Libby and Ryan back to Nags Head? You can concentrate on Sophie. And Darren."

Allison's head popped up and her hand tightened around Harper's. "What about Gail?"

"Mom will love it. I'll have her grab some extra canvases and the kids can paint with her. It'll be like art camp. We'll go to the beach and the dock to fish. It'll be . . ." "Fun" was probably overstating it considering the situation. "A distraction."

"That would be amazing. Thank you."

Harper slipped an arm around Allison's shoulders. "Let's go see if Sophie is settled and ready for visitors."

They walked side by side to the waiting room. Darren was gone. Harper grabbed the first nurse she could find and got directions to Sophie's room. Darren was already by her side, holding the hand that wasn't in a cast, his forehead resting on the back of her delicate fingers.

Lines and wires connected Sophie to machines that beeped and hummed and clicked around her. Her face was almost as white as the bandage wrapped around her head. A tube was under her nose, but she wasn't on a ventilator. Her leg was in a sling and raised off the bed, her left hand in a blue cast from her fingers to her elbow. She looked like a little shake would wake her right up, but it wouldn't. She was Sleeping Beauty.

Allison shuffled to the other side of Sophie's bed. Harper stayed in the doorway, telling herself the room was stuffed with equipment and small, but her leaden feet didn't move for selfish reasons.

Imagining Ben in Sophie's place made her stomach heave and an acidic burn of coffee creep up her throat. Yet through the stew, a sliver of thankfulness rose. It wasn't Ben; he was safe. She pressed her cheek into the cool metal of the doorframe.

Allison brushed her hand over Sophie's face. "I suppose they had to shave her head. She's going to hate that when she wakes up."

"*If* she wakes up," Darren rumbled.

"Shut your mouth," Allison ground out between her teeth, quietly but with a bite.

Darren rose and ambled out of the room. He stood in the hallway, looking down one side of the hall and then the other, obviously disoriented. "I need air."

Harper watched him disappear around the corner before entering Sophie's room and laying her hand on Allison's shoulder. "I'm going to make some calls and meet the kids at the house. I'll get them packed and bring them by here on our way out of town. Is that okay?"

Allison didn't look away from Sophie's face or stop stroking her cheek. "There's a key under the red flowerpot. I'm going to sleep here as long as she needs me."

"I'll bring you a bag, too."

Allison nodded and Harper backed into the hallway. On the sidewalk outside the hospital, Harper closed her eyes and lifted her face toward the early afternoon sun. The hospital seemed to exist on a different space-time plane. The brightness chased away the chill that had settled near her bones and around her heart and had nothing to do with temperature.

Darren sat on a bench set under a crepe myrtle that was beginning to leaf out. She joined him.

"She hates me." Darren's voice was devoid of emotion.

Harper didn't believe for a millisecond that losing Allison wouldn't devastate him. "She's as upset with herself as she is with you about the accident."

"Is she leaving me?" Darren turned his gaze on her.

"She'll be staying here with Sophie."

"And afterward?"

"I don't know." What Allison declared in the shadow of an emotional tsunami wouldn't necessarily come to pass. "I'm going to pick up Libby and Ryan and bring them back to Nags Head for spring break. I'll try to make things easier for them."

"You've been a good friend to her."

"Allison's been a good friend to me."

His chin dropped to his chest. "What if she dies?"

"She won't." Harper wasn't a doctor or a prognosticator, but sometimes people needed something to hang on to and not the barren facts. "Sophie will be running and playing princess before you know it and this will all be a bad memory."

"My life is a bad memory." His laugh was self-deprecating, but the message worried her.

"That's not true. Remember how happy you were when Sophie was born?"

Harper remembered his euphoria and the kisses he kept giving a tired Allison propped up in the hospital bed and the baby he showed off in his arms to visitors.

"It hurts to remember that," he said softly. "It feels like someone else's life."

She was at a loss, unable and unqualified to drag him back into the light. After Noah had died, she'd had Ben to take care of and eventually he'd swamped her grief with the strength of a love she'd never imagined before she'd had him. Ben had saved her.

She worried Darren was beyond saving. He was falling apart before her very eyes. A decrepit ghetto of lies believed and lies told.

Depression scurried and crept into every nook and cranny like rats. The slow decay of hope. Sophie's accident only sped the process.

When the right words didn't come, she covered his hand with hers, and they sat in silence, the sun bright, the birds chirping, the sound of laughter carrying from the parking lot.

He pulled his hand away from hers. "By the time you get down there, the kids will be getting off the bus."

"We'll stop to see Sophie before we head to Nags Head. Will you be here?"

"I don't know." Darren squinted and looked to the far distance where there was nothing but blue sky.

Disappointed but not surprised, Harper walked away. She collected the kids from the bus stop and filled them in on the basics of the situation, painting it with as rosy a brush as possible while preparing them to see their sister in a hospital bed. Libby and Ryan were quiet as Harper pulled in to the driveway of their house.

They stepped inside. The silence had an eerie cast as if the house was haunted. A shiver ran down Harper's spine. Forcing an upbeat tone, she said, "Let's get packed up. And don't forget a swimsuit."

Libby and Ryan retreated to their respective rooms. Once Harper was assured they had a handle on packing, she sidled into Allison and Darren's room. On the surface, nothing hinted at the explosive undercurrents of their marriage. A framed wedding picture sat in a place of honor on the dresser.

She didn't know Darren and Allison back then, but they looked happy. Their love had been tangible the first time Harper had met them. Anything could die, though, no matter how strong.

She ignored the rest of the pictures scattered on the dresser and nightstand and focused on the practicality of packing a small bag with several changes of clothes, underthings, and toiletries.

When she was finished, she stopped in the doorway of Libby's room first. Libby met Harper's gaze in the mirror. "We're not leaving for good, are we?"

In that moment Libby reminded her so much of Bennett. Not in any physical way, of course, but her soul was eons older than her years. The same life experiences yoked Bennett. Hardships faced when they were too young.

Harper sat on the edge of Libby's bed and gestured her over, but the girl stayed planted

379

out of reach. Lies would only drive Libby further into a shell. "I think you'll be back. I hope so. Your parents —"

"Are they getting a divorce?" Libby's voice was mechanical, but her hands were clenched into tight balls at her sides. "My friend David's parents divorced and he moved away."

Harper swallowed. "I don't know, but I do know they love each other despite what's going on right now."

Libby dropped her piercing gaze and gnawed her bottom lip, her shoulders slumping. Years sloughed off and she was back to being a kid again, her voice tinny. "Will Sophie really be okay?"

Harper closed the distance and hugged her. Libby's stiffness melted away and her skinny arms came up around Harper's back with a grip that squeezed the air out of her. "Once she wakes up, we'll know."

"What if she never wakes up?" Libby whispered near Harper's heart.

"She will." Like with Darren, Harper abandoned truth and lied for hope. Imagining sassy, sweet Sophie forever locked in sleep was no fairy tale; it was a tragedy.

They stood there until Libby pulled away. "Don't tell Ryan about Mom and Dad or Sophie. He wants to believe everything is okay." Libby's adult-like resignation made tears spring to Harper's eyes. It wasn't fair, but life never promised fairness. Life promised nothing.

CHAPTER 19

Past

The pain, sharper now and drawn out, extended beyond what was tolerable. Harper grabbed hold of the kitchen counter with one hand and pressed at her lower back with the other, her distended belly tight and hard. She was in denial, but she wasn't an idiot. Ready or not, the baby was coming.

The pains had woken her up in the middle of the night, but she'd done her best to ignore them, attempting to re-create a dreamscape with Noah waiting to hold her and talk to her about the baby and their future together.

That future had been full of promises Noah had broken when he'd gotten himself killed. Underneath the grief was a wellspring of anger that felt all kinds of wrong. She'd known the risks of marrying a SEAL. Except those risks had seemed abstract and unable to touch them. Instead, luck or Fate or God had drawn Noah's number, and she was left to suffer.

Other women nodded in that special way and murmured a similar message: Noah would live on in the child she was carrying. Harper had wanted to scream at them to get the hell away from her. They didn't understand. No one understood.

A guttural groan hit her ears as if it had come from someone else. But no, that was her. A few choice words overlay her short bursts of breath.

The shock of losing Noah had faded into an ambivalence about the baby the last month of her pregnancy. The baby was a distraction from her grief, and not a welcome one.

The past few days, Allison and her mom had to remind her to eat and drink. "For the baby," they'd say. "Think of the baby." Like she could forget. She had to pee constantly, her back ached, and she couldn't see her feet. The baby was a constant reminder of what she'd lost.

Her due date had come and gone. Harper had convinced herself she was willing the baby to stay put, but apparently, nature didn't take cues from Harper's emotional state.

Another contraction. Dawn light suffused

the sky as she puffed and groaned through the strongest one yet. Harper shuffled out of the kitchen. Her mom and Allison were asleep upstairs. She stopped at her mom's room first and knocked.

The door jerked open. Her mom was already awake and half-dressed, her night-gown bunched around her waist over a pair of jeans. Her face morphed from worry to determination. "It's time."

Even though it wasn't a question, Harper nodded. Her mom jerked her nightgown off and finished dressing in a T-shirt, half tuck-ing it in. Nimble fingers braided hair that was streaked with gray. Tears pricked Har-per's eyes. She'd played in her mom's hair countless times as a child or sat still while her own hair was braided by those same fingers.

Harper had the urge to crawl under the covers on her mom's bed and pretend she was ten years old again, her responsibilities at zero and an endless summer of discovery stretching to the horizon.

A contraction had her scrunching around her stomach and grabbing the doorjamb for support. The pain weakened her knees and left her trembling. Her mother brushed Harper's hair off her sweaty forehead.

"I can't do this," Harper gasped in the

aftermath.

"Of course you can. And you will. You have no choice but to go forward, sweets."

If her mom's voice had wavered or shown any weakness at all, Harper would have collapsed. But the steel in her mom's expression sent a wave of strength through Harper. Maybe it was borrowed or even false, but it worked. A sense of inevitability, as if the outcome had been preordained, calmed her panic.

"Let's get your bag and wake Allison up." Her mom wrapped an arm around her waist and guided her out, knocking on Allison's door as they passed.

Allison too was dressed. "I woke up about twenty minutes ago thinking I heard something."

"Probably me," Harper said.

"Grab her hospital bag and let's go, Allison."

Even though Allison had birthed three kids, she moved with an energy that danced on the edge of panic.

A dense mugginess characteristic of July on the beach permeated the morning air already. Noon would see the temperature hit triple digits. A replica of the day she'd met Noah.

Halfway down the sidewalk to the car, she

burst into tears. She had never considered herself much of a crier, but the smallest thing set her off these days. Her mom had stopped asking because most of the time she couldn't pinpoint a problem, which meant it was unfixable.

Her mom's arm tightened around her midsection — her waist no longer in existence — and they plowed on. Her mom guided her to the front passenger seat.

Cars on the road were sparse, which would change as day-trippers flooded the narrow strip of land. A contraction stopped her tears. Self-pity was an extravagance she couldn't afford at the moment.

Their arrival at the hospital was a blur. While her mom spoke to a woman behind a glass partition, a man in white came out with a wheelchair and rolled Harper straight past the check-in desk and through swinging doors he opened by hitting a button on the wall. She craned around to keep her mom in sight.

"Can we wait for my mom?" The pitifulness of her request wasn't lost on her, but she couldn't help it.

"I'm here." Allison grabbed her hand and walked at her side.

Harper squeezed Allison's hand as pain shrouded her reality.

Time was measured by her contractions, a pain-relief cycle that stole her ability to function. Allison and the nurse helped her into a hospital gown and onto the bed.

The fact that a male nurse, the only man besides Noah to ever see her naked, helped her undress didn't even faze her. Pain obliterated any sense of modesty.

"Epidural. Now." She clutched the nurse's arm.

"Dr. Marks should be here any minute." The man's voice was low and was probably meant to be soothing. It didn't work.

"I want a freaking epidural." She tightened her hold.

Her ob-gyn, Dr. Adele Marks, breezed in on a cloud of light perfume. She was in her midfifties, her former life as a sought-after Virginia debutante apparent in her perfectly coiffed blond-gray bob, dress, and heels. As a regular library patron, she was a long-standing family friend with impeccable taste in books. Harper trusted her.

"Harper. As I live and breathe, I thought for sure we'd have to induce you. Legs up and let's check baby's progress."

"I want a freaking epidural," Harper repeated like a broken record, her voice scratching at the end as another contraction racked her body.

The nurse said, "Contractions are two minutes apart, Doc."

"Oh my. Let's see where we are."

Harper was only distantly aware of the hands shifting her. The voices around her gained in volume and urgency, and she opened her eyes to find two more nurses — women this time — flanking her bed and pulling it apart. Adele was putting on a blue surgical-type robe and gloves. The swiftness of the situation scared Harper.

"I want my mom," Harper said, "and an epidural."

At first she thought no one had heard, but Adele came around the bed and took her hands. "Darlin', it's too late for an epidural. Baby's crowning."

"But . . . but you said, first-time births usually take forever."

"Seems like your little boy or girl wants to blow the curve."

"My mom. Where is she?"

"I sent for her. Paperwork can wait. This baby won't." Adele smiled.

"I can't do this. Not without Noah."

Adele's smile wilted. "Oh, darlin', you have to. But remember women have had to bear this burden since time began. You aren't alone. A long line of strong women stand to support you."

Her mom took her other hand, Allison beside her. She had lost Noah, but three strong women stood with her today. She took a deep, shuddery breath. "I'm ready."

Adele moved to Harper's feet, helping position them in the stirrups, and gave orders in a sweetly Southern but authoritative voice.

"Time to push, Harper dear, but softly. We don't want baby to squirt out and shoot across the room."

If she could have laughed, she would have, but her life was pain and pain was her life. Breathing was a success.

Her mom put an arm around her back and lifted her slightly. Harper grabbed her knees and crunched forward, pushing. Twice more she repeated the action.

"Perfect, Harper. Head's out. Wait for the next contraction and give me another push."

The contractions didn't seem to end but rolled one into another, so Harper took a deep breath and pushed.

"Yes! Here come the shoulders and . . ."

An ebbing of the constant pain flowed over her. She dropped her head back on the pillow. A flurry of movement between her legs was taking place, but she couldn't summon the energy to sit up and look.

A baby's cry rang out. Harper's emotions

were in tatters, and all she could think was, *Wrong, wrong, wrong.* It all felt wrong without Noah. He'd been so excited.

"It's a boy. A boy." Tears trickled down her mom's cheeks and curved into the grooves of her smile. "He's beautiful. Perfect."

Adele brought the baby to Harper. His eyes were swollen and closed. He squawked and waved an arm around, blood smearing his bald head. He was ugly. Nothing like Noah. Her arms remained at her sides.

"Go on, Harper, take your baby." Adele shoved the baby at her, and she took him instinctively. Everyone stood around her with identical beatific smiles. Harper should be oohing and ahing and forgetting about the pain in her happiness, but it was like her heart was in a deep freeze.

A nurse took him, and all Harper felt was relief. It took another half hour before she was cleaned up and the bed was reassembled with clean sheets. In that time, the baby was measured and weighed and given a sponge bath.

The nurse slipped the baby into her arms. He wasn't as ugly as her first impression. At least he wasn't screaming his tiny head off. And he smelled better. His eyes were still swollen, but they blinked up at her, unfocused. Not Noah's blue, but a shade lighter than her own. His hair was sparse and circled his head like a monk's tonsure but also matched hers.

The nurse helped get the baby latched on to Harper's breast; the pinch and pull of the baby's mouth mounted an echo of a contraction in her womb.

Harper endured. She'd read all the mothering how-to books in the first months of her pregnancy with relish. She knew what she was supposed to do even if she lacked enthusiasm. At the nurse's prodding, Harper switched the baby to the other side. The nurse smiled down at her.

What was it with that smile? She wasn't the Madonna with Child. Harper dropped her gaze, but the view of the baby going to town on her boob wasn't any more comfortable. She closed her eyes.

"Have you picked a name yet?"

Without opening her eyes, Harper whispered, "Ben. Ben Wilcox."

It was the name Noah had wanted. The name he'd whispered in her ear the night they had been discussing possibilities. It had seemed important to him, and she'd liked it, too.

The nurse took Ben and, after changing his diaper, laid him in a rolling bassinet next to the bed. It wasn't even noon. The sun shined into the windows, but the abrupt change in scenery from her dark belly to the bright world didn't seem to bother Ben, who closed his eyes and slept.

Harper turned to her side, feeling like she'd been dropped over a cliff and then hit with an anvil. She stared at Ben and waited for a miraculous connection to form. Nothing happened. No hope or enthusiasm, only a bone-tired relief the actual birth was over with. She slept and didn't dream.

The next days followed the same pattern except she was home. She slept when Ben slept and woke with him for feedings but otherwise didn't have a desire to hold and cuddle him. Allison went back to her family, but her reluctance was palpable. Harper had interrupted more than one whispered conversation between Allison and her mom.

Her mom pressed her to pick a date for Noah's parents to come see their grandchild, but Harper put her off each time the subject came up. The last time she'd seen them had been at Noah's funeral, and facing them again would bring back that awful day.

She felt detached, as if the birth had cut her tether to reality. She bathed and ate and did the minimum amount of work to keep

Ben happy and growing. Her mom picked up the slack, giving Ben the cuddles and attention Harper couldn't spare.

Adele stopped by, ostensibly for a social call, but unlike Ben, Harper hadn't been born almost yesterday. Her mom showed Ben off to Adele, who cooed and kissed cheeks that had already grown chubbier.

After Harper put Ben down for a nap in the crib next to her bed, she lay down, too, savoring the silence. Adele knocked softly and poked her head around the door before Harper could respond or pretend to be sleeping.

She glided across the carpet with a grace that was becoming a lost art and arranged herself on the side of the bed. "Most women suffer from some level of postpartum depression, darlin'."

"I know." She remembered the chapter in her baby user's manual. "That's not what this is, though."

Adele gazed toward Ben. "Maybe not entirely, but the hormones could be amplifying your grief. I can't imagine what you've been through on top of giving birth. There's no shame in asking for help."

"I don't need help." Harper stared toward the window. "I'm tired."

"Of course." Adele patted her hand and

slipped out the door, but not before casting a worried look over her shoulder. Harper ignored the little voice in her head that wondered if Adele was right and drifted into the only solace she had left — sleep.

Three weeks after coming home from the hospital, she was jerked from a dream about Noah by Ben's soft mewling. It was dark outside, and she pulled a pillow over her head. Would she ever get a decent night's sleep again?

His mewl turned into a cry. Her body responded without her moving, her breasts leaking and aching. She hated the fact that her body no longer belonged to her but to the baby. Ben's cry ratcheted up another few decibels. Better to respond before DEFCON 1 was reached.

She scooped Ben up and settled into the rocking chair by the window. While Ben nursed, she stared into the sky, the stars bright around the sliver of a moon. If it weren't for the exhaustion she faced in the morning, she might enjoy the peace.

Instead of putting him into a milk-induced coma like usual, the feeding energized Ben. He kicked his legs and took hold of a hank of Harper's hair, yanking with a strength that made her yelp more out of surprise than pain.

A gummy smile crinkled Ben's face. Harper smiled back automatically, the motion stiff as if her smile muscles had atrophied. His smile faded. It was probably gas. She made a funny sound. He smiled again, even bigger.

A warmth bloomed in her chest as her heart skipped ahead, making itself felt for the first time in weeks. Maybe it was the exhaustion or her grief or simply the shadows, but Ben had inherited something from Noah. His grin. The one that made his eyes twinkle.

The next morning, instead of handing Ben off to her mom and retreating for more sleep, she sat with him and tried to get him to smile again by making funny faces and noises. Just when she convinced herself she'd imagined it all, his gummy smile lit her up like sparklers.

She cradled him in the crook of her arm and quick-walked to the kitchen. "Mom! He smiled."

Her mom turned from washing dishes, drying her hands on a dish towel. "Honey. He's too young. He probably has gas."

"That's what I thought, too, but look. . . ." She chuffed like a horse and brought her nose to his. He grinned and waved his fists as if he couldn't contain his good humor.

"Oh my goodness." Her mom covered her mouth and stood over Harper's shoulder.

Harper repeated her chuff and got the same response. "Do you see it, too?" she whispered.

"He looks like Noah when he smiles, doesn't he?" Her mom put an arm around Harper's shoulders and leaned her head to put them temple to temple.

Tears rushed to Harper's eyes. It wasn't an unusual state for her these days, but she'd gotten good at sandbagging her emotions. Like a river jumping its banks, she had no control this time. Sobs racked her body. She cradled Ben close to her heart. Her mom's arms wrapped around her from behind and rocked them, a protective force.

That's what she had to be for Ben. He would grow up without a father. The least she could do was try to be the best mother possible.

After her body was drained of tears, she cradled Ben's head and leaned down to kiss him. He took her outburst in stride and rooted for her breast. "Will you make me an appointment with Adele?" In a whisper, she added, "I think I need help."

Her mom gave her one more squeeze around the shoulders and went straight for the phone.

The medicine and therapy weren't a cure-all, but instead of feeling like she was on a roller coaster spiraling constantly downward, the upswings made her grief bearable. She laughed and smiled as much as she cried, and caring for Ben was done out of joy and not duty.

The week Noah's parents visited was difficult. Moments of happiness were interspersed equally with a heart-swallowing sadness. But she gladly promised frequent access to their grandchild, knowing how important it would be to them and to Ben in the coming years.

The days passed as if time was fluid, flowing rapidly at some points, meandering slowly at others, and marked by the milestones Ben reached. His first bite of baby food — pureed sweet potatoes, which he loved. His first word — "Mama." His first step. His first haircut. His first birthday. Each one bittersweet because Noah wasn't there to bear witness.

She weaned herself off the antidepressant, afraid of backsliding into soul-crushing sadness, but she felt strong, her good days outnumbering her bad. Time didn't heal her wounds but grew scar tissue over them, and she and Ben survived.

Chapter 20

Present Day

Jack London bounded down the beach after Libby and Ryan and Ben. The surf was too cold for Harper's blood, but the sun was out and a warm breeze ruffled her hair. She and Bennett had slipped their shoes off and rolled up their pants.

"Thanks for coming down." Harper slipped her hand into his for a squeeze. She half-expected him to shake her off. He didn't seem the hand-holding type, but he only linked their fingers and tightened his grip.

"I hate that I was off in the woods and you had to deal with everything by yourself." His voice was strong and rumbly and re-assuring.

She'd forgotten what it was like to have someone to lean on who wouldn't fall. It was nice. "You were working. I'm used to handling things on my own."

"Yeah." The way he drew the word out had her gaze sweeping to his face, but before she could question him he asked, "Any change in Sophie?"

"Not yet, but it's only been three days." *Only* three days. A lifetime. Every hour that ticked off without her regaining consciousness increased the grim reality of her never waking.

Libby fell to her knees next to Jack London and untied the ribbon in her hair. Ben and Ryan played tag, squealing when the cold water lapped at their legs. Jack didn't run after the boys but stayed with Libby as if he sensed her need. She tied the pink ribbon in Jack's fur, giving him a hornlike ponytail on top of his head.

"Jack is so good with Libby. Was he trained as a therapy dog?" Harper pulled Bennett to a stop so they wouldn't interrupt girl and dog.

Bennett dug his toes into the sand, his gaze down. Harper turned to face him without letting go of his hand, bending down to catch his eye.

"No. I got him as a puppy at a shelter," he said. "A SEAL friend suggested I get a dog after I got out. With everything that happened, I was having a . . . rough time."

While he wasn't throwing a door open on

the past, a tiny window cracked. He was at least acknowledging something traumatic had happened. She had promised herself and him she wouldn't push him. She planned to keep that promise no matter how many questions threatened to launch. She kept silent.

"I dismissed the idea of a dog at first. I could barely take care of myself. But then I was driving and saw a sign for a shelter. My truck ended up in the parking lot. I sat there awhile. Maybe more than a while," he said on a small laugh.

"Eventually, I went in and almost turned around. It was overwhelming. I walked down a long row of cages stacked on top of one another and filled with dogs. At the end a big puppy was lying there with his chin on his paws. Not barking or whining. He looked at me like he knew me and was waiting for me." His laugh bordered on uncomfortable. "That makes me sound crazy, doesn't it?"

"You sound like you stumbled across something you didn't know you needed." As soon as the words were out of her mouth, she recognized them as her truth as well as his. A frisson of energy coursed through her. Could he tell?

"I guess so. I adopted him that day. The

people at the shelter said that he'd been passed over for weeks because no one wanted a dog his size. He was scheduled to be put down the next day. If I hadn't walked in . . ."

"But you did." She'd learned the futility of what-ifs even though in the dark of night she fell into the bad habit.

"We both got lucky." He let go of her hand and joined Libby. Jack gave his hand a lick as soon as he was within reach.

Harper hung back. What made luck good or bad? And could it change? Maybe something that classified as bad luck at the time later took on the cast of good luck because that pivotal moment changed the course of a life forever in ways no one could foresee.

Ben ran over to her and wrapped himself around her legs. She squatted down and hugged him. He was wet and grainy with sand, but she didn't care. If luck existed, then he was the best kind.

He was gone again in a flash, chasing Ryan along the high-tide line. Bennett pulled a tennis ball out of a pocket in his cargo pants and handed it to Libby. Jack spotted the ball and bounced around, panting and excited.

"Want to throw it for Jack? He's gotten chubby this winter and needs to run,"

Bennett said.

A childish joy crossed her face as she took the ball, Jack on her heels.

"Ryan doesn't seem fazed by Sophie and Darren and Allison, but I worry about Libby. She's too perceptive and internalizes her feelings."

"She'll survive." Bennett's voice contained a certainty she didn't share. "Most of us do."

Surely survival wasn't all anyone could hope for. Harper had survived, but now that she'd had a taste of happiness, she craved more.

"I want her to do more than survive; I want her to be happy." She stared at Bennett, wondering what was going on behind his dark, secretive eyes. "Don't you want more than to just survive? Don't you want to be happy?"

"Not sure what that means." He stroked her cheek with the backs of his fingers. "Happiness has always been elusive. Like an exclusive club I was barred from by accident of birth."

She wrapped her hand around his wrist and nuzzled into his palm, laying a kiss on his life line. "You've never been happy?"

"I was happy with Sarge, I suppose. But he died." He hesitated, looking out over the vast ocean and not at her. His voice dropped to a whisper. "And with you. You make me happy. So much so, it scares me."

She held still even as she wanted to throw herself into his arms to kiss away the years of loneliness etched on his bones. Her heart danced a jig even as his word choice pulled the plug on the triumphant music. "Scares" was a far cry from "amazes" or "exhilarates" but better than "makes me feel doomed."

"You make me happy, too. After Noah, I wasn't sure if it was possible."

Troubles shadowed his eyes. His hand tightened around her nape as if she were a flight risk, yet he didn't speak.

Her phone buzzed in her pocket. Every time it had rung over the weekend, her stomach flipped like an Olympic gymnast on speed. She fumbled it out of her pocket. Allison's name stared back at her.

A tremble affected her voice. "H-hello?"

"She's awake. And she knows me. She's going to be okay." Allison was laugh-crying. "Can you bring the kids back?"

Bone-melting relief had her leaning into Bennett. His arm came around her. "Of course. As soon as I can get us packed up."

"Thank you, Harper. For everything. I'll be waiting." Allison disconnected.

Harper didn't hesitate this time but fell

into Bennett's chest, borrowing from his strength. "Sophie's awake."

"Thank God." He rubbed his chin alongside her temple, her senses heightened from the shot of fear.

"Allison wants to see the kids."

"I'll drive."

She pulled back. "Are you sure? I thought you had to work tomorrow?"

"I'll call Andrew in to open the store. You're more important."

She buried her face in his neck so he wouldn't see how much his declaration meant.

"You ready to tell Libby and Ryan?" he asked while rubbing circles on her back.

"Yep." At least this was one tragedy she could spare the kids. Maybe Sophie's recovery would spur the mending of Darren and Allison's marriage.

When they heard the good news, Ryan whooped and ran circles around Harper and Bennett while Libby only smiled, but she skipped next to Jack London on the way back to the house.

The next hour was a flurry of activity as everyone showered off the salt and sand and gathered up items that had migrated all over the house.

Harper's mom gave each kid an enveloping hug along with a paper-bag lunch. She pressed a larger bag into Harper's hands. Harper rolled her eyes toward Bennett, who stooped to give her mom a kiss on the cheek. "Thanks, Gail."

Her mom patted his arm. "I put in an extra oatmeal cookie for you, Bennett. Don't let Harper steal it."

"Hey!" Harper's protest lacked heat. Seeing her mom and Bennett interact settled a warm fist around her heart.

Ben blocked the door, his bottom lip pouched out. "I wanna come, too."

Harper dropped to one knee to put them at eye level. "We're going to the hospital, pumpkin. It won't be any fun."

"You're always leaving me behind with Yaya."

Harper sent a panicked look toward Bennett and her mom. She couldn't even argue the point, because since meeting Bennett and working to get the coffee business off the ground she had been leaving Ben more often. Guilt sprouted like a pervasive weed that was impossible to eradicate.

Bennett knelt next to her. "Someone has to take care of Jack London while we're gone. I was counting on you, big guy."

"You want me to feed him?" Ben's voice lost some of its waver.

"Feed him, walk him, and" — Bennett leaned closer and whispered, "pick up his poop."

Ben made an *eww* noise, but the hint of a smile snuck back on his face. "I can do that."

Bennett stood and ruffled Ben's hair. "I know you can."

Harper drew Ben in for a hug. He laid his head on her shoulder and she took a deep breath, drawing in his distinctive little-boy smell to take with her. "I'll miss you every minute I'm gone, but I'll be home soon. Promise. Take care of Jack and Yaya, okay?"

His arms tightened around her neck to the point of being uncomfortable. Not that she planned to complain. How much longer would he freely give her hugs? While time could heal, it also meant growing up and change.

Disentangling herself from Ben and walking away was like leaving him the first day of preschool. Out of her arms, he retreated to hold her mom's hand. She gave her mom a quick hug and kiss and followed Bennett to his truck before her sappy tears had a chance to make an appearance.

The kids were already in the backseat with everyone's bags stored in the bed. Jack's deep-chested bark from the front window was like a hammer to her already-fragile emotions. Bennett didn't speak as he steered them down the road, but he took her hand in his and linked their fingers. His steadiness in turn steadied her.

The drive seemed to take forever, yet as they pulled in to the hospital parking lot she searched for the right words to prepare Libby and Ryan.

Turning, she laid her arm over the backs of the seats. "Guys, I'm not sure how tired your mom and dad and Sophie will be or if Sophie will even be up to talking at this point."

"Are the tubes all gone?" Libby's gaze was fixed out the window at the hospital, her voice flat and emotionless.

"Probably not. The doctors will still need to monitor her."

"Do you think her hair has grown back?" Ryan perched on the edge of the seat, ready to go.

"That's going to take a while, I'm afraid."

"I wonder if she knows yet," Libby said.

"Knows what?" Harper tensed.

"That her hair is gone. She wanted to grow it out like Rapunzel. She's going to be really sad."

"Then you'll have to do your best to cheer her up, won't you?"

Libby gave a brusque nod, and Harper fought not to reach for her. Libby's stoicism didn't mean she didn't care; it meant she cared so much she was overwhelmed.

"Listen, guys, everything might be different for a while, but it will be okay. Not today. Maybe not even next week. But eventually. Can you trust me on that?"

Libby finally met her eyes. "Promise?" she whispered so softly, only the movement of her lips revealed the word.

"I promise." Harper didn't let her own roiling emotions waver her voice or her gaze.

Libby's shoulders fell an inch, a portion of her anxiety appeased. "I'm ready."

They piled out and made their way to the children's floor. Harper led them through the halls to Sophie's room. It didn't look much different except for one huge exception: Sophie was propped up and her eyes were open.

"L-Libby." Sophie's voice was hesitant and stuttered a little, but her arms flew up and she made grabby hands toward her sister.

Libby hugged Sophie like she was as precious and delicate as a butterfly. Allison gave Ryan a quick hug, guided him to the other side of Sophie's bed, then stood back and watched with a hand over her mouth.

Shock and relief and happiness crashed through Harper, leaving room for hope.

"Wh-where's Da-dee?" Sophie's big blue eyes peered beyond Harper and into the hall where Bennett waited.

"He'll be back soon, darling." Allison's voice cracked and revealed the lie.

Harper touched Allison's arm and mouthed his name. Allison's mouth tightened, and she nudged her head toward the hallway. Harper followed and they gathered with Bennett, who had propped a shoulder on the wall outside the room.

"Where's Darren?" Harper asked.

"I don't know." Allison ran a hand through her lank hair. The week had aged her a decade. "As soon as Sophie woke up and the doctors assured us she would make a full recovery, he left."

"Are you still mad at him?"

"No. Yes." Allison's laugh contained equal amounts of irony and exhaustion. "I don't know. I've called and left him a half-dozen messages. I thought about going after him, but Sophie needs me right now."

"What do you need from us?" Harper asked.

Allison watched the kids interact. Sophie's soft giggles were the sweetest music. "I want my family together. Could you track down

Darren and bring him back?"

Bennett's face was grimmer than normal. "I'll find him and bring him home."

CHAPTER 21

Present Day

Adrenaline careened through Bennett, lengthening his stride as he punched Darren's name into his phone. No answer. He muttered a curse. Harper alternated between a fast walk and jog at his side, her face flushed and drawn with worry. He forced himself to slow.

It had been a long time since the dread and anticipation of a mission hovered over him. He was not handling it well. Maybe he was out of practice or maybe he was old, but his stomach felt ready to expel the sandwich and oatmeal cookies he'd scarfed down on the road.

"Do you think something is wrong?" Her question came out breathless.

He stopped. Her hair was pulled back into a ponytail, but wisps had escaped. Brushing a piece behind her ear, he caressed her cheek with his thumb. Her skin was soft and sweet smelling. Too many nights he woke from erotically charged dreams starring her, his senses tricking him and making him believe she was with him, her scent lingering like a memory.

"The sooner we find him the better." It was a nonanswer, but she didn't call him on it. He walked on but at a slower, although still brisk, pace.

"It's weird he wouldn't stay to see Libby and Ryan, isn't it?" she asked with the same worry growing ulcers in his stomach.

"We'll start at their house."

Negotiating the checkpoints grew his impatience. Bennett had to keep his voice from betraying his agitation. The MPs were only doing their job. Finally, he and Harper were free and he pulled up to Darren and Allison's house.

"His SUV is here. Thank goodness." Harper hopped out of the truck and ran to the front door. A quiet pall hung over the street, and Bennett scanned in all directions as if an attack could come from any direction. The hairs along his neck stood on end, his fight-or-flight instincts awakened even though he couldn't pinpoint why. Certainly he didn't anticipate an enemy combatant jumping out of the azalea bush.

Harper rang the doorbell, knocked, and

cupped her hands to look through the mottled glass insert of the window. "I can't see or hear anyone. Maybe he's out for a walk?"

He tried the knob, but the door was locked. "Do you know if Allison leaves a key anywhere?"

Harper flipped up the red pot. Metal glinted through dirt. Bennett picked up the key and wiped it on his pants. He unlocked the door and cracked it open, instinctively crouching down, his hand going to his hip for a gun that wasn't there and hadn't been for years. His throat was parched, and when he called Darren's name it sounded rough and creaky.

No answer. He stepped farther into the foyer and listened. Nothing. The house had an abandoned feel even as he nudged a pair of tennis shoes out of the way. Onward he scouted, expecting the worst.

The den and kitchen were clear. "Wait here while I check upstairs."

"I'll come with you." Harper took a step backward, but he stopped her with his arm, blocking the way back.

"No. Let me. In case . . ." He couldn't bring himself to say what he was thinking, but by the way her eyes widened and fear flickered across her face he didn't have to.

He waited for her to nod before he returned to the stairs and took them on soft feet, only a slight creak giving him away. He pushed each door along the hallway open, revealing nothing more than empty rooms. In front of the master bedroom, he hesitated, preparing himself. The door swung open with a whine of the hinges.

It took a heartbeat for reality to crash with expectation. His knees trembled and he expelled a long breath he didn't realize he was holding.

Darren stood at the open back window, the flowered curtains fluttering with the breeze. He was barefoot in worn-out jeans and a T-shirt. Bennett's gaze hung on the matte black 9mm in his hand. It was pointed at the floor. Even though Darren hadn't acknowledged Bennett's presence, he was too well trained not to be aware he was no longer alone.

"Why didn't you answer the door, man?" Bennett approached like the gun was a water moccasin, ready to strike at any moment.

"Because I don't want you here." Darren continued to stare out the window.

"Harsh, but I appreciate the honesty. Whatcha you doing with that gun? Shooting squirrels?" Easing ever closer, Bennett forced a false casualness into his voice the same time his heart was clawing its way out of his chest.

Darren raised the gun and Bennett froze, but he just looked at it as if surprised to see it in his hand. He let it fall to rest against his leg once more. "Not really any of your business, Griz."

"Seeing as how you're my brother-in-arms, I'm making it my business."

"Fuck off." He might have been wishing a stranger a nice day by the tone of his voice.

His cold calmness scared Bennett almost as much as the gun. "Not gonna happen."

"I don't need witnesses." Darren waved the gun to the side, and Bennett stepped backward, tripping over the clawed foot of the old-fashioned mahogany bed frame, but no bullet erupted from the barrel. "I left a note."

Bennett's gaze shot to the dresser. A white envelope leaned against Allison and Darren's wedding picture, the front scrawled with her name.

"Letter ain't good enough. She wants *you*. Sent me and Harper to find you and bring you back."

His pronouncement elicited a response from Darren. He half-turned so he could peer at Bennett. Sunlight limned his body

415

and left his expression a mystery, but his voice pitched higher. "Bullshit. She hates me."

"She doesn't hate you. She's hurting and confused, but she still loves you."

"Sophie is going to be okay."

"I know. We dropped Libby and Ryan at the hospital so they could hug up on her. We left Sophie giggling." Bennett paused for effect. "She asked for you. Sophie wanted her daddy."

Darren didn't speak, only turned back to the window and brought the gun up to rest on the sill.

Bennett continued. "They're great kids, all three of them. Libby's so smart. Older than her years, though, because she's worried about you and Allison. Ryan bounds around with the energy of a puppy. Speaking of, he really took to Jack London; you should get him a dog. And Sophie's sweet and innocent enough to still believe her daddy can conquer all."

"I can't, though. I can't even conquer what's in my own head." He rubbed the barrel of the gun against his forehead. Bennett measured the distance to Darren and wondered if he was strong and fast enough to wrest the gun away before one of them got shot. Darren was leaner than his time in the SEALs but as fit as he'd always been. The odds were not in Bennett's favor.

"How about you give me the gun? You're making me nervous," Bennett said.

"Afraid I'm going to shoot myself in front of you?"

"The way you're waving it around, I'm afraid you'll accidently shoot me."

A rusty laugh came from Darren. Bennett took that as a positive sign.

"I wouldn't kill myself in the house. Too messy. I was trying to decide whether to do it by the fence, in the middle of the yard, or in the toolshed." Darren's voice was back to being supernaturally calm.

Bennett debated his options. Maybe the best one was to play along until he could get the gun away from Darren. "You want Allison or one of the kids to find you with your brains blown all over the fence or grass or gardening equipment? Less mess if you hang yourself."

"I deserve a bullet."

Bennett swallowed and joined Darren to look out the window but didn't attempt to wrest the gun from him. Time to dissect to the dark heart at the center. "Why do you think that?"

"Because that's how those boys died. The ones I sent in."

"It's the job. We all knew the risks when we joined up."

"Risk versus reality is different." Darren caressed the gun. "You got out after Noah was killed. Cut yourself off from the team. Are you telling me you never thought about it?"

Suicide would have been the easy way out, and Bennett's way had never been easy. From his time in foster care and beyond, the struggle to survive was familiar if not welcome. Living was his penance.

Besides, now there were other reasons to live that included a woman with enveloping hazel eyes and a warm laugh, even if those were more recent discoveries. "I made Noah a promise."

Darren squinted as if looking far beyond the line of pine trees at the fence line. "I'd say you've gone above and beyond what Noah asked of you."

Bennett rubbed the back of his neck. "Yeah, well —"

A noise, as slight as it was, whipped him around, his senses heightened. Harper stood in the doorway, her hand around her neck. Her eyes were wide, but he couldn't discern surprise from hurt from anger. Or maybe she was all three. His stomach squirmed. Later. He would explain later. Right now, his mission was Darren.

Her demeanor changed as she took in the scene. He gave a slight shake of his head, and she backed from the doorway but stayed in the hall. Having her there gave him courage. It had not been since his SEAL days — since Noah — that someone he trusted had his back. The irony wasn't lost on him.

"You don't really want to kill yourself, do you?" Bennett asked.

Darren shot him a side-eye and shrugged. "I wrote a note. I'm standing here with a gun."

"How long have you been standing here?"

Darren stared out the window like he'd spotted an extinct dodo bird and didn't answer.

Bennett stepped closer, within reach of the gun now. "I know someone who might be able to help you."

"I'm not going to see a goddamn shrink. Everyone would know."

"You don't think everyone isn't already wondering what the hell is going on with you? You're a fucking mess, man." Bennett would wrestle the gun away if it came to that, but he hoped it wouldn't. "Give me the gun."

Darren held the gun in both hands, caressing it like a talisman, before holding it out butt first. Bennett let a long breath out and took the gun, hefting it in his hand. Something was off. He checked the magazine. Empty.

"No bullets," Bennett murmured.

"I was going to practice a few times. Work on the angle."

Or he really didn't want to kill himself; he just couldn't see another way out. Bennett could give him that. "How about this . . . no shrinks, no base support group. You remember Alex Ramirez?"

"Sure. What's he doing now?"

"He's a SEAL instructor but also works with current and ex-military who have been injured physically, mentally, and emotionally."

"You think he can help me?"

"If he can't, then he'll point you to someone who can. Your kids need you. Sophie especially."

"I've been a shitty dad."

"Then work toward not being so shitty." Bennett stuffed the gun in his waistband at the small of his back. "Look, I grew up without a dad, and my mom OD'd when I was nine."

For the first time, Darren came out of his selfish stupor to send him a sympathetic glance. "I never knew that."

"I went through the foster-care system in Mississippi, passed from family to family. Having a dad would have been a dream come true. Even if he wasn't perfect."

Darren leaned his hands on the windowsill and dropped his head. "You think I have a chance to make things right with Allison?"

"There's always a chance to make things right." Bennett glanced down the hall. Harper still stood sentinel at the top of the staircase.

"Okay. I'll talk to Alex."

Bennett pulled his phone out of his back pocket.

"Not right now." A hint of panic sailed Darren's voice high.

"You need help right now. Alex can recommend a doctor who understands the military mind-set. You will do everything he recommends. If you don't, I'll talk Allison into having you committed on a fifty-one-fifty." Bennett wasn't bluffing. He'd hog-tie Darren and put him on a psychiatric hold himself, if necessary.

Bennett punched Alex's number. A measure of tension bled away when he answered with a clipped "hello" on the second ring. Someone else to help shoulder the burden. The briefest of explanations followed; then

Bennett handed the phone to Darren. "You don't have to hide anything. Alex has heard it all and worse."

Darren took the phone and sat on the edge of the bed, his voice hoarse and stuttering. Bennett backed out of the room but left the door open. Harper straightened from where she leaned against the wall, full of worry and questions.

He nudged his head and went downstairs. Harper stayed on his heels but didn't speak until they were in the kitchen. "You're going to leave him alone?" The fire in her eyes burned into him.

Bennett took the gun from his waistband and laid it on the table with a thud. "Not even loaded."

"You don't think he would have gone through with it even if we hadn't found him?"

The letter against Darren and Allison's wedding picture flashed in his mind. "Honestly, I don't know. But I do know he wants help and hopefully Alex can give it to him."

She cocked her head. "Wounded Warriors?"

"He works with them but also does outreach. His brother was ex–Special Forces and committed suicide."

"That's terrible."

"Yeah." Bennett rubbed a hand over his jaw and looked at her through his lashes. "Listen, I know you overheard us talking about Noah. And you."

She rubbed her arm and drew in on herself. "I love you, Bennett, but I can't live with this secret between us. I thought I could give you time — years even — but I can't. If that makes me selfish or stupid or whatever, then I guess that's what I am."

Everything after "I love you" blurred together. "Wait. What?"

"I said, if you don't trust me enough to —"

He grabbed her shoulders and squeezed hard enough to get her to look up at him. "You said that you . . ."

He was a SEAL. Four-letter words were an art form. He could practically carry on a conversation only using four-letter words and their variants. But this particular four-letter word shocked him to the core. It made his bones rattle and his blood sprint through his body at a breakneck, sickening speed.

Harper took his forearms in a tight grip and searched his face. "You don't look too good. You'd best sit before you pass out."

She steered him backward. The edge of the chair hit the back of his legs and he slumped down. "You love me?" The words felt unreal. "*Me?* Why?"

Everything about her softened, and instead of leaving like every other important person in his life, she plopped down on his lap and wound her arms around his neck.

"Why not you?"

"Because no one ever has before." Bennett didn't want to admit he'd never heard anyone say the words outside of movies, and certainly not in reference to him. Sarge had been a less talk, more action kind of father figure.

Her chin quivered as she shuffled her hand through his hair. "That's not true. Your sergeant loved you. Noah loved you. Jack London and Ben and my mom love you."

It's funny what a different perspective could do. He wasn't alone anymore. Even more important, he wasn't lonely anymore. He wrapped an arm around her waist and brought her flush against him, burying his face in her nape, his lips against her skin. "And you."

"Of course me. How could I help but fall for you?"

"I love you, too. Just so you know."

She relaxed into him, her back curling, and he took her weight with a gratefulness that was overwhelming. Overwhelming too was the realization he might lose her if he didn't tell her the truth.

"I promised Noah to look out for you if anything happened to him." His voice was rough. "He asked me to be Ben's god-father."

"That's why Noah picked the name Ben." She huffed a sigh before forcing eye contact. "The money was your way of taking care of us?"

"Yep."

"You weren't intending to get in a relation-ship with me, though, as a means of keep-ing your promise?"

"Lord, no, in fact —" He bit the inside of his mouth.

"Spill it."

Spill, excise . . . what was the difference at this point? "I've been feeling guilty as hell."

"I think Noah would have given his bless-ing. He loved you like a brother."

"It's not only that. It's . . ." He blew out a long, slow breath. "Even when he was alive, I felt a weird draw to you."

She put some distance between them, her hands resting on his shoulders. "But we'd never met."

"Your letters."

She took a quick intake but didn't speak. Nerves had him filling the silence. "I built this picture of you through your letters and emails to Noah. Funny, irreverent, sweet. It was something I kept to myself. Noah didn't know how I felt, but it's why I avoided meeting you all those years. I was afraid he'd figure it out. Anyway, it wasn't real. I understood that when you drove to my shop and confronted me."

"What do you mean?"

"I mean, the real you is more complicated and amazing and beautiful . . . basically, more *everything* than my imagination conjured all those years ago."

"Will you tell me how he died? I need to know and you need to tell me. Then, we can move on together."

He wanted to believe the surety in her voice but didn't.

CHAPTER 22

As always and forever, I love you. Make sure you come home safe to me and our baby. We both need you now.

Harper

Bennett hopped out of the helicopter, hitched his bag over his shoulder, and hunched over in a walk-run away from the whirring blades. Dust rose and obscured his range of vision to just a few feet, the grit irritatingly familiar. It worked its way into every crack and crevice, even the most personal ones.

Darren, the platoon officer in charge, was in front of him, and Noah and the rest of the men were on his heels. Stepping out of the shade of the two helicopters was like sticking your head into a preheated oven. As the dust settled, the base came into view and they weaved their way to the briefing room. Gear rattled as they jogged. The helicopters took off, throwing up another wall of lung-clogging dust.

Their SEAL team operated out of Camp Lemonnier in North Africa. They were set apart from the other men. Untouchables who inspired awe. But Bennett felt like just another grunt in a godforsaken desert. Not what he had in mind when he'd joined up to see the world. Nostalgia for the green lushness of the Mississippi swamps reared up to bite his ass at the funniest times.

They had gotten word on the way back to base from their most recent direct-action mission that a high-value target had been identified. A briefing and a few hours' rest was all they would get before they loaded up and headed out in the dark of night.

Folding chairs were scattered around the room. An AC unit hummed and pumped in blessedly cool air. One corner was taken up with an L-shaped desk that acted as their communication center with laptops and sat-com capabilities.

The primary target was a purveyor of secrets and information. Unaffiliated with any group or religious sect, he spoke one language and worshiped one god — money. The village he'd holed up in was full of his blood kin who might well be unaware of his activities on the dark web. A village full of innocents made the mission especially precarious.

"Take a seat." Darren's voice boomed through the room.

Bennett grabbed a folding chair and opened it on the flanking side, facing Darren. Noah joined him and the rest of the men fanned out in a semicircle.

Darren reviewed the information that had been collected by intelligence sources. Pictures flashed up on the screen of the man and his suspected cohorts. Eight total. The question was how hard would they defend the racket they had created? Under the cover of darkness and during the chaos of a firefight, their faces would blend into one another and the enemy would be determined by who was trying to kill them. Kill or be killed.

Bennett, Noah, and a few others would be sent straight to where the leader was thought to be living, a compound in the heart of the village. The man's picture had been taken from his university photo. He was clean shaven, smiling, and preppy looking. Since then, he might have grown a beard and gone to fat. No one knew. The man was less important than his machines. The computers and cell phones would be a trove of information to root out bigger fish.

That was the hope, anyway. Except for every secret seller they eliminated more rushed in to take their place. A nightmarish carousel going round and round. A weariness no amount of sleep could alleviate had worked its way into Bennett's bones.

Now they would wait until dark. Men handled the wait differently. Some paced; some slept; some joked too loud. One guy meditated. Bennett preferred to find a deserted corner with a deck of cards. Keeping his hands and subconscious busy helped. Noah joined him. Sometimes they talked, sometimes they didn't, but it was always comfortable.

Noah pulled out a folded-up piece of paper. A black-and-white photo fell out. He held it up and stared so intently, Bennett grew curious.

"What's so interesting?"

Noah held it out. It looked like some new age modern art. Wavery lines and gradients.

Bennett squinted at it. "What is it?"

"An ultrasound," Noah whispered.

Now that he realized what it was, a curved line revealed itself as a head. "What is it?"

"A baby, dumbass." Noah slipped him a sly grin.

"Boy or girl, smartass?"

"We decided to find out together once I'm

home." Noah plucked the ultrasound out of Bennett's hand. "Keep your mouth shut about it for a while longer. I don't want to make a big announcement. I feel like I'll jinx it or something."

"Of course. Dude, I'm superhappy for you and Harper."

"Yeah. It's a dream come true." Noah's smile held secrets shared with his wife.

Noah was a great guy and friend and Bennett *was* happy for him, but the tiniest sliver of him was jealous, too. Not that he wanted to take what Noah had, but Bennett's life back in the states was solitary. Lonely. He only had himself to blame.

"Still leaning toward 'Benjamina' if it's a girl?"

Noah barked a laugh. "That's exactly the name I suggested to Harper before we deployed. She loved it."

Bennett smiled and shuffled the cards. Noah smoothed a letter over his knee, and Bennett recognized Harper's handwriting.

While she and Noah exchanged countless emails, it was her letters that were high points. She had declared letter writing a dying art that she must upheld. Her letters were never about urgent matters but the day-to-day interactions with a cast of people made more amusing by her observations.

"What's Harper got to say? Or is this too private?"

Noah didn't always share her letters, and Bennett could only imagine what was in them with a small crimp around his heart that he did his best to ignore. She wasn't his and never would be.

Noah read, and Bennett closed his eyes.

"Dear Noah,

"Well, it happened on a Tuesday at two PM sharp. Total humiliation standing between the Ms and Ps. Perhaps I should back up a bit and inform you that the creature in my stomach — I've bequeathed him/her the name Mongo (temporarily, of course) — has been putting up quite the fuss.

"I thought I had escaped 'morning sickness.' Which, by the way, is complete and utter bullshit. I was at the library browsing for more books to fill the time while you're away and before Mongo makes a grand entrance. There I was holding Anne Perry's latest when Mrs. Hempshaw approached.

"Let me describe her for you: short and round in every way. Her head; her belly; even her glasses have round black frames. She's very nice and knowledgeable and I enjoy talking books with her. There's just one problem: she always smells faintly of cabbage. And while cabbage is an excellent vegetable (you know how much I love coleslaw), this particular morning the smell made Mongo angry. And you won't like Mongo when he/she is angry.

"First I belched. And not a ladylike one. A trucker who's been on the road eating pork rinds and Slim Jims for days kind of belch. Mrs. Hempshaw might have performed the classic Southern lady taken-aback pearl clutch.

"If that was all then I could have retreated with only mild embarrassment. But, oh no, Mongo threw his/her first temper tantrum. Before I could even take a step toward the bathroom, I threw up. A Linda Blair–*Exorcist* puke.

"I had the wherewithal to not turn my head toward the two stacks lined with books. That would have been a real tragedy. As it was, the Anne Perry I was holding was charged to my account and a hazmat team was called in to decontaminate Mrs. Hempshaw. (That last part isn't true. But she might be traumatized and seeking other work. Or therapy.)

"But wait, it gets worse. Mrs. Hempshaw took a step back to escape the carnage, but her foot slipped in the deposit I'd made on the floor. I took a step forward and grabbed hold of her arm to steady her, but I too went sliding. It was like we were dancing and I didn't know whether to laugh or cry. We steadied ourselves and locked eyes, the message in Mrs. Hempshaw's clear — 'we shall never speak of this again.'

"As always —"

Noah cleared his throat. Bennett opened his eyes, no longer in North Carolina but North Africa. A pang of something resembling homesickness washed through Bennett, leaving him feeling hollowed out. It was a strange sensation considering he'd never really had a home until Sarge adopted him. And even then, he'd left Mississippi with no urge to look back. Not enough good memories to outweigh the years of bad.

Noah skimmed the rest of the letter with a tender smile on his face. As much as Bennett wanted to know what else Harper had written, it wasn't for his eyes.

A rustle of men shifting and gathering gear rolled through the room. It was time. Harper's funny, mundane vignette from home would be followed by violence.

A few jokes could be heard bandied between men, usually the younger ones with something to prove or nothing back home to lose. Mostly it was silent except for the noise of the choppers. The minutes before a mission were fraught with a nervous excitement.

This was what they'd trained for. The hours and days and weeks spent learning to sight an enemy through a gun scope. The grueling physical challenges they'd faced during BUD/S. But no amount of training could prepare them for unknown variables that entered the field. The unpredictable nature of man could send things straight to hell.

The village they targeted looked like a hundred other places scattered throughout North Africa. Bennett closed his eyes and strolled through the memorized map in his mind, noting places where a sniper could hide or an ambush might originate from. Even with their night-vision capability, night raids could turn chaotic in a heartbeat.

Bricks and stone of varying shades of the surrounding sand blended the houses into the hills that formed a backdrop. They came in at low altitude over the flat stretch of desert leading up to the village. A narrow road cut a dark gash through the land.

Darren signaled their approach. Bennett took several deep breaths. He was in charge of clearing the leader's house, hopefully with him in it. His heart played ping-pong, but from experience he knew as soon as he was on the ground instinct would trump any nerves.

They unloaded and formed two lines, moving fast and keeping down. The helicopters took off to await extraction. A woman screamed. Muffled words snaked through the night. The first gunshots came from on top of one of the houses — erratic and not well aimed.

Bennett ignored the fire and concentrated on locating the leader's stronghold. His insides crackled. It wasn't nerves. The Navy had trained the nerves out of him and taught him to harness the adrenaline pumping through his body. His senses heightened and reacted to every stimulus — sight, sound, smell. The smallest clue could be the difference between success and failure, life and death.

The pops of gunfire overlay the yells of men. *Hide. Death. Gun.*

On the ground at night, with chaos around him, everything looked slightly different from the map. More ominous and not as easily discernible. He stopped at the corner. The shuffle and vibration of five other men hitting the wall behind him barely registered.

If the intelligence was correct, the leader's house was around the corner, and Bennett expected it to be protected. Or did the leader think a village full of human shields enough protection? Bennett kicked rocks out into the middle of the street. Bullets thudded into the ground, kicking up dirt and rocks. The angle of impact suggested one or two men were on top of the buildings.

Bennett motioned behind him, and like a choreographed dance, they moved in synchronicity, each with a role. Bennett stayed focused on the door while the others laid down heavy fire into the rooftops.

Motion at the far end of the street drew his attention. His night-vision glasses tinted everything in an eerie green. Bennett raised his gun and sighted a figure. It was a kid in jeans. Or what Bennett would have considered a kid. Eighteen or nineteen.

The kid had a gun and it was trained on him. Bennett fired. The kid hit the ground and didn't move. It had taken only seconds, but those seconds would haunt Bennett like so many others.

Bennett shot the door latch and shouldered it open, dropping to a squat to surveil the area. Noah was doing the same over his head. A man rushed them from an open doorway at the end of a short hall. Noah took him down.

"Clear the hall and the downstairs," Bennett barked to the men behind him.

A set of stairs led to a second floor. Bennett climbed them, took them two at a time with his gun trained at the top. Noah was on his heels. A spate of gunfire sounded from the back of the house, but Bennett stayed focused. He trusted the rest of the men to do their jobs.

Darkness enveloped the top of the stairs. He paused, his breathing loud in his ears. The whine of a child punched through the silence. The noise was quickly muffled, but it came from his left. Bennett gestured to the door with his gun barrel. Noah nodded and joined him on the other side of the door.

Bennett shoved his shoulder against the thin wood and a cracking sound accompanied the swing open. Two women scooched back against the wall, hands covering their faces. Mattresses on the floor lined the wall. At least two children huddled against the women. No sign of weapons.

To be sure, he strode forward and used

his foot to search around the women and in the covers. The women scurried out of his way like animals trying to escape the clutches of a predator. A sick feeling turned his stomach. He ignored it.

"Stay down. Stay down." Bennett barked the orders to the women unsure if they understood. He made one last scan over the room, identifying nothing threatening.

He backed out and followed Noah to the only other door on the hall. This time Noah led the way into the room. A man huddled over a computer. He was wearing a pair of khaki cargo pants and no shirt.

"Move away from the computer. Now." Bennett clipped the words out loud and slow, even though the information they'd been given indicated the man was fluent in several languages including English.

The man didn't move except to throw a glance in their direction, still frantically typing.

"Move." The force in Bennett's voice did nothing. He couldn't let the man delete or corrupt the information on the computer.

"On the floor, hands over your head." Bennett grabbed the back of the man's neck and forced his compliance.

The man went to his knees but no farther. Noah put a boot in the middle of his back and pushed him down, letting his gun drop to pat the man down. He pulled a knife from a holster strapped to his leg but no gun.

Bennett scanned the small room again. Nothing. The man had left himself unprotected. Inner alarms rang.

Time ceased to abide by the laws of physics. Noah reacted to something over Bennett's shoulder, a curse rolling out of his mouth like molasses to Bennett's ears. Noah launched himself at Bennett, their shoulders making jarring contact. The move shoved Bennett off his feet. He landed hard on his opposite shoulder and elbow. The report of gunfire echoed against the walls and reverberated in his head.

Adrenaline pumped his heart and masked any pain. He couldn't tell whether he'd been hit or not. He flipped to his back and brought his gun up. A woman stood in the doorway with a gun she was fitting another magazine into.

Bennett didn't hesitate. The force of the bullets sent the woman backward into the hall. A wail came from the leader as he scrambled toward the woman. The gun was at her side. Bennett fired again, putting two bullets in the man's legs. He crumpled over and grabbed his legs with a high-pitched scream, blood welling through his fingers.

Noah was sitting up, his hand around his throat, his torso wavering. The *clomp* of boots up the stairs put Bennett on alert, and he trained his gun on the doorway. Darren appeared, the shadows of other team members behind him.

"We need a medic!" Bennett yelled.

Darren called the same to a team member down the hall.

"Secure the women in the other room. Here's our guy. I only hope he didn't have the chance to delete everything." Bennett gestured to the man on the floor. "What's the situation outside?"

"All secure. Get him out of here." Darren gestured two men into the room, stepped back, and radioed as Bennett turned back to Noah.

Two team members grabbed the leader under his arms and dragged him out of the room, red streaking the floor like a gruesome finger painting.

Blood slicked Noah's fingers and pooled on the floor. A neck shot. Bennett eased off Noah's headgear and helped him stay upright. Keeping the wound above his heart to minimize blood loss was crucial. Noah's hand trembled.

"Let me. I can put more pressure on it."

Bennett's voice was rough.

The brief moment the wound was revealed sent ice through Bennett's veins. Blood pulsed from Noah's neck with every beat of his heart. An artery had been hit. Bennett slapped his fingers over the gash and pressed hard, but blood leaked through.

"Fuck. Where's Doc at?" he yelled.

Now that the situation was secure, the moment scrolled through his head on repeat. Noah had sacrificed his own life to save Bennett. Noah was the one with a wife and a baby on the way. Bennett had nothing and no one to miss him. He was the one who was supposed to take a bullet to save Noah, not the other way around.

"Why'd you do that, man? Why?" Bennett whispered, not expecting an answer. Someone turned on lights and Bennett ripped off his headgear.

Noah's bloodied hand circled Bennett's wrist with a surprising strength. His mouth opened and closed before words emerged on the wisp of a breath. "Tell . . . tell Harper . . . love."

"You're going to fucking tell her yourself. I'm not going to let you die."

They locked eyes. Noah blinked and looked straight through Bennett.

Bennett gave him a little shake. "Hang on.

Doc's coming." He yelled over his shoulder, "Where's the fucking medic?"

"On his way." Darren knelt on Noah's other side.

"Baby," Noah whispered.

"You'll see your baby. Just hang on."

Noah gave a small shake of his head and a slow blink.

Emotion stripped away the platitudes and reassurances and lies. Bennett's boots slipped in blood. The reality was stark and devastating.

"R-remember your promise."

"I'll make sure Harper and the baby are taken care of." He swallowed but couldn't stop the tears from stinging his eyes.

Promise? Noah mouthed the word as if the strength to even speak was too much.

"I promise."

The fight went out of Noah, his body growing slack in Bennett's arms. He drew Noah into his chest but kept his hand clamped over his neck. The flow of blood slowed and eventually stopped as Noah's heart ceased pumping.

Bennett rocked him back and forth and held him tight. The medic arrived with a clatter and fell to his knees next to Darren. He was young, with acne scars along his cheeks and a gaunt face that made Bennett wonder how long out of training he was. They tried to ease Noah out of Bennett's arms, but he growled at them like a wild animal protecting its young.

The medic checked for a pulse and shook his head. "I'm sorry, man. He's gone."

Bennett didn't need professional confirmation. He'd felt the final beats of Noah's heart against his fingers. The man who'd been by his side from the first day of BUD/S training, for every deployment, his best friend. His only friend.

The mission continued around his personal tragedy. Two SEALs entered the room and began packing up the computer along with every single document or item of that might hold clues to the far-reaching tendrils of the man's influence. The leader would be taken to the base and handed over to the big dogs for questioning.

Darren touched Bennett's shoulder. "We need to load up."

He was right. SEAL missions were quick and surgical. Bennett stood and heaved Noah into his arms, his right leg wobbling and giving out on him, sending him to one knee. He forced himself to rise again.

"Fuck, dude, your leg's a mess." Darren grabbed his arm. "I'll take him."

Bennett clutched Noah's body closer.

"No. Just lead me out of here. I'll be fine."

He felt no pain, which meant either the wound was superficial or the adrenaline was masking the severity. It didn't fucking matter. He was alive, and Noah was dead. The universe was all mixed up.

He stepped into the hallway. The woman who'd killed Noah lay in a heap on the floor. No regret for killing the woman surfaced. Would it all prove to be worth it? Would the information they'd recovered prove valuable? Would it save lives?

It didn't matter. Burgeoning grief rolled through him like the leading edge of a storm. He made it down the stairs and into the dusty street. Chopper blades sliced through the air and made his heart thump. Each beat mocked him. He should have died, not Noah.

He rounded the corners of the buildings, giving him a straight shot to the choppers. The black machines blurred and the noises around him grew muffled. He blinked to clear the dust and debris flying around them. Black crept from his peripheral vision until he felt like he was looking out the wrong end of a pair of binoculars. His vision snuffed like a candle.

He came to on a bed. The smell was antiseptic and bleach. Bright lights made it difficult to focus. IV lines were taped down to both arms. His nose hurt and he swiped at it, pulling away an oxygen tube.

A man-sized lump was under white sheets in the bed to his right. Blond hair peeked out at the pillow. *Noah.* His memories were fuzzy. Had Noah made it after all?

He forced himself to sitting. Pain shot through his leg and left hip. He groaned and pushed through the pain like he'd been trained to do. He reached over and grabbed the edge of the sheet.

"Noah." His voice rasped, his throat desert dry.

The man in the bed flipped to his back and looked over at Bennett. Half his face was covered in gauze, but the raw skin of a burn edged the white, his lips a macabre scarred slash.

Bennett fell back onto his pillow. "Sorry, man, thought you were someone else."

"I wish I were." The words came out as if his lungs, too, had been charred from the inside. The man turned back over and huddled into himself.

How long had Bennett been laid up? Where was Noah? He sat back up, this time prepared for the pain, and swung his legs over the side of the bed. His left leg was stiff and bandaged from upper thigh to below his knee. More bandages were taped to his hip. Would his body support him? It would have to.

He had to . . . What? He hesitated, his mind as muddy as a Mississippi marsh. What was he doing? Noah was beyond saving.

An alarm beeped on one of the machines at his head. A nurse bustled in, her mouth set in a disapproving line.

"Back in bed, Caldwell." Her voice was brisk, but her hands were gentle as she eased him back in the bed and reattached the O2 sensor on his finger. When she tried to put the tube back into his nose, he grabbed her wrist. A staring contest commenced. She huffed and set the tube aside.

"You SEALs are extraordinarily stubborn." She took up a clipboard and made notes, pressing buttons on the monitor. "Are you thirsty?"

He was parched. "How long have I been out? Where have they taken Noah?"

He half-expected her to plead ignorance. And maybe a regular nurse would have, but this was a Navy nurse. As she held out a bottle of water with a bendy straw for him, she said, "You've been out nearly twenty-four hours. Your fellow SEAL's body left on a transport to Germany."

Noah was gone. A gaping black hole in his chest sucked away any hope. The future stretched as bleak and barren as the land around them.

"He was my friend."

The lines around her mouth smoothed. "I know, and I'm sorry."

Loss and regret and guilt battered him. His mind flitted to a woman he'd never met. Had Harper been told? What would she say if she knew Noah shouldn't have died? It should have been him.

"When I can get back to my team?"

"You took two bullets to your leg, Caldwell."

Bennett closed his eyes, but light danced stars behind his eyelids.

"And another bullet creased your hip."

His heartbeat was a little fast but strong.

The nurse checked the bandage on his hip. The tug of the gauze on the wound was an irritant he wanted to swat away.

"You lost a lot of blood and will need physical therapy. They're sending you stateside."

His lungs worked, heaving in one deep breath after another.

The nurse poked his arm. "Did you hear me, Caldwell?"

"Leave me alone." His tone was harsh. Later, he would apologize. Maybe. It was hard to accept the fact that Noah was packed away in a casket on his way home with no light, no heartbeat, no life.

The promises he'd made Noah circled like carrion. Bennett would take care of Harper and their unborn child. But she could never know it was him. The man who should have died.

CHAPTER 23

Present Day

Harper shifted on Bennett's lap as the story of Noah's death rewrote itself. Or, more accurately, filled in the blanks. Noah had sacrificed his life to save Bennett. Fate had twisted and knotted their lives together like a kindergartener trying to macramé.

She shoved the useless what-ifs away. She loved Bennett, but that didn't supersede her love for Noah. While they were both exceptional men, they were very different. If Noah had lived, she hoped their relationship would have deepened and grown as they matured. As it was, she'd matured without Noah, and as a different woman she'd found Bennett.

Life was all about timing and could change with the speed of a bullet.

"Do you hate me? Do you wish he'd lived and I'd died?" Bennett's voice was rough and his eyes shined with unshed tears. Three months ago, she'd have sworn he wasn't capable of such emotion.

"Of course not." She rubbed his cheek, the hair scratchy in a good way. "Life has a way of giving us what we need at the right time."

He slumped over her, his grip biting. "I thought for sure you'd leave me."

With a jolt, she understood. Everyone in his life had left him through choice or death. She tightened her hold on him with a matching fierceness. "Never."

A knock on the doorjamb brought them out of their reverie, and Harper shot off Bennett's lap. Darren looked worn down, his eyes red rimmed, but the ghost of a smile touched his lips. "Sorry to interrupt. I was hoping — if it's not too much trouble — you'd run me up to the hospital to see Allison and the kids."

"Course not. You feel steadier?" Bennett asked.

A real smile manifested itself, although it was dry. "You mean, am I getting ready to off myself?"

"Well, yeah." Bennett only shrugged.

"No." He held up a white envelope, his hand trembling. "Alex suggested I read the letter I wrote to Allison. Tell her everything. I'm not sure she wants to hear it or if she can handle it, though."

Harper exchanged a telling glance with Bennett. She touched the back of Darren's hand. "Allison is the strongest woman I know. She can handle it and then some. Tell her. Trust her."

Darren nodded, and Harper hoped he would have the strength to follow through and share his burdens with Allison. She followed the two men to Bennett's truck and wondered if it was training or birth that set men who chose to be SEALs apart. Their independence and mental steel was both a strength and a weakness. When times got more than they could bear, it was nearly impossible for them to ask for help.

At the hospital, the transparent relief on Allison's face before she pulled Darren into her arms portended what was to come. Somehow she seemed to sense how close she'd come to losing him for good.

"Y'all go talk. Bennett and I will hang out with the kids." Harper tried to impart to Allison without words how important this moment was. Allison hung on to Darren's hand and nodded.

After they retreated to a small chapel to talk, Harper pasted on a smile and picked up the pack of cards on a rolling table. "Did you guys know that we have a trickster in our midst?"

Sophie pushed taller on the pillows, her eyes big and blue against all the hospital white, including the bandage that wrapped her head like a turban. "W-who?"

She held out the cards to Bennett. "Let's see what you've got, Grizzly."

Bennett entertained them for more than half an hour. Even Libby was transfixed by the sleight-of-hand tricks. Bennett was a natural with the kids.

He'll make a good father. As soon as the thought popped into her head, a blush spread like wildfire, and she flapped her shirt to keep from breaking out into a sweat. They hadn't discussed the future, but much like she'd known Noah would be an important part of her life the day they'd met, she knew Bennett was here to stay.

The implications were obvious but too startling to examine.

"Hey. You okay over there?" Bennett had backed away from the bed and was shuffling the cards from one hand to the other.

"Just peachy," she said with a forced smile.

"W-will you . . ." — Sophie struggled for long seconds with the next word — "t-tell me a story, Harper?"

"Of course I will. What would you like to hear about? Sleeping Beauty? Rapunzel?"

Harper lay down on her side in the bed with Sophie, careful not to jostle the IV or tubes.

"N-no princesses." Sophie didn't meet her eyes as she played with the end of Harper's ponytail.

"How about a story about a little girl who's strong and brave and tames a dragon even though no one thinks she can?"

Sophie smiled and nodded, settling against Harper's chest. Harper closed her eyes and let a story ramble from her mind to her mouth. She wasn't sure how long she talked, but after she uttered the final "and she lived happily ever after" the silence that followed was peaceful. Sophie was lax and breathing deeply, Libby and Ryan were sitting close to the bed staring at Harper raptly, and Bennett leaned against the wall wearing a slight smile.

She slipped out of bed, careful not to wake Sophie, and whispered, "How about we go get some ice cream downstairs?"

Libby shook her head. "I think I should stay. In case she wakes up. I don't want her to be afraid."

"I'll stay, too." Ryan scooched his chair closer to Sophie's bed.

Harper and Bennett retreated to the hallway, but she kept her eye on the kids. She had to believe they would get through this with scars but no lasting wounds.

With the walls and secrets swept aside, Harper didn't hesitate to notch herself into Bennett's arms. Burying her face in the warmth of his neck, she inhaled, and like he'd imprinted on her, her heart recognized home.

"They're coming." His chest rumbled against her.

She shifted but didn't pull away. Allison had been crying — Darren too. "What do you need?" Harper directed her question to Allison.

"Prayers?" Allison gave a little laugh. Although she seemed lighter and reconnected with her husband, the road back to a new normal would be long and difficult.

"I appreciate everything you've done, man." Darren dropped Allison's hand to clasp Bennett's in a shake. Instead, Bennett pulled Darren into a bear hug.

"I wish I'd been there for you sooner. We all have our ways of coping, I guess. What's your plan?"

"I want to see my little girl home, and then I'm going to take a leave of absence and work out my problems or at least learn to manage them. Alex said he'd help. He also invited me to the survival weekend he's put together with you."

"Good. I was going to suggest that my-self."

While the men discussed particulars of the trip, Harper pulled Allison to the side. "Are you two going to be okay tonight?"

" 'Okay' might be overstating things, but I think — I hope — we've reached a turning point. The things he told me, I can't imagine . . . But I'm glad he trusted me." Allison squeezed her mouth closed, her chin wobbling. "How close was he to finishing it?"

"The gun wasn't loaded, if that's any consolation." Harper rubbed circles on Allison's back like she did for Ben when he woke from a nightmare. Unfortunately, Allison's nightmare was all too real.

"Maybe it shouldn't, but that does make me feel better."

"What happens now?"

"Darren is going to stay with Sophie. He'll be safe here. I'll take the kids home and try to get a decent night's sleep. Tomorrow is a new day." Allison flashed a brief watery smile before looking to the floor. "I appreciate everything you've done for me and Darren and the kids. I don't know what I would do without you."

"You won't have to find out. And I'll be back and forth for the opening of the café. Let me know if I can watch the kids or take you out to vent or whatever. Call or text me in the morning."

Bennett slipped an arm around her shoulders and Darren retreated to Sophie's bedside. Allison joined him, her hand on his shoulder.

"I guess that's it," Harper whispered.

"For now."

They didn't speak again until they were outside. Even though the children's wing of the hospital did its best to be open and welcoming, tension was sloughed away by the swaying trees and endless night sky. Relief coupled with worry, but she and Bennett had done everything in their power to help. It was up to Darren to fight for his life both literally and abstractly.

"What do you want to do? We could get a hotel room for the night or drive back."

Part of her longed for the privacy of a night together after the turmoil of the day. But a driving need to be with Ben when he woke seeded impatience.

She pulled Bennett to a stop and met his gaze. "As much as I want to frolic all night in a king-size bed with you, I need to be home."

"Because of Sophie." It was a statement, not a question.

"Yes and because of how I left things this

morning with Ben."

"With Ben and Sophie close in age and seeing her . . . like that. It's scary."

He was right. Call it mother's instinct, but she needed to make sure Ben was safe. "You don't mind?"

"As long as I can get a rain check. I don't know that I've ever frolicked in bed, but as long as it involves you naked, I'm all in."

Harper muffled laughter. Bennett was a surprise on so many levels, not least of all the sly, sexual tease in his voice.

"Rain check it is."

"But I'd also be good with some covert action in the dead of night if you're up for it."

"I might be up for hunting bear later." She popped to her toes to press a kiss on his smiling mouth. "Grizzly."

CHAPTER 24

Two months later . . .

Harper paced next to the coffee roaster in the back of the café. It was five in the morning opening day of Home Front Coffee. Sleep had been not just elusive but nonexistent. The aroma from the roaster filled the room. She and Joyce and Madeline had roasted countless small batches of beans, ground them, made coffee, and sampled it. They had agreed the medium dark roast was the most appealing. Eventually, Home Front might offer a variety of roastings, but keeping it simple at the start held its appeal.

Fresh beans for the first customers would be good PR. Except what if no one showed up? What if her tiny venture folded in Guinness world record time?

Thinking about the possibilities made her sick. Literally. On her run to the bathroom, she hit her shoulder on the doorjamb, fell to her knees in front of the toilet, and heaved. She cleaned up and rinsed her mouth out with water. The lights emphasized her sallow complexion and dark circles under her eyes. She'd been sick with nerves for the last week and tired. So tired. Stress was a killer.

One way or another, she'd feel better after today. It was the not knowing if her business plan was amateurish or brilliant or something in between that was taking a toll. The turn of the lock out front brought her out of the bathroom. Madeline had arrived. Energy and good humor and optimism crackled around her. Harper wanted to give her a hug. Without Madeline, Harper might have given up.

Madeline took a deep breath and hummed. "You've already got the roaster going. It smells divine in here."

"I couldn't sleep."

Madeline's smile didn't infect Harper. "I know. I'm excited, too."

Instead of admitting her mood had shifted toward the dread end of the scale, she said, "Do you think I ordered too many bakery items?"

The bakery across the street had provided muffins and scones and coffee cake to Home Front Coffee at wholesale prices. In return, the bakery would stock bags of freshly roasted Home Front Coffee in their bakery for a tidy profit. Hopefully, a win-win in terms of advertising and making a name for themselves.

"You ordered the perfect amount. T-minus one hour. Let's put several of each on display. We can restock as we sell out." Madeline's enthusiasm only made Harper feel like a Jenga tower one turn away from collapse.

She went into the back where a corner of the storeroom had been commandeered as office space. A safe held the petty cash she'd taken out of the bank to load the register. After she did that, she checked and rechecked the credit card reader link. Considering how few people carried cash these days, a malfunction would be disastrous. She still had nightmares about the defective machine at Wilbur's when she worked at the ice-cream store during the summers.

Two young wives from the military support group knocked on the door. While Madeline and Harper's job was to put out the inevitable fires and man the roaster the first day in operation, Harper had hired the two women to handle the behind-the-counter work. Both had experience as waitresses and in retail, plus they were friendly and excited about working at Home Front. Joyce would come toward the end of the shift and help with closing out the register and deciding what they needed to reorder and when.

Madeline let the two women inside and they put on aprons and chattered while they prepared for the opening. Allison was the next to arrive. She and Harper exchanged hugs.

The two months following Sophie's release from the hospital had brought stability and healing to Allison and Darren and their family. Darren still struggled with PTSD, but through the combination of medicine, his Wounded Warriors group outings, and Allison's support, he was managing his anxiety and depression.

Harper retreated to the coffee roaster. The smell of coffee was usually her morning siren song, but she couldn't quell the roil of her stomach. The roasting cycle was complete and the beans were cooling. Some they would use that morning, and some they would bag to sell.

Allison joined her at the roaster. "Almost time, Boss."

Oh God, she was in charge. The pressure threatened to crush her. She took a deep breath, but the freshly roasted coffee made her choke. She slapped a hand over her mouth and, knowing she wouldn't make it to the bathroom this time, scurried around boxes for the back door. She made it by an inch. Not that she had anything left but bile.

She returned, feeling wrung-out and put-up wet. "Sorry. I'm battling a severe case of nerves."

The worry on Allison's face was replaced by amusement. "Oh, is that what it is? I thought you might be pregnant."

Harper made a scoffing noise, but a roar had filled her ears, muffling whatever else Allison said. Pregnant? She couldn't be. It was impossible. Yet was it?

She and Bennett hadn't been able to keep their hands off each other the last two months. Sure, they had been careful, but there was that one time on a secluded dirt road. Serious frolicking had taken place in the cab of his truck. Anyone could have driven by. It had been on the edge of wild and reckless, and she'd loved every minute.

When was her last period? It wasn't something she normally tracked. They were irregular and on the light side, anyway. Had it been more than four weeks? Maybe.

At some point, Harper's inattention registered with Allison. "Harper! Are you pregnant?"

"I don't know." She must have looked like she felt — scared, shell-shocked, but with a hint of wonder, too.

"Well, bless your heart." Allison said it in a non-ironic way and seemed to possess knowledge Harper lacked.

"A baby is really unlikely."

"Is it? You're still young, and Bennett has been rocking your panties off for months now." She waggled her eyebrows.

Harper shushed her between clenched teeth. Her stomach was trying to tear its way out of her body like in *Alien*. "What should I do?"

"Let's have a great opening day. Then, we'll grab a pregnancy test and some pizza on the way home."

"I meant, long term if it turns out . . ." Harper already knew what the pregnancy test would say, and she'd been a fool not to suspect earlier.

"Tell Bennett. You don't think he's going to be excited?"

"He brought up marriage about a month ago."

Allison grabbed her hands. "In general or specifically related to the two of you getting married?"

"Specifically us."

"What did you say? Obviously, not yes, or

he would have put a ring on it already."

"It felt like less of a yes-no situation and more like he was feeling me out. Like he didn't want to outright ask if I wasn't open to the idea."

"And are you?"

"Of course I am. I love him, but we haven't been together long, and he's never wanted to settle down."

"That's because he was waiting for you." Even though Allison was only a couple of years older than Harper, she possessed a wisdom that far outstripped her. "How did you leave things?"

"I did some babbling about Ben and needing time and went to the bathroom to regroup."

Allison burst out laughing. "Smooth."

Madeline stuck her head through the connecting door. "It's time, ladies."

Harper grabbed Allison's wrist as she was turning toward the door. "I'm scared."

She wasn't sure if she was referring to the prospect of an unplanned pregnancy or the opening of Home Front. In a few short months, her easy, boring life had been upended, by chance and choice.

"I know. But isn't it exciting?" A slow grin spread across Allison's face.

Now threaded alongside her nerves was

excitement. The possibility for failure hovered, but she would reach for success, both personally and professionally. "Yeah, I guess it is."

They entered the café side by side. Two customers stood at the counter ordering coffee, while a carload of four more people in office attire piled inside, their chattering filling the space.

The next eight hours went by at warp speed. When two o'clock rolled around, Harper flipped the sign to *Closed* and pulled the shade on the front door. Until the shop got its footing and she could hire and train more wives from the base, they would close after lunch.

It was another two hours before she and Joyce had balanced the register and cleaned up, readying everything for the next morning. They'd had more customers than she'd anticipated, which was good, but Joyce needed to up their order for bakery items the next morning.

"I'm exhausted." Harper stretched her back as they stepped out into the hot presummer sun.

"You stop at a pharmacy, and I'll head home and order pizza." Allison gave her a pointed look.

Harper did as she was told, then drove to

Allison's, glancing periodically at the small box on her passenger seat like it was an unexploded bomb.

It was like an evil witch's curse had been lifted off Allison and Darren's house. Sophie and Libby were playing dress up and chasing each other up and down the stairs. Darren was in the backyard throwing soft underhanded pitches to Ryan, their laughter carrying through the screen door to the back patio. Allison flipped the pizza box open and glanced over her shoulder as Harper walked in.

"Go take it before the kids descend on the kitchen like locusts."

Harper slipped into the powder room and ripped the package open. Peeing on the stick was an uncomfortable, messy affair. She capped it and washed her hands, staring at the little window. Her future might change in a matter of minutes.

The seconds ticked off. Light blue appeared. She picked up the stick and blinked. A plus. She was pregnant. Not surprising, but shocking nonetheless. Her already-complicated life was about to get more tangled.

She walked out of the bathroom and held up the stick for Allison to see the result.

"Oh my god, you're pregnant!" Allison

gave a whoop.

Harper burst into tears.

"Are you upset?" Allison rubbed her back.

Harper couldn't get a word past the hiccups.

"That was a dumb thing to ask. Obviously, you're upset. Are you worried about what Bennett will say?"

"B-Bennett. The café. Ben."

Allison's mouth formed an O. "I get it. It's complicated, but all the kinks will work themselves out. As far as the coffee shop, you could offer Madeline and Joyce bigger stakes in the company. Take some of the responsibility off you."

"I need to call Bennett."

"Are you sure you don't want to wait until you" — Allison waved a hand over Harper — "get yourself together?"

The need to talk to him, share her burden, even though it would become his burden soon enough, was overwhelming. Without becoming aware, he'd become her partner, and she hoped he would continue to be her partner into this brave new world.

She tapped his name and waited through three rings.

"How did the first day go?" The deep rumble of his voice, even through the distance, was like a lifeline.

Tears clogged her throat and all that emerged were a few stuttered words.

"I can't understand you, sweetheart. Can you take a deep breath and tell me what happened?" Love and worry transmitted behind his words.

She took one deep, shuddery breath. "Our first day was a smashing success. More customers than we anticipated. We sold out of muffins and cookies and bagged, roasted beans."

"That's amazing. I'm so proud of you."

A sob slipped out of her.

"What the hell is wrong? Is it Ben? Allison or Darren? The kids?" An urgency thrummed like he wanted to bust through the line and tackle the problems.

"No. Everyone here is good. Great, in fact. It's . . . it's me. And, well . . . I've been feeling sick this week. I threw up this morning."

"Stress is a killer. You'll feel better now the shop is open."

"Nope. I don't think I'll feel better for like seven months. Maybe seven and a half."

"What are you talking about?"

"I'm pregnant."

A thud sounded on the other end followed by heavy breathing.

"Bennett? Are you still there?"

"Sorry, I dropped the phone. I'm here and shocked. How? When?"

"I'm pretty sure you know how. You're pretty amazing at the how part. As far as when, I think it was that time in your truck. We took a chance, remember?"

A long spate of silence. "Are you happy about this?" His voice was soft.

She took inventory. Fear was there in spades, but also satisfaction and, yes, happiness. A second chance at love had snuck up on her. She'd assumed her one shot had died with Noah.

"Yeah, I am happy." She inhaled sharply as the truth arrowed through her.

"*Now* will you marry me?"

Her head swam and she sank down on the edge of the couch and folded over her knees. "What about Ben? Where will we live? And, what about —"

"We'll figure it out. Together."

The surety of his words and voice sloughed away her panic. The alternative to not figuring it out wasn't an option. Their history wound through the years, their connection fated.

"Unless you don't want to get married?" Uncertainty crept across the line in his voice.

She wanted to teleport into his arms to

offer reassurances, but she had to content herself with words. "You're not getting off that easy, Mr. Caldwell. I'm going to marry you and make you the happiest man alive."

"Too late for that. I'm already the happiest man alive."

EPILOGUE

Harper's eyes popped open. A dull pain rippled through her belly. She was a week overdue, so going into labor wasn't a surprise. In fact, she'd been scheduled for an induction that afternoon. It seemed the baby wasn't going to wait. The tightness and pain eased.

She and Bennett and Ben were living at her mom's house in Nags Head, waiting for the contractors to finish the house they'd had built outside of Virginia Beach, close to Bennett's business. Of course, it was supposed to be done a month ago with plenty of time to get moved in and settled before the baby came, but a rainy summer had delayed the work.

Harper wasn't upset, though. Honestly, being home with her mom was comforting, and she had desperately wanted Adele to deliver her baby. She heaved herself off the bed and stumbled toward the window, her balance compromised and her back aching.

The rising sun streaked the sky with pinks and oranges. It was December. Another winter had come. The leaves had dropped and been swept away by the wind, leaving the grass barren and the beaches lonely.

Yet her familiar melancholy had stayed at bay. She and Bennett had walked down to the dock the night before, the air crisp and her mood high. The site of their first kiss. In spite of her stomach making things difficult, they had re-created the moment.

She glanced over her shoulder and smiled. Bennett was a massive lump under the covers, only his arm visible where it lay in the spot she'd left as if seeking her.

The last months had brought enormous change. Ben had been ecstatic at the news of the baby and the fact that he was gaining Bennett as a stepfather. But his enthusiasm had waned when he'd discovered he would have to change schools and leave Yaya's house.

Bennett's loft above the shop was perfect for one but not a sudden family of four. And it made sense for them to move to Virginia Beach. She was already working remotely, running the internet sales side of the café and planning for their expansion, but Bennett needed to be on-site to run his business.

She braced a hand on the sill as the next pain took hold. Time to wake the soldiers. She sat on the edge of the bed and put her hand on Bennett's shoulder. He startled awake, his eyes wide, his mind back in his dream. Was he with Noah?

"It's time," she said softly.

"Time?" At first confusion clouded his face, but it cleared as sleep was cast off. "It's time. Holy shit, it's time." He jumped up, more agile than she was, and stood in the middle of the floor, his hands up as if frozen in indecision, which was very unlike him.

"Get dressed." She gave his butt a pat. While she was sure the female staff at the hospital would appreciate Bennett Caldwell in nothing but boxer briefs, she didn't want Adele distracted with a spate of heart attacks.

She did the same, pulling on stretchy yoga pants and a T-shirt that hugged her belly. Bennett returned, buttoning his jeans, a lost look on his face.

"Grab my ba-a-a-ahhh . . . dammit." Another contraction took hold, this one stronger. She grabbed Bennett's forearms.

The pain faded and she loosened her grip,

but her fingernails left indentations on his skin. Color had drained from his face. "Is this normal?"

"Totally, but we'd better hustle."

She'd never seen Bennett move so fast. Laughter bubbled up, as did anticipation. She couldn't wait to meet their son or daughter. The contrast to her labor with Ben was stark. That day had been filled with dread and fear. While there was still fear present today, a well of optimism had filled over the last year.

Her mom came out into the hallway, holding her robe together. "What's going on?"

"The baby didn't want to wait until this afternoon." Another pain shot through her body, no longer confined to her belly. She puffed until it waned. "Contractions are coming on fast. We need to go. I don't think it will be long. Could you call Adele and let her know we're on the way?"

"Of course." Her mom gave her a brief hug, shooing them away. "I'll bring Ben up afterward. Love you, Harper Lee."

"Love you, too. I don't know what I would have done without you." Tears blurred her vision, her emotions careening like a pinball machine.

They made it to the hospital — barely. Adele whisked in as Harper was ready to push. The nurses were still scurrying around the room preparing the bed and everything the baby would need.

Holding on to Bennett's hand and with his words of encouragement in her ear, Harper gave birth to a healthy nine-pound baby boy. After he was cleaned up and placed in her arms, she and Bennett admired his perfect fingers and toes. The baby blinked up at them with unfocused blue eyes. Blue eyes. The unexpected color left her reeling.

"We need a name, huh?" Bennett stroked over the baby's delicate head with his big hand.

"I was sure it was a girl. I guess 'Evangeline' is a no-go."

He huffed a laugh but turned serious. "I thought of a name, but I'm not sure how you'll feel about it."

"Try me."

"What about . . . Noah?" Bennett whispered.

Her wave of surprise ebbed. After all, she had named Noah's son after Bennett. The name clicked into place like the last piece of a puzzle. She leaned over to brush her lips over the straggle of baby hair, breathing in his essence. "Perfect. I love you, Noah."

AUTHOR'S NOTE

This book wouldn't have been possible without my editor, Eileen Rothschild, having the confidence that I could branch out and tackle a new genre. It's a true joy to brainstorm with her. Big thanks to Monique Patterson and Tiffany Shelton and to the copy editors and proofreaders and cover artists at St. Martin's Press who make the machine run smoothly.

I also need to thank Brandon Webb for providing his expertise as a former SEAL and SEAL instructor to make the path my characters followed as accurate as possible. Brandon's book *The Red Circle,* detailing his training as a SEAL, proved invaluable to get the feel and details of the harrowing BUD/S training every SEAL must complete.

I am not a military wife myself, so I have to send a huge, ginormous thank-you to Michelle Tonsmeire! Not only is she my bestie, but she is a military wife. Through the years I've witnessed her sacrifices on the home front as she moved from base to base with her family and survived as a single mom when her husband was deployed. I hope I portrayed her strength — and that of all the wives and husbands who keep things running at home when their partner is deployed — with truth and compassion.

My goal, when writing as Harper Lee Wilcox, the woman at the center of *The Military Wife,* was to portray her as a complex individual with her own goals and needs apart from being a wife and mother. The obstacles I threw at Harper, from having to choose between her own ambitions and her marriage to making new friends to raising a child without her husband, aren't all that unusual. They are challenges faced by women every single day.

One exchange in particular highlights the unique challenges of being married to a man in the military, particularly a SEAL. "Most people don't get it. The threat of death is abstract, but for women like us, the threat has moved into the spare bedroom." Military spouses learn to deal with the underlying threat of losing their husband or wife while still working and raising their kids and living their lives. It's a sacrifice not many of us will ever understand. For just a little while, I tried to put myself in Harper's heart.

Through all the challenges Harper overcomes, I hope the reader will recognize her strength is not what she can handle on her own but what she accomplishes when she leans on others, and in turn, the help she extends to others when they are in need. Above all, *The Military Wife* is about the connections, big and small, that make life worth living.

ABOUT THE AUTHOR

Laura Trentham is an award winning romance author. *The Military Wife* is her debut women's fiction novel. A chemical engineer by training and a lover of books by nature, she lives in South Carolina.

The employees of Thorndike Press hope you have enjoyed this Large Print book. All our Thorndike, Wheeler, and Kennebec Large Print titles are designed for easy reading, and all our books are made to last. Other Thorndike Press Large Print books are available at your library, through selected bookstores, or directly from us.

For information about titles, please call:
(800) 223-1244

or visit our website at:
gale.com/thorndike

To share your comments, please write:
Publisher
Thorndike Press
10 Water St., Suite 310
Waterville, ME 04901